THE HERO COMPLEX, BOOK I

HERO, SECOND CLASS

MITCHELL BONDS

HERO, SECOND CLASS by Mitchell Bonds
Published by Marcher Lord Press
8345 Pepperridge Drive
Colorado Springs, CO 80920
www.marcherlordpress.com

This is a work of fiction. Names, characters, places, and incidents are products of the author's imagination or are used fictitiously. Any similarity to actual people, organizations, and/or events is purely coincidental.

Cover Designer: Kirk DouPonce, Dog-Eared Design,
    www.dogeareddesign.com
Cover Illustrator: Kirk DouPonce
Map Designer: Gary Tompkins
Creative Team: Jeff Gerke, Pat Reinheimer

Library of Congress Cataloging-in-Publication Data
An application to register this book for cataloging has been filed with the Library of Congress.
International Standard Book Number: 978-0-9821049-1-0

Printed in the United States of America

DEDICATION

To LeeAnn Bonds,
for instilling in me a sense of creative insanity
and for encouraging me to attend college.

To my friends at Hillsdale College,
who provided Constructive Criticism.

To the guys at TBC,
who are some of the characters.

And to Patricia C. Wrede,
for being a veritable font of inspiration.

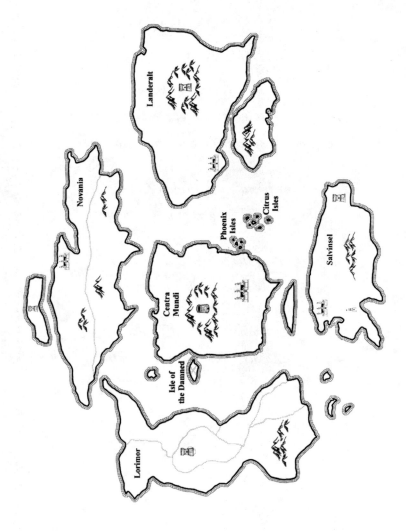

PART ONE

APPRENTICED TO A HERO

THE PROPHECY OF THE . . .

Extracted from "The Chronicle of Saint Michael"

The Stars that Fell from Heaven
Those Frozen spheres of Flame
A terrible Commotion
Invoked in Evil's name

As Strength against the Falling
Stood Michael, Helm, and Greaves
They blew away the Comets
As Autumn winds blow Leaves

One shattered 'cross the Eastern sky
Another shattered West
One landed in the Ocean
As Mankind's Final Test

A Light comes from the Fallen
In form of Hero strong
His Might in Sword and Magic
Shall make a tale fair long

He meeteth then the Huntress
Though She is not his Kind
Together in the Starlight
Their Destiny shall Find

From them, the Two of Balance
Shall spring, and then shall grow
In Power and in Stature
Their Fates they do not Know

The One Combats the Darkness
The other Fights within
Then Dire Things shall Happen
And they shall fight as Kin

The Balance then is Shattered
Creator's Will be Done
All Races then United
In bright Eternal Sun

PROLOGUE

AWN POKED HER rosy fingers across the sky.

And promptly tore two small holes in it.

Vertis the Sky god repaired the holes and scolded Dawn, sending her off to get a manicure. He took over from there and cast the sun's early rays into the stone-paved courtyard of Bryath Castle, the hub of Centra Mundi's government. Blue and silver pennants flapped merrily in the gentle breeze, and the cold stones of the ancient fortress began warming in the sunlight.

But light creates shadows, and from them slipped a man in a black cloak, clutching a dagger in his bony hand. The man crept up behind a bleary-eyed sentry, dagger poised to strike. The sentry standing near the massive oaken gate was still half-asleep and had begun his shift only minutes ago, as evidenced by the creases in his recently folded, blue-and-white uniform. With a swift and silent swipe, the black-garbed man slashed open the sentry's throat. The sentry gurgled and collapsed, caught as he fell by his killer.

Across the gate from the assassin, a similar man slew the other sentry quietly and leaned the corpse against the wall. The assassins atop the wall had done their work also, so not a single soul watched the western approach to the castle, nor guarded it.

It was not until the gate opened and the drawbridge rattled down that the Castle Guard realized something was amiss. And by then, it was too late. A hundred black-clad men wielding swords and crossbows flooded through the West Gate, slaying anyone they ran across. Finally a bleeding sentry raised his head and sounded the alarm on a bent trumpet. Men scrambled to respond, and the palace guard hastily armed themselves, storming out to meet the invaders.

"They've breached the gate!"

"Get down here, *now!*"

"Protect the King!"

"Anyone seen my shoes?"

A sergeant stopped barking orders to his men and glared at the shoeless guard. "This is no time for footwear problems, man! Just get off your posterior and fight those GYAAIIEE!"

A wickedly flanged mace slammed down on an unfortunate sergeant. "Yes, you pathetic fools," the mace's wielder said with a horrible chuckle, "come and fight us Gyaaiiee."

Outside the barracks, the host of black-clad invaders brought in a battering ram to attack the gates of the inner keep. They set fire to the stables for good measure, throwing the horses into a panic. The flagstones of the courtyard flowed with the blood of many members of the Palace Guard.

The shoeless soldier backed up, gibbering in fear. The man standing over him stood easily over six feet tall. Blood dripped from the man's silver armor and red beard, and the frightened soldier got the impression that none of that blood belonged to the man.

"Mwahaha! Fear me, you worm!" the towering man said with a laugh. "Now prepare to meet your doom!"

A second invader stepped up behind the red-bearded man and slapped him across the back of his helm. "Stop fooling around with the common soldiers and help me get to the throne room," he ordered. The new arrival was much shorter, about five and a half feet tall, clad in armor of midnight black, with a helm that resembled the horned head of a demon. "We've no time for your idiotic catchphrases."

The tall man sighed and slew the shoeless soldier with a single solid swipe. "Fine," he said, shaking a bit of brain loose from a flange of his mace, "but promise me I get to kill some innocents later. I'm enjoying this Villain business already."

"Too much, it seems," said the man in black. "Let's just get this done before they can summon reinforcements. Where did those blasted Manticores disappear to? They'd better not be fooling around scaring horses, or I'll have to have a word with our beast master . . . "

" . . . and so then the bartender says, 'That's not a gryphon, that's a chicken glued to a cat!'"

The men at the table laughed politely, not wishing to offend their monarch. It was a privilege to eat with the King of Bryath, and the food was good, if not the humor.

King Ataraxes Zamindar Bryath the Third wiped away a tear as he continued chuckling to himself over his joke. "Oh, I love that one so very much." He wore a heavy gold crown atop his greying blond head, and velvet robes of a deep vermillion hue, currently bedecked with crumbs from the strawberry tart he had been eating.

The men who ate with the King on that day were Sir Grant, the Captain of the King's Own Guard, Salidor Goldwater of the Seafarer's Union, and their special guest, a professional Hero, behind whose chair stood a page boy bearing the Hero's shield.

The four men sat in a cavernous dining hall, one built to accommodate a hundred or more nobles during official dinners. Morning sunlight filtered into the room in myriad colors through exquisite stained-glass windows depicting previous Kings of Centra Mundi and their deeds. The men's conversation echoed in the mostly empty room, the sound absorbed only by the long table in the center of the room and the many chairs that lined it. The rest echoed about the carved marble buttresses holding up the tiled roof. A small fire danced cheerfully in the fireplace at the south end of the room, for despite the heat of summer, Bryath Castle was a terribly chilly and drafty place.

The Hero in question went by the name of the Crimson Slash, though his real name was Reginald Ogleby. Or, more correctly, *Sir* Reginald Ogleby, after being knighted by the current King for his courageous actions during the Battle of Three Streams. He was a well-known warrior who had, the day before, delivered a gift for the King's birthday celebration. The gift was from the International Guild of Heroes, whose headquarters sat near the center of Bryath's castle town. The King hadn't opened it yet.

Reginald himself was an impressive figure, an enormous fellow, over six feet tall, with shoulders as broad as an ox. He had a kind face, if a bit rough. Today, his thick black hair looked as if it hadn't been combed yet, but the beard covering his cheeks was neatly trimmed. His silver armor gleamed with a professional sheen, and the bar of crimson paint across the breastplate's surface appeared freshly painted.

The King leaned over to Reginald and smiled. "Sir Ogleby, I must ask: what have you brought from the Guild for me?"

Reginald shook his head and smiled. "My apologies, your Majesty, but I am sworn to secrecy on that score. Your Majesty will simply have to wait until your birthday." The Hero's voice was a gravelly base rumble, pleasant, but obviously not a singing voice.

The King stuck out his lip briefly in jest, then chuckled. "Ah, I suppose I shall. So, will the Guildmaster be attending this year, or do his legs pain him too much?"

"Guardian is in fine health, your Majesty, and was delighted to receive your invitation," Reginald replied. "He would not miss your birthday for all the gold in—"

A soldier, one of the Palace Guard, burst into the room, breathing heavily. All the men at the table turned to look at him. The soldier bowed to the King, then turned to Sir Grant, a panicked look on his freckled face. "Sir Grant! There's been an attack on the West Gate, and they have already breached the outer keep!" he said breathlessly.

Grant, clad in the silver and blue of the King's Own Guard, immediately leapt up from the table and grabbed his sword from where it had been resting beside his chair. "How many?"

"Near a hundred, sir," the soldier said, "plus some of those nasty Mythologicals. There's a Manticore or two down there, and we spotted a Chimera earlier. Pike and Harding request your assistance."

Grant turned to the King. "Your Majesty, I request that you take shelter until we resolve this matter."

The King shook his head. "A mere attack? Bah. What is this, the third this month? I'll worry when they break through into the inner Keep. You can certainly deal with a few would-be assassins, yes?"

Grant bowed. "Yes, your Majesty. I will ensure this action comes to naught. If you will excuse me." He turned and followed the soldier out of the room.

Reginald's eyes strayed to his massive sword, which leaned against the wall. The Hero clenched a fist and sighed, as if he very much wanted to join in the fray instead of endure the King's attempts at comedy. But he had neither been invited nor ordered to, and instead leaned back in his chair and took another bite of sausage.

"So, where was I?" the King said. "Ah, yes, chicken glued to a cat. And so the first man rolls his eyes and says . . . "

"Sphere of Annihilation!"

A ball of swirling blue mist sprang into existence in front of a group of soldiers, then burst. The corrosive mist burned their flesh and rusted their armor in seconds, sending the men reeling in agony.

The man in the demon-helm snorted in derision. He turned to face another soldier, holding his dull grey falchion high. The falchion was a slightly curved sword, both wide and heavy, and gutted the soldier cleanly as the invader brought it down across the man's chest.

"Anthony," he said to the red-bearded man, gesturing with his ebon gauntlet, "send more Minions to secure the west hallway. I dislike being flanked. And get those Manticores to stop fooling around with the horses and send them to cause a diversion in the southern corridor. When you're done, grab a dozen Minions and join me in the east hallway. The inner keep isn't far."

"Yes, milord." Anthony's face took on a triumphant grin, and he raised a clenched fist in a triumphant gesture. "Once we breach the inner keep, it's only a short while until you get your hands on the King's ring, and then you have what you need to take over the world!"

"Yes, Anthony, I know," the demon-helmed man said. "I can do my own exposition well enough, thank you. Now do as I say, and be quick about it."

The bearded man grumbled, but turned to do his lord's bidding. "Yes, milord. Can you hold here until I return?"

"Of course. Now go. There is much havoc to be wrought and little time to wreak it in." The helmed man smiled as a fresh wave of Palace Guard stormed toward him and began a dance of death, complete with theme music. Disturbing, minor-key organ blasted from around him as he took his first step forward.

That step brought him inside the first man's guard, and the invader opened the man's chest before he could raise his shield. Two more went down before the others had time to react. The man in the demon helmet was too fast for them. And too strong, as well, for any shield or weapon raised in defense shattered under his onslaught.

The man in the helm laughed, a malevolent and resounding chuckle, the unearthly sound echoing from the helmet in a cascade of black noise.

"Mwahahaha!"

" . . . and said 'No, no, not *that* horse!'"

Reginald sighed, not even pretending to laugh this time. He'd heard the noise of battle from below them in the courtyard and was barely resisting the temptation to leave the table and look out the window.

The merchant from the Seafarer's Union still chuckled sycophantically. "Oh, your Majesty, you are so amusing."

"Cease your fawning," the King said, scowling at the thin, overdressed man. "Sir Ogleby, is aught amiss?"

"No, your Majesty, it's probably nothing. After all, Sir Grant is more than competent." Reginald settled back in his chair and looked unhappy.

"'Tis a shame that your Guild dictates noninvolvement in our mundane affairs unless Villains are involved," the King said, taking a bite of a strawberry-filled pastry. "I would let you go in a heartbeat if it were the case, but for an everyday assassination attempt . . . "

The merchant Goldwater turned to Reginald, a quizzical expression on his pale face. "The Guild of Heroes won't let you protect the King?" he said, squeaking slightly in growing fear. "Whyever not?"

"What do you think the Palace Guard and the King's Own are for?" Reginald replied, leaning back uneasily. "If a Hero came by and did their job for them every time someone attacked the castle, what do you think that would do to their morale?"

The merchant nodded. "Not anything good. And you Heroes have better things to do than hang around waiting for assassination attempts."

"And it's not sportsmanlike," the King said, popping the rest of the tart into his mouth and reaching for another. "The guard would feel unmanned, but having a Hero spoil your careful planning is just unfair. Now, if there were a Villain involved, that would change things . . . "

"Indeed," Reginald said with a sigh.

"What, how so?" the merchant asked. "I would classify anyone attempting to kill the King as a villain. What do you—"

Reginald held up a hand to cut the merchant off. "There are villains, and then there are Villains," he explained. "The kind that run their own guild and command entire armies of henchmen are Villains. Any buffoon who beats his wife or throws rocks at a parade is a villain. They are totally different in orders of magnitude. They've even their own guild like ours, but it's evil, and . . . bah, it's complicated." The Hero waved a hand dismissively. "All you need know now is that the situation is not dire enough for me to be allowed to step in."

"I'd feel safer if you did," the King said, a gleam in his eye. "Almost makes me wish there was a Villain involved, eh, Sir Ogleby?"

Reginald nodded. "Aye. It's been far too—"

The door slammed open, and Sir Grant staggered in, bleeding from multiple sword-wounds. His armor had been rusted away in places, and he bore a look of fear on his face. Several members of the King's Own Guard followed Grant in and took places around their liege, swords drawn.

"Your Majesty!" Grant said, pulling the King up from his chair. "We must hurry from this place! They have breached the inner Keep and are headed for the throne room as we speak. Their commander wields strange magic beyond anything I have seen. He and his men have slain over half of the Palace Guard!"

Reginald leapt to his feet, palms flat on the table. "Strange magics, you say?"

Grant nodded wearily. "Spells far beyond the power these types would naturally have. And that infernal music! An eldritch melody that sucked the courage from my bravest men."

Reginald knocked the table aside and grabbed Grant by the shoulders, scattering breakfast foods all over the flagstones in his excitement. "When you say music, do you mean actual, audible music?"

"Aye, a sinister tune. As if played by demons in Hell's Organworks."

"Nonsense," the King said, clucking over the spilled food and retrieving yet another strawberry tart from the mess on the floor. "The castle doesn't have an organ. We haven't had an organist since Friar Belham quit over the Hydra-in-his-bathtub incident."

"Think very carefully," Reginald said, looking into Grant's weary eyes. "The music . . . is it in a major or minor key?"

"Minor, C minor," the knight replied. "Why?"

Reginald grinned and took his shield from the page boy, then picked up his enormous sword from its place by the wall. "Theme music, my friend. Their leader is a Villain for certain. Get the King to the throne room, and set up what defenses you can muster. I shall make short work of this Villain when he arrives."

"Change of plans, men," Grant barked. "We escort the King to his throne room. Ranulf, you prepare the Route of Emergency Escapes. The rest of you take up Penultimate and Ultimate Defensive Perimeter stations inside the throne room. The Crimson Slash will confront the Villain."

The King's Own saluted—looking markedly relieved—and led the protesting King of Bryath from the room.

Reginald smiled, and ate the rest of the strawberry pastry.

"We must be almost there," the demon-helmed man said, looking down at the corpse of a soldier with slightly different armor than the others he'd just slain. "I think this one was one of the King's Own."

Anthony spared a glance at his lord. "Good. Then we can get on with the taking over the world thing." The large man spun and knocked down a door with his flanged mace. Five soldiers had been hiding behind it, preparing to make a brave attempt at ambushing the intruders. Now they fell backward under the impact, and a half-dozen black-clad Minions leapt forward and slew them where they lay.

"Exactly," the man in the demon-helm said. "I shall have civilization under my thumb before you can say Worldwide Domination."

Anthony grinned. "Worldwide Domina—"

"Silence, Anthony. Your strong point is smashing things, not witticisms. Now, where's the throne room?"

"We could follow the map, milord."

"Map? What in the Nine Hells are you—"

Anthony pointed. The demon-helmed man turned and saw a plaque on the wall with a simplified floor plan of the surrounding area, with an X stating "You are Here."

"Oh."

Down a corridor and to the right was a room labeled "Throne Room: Audience hours 10–12, 3–5, weekdays only."

"Oh good," Anthony said. "They're open."

"Or they will be," the helmed man said, shaking his head and striding down the hallway. "Onward!"

"Listen!"

Reginald and the King's Own stood in the red-carpeted throne room, spread in a V formation between the throne and the entrance. Two knights slammed the crossbar down from the inside to secure the door, then scrambled back to their places. The assembled Kingsguard fell into a hushed silence, straining to hear what the Hero spoke of. Faintly, and growing louder by the moment, they began to hear strains of a complicated and sinister music, as if a powerful pipe organ below the castle's foundation was blasting at its top volume.

"Ready yourselves," Reginald said. "That music will hit top volume just as the doors burst open. And the first thing that will come in will be a dozen Minions. They are weak, but do not let them catch you off guard. Now, hold fast. For the King!" The Hero raised his titanic sword into the air and accidentally poked a hole in the ceiling panels with it. He pretended not to notice.

The Kingsguard chuckled grimly and braced themselves for the onslaught.

"Dark Fog of Sinister Entrances," said the man in the helmet. A misshapen blob of black mist appeared between his hands. "Cue the music," he ordered, "and open that door!"

Anthony delivered a grievous blow to the doors with his mace. Simultaneously, the helmed man released his spell, sending a rush of Sinister Fog into the room, followed by a dozen of his remaining Minions.

The music, which had inexplicably been following them around, crescendoed, adding its noise to the sounds of yells and metal on metal.

The helmed man removed his helm and tossed it aside. Beneath the demon-horned helm the Villain was quite handsome, with wavy, raven-black, glossy hair and pointed facial features. He was not an Elf, for his eyes glowed a soft green. The Villain strode into the smoky room, sword drawn and a confident, smug smile on his face.

"Happy birthday, your Majesty. Surrender your ring or Prepare to Face your D— *Orsobu Pitchi!*"

The smoke cleared, and the Villain's demands became a curse instead. All twelve of his Minions lay dead, slaughtered by the efficient hands of the Kingsguard. And in the center of those men stood something that threw his plan out the window.

A Hero, clad in shining armor and wielding a tremendous sword, stood in the center of the room, staring the Villain down.

"Greetings, foul Villain," the Hero said with a smile. "What brings you to Bryath Castle on this fine day?"

The Villain scowled. "You! Who are you, and how did you know I was coming?"

"Mine name is the Crimson Slash," the Hero said, locking eyes with the Villain. "And I didn't know you were coming. Poor timing on your part, methinks."

"Bah. It matters not," the Villain said, and raised his arms in his best sorcerer's pose. "You have heard of me, no doubt. I am a Villain from a long line of dastardly Villains. My name strikes fear into the hearts of those who hear it, and you will shriek it with your last breath as I slay you."

"But what is it?" the Crimson Slash asked.

"I'm getting there," the Villain replied, peeved. "Don't interrupt."

The Crimson Slash bowed slightly. "My apologies. Continue."

"Thank you. Where was I?"

"Shrieking with my last breath."

"Ah. You will shriek it with your last breath as I slay you," the Villain continued. To the Dwarves, I am *Kon Borok gat mors*, son of the Killing Stones. To the Elves I am *Malikinolar*, Bringer of the Darkness. And to the Orcs, I am *Vorsch Kraam*, the Eater of Souls."

"And I suppose the Istaka call you *Kriha beridakh*, One who Tires the Ears," the Crimson Slash said, leaning on his sword.

The Villain scowled, dropping his pose and putting his hands on his hips in frustration. "Do you want to hear my name or not?"

"Well, if I'm to shriek it as you slay me, I'll have to know it, I suppose."

"Very well. To the Census Keepers, I am Voshtyr von Steinadler, son of Benjamin von Steinadler. But to Heroes and commoners alike, I am Voshtyr Demonkin." He raised his arms again. "Prepare to Meet your Doom, Crimson Slash!"

"My Doom?" the Crimson Slash said with a laugh. "No, sirrah, you are outnumbered by more than eight to one. Prepare to Face Justice!"

Voshtyr snorted. "You fool. You think mere odds can stop me? Well, let me even them out somewhat!" With a diabolical laugh, he flung his left arm out at the Kingsguard. A wave of crackling purple energy blasted forth from his hand, striking four of the men and knocking them to the floor in writhing convulsions. With another gesture, they stiffened and rose, blank stares on their faces.

The Crimson Slash almost dropped his sword, and Voshtyr laughed at his facial expression. The blast was nothing less than combined *Soul Burnout* and *Penultimate Reanimation* spells. The blood drained from the Crimson Slash's face. "Grant!" he yelled. "He's not a Villain—he's an Arch-Villain! Take the King and run!"

"Anthony!" Voshtyr barked at his red-bearded thug. "I have a Hero to slaughter. Get that ring for me!"

Anthony threw himself at a wall of remaining Kingsguards, his mace a silver blur.

The captain of the Kingsguard hurried his monarch toward an antechamber while fighting off the red-bearded man and his former comrades. The reanimated corpses of the Kingsguard were fresh enough to retain their muscle memory.

They fought almost as well against their erstwhile friends as they had while they were alive.

Voshtyr turned to the Crimson Slash. "And now, you will learn a lesson you shall take with you to your grave: why a mere Hero should not trifle with an Arch-Villain."

"You cannot defeat me!" Anthony shouted at two Kingsguards as they both moved to protect their king. Anthony brought his mace down on them with a rush of air. "I am Sir Anthony the Mace, and thousands have fallen beneath my blade!"

The two men combined their strength to ward off the Villain's blow. One of them laughed. "Well, I am Ranulf of the King's Own. And that's not a blade, that's a mace."

"True," the other guard said. "I am James of the King's Own, foul Villain. And last I heard, your Villainy Rating said that you were at forty-seven murders." He threw his weight into his shield, sending the Villain staggering back. "That's more like dozens than thousands."

"*Silence!*" Anthony bellowed. "My slight exaggeration matters not. What matters is that two common men such as yourselves cannot hope to best a Villain!"

"How about three?" asked another Kingsguard, stabbing at Anthony from behind.

Anthony the Mace snorted, spinning and parrying the attack. "Bah, one more means little. You could have four or five, or, er, six . . . " His bluster trailed off as several more knights surrounded him.

"Stand your ground, Villain," Ranulf demanded.

"I'll stand where I want," Anthony said. "My armor is nigh invulnerable to common weapons. Only a magical blade could have any hope of—"

With a nod from Ranulf, all six of the Kingsguard twisted the pommels of their weapons. Shimmering blue light blazed around the cold steel of the swords.

Anthony's eyes grew wider, and he backed up a pace. "Magical weapons? Bryath must have a high equipment budget . . . " Then he shook his head. "Fie! Your weapons matter not. Eat elemental death, fools!" Anthony gestured with his gauntleted hands. *"Underworld's Own . . . "*

"Brace yourselves, men!" Ranulf shouted, raising his shield.

" *. . . Crushing Sphere of . . . "*

The Kingsguard hunkered down against incoming magic.

" *. . . Incredibly Mighty . . . Cowardice!* Yaaah!" The Villain shoved aside one of the Kingsguard and ran back down the hallway the way he had come.

Perplexed, the knights stood staring for a few moments. Then with a shout, several leapt to pursue the fleeing Villain. The rest returned to guard their monarch and escort him from the scene of carnage.

Voshtyr snarled and threw himself at Reginald. At the same time, he withdrew a short, straight-edged dagger and threw it at his target's head.

The Crimson Slash saw it coming. He caught the falchion on his shield, but the dagger laid open his left cheek.

"A crimson slash for the Crimson Slash," Voshtyr said with a sneer.

"It's just another scar, Demonkin. One I shall live to see heal and you will not." The Hero winced as the blood flowed into his beard, but he immediately counterattacked. "The Crimson

Slash pressed his counterattack, raining furious blows on the dastardly Villain!" he shouted, striking repeatedly at Voshtyr.

Voshtyr had to retreat beneath the hammerlike blows of the Hero's oversized sword. "What in the Ninth Abyss are you doing?" the Villain demanded, dodging behind a pillar and clutching his right wrist.

"Narrating!" Reginald replied. "What is an Epic Battle without narration?"

"Significantly less annoying!"

Reginald laughed heroically.

Voshtyr ran at the Hero and ducked under another Standard Horizontal Slash. As he came up, he bashed aside the Crimson Slash's shield with his left gauntlet and lunged for an opening.

"The Crimson Slash punched Voshtyr in the face. The Villain's attempt at catching the Hero off guard failed, gaining the foul man naught but a bloody nose."

"*Graah!* Stop that narration or I'll render you incapable of speech!"

"The Hero was unafraid of the Villain's bluster, knowing that words never suffice in place of action."

Voshtyr's eyes narrowed to slits. "Fine, then, action it is." He leapt high, his falchion crackling with dark purple energy as he brought the blade down from above.

"The Crimson Slash blocked the cut with his massive sword, absorbing the impact, and the dark magic disappeared with an ineffective sigh. Now the Hero's face was mere inches from Voshtyr's!"

"Yes, and there's something stuck to it," Voshtyr said, raising an eyebrow. "Is that . . . cherry filling?"

Reginald felt his face go red with embarrassment. "Strawberry, most like." With a swing of his shield, he knocked Voshtyr off balance.

But off balance did not mean unprepared. Throwing his left hand out as he fell, Voshtyr shouted, *"Impact Beam!"* A coherent beam of distorted air lanced out from his hand and Reginald found himself knocked backward, a smoking ding in his breastplate.

Recovering rapidly, Reginald spun backward, his blade bisecting a hopefully non-load-bearing column to the side of the room. It fell toward Voshtyr with a grinding groan.

Voshtyr leapt deftly to the side to avoid the falling column. "Do you think such a pathetic trick will work on me?"

Unfortunately for the Arch-Villain, the falling column was not the trick. It was the distraction.

"The Crimson Slash intercepted the Arch-Villain as he dodged the column. With one sweeping blow the Hero lopped off the foul Demonkin's entire left arm!"

Voshtyr screamed in agony. His left arm fell to the floor, severed cleanly at the shoulder. Black blood spattered the red carpet. He fell to his knees, clamping his other hand tightly over the wound to stanch the bleeding.

"Well, it seems you may have to change your Villain name after this," the Crimson Slash said, leaning on his sword and smirking at Voshtyr. "How does 'Voshtyr Tripod' sound?"

Voshtyr growled, his face a hideous mask of pain and hate. "You Heroes need to learn when to taunt and when not to," he hissed through clenched teeth. "This is a when-not-to."

"On the contrary," Reginald replied. "I quote *The Complete Guide to Heroics,* volume 3, chapter 17, paragraph 22: 'Another opportune time to Taunt your Foe is when you have just delivered a successful attack and have the Advantage over your Opponent.'"

"Advantage?" Voshtyr said slowly. "What advantage? You think depriving me of a weak corporeal limb will slow me down? You fool. You have only made me stronger."

"Then let's see how strong you get when I remove the other," the Hero said, readying his sword once more. "Prepare to face Jus—"

Pain seared his mind. Voshtyr filled it with his sinister magic, and it had just hit its breaking point. The Villain's green eyes changed to a malevolent red glow as the power of his magic increased tenfold.

"Now," Voshtyr said, rising from the floor, "remind me again who has the advantage here?" Dust and shreds of red carpeting began to swirl around him, and the light from outside the windows dimmed.

"Your . . . your eyes . . . " Reginald said, backing away and holding his head.

"Lovely, aren't they? Got them from my mother." Voshtyr pulled his gauntlet away from his bleeding shoulder and licked his own blood from his finger.

"Red eyes . . . ? You're not . . . " the Crimson Slash swallowed. "You're not—"

"Human?" Voshtyr replied, advancing. "Not entirely, no. You have no idea with whom you are dealing. Indeed, any Arch-Villain outmatches a Hero, but I am far above pathetic Arch-Villains as well!"

Voshtyr's eyes flared brighter, and he pulled from inside his armor a necklace made of what looked like rough-cut beads. Reginald saw they were actually tiny gemstones, each one flickering with inner light. Voshtyr held the necklace up to the heavens. "No, you have *no* idea."

The sky outside the castle walls darkened as the sun eclipsed itself. The castle shook violently, shattering the stained-glass windows of the throne room. The Crimson Slash staggered backward and braced himself against the empty throne.

With a deafening roar, the castle tore itself apart. Explosions blossomed all around, blowing chunks out of the walls, enormous gouges in the exterior stonework. The entire top of the throne room spun off, swirling upward into an enormous hole in the sky, the grey stones disappearing as they entered its maw. Lightning a horrendous shade of purple streaked across the damaged sky.

Reginald stared at Voshtyr in amazement. Where was the fiend getting all the magic to wreak such havoc? In determination he dug a slim silver token—it looked almost like a coin of the realm—from his pocket and pressed it hard in the center.

Reginald knew Voshtyr would know what the Token meant. But the Arch-Villain didn't quail, as he'd hoped, but instead smiled wickedly.

"Thank you, my dear Hero," Voshtyr said, "for calling more Heroes for me to toy with before I slaughter them. What a pleasant day this is becoming."

Reginald heard a voice boom from the Token. "Crimson Slash! Your location reads as right in the center of the cataclysm on Centra Mundi! Are you all right?"

"No! I require immediate assistance!" the Crimson Slash yelled over the howling of the wind and the vortex above. "AVA-RIA, I repeat, AVA-RIA! Send whoever you can, whatever you can, as fast as you can!"

The reader should note that AVA-RIA is not some form of obscure chanted prayer, nor is it a type of fruit juice, nor even an Elven word for a botched opera solo.

It is instead a code word used by professional Heroes to warn each other of an Arch-Villain Attack (AVA), and that he or she Requires Immediate Assistance (RIA).

Whereas Reginald had little use for a glass of fruit juice at the moment, had no prayer beads within easy reach, and had as much appreciation of opera as he did of feline caterwauling, he certainly needed backup.

"AVA-RIA acknowledged, Crimson Slash," the voice said from the coin. "Help is on the way. Delay the Arch-Villain if possible."

Reginald nodded and severed the connection and glanced around. The situation had not gotten any better. The hole in the sky continued to pull bits of the castle into its maw, and had indeed grown to the point where it was ripping trees from the castle courtyard out by their roots. The sun was a black circle wreathed in fire. The howling of the wind had increased in both volume and pitch, now shrieking around the shattered stones. The King and his Guard had abandoned the darkened throne room entirely, leaving only the beleaguered Hero and his diabolical opponent.

Voshtyr stood in a pose of manic ecstasy, produced by the power of his terrible magics, no doubt. A fiendish smile lit his features, as did the flaming glow of his red eyes. His shoulder had ceased bleeding, as the blood had blackened and scorched to his wounded flesh. The Arch-Villain's black cloak swirled about him in the wind as he raised his remaining arm to the vortex, laughing inhumanly.

"Demonkin!" Reginald shouted, raising his sword. "This has gone far enough! Taste My Blade!"

The Arch-Villain, entranced by his own magically induced chaos, barely had time to raise his own weapon in defense as Reginald's titanic blade descended on him. With a resounding clang, Voshtyr's falchion lost half its length.

Voshtyr scowled, his glowing eyes flaring brighter. "Excuse me, I was enjoying my Moment of Triumph."

"No one else was," Reginald said, squaring off against the Arch-Villain.

"That matters not." Voshtyr turned to face him. "You are an interfering nuisance, Crimson Slash. Do you know what I do to interfering nuisances?"

"Shake their hand and swap stories with them over a flask of brandy?"

"No, you fool! I slay them without mercy. Now, have at you!" Voshtyr slashed at Reginald with the broken-but-still-sharp falchion, its blade dancing with spectral fire.

"The Crimson Slash blocked the shorter blade easily. The evil Voshtyr found the task of getting through the Hero's guard nearly impossible. Even the repeated blasts of dark flame failed to penetrate the Hero's shield. The Crimson Slash now had the Advantage over his Foe and would soon defeat him entirely!" Reginald put his entire weight into a horizontal sword-cut. "With a single mighty blow, he knocked the Arch-Villain backward into a stone column!"

Voshtyr flew backward, slamming into one of the few pillars that hadn't yet been ripped from its anchors by the vortex above. But this time the Arch-Villain was more prepared. Instead of striking the pillar in an uncontrolled trajectory, he landed feet first on the marble surface, pushing off in an incredible lunge at Reginald's shield.

Reginald raised his sword but Voshtyr's rebound had surprised him. The Arch-Villain's hand clamped around his throat. "*Ghug!*" Reginald choked out as Voshtyr put pressure on his windpipe.

"Ah, not so cocky now, eh, Hero?" Voshtyr said, a malevolent grin on his pointed features. A flash of purple energy crackled down his arm. "What, no plucky narration for posterity? Or does your final battle fade into obscurity? Ah, here's some for you: The pathetic Hero gasped and choked, realizing, as he died, his foolishness in daring to challenge the mighty Voshtyr Demonkin."

Reginald convulsed. His throat ached around where Voshtyr's fingers grasped. He could feel himself dying. With tremendous effort, he swung his sword in a desperate attempt to free himself from the life-draining grasp.

"None of that," Voshtyr said, his eyes flaring a shimmering blood-red. Reginald's blade flashed a dull and toxic green and spun from his weakening grasp. The Arch-Villain turned his blazing gaze back on Reginald and increased both the grip and the magic.

Reginald gurgled, feeling pressure spread up his face and burst blood vessels in his eyes. He sank to his knees as darkness clawed at the edges of his vision.

Then, with the convenience of a *Deus Ex Machina*, two things happened.

First, Reginald's reinforcements arrived. Three Heroes in Heroic Armor appeared with a sparkle and rush of air, all armed for combat. Emblems of varying shapes and colors adorned their armor, and their weapons glowed with the effulgent sheen of elemental magics.

Reginald knew them by both name and reputation. The knight in dark purple-tinted platemail was the Purple Paladin. He knew the woman in white-lacquered riding armor as the White Shrike. And the third he had met only once, when the Turquoise Templar had amused his guests by creating the largest magical light show in anyone's memory.

In the same moment, three very irritable Villains appeared amidst a rush of black wind, a signature teleportation mark for the Brotherhood of the Black Hand. The three newly arrived Heroes found themselves standing shoulder to shoulder with a seven-foot-tall Orc in nightdark robes, a knight in black armor, and a weedy-looking fellow with spectacles and a heavy, leatherbound book. The swirling ruins of Bryath Castle had suddenly become a very popular locale.

"Voshtyr Demonkin," the weedy man demanded, "drop that Hero at once!"

Reginald felt the Arch-Villain's grasp release. He fell to the flagstones with a heavy thud and rubbed his throat.

Voshtyr threw up his hands in confusion. "What are you three doing here?"

"Dealing with that," the weedy man said, pointing up at the hole in the sky and the eclipsed sun. He opened his book and ran a slim finger down the page. "Voshtyr Demonkin, you have already used up your solar eclipse for the quarter—and you haven't paid for a second one. Furthermore, if you're going to cause Epic Destruction on this scale, you need to fill out Environmental Impact forms 32-A and 44-QZ. You could have filled these out ahead of time if you'd shared your plan with the Brotherhood, but no!" He slammed the weighty book shut and glared at the Arch-Villain. "You had to go and do it yourself."

"But I—"

The weedy man held up a hand, pointing at the wounded sky. "The vortex, Voshtyr."

Voshtyr scowled, but cut the power from his potent spell. The sun brightened, and the hole in the sky closed with a muted burp. Pieces of the castle began descending to the ruined landscape. "All right, all right, I'll sign your papers. Just hurry it up. If the king and his ring get away now—"

"The King's not going anywhere," the Purple Paladin said. "You are." He pointed a thick finger coated with tiny overlapping plates into Voshtyr's face. "You're going to spend a little time in a special prison for what you've done here today."

"What, for wrecking this pathetic castle and slaying a few of the palace guard?" Voshtyr sneered. "Those mean naught to me."

"No, those are merely the civil charges," the Turquoise Templar said, taking a scroll out of a belt-pouch and looking at it. "You're also charged with Overuse of Magic, Illegal Magics, Grand Theft Soul, and," he glanced around himself, "first-class Environmental Damage. White Shrike," he said to their third companion, "see to the Crimson Slash."

The third Hero, a woman clad in sparkling white armor, knelt beside Reginald. She placed three fingers on his neck and closed her eyes.

Reginald caught his reflection in a large fragment of shattered mirror amidst the rubble. His cheek bled from a nasty cut, his neck and face were a leprous white save for purple finger marks, and his eyes were so bloodshot it seemed they had no whites. As he watched, the purple discoloration faded and normal color slowly returned to his cheeks. Reginald coughed and sat up, his bloodshot eyes gradually returning to their normal hazel.

Voshtyr turned to the other three Villains, the red glow fading from his eyes. "What is this nonsense? You three— don't you see this opportunity? These Heroes are at our mercy and the King is but moments away! Come, help me slay these buffoons, and together we can Rule the World!"

"No can do, Demonkin," the Orc said, shaking his green-skinned head. "You started this without involving the Brotherhood, and we can't intervene in any non-sanctioned activities. And . . . didn't you used to have two arms?"

"Fools! So you're going to let them take me? I'm—"

"Now under the jurisdiction of the Greater Bryath Heroic Court District," the Purple Paladin said. "Stand down, Voshtyr von Steinadler, and your compliance will be taken into account at your trial." Purple placed his hand on the hilt of his sword, just in case the Villain resisted.

Voshtyr looked back and forth between the Heroes and Villains. Finally, he looked at the Villainous Knight in black armor. "Can't you even . . . "

The knight shook his head. "The most I can do is ensure that your accomplice, Sir Anthony the Mace, finds temporary shelter. Perhaps he can free you from these men in a few days."

The Heroes laughed in derision. "Anthony the Mace?" the White Shrike said, looking up from her healing. "The one who used to be the Silver Talon? That meathead couldn't stage a jailbreak at a nursery."

Voshtyr sighed melodramatically and raised his hand in surrender. "All right. I admit defeat. For now." He dropped the glowing necklace of gems and glared at Reginald.

"Good choice, von Steinadler," the Purple Paladin said. "Take him away."

As Voshtyr was led past Reginald, he stopped and stared into the Hero's face, his eyes narrowed. "This does not end here, Crimson Slash. A week, a year, five years—it matters not. I will find you. And when I do, I shall make you suffer."

Reginald returned the Arch-Villain's gaze calmly. "Sorry, Demonkin. This is a do-not-taunt moment. You need to read the book again." He leaned toward Voshtyr's face. "You may try, but you shall fail next time as well. Justice always prevails."

And with that, the Turquoise Templar led Voshtyr off to a maximum security Villain Detention Center and a heavily magic-proofed holding cell.

Reginald sat wearily on a pile of shattered stone and sighed. He watched with growing fatigue as the group of Heroes and Villains worked out details of custody of Voshtyr for his trial.

There was much shouting and finger-pointing, but thankfully no drawn weapons. Such matters were regulated by the Guild of Heroes and the Brotherhood of the Black Hand, after all.

The King and Kingsguard slowly filtered back into the castle, gawking at the destruction.

"A thousand thanks, Crimson Slash," Sir Grant said. The knight was bandaged and pale, but he clapped Reginald on the shoulder. "We of the Kingsguard could not have held that demon off without your help, and our King would now lie dead if you had not been here. You have the gratitude of the entire kingdom of Bryath."

Reginald chuckled. "I'd rather have a bottle of brandy. Or another of those strawberry tarts." He sighed. "I hope that Arch-Villain cannot make good on his threats. I'd not wish to fight him again."

Something buzzed in Reginald's equipment pouch. "Just one moment, Sir Grant, I'm being called." He dug into the leather bag and retrieved a small silver token bearing an hourglass and eye painted on it. He pressed it gently and held it in his palm.

An almost transparent figure of a woman appeared in miniature, standing atop the token. "Crimson Slash," she said, "this is the Guild. We have a new duty for you."

"Yes, of course," Reginald said. "Shall I escort Demonkin to the VDC?"

"No, Sir Ogleby, 'tis a task far more dangerous." The woman raised her arm and pointed directly at Reginald, pausing dramatically.

"It is time for you, the Crimson Slash, to take a new apprentice."

Chapter I

THE TIME WHICH ONCE
WAS UPON

*In which the Reader first Meets the Protagonist,
and he Passes a Test*

NCE UPON A Time, in a faraway king-
dom, there lived an old man and his wife.
They had no children, and the old man
prayed every day that he and his wife would
have a son.

This story has absolutely nothing to do with them.

It is instead the tale of a boy who wanted to become a
Hero.

On the tropical island of Starspeak, the second largest of
the Citrus Island chain, lived Cyrus Solburg, a red-haired lad
of fifteen years. His residence was a small house near the piers,
with his Uncle Jacob, Aunt Catherine, and his cousin Marco.

Ever since he had been a little boy, Cyrus wanted to grow
up and be a Hero like his father had been. And on the day our
story starts, the isolated island of Starspeak received a visit
from two members of the International Guild of Heroes.

The small ship in which they traveled glided into the
cerulean water of the bay and gently pulled up to the quay, its

sails flapping in the salty breeze. The sailors lashed the ropes to the dock and dropped the anchor, and a man of medium height wearing all red—from his cloak and soft boots to the brass-studded felt shirt and trousers—stepped onto the deck and slid down a rope to the docks.

The weathered planks of the pier ran a short distance to the glistening white beach of Stasrpeak island. The island itself was a pretty place, the very picture of a tropical paradise. There were palm trees on the beach and citrus-bearing trees farther inland. The waters offshore were a brilliant turquoise, dotted by the boats of local small-time fishermen seeking the day's catch.

A small stone path led from the pier, up a gentle incline, and into the town. The one small town on Starspeak contained houses made of many materials, from driftwood to sandstone. The smell of ripe oranges drifted down to the pier, mingled, unfortunately, with the smells of tar from the boat repair yard and fish from the market. Several children of assorted ages ran about, laughing and shouting as they played a silly game that involved beating a leather ball around the beach with a pair of flat sticks.

"Oy! Yellow!" the man in red shouted to another man, who had just appeared from below the deck. "Get down here so we can check for talent and get off this godsforsaken rock!"

The other man, a young blond dressed in a white cassock with golden embroidery, sighed and watched the wind blow through the palm trees on the shore. "I rather like it here, Red. It's quiet, sunny, and peaceful. Besides," he said as he lowered and clambered down a rope ladder, "Starspeak has produced two noteworthy talents recently, so it is undoubtedly worth our time."

"Bah. It was the family, not the island," Red replied. The breeze playfully blew his long black hair into his face, and he yanked it back harshly, tying it into a ponytail with a thin strip of leather. "Both of them were Weatherblades, right? I don't see the point in coming back here year after year, Yellow. There's going to be no one here worth their salt, just like the last two years."

"Well, you could be right. But look on the bright side, Red: even if we fail to find any prospects, we're still on a two-day paid vacation to a tropical paradise." Yellow inhaled the salt air and smiled. "And don't forget, there's that one boy who sent us a letter. We should at least visit his house."

"His house? Nine Fires, Yellow. Let's just do a sweep of the town like usual and save ourselves the trouble of wandering all over trying to find one brat."

"Very well. They already know that we're coming. We may as well hold the event in the town square."

A red-haired boy watched as the sleek ship sailed into the harbor, but soon turned back to his work in his own boat. It was probably another tourist or merchant here to see what fruit grew on this island. He actually preferred it be a merchant. At least they brought strange things from foreign countries. Tourists merely came, ate, and littered.

The salt wind flapped the white homespun shirt he wore and tousled his hair, carrying with it smells of tar and hempen rope from the newly arrived vessel. At a nod from his uncle, the boy heaved his end of the net overboard and watched it sink. "Which do you think that boat's here for, Uncle Jacob? Trade or Tourism?"

His uncle shrugged. "Merchants, most like. It's almost fruit season, and they're bound to show up to scout out the best crops."

The boy looked the ship up and down. "I hope they brought a monkey. Or a lesser basilisk. Or maybe they'll have some amras seeds! The sailors might have some stories to tell, or maybe there's a Hero on board, or—"

"Or maybe you'll sprout wings and fly away," Jacob said, chuckling softly. "Calm down, Cyrus. It's just a ship like any other."

"Har har, Uncle Jacob. Can I go see them now?" The boy, Cyrus, tapped his fingers anxiously on the gunwale of the small fishing boat.

Jacob shook his head. "We've got work to do, boy. You can play around at the docks when we get done."

"But Uncle, they might be gone when we get done!"

Jacob turned a flat, tired gaze on Cyrus. "Not until we get today's catch in, boy. No fish in the market, no food on the table, you know. Now haul on that line there."

Cyrus sighed and began spreading his corner of the net.

"Augh! My knee!" a little boy screamed, and began sobbing for his mother.

"Ezra Sandbar, negative. Failure in Jumping," said Red, gleefully hashing a large red X across the success/failure box on his clipboard. He pulled at the collar of his heavy red tunic. "Whew, I should have worn something lighter. This sun is too much."

Yellow wiped his blond hair out of his eyes and knelt in the sand outside the city square. "Well, you could take a layer off, Dante," he said to Red, and pressed two fingers to little

Ezra's knee. A pale blue glow spread across his skin. The boy stopped crying. Yellow smiled. "Go on now, Ezra. Go play with your sister."

The boy ran off to join his older sister, who had just failed the Strength test.

Red thumped Yellow's shoulder with the clipboard. "Yeah, I could, Joseph, but I look better with my whole outfit on. Anyway," he said, looking down at the clipboard, "we're five down, with seven to go. At this rate, we'll be done before sundown. And good riddance. We'll be off this rock by nightfall."

"A pity," Yellow said, looking at the small cluster of sandstone buildings tinged orange by the slowly setting sun, "but I suppose it can't be helped."

As the sun dipped below the horizon in a flash of green, Cyrus and his uncle dumped the day's catch into a deep trough for salting-down.

Cyrus's cousin Marco, a dark-haired boy two years his junior, came running down from the house.

"Hey, Cyrus, guess what!"

"You found a live crab in your bed," Cyrus guessed.

Marco shook his head. "Nope, guess again!"

Cyrus looked at his cousin with a grin. "Well, you will find a crab in your bed if you don't tell me what you're all excited about." He dumped a thin layer of salt across the fish.

"There were Heroes here today! And I *almost* passed their speed test!"

"Heroes?" Cyrus dropped the bag of salt. "There were Heroes here today? They must have got my letter! Wait, that means that ship . . . "

Uncle Jacob glanced at Cyrus. "A little more urgent than merchants, eh? Get thee gone, boy. I can handle the rest. Go and see if those Heroes are still here."

Cyrus grinned and dashed off to the town square.

Upon his arrival, he found it deserted. The majority of the sandstone buildings were closed up for the night, light filtering out through the shuttered windows. Many footprints spattered the sand and stones, but there was not a soul to be seen. Biting back his frustration, he ran for the docks, on the off-chance that the Heroes had not left yet.

The repairmen and carpenters had gone home for the night, leaving the pier all but deserted. The sea was now the inky black it always became at night, and the breeze blew from behind him as the warm air from the island fled for the cooler clime of the ocean. A few seagulls hopped across the beach, squabbling noisily over some moldy scraps of bread that must have been tossed overboard. No movement was visible on any of the few ships docked at Starspeak.

But it was Cyrus's lucky day. Or perhaps it was Fate that the crew had discovered a minor leak in the ship's hull that delayed their departure. Either way, Cyrus spotted two Heroes sitting on the pier—one in red and the other in white and gold. The red one sat shaking stones out of his boots.

Cyrus stepped cautiously out onto the pier. "Excuse me, are you two the Heroes who came in on this ship?"

"No, we're traveling rock salesmen," replied the man in red, handing the boy a pebble from his boot. "This one is a free sample. Now get out of here, we're busy."

Cyrus frowned and was about to reply, when the white-robed Hero stood up and walked over.

"Yes, we are," he said, "and unless I miss my guess, you must be Cyrus Solburg."

Cyrus gasped. "You know me?"

"Aye. We know all about you. I've even read your letter. I'm Joseph Evinmar, known as the Yellow Sun. What say you, Red?" he asked his companion. "Shall we test the boy?"

"Not interested," said the red-garbed swordsman, banging on the heel of his calf-length boot. Sand and stones fell into a pile on the sun-bleached boards of the pier.

The Yellow Sun frowned. "Come on, Red, we must give the boy a chance . . . "

"Must?" Red retorted. "You see the sky? You see the sun anywhere in it? No, I'm done for the day. Try again next year, kid."

Tears pricked at the back of Cyrus's eyes, and he clenched his fists. "You're not even going to let me try?" He tried hard to keep his voice even, but it cracked on the word *try*.

Red snorted. "Only if you could beat me in a footrace, kid."

Yellow laughed. "What an excellent idea, Red! If the lad can beat you in a footrace, will you test him?"

"What?" The man in red started. "I wasn't serious, Yellow. I mean, sure, but there's no way a kid like him could—"

"Excuse me, Hero," Cyrus said, "but I have to ask two things. First, what's your name, and second, can I borrow one of your gloves?"

"I'm Dante Vertigo, known as the Red Death," said the man in red, absently handing one of his felt gloves to the boy. "What did you want the glove f—"

Cyrus slapped the glove across the Red Death's face. "I challenge you to a footrace, Red Death."

• • •

Twilight had dimmed to dark by the time the Yellow Sun managed to separate the Hero and the boy and set up an agreed-upon starting line.

The two Heroes and Cyrus stood on the southern coast of Starspeak, just past the pier. To their left was the sea, to the right, the island's interior.

"Now, the rules are simple," Yellow said, glancing back and forth between the two competitors. "You start when I say go, and the first one to make a complete circuit of the island wins. No shortcuts. Just the circumference. Understand?"

Both nodded.

"Good. *Go!*"

Before Cyrus could react, the Red Death shot forward as a crimson blur, deliberately veering in front of the boy and spraying sand in his eyes. Cyrus wiped the grit from his eyes and ran as well.

The Yellow Sun watched the boy with pity. The Red Death was too fast and too well trained for a rank amateur to defeat. Neither could Cyrus know that the Red Death's specialty was supersonic movement, unless he'd read some of those ridiculously exaggerated adventure stories that bards were always writing about Heroes. But no matter what the stories said, they couldn't exaggerate his speed. Dante Vertigo lacked the enormous physical strength most Heroes had, but he made up for it with finesse and velocity. He was soon out of sight.

Not that Cyrus was slow, Yellow noted. The boy ran at a clip that would shame a healthy horse. Maybe next year, if he showed up on time, he'd pass the tests.

• • •

Trees passed by Cyrus as amorphous dark blurs. Rocks large and small shot by at an incredible rate as he circled the island. Cliffs to his left, forest to the right, Cyrus struggled to catch up to, or at least keep pace with the Red Death.

He was two-thirds of the way around when he heard a shout. Halting, and nearly falling over thanks to a little-remembered law of physics, Cyrus turned around and walked back to the cliff. There were two sets of four fingers sticking up over the edge.

"Boy! Help me out of here, will you?" called a voice from below. It was the Red Death. The Hero hung in midair, a hundred and eighty spans above the rocky sea below. "I'm going to fall if you don't help me!"

Cyrus hesitated, pondering what to do. If he helped the Hero, he might still lose the race. If he left the man to his possible demise, it would be un-Hero-like behavior in the extreme.

As usual, the choice was easy. He reached a hand down and pulled the struggling Hero out of the chasm.

"Heh, thanks, kid. I wasn't expecting you to help me out of there," Red said, catching his breath. "I don't know *bok* about Starspeak's geography, and it's dark as a bag of bats out here. I just barely managed to catch hold of the edge . . . " Standing up, Dante saluted Cyrus with two fingers. "Well, we got a race to finish. Toodles!" he said, and sped off again, leaving rock-dust in his wake.

Cyrus picked up the pace as well, keeping the Red Death in sight until the Hero crossed the finish line. At that point, the boy slowed down. By the time he arrived at the pier, he'd slowed to a disillusioned plod.

"Well, kiddo," the red-garbed Hero said, ruffling Cyrus's hair, "you didn't really expect to beat the Red Death at a foot-race now, did you? I mean, you're what, fourteen years old?"

"Fifteen," Cyrus said wearily, turning to walk away. "I have to get home now. There's fish to salt."

"Whoa, whoa, where do you think you're going?" The Yellow Sun grabbed Cyrus's shoulder. "I talked with Dante before you got here. He told me about the cliff, and we agree— you have the heart to be a Hero. We'll test you for the other required abilities tomorrow, if you're willing to come back."

Cyrus's eyes widened until they seemed fit to pop out of his head. "Really? You're not leaving yet? You w-want me to be a Hero?"

"I speak nothing but the truth," Yellow said, patting the flanged mace in its sling by his side. The weapon had the word *Veritas* etched in the handle. "Come back tomorrow after sunrise, and we'll start. Go, tell your family!"

Cyrus didn't hesitate. He sped off, unadulterated joy putting a spring in his step.

The Yellow Sun and the Red Death watched the boy go, the latter chuckling a bit as he did so.

"So," Yellow said, "it looks like you're going to have to endure another night on this godsforsaken rock."

Red shrugged. "I don't know about the *endure* bit. I'm starting to like the place. It kind of grows on you."

The Heroes were as good as their word. When Cyrus ran down to the docks early the next morning, the Yellow Sun and the Red Death awaited him.

They tested his strength by having him lift a cow. Though terrifying for the animal, it was easy for Cyrus. He had been able to pick up extremely large objects since he was a boy of eight years. Red tested him in skill by staging a three-minute swordfight. Despite the Hero's speed, Cyrus held up for two minutes and fifteen seconds. Cyrus successfully navigated a jumping obstacle course, and, Yellow said, in record time, to boot. He had already passed the speed test, Red said with a chuckle.

Yellow cast a spell to test Cyrus's magical capacity and resonance. When he got the feedback, he frowned, retried, blanched, and kept the final results to himself.

When the tests were done, Cyrus flopped into the sand, panting, but with a smile pasted all over his face.

The Yellow Sun walked a short distance away and pulled a silver disk from his pocket. The imprint was that of an eye, which had an hourglass for a pupil. He gently pressed the center of the token, then stared out at the cerulean waves as they crashed onto the sandy shore. In a few moments, a tiny pale figure stood atop the coin.

"Yellow Sun, have you found a likely prospect?" the translucent woman asked.

He nodded. "That we have, Destiny. It's the lad who sent us that letter a few years back. He's Jeremiah Solburg's son. Take a look for yourself." He held the token out so that it faced the boy lying in the sand.

A soft and ephemeral laugh wafted from the token. "Yes, yes, he will do. He looks just like his father did at that age. You have my approval. Bring me the paperwork." The woman looked privately amused. "I think I have just the Hero for him."

"All right, Destiny. Thank you. We'll see you tomorrow."

"You're welcome. Good day and good luck."

With that, the Yellow Sun pocketed the token and approached Cyrus.

He extended a hand and pulled the lad up. "Cyrus Solburg of Starspeak," he said formally, "you have been Chosen by Destiny to become a Hero. Do you have the courage to carry through?"

Cyrus's eyes widened with his smile. "Yes, I do. Absolutely!"

"Good!" He clapped Cyrus soundly on the shoulder. "We have some paperwork to do, and then you'll meet your mentor within the week." He turned to the Red Death, who had apparently been attempting to see how many coconuts he could impale on his blade. "Come on, Dante, we've work to do."

Red grumbled but began removing the fruit from his sword.

Yellow turned back to Cyrus. "We must first speak with your guardians. Lead us to them, Mr. Solburg, if you please."

Cyrus's mind was a blur. The Heroes had met Uncle Jacob and Aunt Catherine and had set sail on the evening tide.

They'd left Cyrus with a letter, which he was to deliver to one Sir Reginald Ogleby, known as the Crimson Slash. Apparently the Crimson Slash was coming to Starspeak—but when? Not knowing what to make of it, Cyrus kept the piece of paper under his pillow. But he took it out and read it again every couple of hours. It contained words such as "courageous," "competent," and "principled"—describing *him*, of all people.

But aside from the glowing letter, nothing had changed. He still had to be out at sea before dawn with his uncle, in for lunch, out again until dusk, and then more fish to salt than anyone in his right mind would ever want to handle. Ships came and went, with no Heroes aboard. After the tenth day, the boy stopped looking. Maybe it had been some kind of cruel joke.

So it was a surprise when Cyrus came home one evening to find a very large man sitting at his kitchen table, talking amiably with his Aunt Catherine and cousin Marco. As soon as Cyrus entered the house, the man stood up and smiled, nearly striking his head on the oil lamp hanging from the ceiling.

The Hero was an enormous fellow, over six feet tall, with shoulders broad as an ox. He had a kind face, if a bit rough. His thick black hair and the neatly trimmed beard that covered his cheeks failed to obscure a long, thin, newly healed scar running down the left side of his face and neck.

"Greetings, lad!" the man boomed. His voice was a gravelly bass, a mellow tone that Cyrus could feel as well as hear. And there was power behind it, as well. Despite how loud this man was, it was obvious that he was using only a fraction of his lung power. "You must be Cyrus. Mine name is Sir Reginald Ogleby, known far but not wide as the Crimson Slash. Destiny has made you my apprentice. Will you be ready to leave Starspeak tomorrow morning?"

"I . . . um . . . You're . . . ? I mean, of course I will," Cyrus said, looking down at the grey throw rug on which they stood. Good Gryphons! Even the man's *boots* were huge!

"Look up here at my face, lad."

Cyrus did so, looking into the Hero's hazel eyes, which sparkled with hidden mirth.

"There. That's better. That's the first thing about being a Hero: always look people in the eyes. Did you know that you can tell if someone is lying just by holding their gaze? You can also see trust and other emotions in there, clearer than fish in a sunlit pond." The Hero put a large hand on Cyrus's shoulder. "Do you know what I see in your eyes, lad?"

"N-no sir."

"I see two things," Reginald said. "First, I see fear. That won't do. A true Hero has no fear, for fear is a fatal weakness. Second, I see the future. In you may lie the hope of the world someday. In the future, you will be a great Hero, and people will sing songs about you over their ale." He nodded and dropped his hand. "But that day is a ways off yet. Sleep well tonight, for tomorrow we leave here, and you may not see this beautiful little island for a long while." Turning to Catherine, the Hero bowed. "I thank you for your hospitality, madam. See that young Cyrus makes it down to the docks at dawn, would you?"

Catherine agreed and showed Sir Ogleby to the door.

Jacob hurried his nephew off to bed, first helping him pack a few necessary things. "I may never get this chance again, boy," he said, "so I want to tell you now. I'm very proud of you, and I'm sure your father would be too."

Cyrus wrapped his arms around his uncle in a hug that popped some vertebrae. "I'm going to miss you, Uncle Jake."

Jacob shook his head, smiling slightly. "No, boy, I don't think you will. You're going to go become a Hero! Can you believe it? It seems like yesterday that you were sitting on the docks, listening to those silly tales of the Golden Hammer and telling me you were going to be a Hero when you grew up." He ruffled Cyrus's hair and tucked the blanket around his shoulders. "But as I was saying, you simply won't have the time. I imagine you'll think of us fondly from time to time.

But miss us? No, you'll be living your dreams, and when you are doing that, there are no regrets."

And so, the next day, Cyrus left with the Crimson Slash.

As the ship pulled away from the pier and Starspeak faded into the distance, Cyrus Solburg smiled.

He was Apprenticed to a Hero.

Chapter 2

OF VILLAINS AND VOCABULARY

In which the Apprentice Hero Learns some of the
Many Failings of Heroes and Villains
and also Learns to Take Notes

THE BOAT PUT ashore in the rain and fog. The inclement weather masked its deposit of a single Hero and his apprentice on the beach. After dropping off the two, it hurried back to its ship as if aquatic hellhounds pursued it through the water.

The Hero was now armed for combat. He wore an open-faced helm with nose-guard, greaves of shining steel, and a breastplate with a single crimson bar running from his left shoulder to the right side at the waist.

On his back rested a titanic sword, a truly epic weapon.

From pommel to tip, it was almost five and a half feet long. The grip was wrapped in leather, and thicker than one of Cyrus's hands would fit around, though it was about the right size for Reginald's titanic mitts. The blade itself was not only longer than a common iron long-sword, it was also much thicker and wider. In the center, it was almost three times as thick as a great-sword. From the center, the sword narrowed to two cutting edges. A ruby in the eagle-claw pommel sparkled with a tiny inner fire.

Cyrus peered excitedly into the total lack of scenery, trying to pick definite shapes out of the fog. The rain beat down on his oilskin and backpack as Reginald slung his shield over Cyrus's shoulders.

"I'll need you to carry that until we reach the top," Reginald explained, examining the cliffs for a good place to start his climb.

Cyrus looked up the insanely tall cliffs. They began three feet beyond where the beach stopped. Supposedly, an evil fortress waited at the top. "Are we really going to climb those?"

Fog shrouded the tops of the cliffs, and what Cyrus could see looked nigh unclimbable. Veins of granite shot through the stone—an unstable combination. And the rain coated the entire surface of the cliff with a wet sheen. No one in his right mind would attempt such a climb, but here the two stood, their only escape route vanishing into the fog as it returned to the ship.

"Aye," Reginald replied, handing Cyrus a dull metal box attached to a length of rope.

Cyrus looked at the box curiously. "In the rain?"

"Aye, lad. The Villain would never expect someone to be so foolish as to attempt scaling the Called Bluffs during a rainstorm." With a sharp laugh the Crimson Slash began his ascent, unencumbered by climbing gear, safety rope, or, it seemed to Cyrus, common sense.

He watched as Reginald scaled the cliff. A quarter of the way, the Hero looked down. "What are you doing, lad? Get yourself up here."

"How?" Cyrus asked. "I can't climb rocks! We only have maybe two cliffs on Starspeak, and neither of them are good for climbing!"

"That's what I gave you the rope for, lad. Give it a few swings, then throw it at the cliff."

"Throw the box?"

"Aye!"

Cyrus did as his mentor said, spinning the box around in a tight circle, then lobbing it at the sheer cliff face. To his astonishment, the box sailed upward and split apart into three claws, which jetted forward and penetrated the cliff.

The Hero chuckled. "Standard Issue Apprentice-Level Climber's Kit, a must for beginning climbers. Just follow the box's lead, lad. It will find the safest route for you. But make haste—this fog will not last forever."

Cyrus obeyed, scrambling up the rope, which had magically located a narrow ledge just wide enough for him to stand on while he threw the box again. As he clamped a cold, wet hand onto the slick stone and climbed over the edge, he caught up with his new mentor. "Hey, Sir Ogleby . . . "

"'Reginald' will do fine, Cyrus," the Hero said, stretching his burly right arm out and purchasing a tentative hold on a stubby outcropping just above him.

"Right, Reginald. Anyway, if no one would be so foolish as to attempt scaling the Called Bluffs during a rainstorm, why are we doing it?"

Reginald removed his left hand from a precarious bit of rock and hung over the abyss by his right hand. With the left, he stroked his beard thoughtfully. "Well, that's the first thing about being a Hero, lad. You must take Unnecessary Risks. It's part of what makes Daring Heroics so Daring and Heroic. You'd best write that one down."

Cyrus abandoned his tenacious grip on the rocks to fish around in the pack, producing a bedraggled piece of paper and a stick of graphite, nearly losing his footing in the process.

"Never mind, lad," Reginald said. "It seems you have a firm grasp on the concept already."

"All right, but while I have this thing out, is there anything else I should jot down? Like, why do you have so many names?" Cyrus asked. "You're Sir Reginald Ogleby, but you're also called the Crimson Slash. Where did you get that name?"

Reginald grabbed hold of the cliff again and swung right, gaining a toehold and a grip with both hands. "Well, lad, when a Hero completes his first Quest, he chooses a name for himself. It is imperative," he said, searching the rock for another safe place to hold on to, "that you have a basic grasp of the Central language in order to create a proper Heroic Name. Do write this down—it is of some importance. The first thing about being a Hero is to have mastery of a language or three. It is useful more often than one might think."

The boy blinked. "Wait, I thought the first thing was—"

"A proper Heroic Name," Reginald said, motioning for Cyrus to continue climbing, "consists of an adjective and the noun it describes, prefaced by the word 'the.' For example, I am known as the Crimson Slash. A good friend of mine is the Black Viper, and your father was called the Bronze Gryphon."

"You knew my father?" Cyrus asked, detaching the box from the cliff and throwing it upward once more. The rain continued coming down, pattering metallically off the shield on Cyrus's back.

Reginald shifted sideways on the cliff face with a grunt, working his way toward a broad ledge a little higher up. "Yes, I knew him. A fine Hero, Bronze was. Always kept his head about him, could stare down a demon, and was no slouch in a swordfight. You look quite a bit like him, you know." Reginald regained his hold on the cliff and moved up another two handspans. "I suppose I had best tell you who we go to fight."

"A Villain?"

"Sharp lad. Aye, a Villain Most Foul. He calls himself Berrik Sawface, and inhabits the Fortress of Misfortune, the very castle that rests atop these bluffs. Allow me to explain Villains to you . . . "

Cyrus clambered up the rope and sat on a wider ledge, preparing himself for blatant exposition.

"Villains have many of the same abilities that we Heroes do," Reginald said, wiping rain from his face, "but they use them for foul purposes, causing suffering and blotting out hope wherever they may be. These miscreants refuse to honor any rule made by the Guild of Heroes. In fact, they tend to do the opposite just to spite us."

Reginald tested handholds in the cliff face until he found one that suited him. "Take our separate naming schemes for example. I've already explained how Heroes do it, but Villains always use their given name followed by a single word, preferably a sinister-sounding one, which describes them or their appearance. A long-time foe of mine, who we will visit tomorrow after we defeat Sawface, provided we survive this cli—"

Reginald slipped on the slick stone and dropped a good five feet before catching himself. He cut his fingers on the jagged rock and inhaled sharply as the stone bit into them.

" . . . calls himself Rish-tak Plainscale. I've also confronted Eldrin Afterglow, Mortimer Clawhand, and the crazed Gemharra Skulleater."

Cyrus tried to take notes, but by this time the rain had soaked his parchment, making it just plain *ment*. How could Reginald continue a sentence after almost falling to his death? He gave up and put the writing gear away. "Visit? We're going to 'visit' a Villain?"

Reginald hefted himself up onto Cyrus's ledge and sat down to catch his breath. "Aye, lad. Plainscale and I are the best of enemies. He's a Villain by familial ties, you see, not by nature. The lizard keeps to himself, mostly. He confines himself to scaring small children and slaughtering tax collectors." Reginald pointed a bleeding thumb toward the top of the cliffs. "Sawface here is a rival of Plainscale's, and I seem to be inadvertently doing my old nemesis a favor by removing him."

"So Villains do a lot of infighting then?" Cyrus asked, pulling out a cloth and wiping blood from Reginald's torn fingers.

"Not so much as you might think," Reginald said, "but they do when they haven't a Hero to fight. Evil is inherently self-destructive, you see, which is why you seldom see a band of Villains working together."

Hero and apprentice completed their climb well before the fog lifted, and crept their way up to the base of the formidable black walls of the Fortress of Misfortune.

The edifice soared above the cliff-top. Reginald explained that the tremendous rectangular wall surrounded an inner keep, with guard towers and wickedly pointed spires adorning it. An air of gloom hung about the structure, and several conveniently placed Human skeletons added nicely to the effect.

"This place gives me the creeps," Cyrus said, shrinking toward his mentor.

"That is the intent, lad," Reginald replied. "The skeletons are new. Sawface must have finally found himself a competent exterior decorator. Last year all he had was a pair of hideous statues."

Several guards of some sort walked back and forth in a regular pattern around the base of the wall, with torches to help them see through the early morning mist and rain. Reginald watched them for several minutes. Cyrus tried to see what he was looking for. He eventually noticed that the guards' pattern never varied, not by a single footstep, and had no proper overlap for the guards to ensure one another's safety.

Reginald chuckled softly and rummaged around in Cyrus's pack. "Sawface is a method Villain, then. Here, lad," he said, handing Cyrus a pocket telescope, "take this and look at one of those guards. Tell me what he's wearing."

Cyrus extended the telescope and peered through it at the guard. "Mostly black, armed with a shortsword, has a raincloak with a serial number of some sort on the sleeve. It . . . doesn't look quite Human. It's too pale, too . . . I don't know. What is it?"

Reginald scoffed. "That, lad, is a Minion. They're quite common in Fortresses and on the Battlefield alike. They're not stupid, precisely, but they are foolish enough to fall for simple tricks. Observe." He picked up a fist-sized rock and hurled it over near the cliff, where it bounced over the edge, making some small amount of noise.

The Minion whirled about, holding his torch up. Cautiously, it approached the cliff and leaned over, looking down. Reginald walked over and gave the creature a shove. With a muted wail, the Minion disappeared down the foggy cliff.

"The poor things never seem to learn basic distraction methods," Reginald said with a sigh. "I have used that trick dozens of times. Now, here comes the other one."

As Reginald snuck back over to the shadow in which he and Cyrus had been hiding, the other Minion walked around the corner, apparently not noticing the other's absence, even though he stood right where the other one had gone over the edge.

"Your turn this time, lad," Reginald said. He handed Cyrus another rock.

Cyrus smiled, took the rock, and hurled it toward the cliff. It struck the Minion in the head. The Minion turned slightly, a dazed expression on its face, and fell off the cliff as well.

"Hmm," Reginald said. "I don't think you've got it yet. You're supposed to use the rock as a distraction."

"I think getting hit in the head with a rock is pretty distracting," Cyrus protested.

Reginald shrugged. "Either way, the lookouts are gone. To the Fortress!"

And in they went.

Reginald swiftly dispatched the small and unprepared resistance they met as they infiltrated the Fortress. Hideous statues lined the walls, along with murals and tapestries depicting massive battles and horrible tortures. The inside of the fortress was hardly less gloomy than the outside, as guttering torches provided but little illumination and threw more shadows than light.

Along the way, Reginald described for Cyrus the various techniques he used to defeat his opponents, such as the Elbow-Room Slash, the basic Tornado attack, and several variations of the classic Multistrike. It was a little difficult to have finesse when using such a large weapon, he explained, but promised to teach Cyrus more about sword-fighting when they reached their next destination.

To be honest, it was too much information for Cyrus to handle all at once. The only swords he had ever played with were toys. All this talk of "special attacks" and "sword styles" was far beyond him and sounded patently ridiculous.

They entered the room with unstable iron grates for flooring. The grates were suspended above a pit of bubbling lava.

Cyrus started. "Wait a minute: lava? Aren't we—"

"Up high on a cliff, nowhere near where molten rock should be?" Reginald finished for him. "Yes. But all Villains have a pool of lava somewhere in their fortress, usually for fighting over. It's imported, of course." He glanced about the roughly circular room and took a deep breath. "We must be in the Duel Room."

Cyrus looked around, concerned. "Uh, Reginald? The floor here looks like it's connected to some kind of pulley system . . . "

Reginald glanced down and shrugged. "It's probably nothing, lad."

A voice boomed out at them from across the pit. "We meet again, Crimson Slash, but this time, the advantage is mine!"

At the far end of the room stood a man in black armor. A jagged scar ran from the right side of his forehead, between his eyebrows and down his nose, terminating below the left side of his jawline. He grasped a wickedly serrated, hook-tipped broadsword in his ebony-gauntleted hands. The blade had what appeared to be a second handle mounted a third of the way up its length, possibly for better control of complicated attacks.

"Berrik Sawface!" Reginald bellowed, a ferocious smile on his face, "Your foul Villainy cannot go unopposed! Prepare to Face Justice!"

"Justice?" the Villain sneered. "Oh, no, you pathetic Hero. I have you exactly where I want you!" Sawface laughed manically and pulled on a lever beside him.

The floor beneath Cyrus and Reginald gave way, sending the two plummeting toward the lava. They both barely managed to get a hold on the sloped walls of the pit, sliding to a halt on a ledge mere inches from the molten rock.

"Mwahahaha! You fools!" Sawface shouted from the grating above. "I am far more intelligent than you! The lava will burn the flesh from your bones, and then my Ultra Golem will smash the Bryath Army to smithereens!"

"Ultra Golem? Bryath Army?" Reginald said, stretching up and trying to get a hold on the crumbling pit wall. "I came here to stop you from building the Metropolis Incinerator, with which you were going to annihilate the Holy City of Beth-Amial. Whatever happened to that?"

"Eh, the Incinerator," Sawface said wistfully. "It burned itself up due to faulty wiring." He scratched the back of his neck. "Curse my incompetent electrician!"

A smile crept onto Reginald's face, just as he and Cyrus crept up higher on the pit wall. "Ah, so you'll be forced to use the Ultra Golem, then. What exactly is it?"

"A golem that could crush a Titan!" the Villain boasted, a malicious sneer on his face. "The world will quake before my might when it is complete! From the top of my creation, I shall rain destruction and terror on the people of the world! The masses will flee, the soldiers will die, and you, pathetic Hero, can do nothing to stop me! Once I attach the right leg . . . "

Reginald turned to his apprentice. "What he is doing right now," the Hero said as the Villain babbled on, "is very important, so pay attention. This is his Primary Monologue. Unlike the Secondary Monologue, in which he will most likely have me at his mercy and yet fail to press his advantage, the Primary Monologue is a carefully prepared speech in which a Villain will tell you of his foul plans in detail, down to the way to defeat him. Hst, listen!"

" . . . but if the Earth crystals are removed, it will lose power, a minor flaw that a dim-witted Hero like yourself could never dream of exploiting . . . "

Cyrus gaped, sliding onto a wider section of the ledge and pulling his boots back from the uncomfortably warm lava. "You're saying that they're all this arrogant and stupid?"

"Aye, lad, most of them are. Especially the less dangerous ones. Not only that, but he's not paying attention to us right now. It gives us time to do this."

Reginald swung his sword up and slashed the support rigging beneath the rusted gratings. With a crash, the entire works tumbled into the lava.

"Curses!" yelled Sawface, landing on one of the floating pieces. "Crimson Slash! Prepare to meet your Doom!"

"Justice shall Prevail!" Reginald bellowed, and leapt out onto the precarious and inexplicably floating ironwork.

"Reginald!" Cyrus shouted. "What do you think you're doing?!"

Reginald glanced over his shoulder. "What's the first thing about being a Hero, lad?"

"Uh, take unnecessary risks?"

"Close, but no," the Hero said. "'Always fight Climactic Duels in Ridiculous Locations.' Like over lava, for instance."

Cyrus put his head in his hands and began thinking that perhaps being a Hero was not the best career choice.

"So now I am curious, Berrik Sawface," Reginald said, advancing on the Villain, "how does one get a name and a scar such as yours?"

The Villain drew the dire claymore and brought it to bear on the Hero. "I received this wound during my slaughter of half the graduating class at the Hero Academy ten years ago."

"Ten years ago?" Reginald stared into the Villain's eyes, then laughed. "You lie. I can see it in your eyes. Besides, my previous apprentice graduated from the Academy ten years ago—there was no such incident!"

Sawface shrugged. "No, but it makes for a better story. Have at you!"

"The Hero leapt forward, landing a crushing blow on the Villain's shoulder-plate!" Reginald bellowed, leaping forward and landing a crushing blow on the Villain's shoulder-plate. "Are you getting this, lad?"

Cyrus started. "Getting what now?"

"My narration!" Reginald said. "The Hero blocked a counterattack by Sawface and took a swipe at the Villain's head!"

"What am I supposed to do?" Cyrus asked.

"The Hero rolled to the side and threw a lava-coated slab of iron at his foe!" Reginald narrated, doing exactly that. Berrik leapt aside, nearly losing his balance, and the chunk of grating splashed harmlessly into the molten rock behind him. "Write it down, Cyrus! How are future generations to know of the Exploits of the Crimson Slash if there's no written record?"

Cyrus fumbled around in his pack for some dry parchment and the graphite stick. "Shouldn't you let minstrels write that sort of thing for you?" he asked.

"Of course not," the Crimson Slash said, snorting in derision as he leapt over Berrik's sword as the Villain aimed a cut at his feet. "You think I'd trust some half-wit bard who's never held a sword to accurately describe epic combat? You might as well ask a blind poet!"

"Dynamo of the Ungodly!" Berrik yelled. Electricity crackled around him, and he began throwing multiple high-voltage slashes at the Hero, using the pivoting second handle on his sword to halve the time between strokes.

"The Hero retreated in the face of such Hellish fury, 'til he neared the edge, where the boiling rock cherried the iron," Reginald said, backing up to avoid numerous electrical lacerations.

Cyrus began writing down his mentor's narration, but cast worried glances back at the combat every few seconds. He saw Reginald lose his balance and nearly fall into the lava. "Reginald! Do you need help?"

"No, lad, I'll be just fine . . . " he said, sounding a bit unsure.

"Your Doom is sealed, Crimson Slash. Now I shall reveal to you the origin of my scar, and it will be the last thing you shall ever hear." The Villain lashed out at Reginald, driving him out onto the last available prong of metal not submerged in liquid stone. "I received this wound . . . because I wasn't familiar with the operation of this sword," he said, hefting the vicious blade.

Reginald gave the Villain an odd look. "You mean . . . that scar was an accident?"

"Yes," the Villain admitted. "I didn't know how to use the pivot-handle yet, and well, now I have the scar. You can see why I never tell anyone still living. Now die!" he said, delivering a final blow to the Hero.

"You amuse me!" Reginald said, laughing. "The Crimson Slash parried the attack and locked blades with the diabolical Sawface!" Reginald grinned at the surprised Villain. "It seems a shame to kill you now that I know. *Meteoric Onslaught of the Ages!* the Hero shouted, leaping over the Villain and striking at him repeatedly from the air!"

The Hero's blade glowed green as he threw a dozen rapid-fire cuts at the Villain. Sawface backed up to avoid polysyllabic aerial decapitation. "The Hero drove his foe across the heated metal, delivering blow after blow. The Crimson Slash had gained the upper hand, and pressed his advantage . . . "

Cyrus sighed and continued taking down his mentor's dictation. Hopefully, he would soon graduate to more important matters than mere notetaking.

Chapter 3

FIVE YEARS LATER

*In which Five Years have passed between This Chapter
and Chapter Two, and the Villains begin to Plot*

"THE FEARLESS HERO stood toe to toe with the scaled monstrosity which confronted him. The dim light of the dense forest barely illuminated the combatants: the Hero in his shining armor and the Dragon in its emerald scales. Sword drawn and shield ready, the Hero circled the Dragon, seeking a weakness to exploit. In a flash, the Hero lunged at the beast's exposed underbelly!

"The evil Dragon quickly parried the attack with its pincer-like tail and countered with a blast of withering flame. The Hero brought his shield up and deflected the furious blaze. As it burned up in his hand, the Hero vowed to wreak his revenge upon the merchant who had sold him the 'fire-proof shield.' Recovering quickly, the Hero vaulted into the air, preparing to deliver his signature 'Blade of Fury' attack! Unfortunately, the Dragon somehow anticipated it and slammed the Hero with its tail, sending him flying into a—*oof*—nearby tree! Ow . . . "

"That's because you keep saying what you're going to do right before you do it," rumbled the Dragon. He was a tremendous beast, over thirty feet in length, with shimmering green scales that caught the patchy sunlight filtering through the forest canopy above them. His enormous wings remained folded to his scaled back, as they most likely would not fit unfolded amidst the trees. "It's rather easy to defeat a Hero who self-narrates."

"See, I *told* you someone was going to catch on eventually," Cyrus said, peeking out from under his floppy blue hat. He struck the parchment with the back of his hand. "Plus it's more than a little irritating to have you narrating in the third person. It's ever so much harder to write it that way."

The overwrought dialogue was not the only irritating thing. There was also the midsummer heat to think about. At least the shade on the packed dirt of the forest path moderated the temperature, though it did nothing to help the dialogue.

"Just you . . . wait . . . fiend . . . " wheezed Reginald as he struggled to remove his dented breastplate. "I'll have you . . . begging for your scaly life as soon as I . . . get this . . . armor . . . " The Hero stood up, then promptly passed out and fell down again.

"Blast, not again," Cyrus muttered. He put down the scroll and quill he had been using to transcribe his mentor's dictation. He rolled his eyes at the Dragon and went over to the Hero on the ground. He attempted to remove the armor, only to find that the impact of the Dragon's tail had bent the armor onto his torso, and it would not come off. "Oy, Dragon!" Cyrus called. "Will you help me get this armor off him?"

The Dragon snorted contemptuously. "I think not. He called me a 'scaled monstrosity,' 'evil,' which I am certainly not, and a 'beast,' a term which applies only to my elder brother. Besides, I don't believe that *helping* the Hero was in the contract."

Cyrus sighed heavily. "Ah, well. I suppose that slab of Chimera jerky will go to waste, then."

The Dragon perked up, raising his pointed ears. "Chimera jerky? He has some?"

"Hmm? Oh, yes."

The Dragon bent his six feet of green-scaled neck down and sniffed the prone form of the Hero. "He doesn't smell like Chimera jerky. He smells like . . . " The Dragon sniffed again and sneezed out a ball of flame, which incinerated a young cedar . . . "cheap cologne."

Cyrus chuckled and began unclasping the hasps on the breastplate. "Well, that he certainly does. But under the armor he has a pouch of emergency rations, part of which is . . . "

"*Chimera jerky!*" exclaimed the Dragon, drooling from one corner of his mouth.

"Exactly. But since I can't get this armor off . . . "

The Dragon shoved Cyrus aside and picked up the breastplate, Reginald still attached, in his teeth and shook it vigorously. With a muffled *pop*, the Hero fell free, regaining consciousness at about the same time that he hit the ground.

"By the Seven Furies that guard the Isle of the Damned, I'll defeat you yet, Dragon!" Reginald hollered.

Cyrus and the Dragon sighed simultaneously, the latter emitting a puff of smoke.

"Cyrus! My sword!" Reginald shouted.

"C'mon, Reg, give it a break," Cyrus protested. "The Dragon just saved your life."

Sir Reginald Ogleby drew himself up to his full heroic six foot four inches, not counting the boots. "Saved my life? What kind of behavior is that for a marauding Dragon?" He attempted to scratch his head but encountered his helmet.

The Dragon made what Cyrus assumed was an embarrassed face, despite it still looking rather ferocious. "Your squire said you had some Chimera jerky under your armor, so I took it off."

Reginald spun and looked at Cyrus. "You did?"

Cyrus merely grinned and straightened his hat.

A look of surprise crossed the Dragon's reptilian face. "What? You mean . . . you don't actually have any?"

"Good thinking, lad!" Reginald said, clapping Cyrus on the back. "You'll make a proper Hero yet!"

The Dragon roared, and before Cyrus could even blink, Reginald rolled across the clearing, snatching up his sword as he did so. The Dragon let loose a mighty gust of wind and flame, blasting the ground that Reginald had just occupied.

"*Hold up!*" Cyrus shouted.

The point of Reginald's enormous sword rested just inside the Dragon's mouth, and a blob of fire smoldered at the back of the reptile's throat. "That's it, Dragon," Reginald said calmly. "One upward thrust and this sword penetrates your brain."

"Thash wha yoo thig," mumbled the Dragon, his tongue having trouble forming syllables with a very large, double-edged sword in his mouth. "Ahll ah haff to goo ish breeth owt an yur koshk!" The blob of flames in his throat burned brighter.

"Just forget it, you two!" Cyrus interrupted. "You've proven that you're evenly matched. Dragon, you can claim that you bested Reg, and leave. Reg, you can claim that you beat the Dragon and claim your reward! It's very simple. You both get what you want, and nobody has to die."

Dragon and Hero regarded each other with a gaze of intense mistrust. "What guarantee have I that he will not roast me if I withdraw my sword?" asked Reginald.

"Yesh, wha adout ish shord? I on't crusht Eerosh."

Cyrus sighed. With an air of mock alarm, he jumped up and pointed into the woods. "Look out! An Ogre!"

Hero and Dragon spun to face the new menace, and Cyrus burst into laughter. The two had broken up their death lock to face a small white rabbit.

Both combatants sheathed their weapons, Reginald returning his to its back-scabbard, the Dragon swallowing his and belching some greyish smoke.

"Well fought, Dragon. Mine name is Sir Reginald Ogleby, the Crimson Slash."

The Dragon bent his shimmering green neck in respect. "It was an honor to fight someone as skilled as you, Crimson. I am Keeth, son of Barinol, whose sire was Kisanth the Great."

Reginald started scratching his helmet again and stopped, irritated. "Keith, you say? Odd name for a Dragon."

Keeth bared his formidable fangs. "It's *Keeth!* Double vowel."

"My apologies, Keeth," Reginald said. "But how could you tell I spelled it—"

"Dragons hear vowels, Sir Ogleby," Keeth explained. "Rather a stupid ability, to tell the truth. It's a mixed blessing at best. It seems the gods couldn't think of anything truly useful to give Dragons as a gift that we didn't already have, so we received magical spelling and grammar detection."

"Well, you'd make a good writer," Cyrus said, retrieving his quill and scroll. "Better you than me." He loaded Reginald's mangled breastplate opposite his spare shield on their pack mule. The mule, Cyrus noted, had been stoically ignoring the fight. "Well, now that proper pleasantries have been exchanged, can we get going?" Cyrus leaned against the mule's furry grey side. "I'm a bit hungry."

Keeth looked at Cyrus. "Are you certain you have no Chimera jerky?" the Dragon asked. He then turned and barbecued the rabbit with a blast of flame. "It would go rather well with roast rabbit."

Cyrus smiled. Things were working out just fine.

Before the reader thinks poorly of the Crimson Slash for failing to defeat a mere Dragon, the author must remind him, or her, as the case may be, that Dragons are the oldest, wisest, and most fearsome of all the Elder Creatures.

The average mature male Dragon measures near eight feet broad and thirty-five or more feet long from head to tail, though they continue to grow slowly during their entire lifespan. The head is sloped, wedge-shaped, and contains a fire-breathing mouth with two rows of incredibly sharp triangular teeth.

Neither are their hind ends less dangerous. The heavily muscled tail of a Dragon is a mighty weapon, capable of felling trees and smashing boulders. At its tip, the tail has a two-pronged pincer of magnificent strength and edge. The head, tail, and everything in between are coated and protected by an ever-growing layer of iridescent scales that rival even Enchanted Armors in their impenetrability and resilience.

But the most impressive feature of an adult Dragon is the pair of wings sprouting from its upper back. Tough but light bones comprise the skeletal structure, and a fire-resistant membrane fills the gaps between the bones. A Dragon regulates its internal body temperature by spreading its wings to collect sun or let excess heat escape, whichever the case may be, and keeps them folded to its back to conserve body heat.

The creatures come in a multitude of colors, from white to black, green to red, and all primary and secondary colors in between. All Dragons breathe fire and are generally amiable toward Humans, save for the occasional foolish treasure hunter who invades their lairs. The exception to this rule is Black Dragons, who are generally grouchy and irritable. But even a Black Dragon will not attack a Human without due provocation.

So, needless to say, a Dragon is a handy addition and a valuable ally for any group of Heroes to run across, or a dire foe should one be so foolish as to get on the bad side of these magnificent creatures.

A woman's scream echoed down the black tunnel, and all the candles went out with a bang. Someone, totally blind in the darkness, tripped over something and fell to the ground with the heavy ring of occupied armor against stone.

"By the Seven Mad Gods that Rule the Sea!" a man cursed. "*Inlumino.*"

A small luminescent globe appeared hovering above his head, casting a pool of light that illuminated the ornate summoning chamber. It was small and dark, made smaller by the ebony carvings of Dragons and demons inlaid in the stone walls. In the gleaming sheen of the shimmering walls, the man caught sight of his reflection: a handsome, raven-haired man of twenty-five years, with a single scar on the left side of his face and neck.

He rubbed his head and cursed mildly. "Nieva, are you all right?"

Nieva, who had screamed a moment before, rose up from the wreckage of a circle of candles. "I'm fine, Serimal. But . . . what happened?"

Serimal surveyed the mess in his Summoning Chamber. "I'm afraid your spell backfired, my love. I didn't know *Channeled Farsight* spells exploded like that."

Nieva rubbed her shoulder. "They do not, normally. But the Dragon killed my rabbit."

Serimal looked at Nieva. The woman's pointed ears betrayed her Elven lineage. She looked quite young, but he knew her real age was difficult to determine. Her high brow and noble nose marked her as a pure-blooded Elven Princess. Her straight, black tresses perfectly complemented her silver eyes. She rearranged her dark robes and gracefully sat down next to him.

"Killed the rabbit?" Serimal asked. "Did you see any weak points before it—"

"I'm afraid not," Nieva replied, her melodious soprano damped by the small room and its ornate contents. "His technique is too perfect. Perhaps we could exploit his temptation to narrate his combat."

"His what?" Serimal rose to his feet, helping Nieva up as he did so.

"He narrates all he does," the Elf said, dusting off her black silk dress. "I've heard it's quite common among Heroes who are too sure of themselves."

Serimal attempted to straighten his tousled black hair. "I suppose that would help a bit, if I knew what he was doing before he tried it. Nothing else?"

Nieva turned her silver eyes away. "Nothing good, milord. The Crimson Slash seems to have befriended the Dragon he was fighting."

Serimal swore again. "Well, we'll just have to find a way to lure him here without the creature's aid. Something better than honorable combat, I would imagine . . . "

"Or something worse." Nieva smiled, and it chilled the room, casting illusory frost across the floor. "This may call for an official Dastardly Plot."

Serimal's smile matched her own. He took Nieva's hand and they walked from the ruined room.

"A *False Quest*?" Torval sputtered. "Why, we don't even have one of those written up right now. False Quests are so outdated that even the most dim-witted of Heroes have known the ins and outs of them since before the Twenty-Minute War!"

Nieva glared at the Purveyor of Evil Products. He was a disgusting, overweight man, with all the money-grubbing qualities of a tax collector but none of the personal hygiene. He occupied a hardwood chair in her sparsely furnished reception room.

Designed to keep semi-unwelcome guests at ill ease and decrease the time of their stay, the room was a dull grey and lacked any vestige of color. A single arrow-slit in the outside wall let in a narrow stream of light. A heavy, brooding black desk sat at the back of the room, with a sword rack on the wall behind it. The only furniture in the room besides the desk was a small end table with a bowl of fruit on it and a pair of vaguely uncomfortable hardwood chairs, one of which Torval occupied.

Nieva eviscerated the piggish man with her gaze. "That's exactly why it will work now," she said. "No Villain has attempted to use a False Quest in so long that Heroes, with their relatively short attention spans, are bound to have forgotten about them."

Torval shifted on his hardwood chair. His pimpled face and corpulent form betrayed his rich, unhealthy lifestyle.

"Well, my lady," he said, "I can get one of our scribes to start writing one right now, if you like. But if you want a good one, it will certainly cost you." The merchant smiled and rubbed his fingers together, then took a pear from a bowl on the table and bit into it, the juice dribbling down his chin into his scraggly red beard.

Nieva looked at Torval with disgust. "Very well, you money-grubbing fool. We'll pay the price, but no more than five thousand gold pieces."

The fat merchant choked on his pear. "F . . . fuh . . . five th-thousand . . . guh . . . "

"Is there a problem?" Nieva's gaze burned into Torval's piggish eyes.

"N-No, milady. Five thousand is sufficient."

"Good." She began to walk away, then turned. "We'll also need a shape-shifter."

"A shifter, milady?" said the merchant, a puzzled expression on his blemished face. "Whatever for?"

"Apprentice Heroes don't just disappear by themselves, you know." With that, she placed her palms together and disappeared, the air rushing to fill the void making a muffled *whump*.

Perhaps the first thing one needs to know in order to survive in the land of Centra Mundi is how to avoid tax collectors. Tax collectors are agents of whatever king, aristocrat, or legislative authority rules the country at the moment. They are the most feared parasite in Centra Mundi, followed by the Grinder Leech at a distant second.

The two, as it happens, are quite similar. While a Grinder Leech attacks your flesh and drains your blood for food, tax collectors take your hard-earned money from you, with or without your consent, and squander it on pointless, bureaucratic projects and nice things for their families.

You can avoid both predators by hiding in bushes, faking your own death, or beating them mercilessly with a large stick. Of these, faking your death is the least effective against tax collectors, as a Grinder prefers live food, but a tax collector will most likely go through your pockets and take everything you have while you lie there.

This discussion of tax collectors leads nicely into a discussion of Heroes, Villains, and the Balance of Light and Dark. Actually, it has very little to do with it, but you must read the following anyway, as it is important to understand the rest of this story.

While tax collectors are ordinary men, usually traveling with an armed escort to keep the peasants from killing them and taking back what is rightfully theirs, Heroes and Villains are so far above ordinary Humans that they make a grown man seem like a newborn baby.

Though no different in looks from an average person, Heroes are far stronger. Even a puny Hero can best a burly peasant in an arm-wrestling match. In combat, a single Hero can defeat a small army of normal soldiers by him- or herself, swinging weapons faster than the eye can follow, or performing near-impossible dynamic attacks. Heroes can leap to the tops of tall buildings from the ground.

Some Heroes cannot perform amazing feats of strength, but can instead use their minds to bend the elemental forces of the world to their wills, making them do incredible things. The common people call this Magic. As it is far more commonplace in this age, it no longer terrifies them as it once did.

Heroes are, in short, superhuman. Not, of course, that all Heroes are. Human, that is. Heroes can also be found among Elves, Dwarves, Orcs, and, though rare, even amongst less plentiful races, such as the Katheni and Ransha.

Heroes travel alone or in groups of no more than five. A group of Heroes, referred to as a "party" for some reason now lost to us, usually contains one or two large, beefy, weapon-wielder types—sometimes called "tanks" or "meat shields" by their compatriots, for reasons also unknown—a slender magic-user, a non-Human or a priest (either is acceptable), and a squire. This arrangement is not by choice. Somehow Fate always throws Heroic parties together in this manner.

All Heroes, no matter the sex, race, or composition of the party, are honor-bound to protect the weak, uphold laws, and combat Evil wherever they find it. The aforementioned Evil is often found in the form of Villains. Villains have much the same abilities that Heroes do, but they use their strength for their own selfish purposes or to deliberately cause mayhem and discord.

Naturally, constant conflict exists between Heroes and Villains and their representative organizations, the International Guild of Heroes and the Brotherhood of the Black Hand, respectively. Their battles often tear up the surrounding area, due to the wide-ranging and excessively violent nature of powerful but opposite equals meeting in combat.

But aside from the massive collateral damage inflicted during Hero and Villain combat, why such a fuss over them? The answer is simple: Balance. If Villains become too numerous, the world will fall into darkness. If Heroes proliferate, then military "justice" will reign, eventually becoming persecution of anyone who even *seems* evil, and war will be fought to free those who feel oppressed.

The Balance shows itself in many ways. Some Villains were once Heroes themselves, now turned to evil purposes, just as some Heroes are reformed Villains. These are the most effective and dangerous types, for they know the other side's strengths and failings. Balance tips gently back and forth during the centuries, but the Legends say that if the Balance were ever tipped too far one way, it would usher in the End of the World.

So how does one live in this Balance? Well, as a rule, it is usually best to befriend Heroes and eschew Villains. One can hire a group of Heroes—seven, perhaps—to defend your city. Heroes are also often hired to clear up diplomatic messes, or even assassinate evildoers who lurk outside the reach of the law.

There are even rumors about Heroes being hired by a king to fight Monsters that *were hired by the same King* to pillage the countryside.

There exists a tacit agreement between Heroes, Kings, and all manner of Talking Beasts that no one ever speaks of this type of agreement. It is deemed perfectly normal, for instance, for Dragons to kidnap princesses and for Heroes to rescue them. As long as the general peasantry knows nothing of these arrangements, everything is fine.

And so the world spins on around its sun, the peasantry spinning tales of Heroes and Villains over their ale. Princesses are rescued, foul plots foiled, and every day someone is saved by some Heroic action or other.

Cyrus Solburg was apprenticed to a Hero. He couldn't think of a more time-consuming, overregulated, tradition-laden, wearisome, and yet tremendously satisfying career.

Chapter 4

AN UNLIKELY GROUP OF HEROES

In which the Party is Attacked and Darkness appears

THE DIM GREEN light of the forest gave it an air of drowsiness and tranquility. But it was a mundane forest and the peacefulness was natural, not having an *Air of Drowsiness* like an enchanted forest would. The party proceeded through it with companionship and camaraderie.

Keeth plodded down the center of the winding forest path. Reginald rode alongside on Wraith, his coal-black charger. Hero and Dragon chatted amiably of ancient battles and drinking songs. In the back, where he habitually rode, was Cyrus.

Cyrus's silver-grey pony, Brisk, was a good-natured beast, but despite her name, she was not very fast. Every thirty seconds or so, she would notice that she was falling behind and would break into a trot in order to catch up with the Hero and Dragon.

Following resolutely behind them all was Toboggan, the pack mule. Toboggan was showing signs of his age. His short grey fur was becoming mangy in places. But he could still almost keep up with Reginald's charger if worst came to worst.

"I tell you what, Brisk," Cyrus said to his horse, "if I ever make Hero status, I'm not putting up with any of this make-believe stuff. I'll just call a spade a spade."

Brisk flicked one ear back. Her Human was making noise again. She hoped it had something to do with a nice big clover patch.

"Right, girl?" Cyrus patted Brisk's neck. "It's obvious that the King hired both Reg and the Dragon. I mean, think about it: the king's in trouble. In Filar, the government is a constitutional monarchy, not a regular hereditary one. Well, King Alfredo is getting to be pretty unpopular with the peasants these days, what with the land taxes and all."

Brisk twitched her ear forward again. Her Human had made almost those same noises last time they'd found a Dragon. If the past was any indication, he'd make noises for another two hundred steps or so, then fall silent. And without yielding any clover, either.

"So what can he do to boost his poll numbers? Actually do something for his peasants? No, too time-consuming. Hold a huge feast and invite everybody? No, too expensive. He needs something cheap and flashy. So he hires a Dragon to start burning small villages, and then hires a Hero to stop the Dragon. 'Problem' solved, the peasants rejoice, the poll numbers go up, and everybody's happy. The only thing is, nobody sees the pattern here. Everybody involved acts like this happened naturally. It's as if they believe that Dragons naturally want to attack small villages, and Heroes have nothing better to do than stop them, and so . . . well . . . " Cyrus petered out.

Brisk shook her mane. It was *exactly* two hundred steps.

• • •

Then a furious midsummer blizzard struck. A blinding snow-storm lashed out of the trees, instantly coating Hero and Dragon in a five-foot drift. An evil laugh drifted out of the storm. "Well, well. Caught off guard, eh, Crimson Slash?"

The Crimson Slash erupted from beneath a snowdrift, sword and shield prepared. "Show yourself, sorcerer!"

"I'm not a sorcerer, I'm a mage," the voice said. "And I'm afraid that isn't very likely. I'm sure that if I did, you'd try to slice me up."

The Crimson Slash scratched his head, which was free of his helmet at the moment, but covered in snow instead. "Well, I . . . I mean . . . That's my job . . . "

"Exactly. That doesn't exactly give me incentive to show myself, does it?"

Cyrus dismounted and shook the snow from his floppy hat. The horses seemed to be all right, and Keeth looked only mildly discomfited by the chill of the snow. The Dragon shook the white precipitation from his large, membranous wings and pivoted his wedge-shaped head to locate the source of the magical snowstorm. Their assailant was either behind one of the trees they'd been riding through or behind the stone out-croppings of the hill to his right, Cyrus guessed.

"But you must show yourself!" shouted the Crimson Slash. "You've got to accept a challenge. It's the rule! Codex Heroic, page 117, paragraph B!"

"Only Heroes abide by the Codex, Crimson."

The Crimson Slash straightened up. "You mean you're . . . "

"Not a Hero. I am a Villain. Many know me as Thomas Frostbite. That said, you die here." A surge of magic so pow-erful that Cyrus could almost taste it wrapped around the Crimson Slash and Keeth.

Cyrus gritted his teeth and straightened his floppy and snow-sodden hat. Sudden, unseasonable snowstorms were one thing. Indeed, given the prevalence of mages these days, they were quite common. But massive energy detonations were something else entirely. Besides, that introductory speech should have lasted at least twice that long before the Villain launched an attack. What lousy manners this Villain had.

With a flick of his wrist, Cyrus removed from the pocket of his robe a pair of silken gloves with large runes on the backs of them. He slipped them on and extended his hands, palms down. He then brought his hands together, and as his right hand slid over his left, he turned both inward. The runes on the back of his gloves glowed bright blue, and the rising surge of power died down to a small trickle.

"What was *that?*" the voice yelled from the forest. Out from behind a tall, broad tree stepped a short, narrow man clad in blue and white robes. The Villain was Human, with a sickly wisp of a brown beard that clung tenaciously to his narrow, pointed chin. He was young. Indeed, he could not have been over the age of twenty-five. But evil burned cold in his grey eyes. "Who just counterspelled me?" he demanded.

Cyrus smiled. "Over here, shorty. You want to use magic? Try me."

The mage smiled back, though in a decidedly more evil fashion. "Insolent whelp! I'll show you a thing or *Five!*"

As he pronounced the last word, he flung his hands out, twisting his arms as he did so. His thin wisp of beard blew forward in the backwash as five fragments of flaming frost flashed through the air.

Cyrus had time either to scream or to drop to the ground before the ice reached him. He opted for the latter, flinging himself into the snowbank. The inexplicably incandescent icicles passed overhead, smashing harmlessly against a large rock.

A slash of flame rent the newly chilled air and carbonized the mage's hiding-tree. Keeth waded out of the drift, shivering massively. "I d-don't l-l-like c-c-cold!"

The Crimson Slash drew himself up to his full Heroic six foot four inches, not counting the boots, and pointed his sword at the now-exposed mage. "Frostbite! I challenge you to a Hero's Combat! Stand your ground!"

Cyrus clapped a hand to his head. *Not again*, he thought.

The Villain turned slightly aside. "You do? I didn't expect that. Very well. I must use the most powerful spell I have left."

The Crimson Slash shifted his shield to *Spell Blocking Position Delta*.

"*Teleport!*" the mage yelled.

"No!" shouted the Crimson Slash, lunging forward.

"Bok in a bucket," Cyrus muttered.

The mage vanished in a shimmer of powdery snow.

"By the Seven Furies . . . " sputtered Reginald.

Keeth sneezed. "I n-need t-t-to get out of th-th-this s-snow . . . "

Ten minutes later, a cheery fire blazed beside the path. Cyrus began rubbing down Wraith's glossy black coat, removing excess moisture. A few patches of snow remained from the unseasonable blizzard, but they were rapidly melting. Keeth plodded about the area, trying to find a sufficiently large dry spot on which to rest his bulk. And Reginald performed a brief scout of the surrounding area.

It was already trailing into the evening, and by the time they would have gotten everything dried out and continued on, it would have been dark. So instead, Reginald ordered that they make camp. It was easy enough. Cyrus selected a place on the lee side of the large rocky outcropping that had provided some cover during their brief battle with Thomas Frostbite.

Reginald leaned back against the slab of rock. "Cyrus?"

Cyrus looked up from his work. "Sir?"

"How did you stop that magic buildup I felt?"

The apprentice Hero looked down, hesitant to answer, then began rubbing Wraith again. "You remember how I told you once that I didn't seem to be much above average Hero strength?"

Reginald looked puzzled. "Yes, lad. But I told you we'd improve that, and you have. You've got some decent muscle mass now, and you're capable of many minor feats of strength. What's it got to do with the magic?"

Cyrus sighed. "Well, I don't think I'm going to end up as a brute force type Hero. I think I'm a magic user."

Reginald gaped. "Now, lad, you don't really mean that. I'm sure it's just a phase. You'll see that the gods intended men to wield swords, not magic."

Cyrus didn't know why that statement hurt so much. "Anyway, when we defeated Venmar Crystalline last summer, I—"

"Ah, yes, Crystalline!" Reginald exclaimed, sitting up. "That was it, Keeth. The Wizard I fought last summer that I was telling you about!"

Keeth opened a scaled eyelid. "Mmm. 'Zat so?" he said lazily.

Reginald turned his attention back to his apprentice. "Sorry, lad. What were you saying about the Wizard?"

Cyrus nodded. "You know how I took his hat after you broke it?"

"That was Crystalline's hat?" Reginald asked, staring at Cyrus's floppy hat. "Wasn't it pointy, like a normal wizard hat?"

"It was, but when you hit him with that flying-disk-sword-spin thing . . . "

Reginald scowled. "It's called *Claymore Roulette*."

" . . . you hit both him and his hat. It killed him, and broke the thing in the middle of the hat that keeps it pointy. So I took it out and kept the hat."

Keeth peered down at Cyrus. "So your hat stopped that frosty mage?"

"No," Cyrus said sheepishly. "I also pulled these out of his back pocket while Reg wasn't looking." He brought the gloves out of his pocket again.

Reginald's complexion turned a strange shade of purple. "Lad, what did I tell you about fooling around with that Wizard's junk?"

"I'm sorry, Reg, they just—"

"That's *Sir Reginald*, squire!"

"Sorry, Sir Reginald. They just kinda called to me. Ever since I put them on, I've been able to do minor Magic Tricks and cast small Spells. I wasn't sure the gloves would counter such a powerful attack, but it worked out okay."

"Oh, it did this time," Reginald said, scowling, "but magic trinkets are inherently dangerous! You never know when one is going to fail, or backfire on you, or—"

"Or work perfectly?" Keeth said. "I for one am grateful for Cyrus's quick thinking. That mage was preparing at least a *Greater Spontaneous Detonation* spell, and my scales could not have withstood that. And neither could your armor, Sir Reginald." The Dragon settled down a few yards from the fire, on a properly dry section of forest loam. "You must admit, the lad did save us a great deal of pain and grief."

Reginald calmed back down. "Well, then. Keep the junk if it's that useful."

"Thanks, Reg."

Keeth winked at Cyrus. Cyrus winked back, then finished rubbing down Wraith, and began setting up camp.

A prison cart slowly creaked out of the shadows of a massive city gate. When it stopped, a portly guard clad in red breeches and purple tunic clambered down from the side seat and produced a ring of keys from somewhere beneath his bulging stomach. He unlocked the back of the iron box that served as a mobile prison cell and yanked on a chain inside. "Come on out, reprobate," he said. "Time to face the ol' daylight again."

The prisoner stepped out of the cart and onto the gravel of the road, blinking against the invasive midday sunlight. "My irons," he said.

Iron, in the singular, would have been more appropriate, as he had but one arm. His drab grey prison shirt hung loosely off his left shoulder, and the sleeve blew about in the gentle breeze. His right wrist was chained to his waist. The prisoner's slightly pointed ears poked through his bedraggled and dirty black hair. He turned his face upward. He looked directly at the sun and smiled disturbingly.

"Patience, malefactor. They'll be off in a moment." The guard unlocked the heavy silver manacle chaining the prisoner's wrist to his waist and pulled the chains from his ankles as well. "There, you're free now. Don't ask me why. If I'd had my way, you'd be executed by now. A little strange, how the council decided you ought to be let go like that . . . "

The one-armed prisoner smiled grimly, his pale skin coated with grime from the prison cell he had so recently inhabited. "Justice is a fickle thing, *pitchi*," he said, spitting at the guard's boots. "For all those idiots on the council know, my release may usher in a new Dark Age."

"Here now, none of that tripe. Just take this cloak and your arm and be going," the guard said, handing a bundle to the prisoner.

"If you will give me a day's worth of trail rations," said the prisoner, "then when I take this city and crush it beneath my heel, your death will be swift and painless."

The guard cuffed the prisoner on one of his pointed ears, knocking him to the ground. "Begone, ruffian. I've no food to spare for the likes of you. Get hence afore I let you have it."

The prisoner rose slowly, retrieving his bundle from the dirt where it had fallen. "Miles, your name was, correct?" he said, looking into the guard's face. His eyes flared from green to a dangerous red. "Farewell, Miles. When we meet again, I shall make sure that you live a very, very, long time while you're dying." With that, he turned and slowly made his way into the forest.

The guard watched the prisoner until he disappeared into the trees. With a sigh, he clambered back up onto the cart beside the driver. "Well, that's that, then. He's gone, and it's time for supper."

The driver scowled. "I still mislike it." He bit a piece of tobacco off the chunk he held in his hand. "Any man that can attempt to murder the king, survive being attacked by the entire Kingsguard and a professional Hero, and finally, get his sentence commuted and get himself released is not the kind of man I want walking the streets."

"Yet he walks," Miles sighed. "This is a dark day, Toby, mark my words. Today's going to go down in history as the day all the trouble started."

Chapter 5

ANOTHER TWIST IN THE TALE

*In which the Reader learns Geography, Cyrus Discusses
Political Economics, and the Villains Set their Plan in Motion*

THE PETTY MONARCHY of Filar is a small country located in the southwestern corner of the Continent of Centra Mundi. Centra Mundi itself lies at what one might easily call the Center of the World, for the landmass is central in relation to the other four continents.

To its West lies Lorimar, ancestral home of the Elves, a land of lakes, rivers, forests, and other diverse terrain. North of Centra Mundi is Novania, a snow-covered land ruled by the ageless Frost King. Snow permanently blankets the northern half of this frigid clime, but it is famed for its belly warming Firewine and refreshing Icewine.

The eastern continent of Landeralt is home to the Hereditary Evil Empire, a massive country whose primary goal is to train and raise Villains. Its primary exports are Evil and Socialism. The two seem to go hand-in-hand quite nicely.

And looking south, one will find Salvinsel, a land rich in mineral resources but poor in population. The von Kamish family holds sway over most of the continent, but leave the deserts and mountains open to miners brave enough to plumb their depths for riches. As a major blemish on its natural beauty and resources, Salvinsel also boasts some of the largest slave markets in the world.

Multitudinous islands surround the five continents as well. Southeast of Centra Mundi and northeast of Salvinsel, the traveler will encounter both the Citrus and Phoenix Islands. Each island group is rich in its namesake, for the former produce the majority of the world's citrus fruit, while the latter are a famous breeding ground for the fiery birds.

Between Centra Mundi and Lorimar lies the Isle of the Damned, rumored to contain a gateway to the Hells themselves. Off the west coast of Landeralt, one will encounter the Eastern Islands, a chain of four islands renowned for their cuisine and producing the strangest but deadliest swordsmen in the world.

Lying at the center of so many places, Centra Mundi is naturally the hub of all sorts of business, from minor wars to intercontinental mercantile arrangements. The government of this continent is complicated, as it is divided into a plethora of small, independently governed kingdoms, each owing fealty to the largest kingdom, Bryath.

One of these kingdoms is the aforementioned Filar. And outside the walls of the township, an apprentice Hero leaned against a sleepy green Dragon.

Cyrus sat just outside the castle, picking grass and making a large pile of it atop Keeth's tail. Keeth himself dozed in the shade cast by castle Filar's massive rough-stone walls.

The gentle breeze pushed small puffy clouds about the sky and rustled through the hayfields outside the township's walls. The midsummer sun beat down on the surrounding area, baking the moisture out of the grasses and producing the smell of drying hay. Not to mention the smell of animal dung from the ill-kept, packed-dirt road leading into the town. Blackflies and other insects buzzed about, some landing on Keeth but finding the Dragon's scales far too thick to get any kind of meal through.

One landed on Cyrus's neck, but he slapped it before it could bite him. "Euuch," he said in disgust. Apparently this fly had bitten someone else before landing on him. Enough of this waiting and inactivity, he thought. They'd already been waiting for two hours, waiting for Reginald to return with the reward money. So he sat up and nudged the Dragon's scaled flank. "Keeth?"

"Mmm?" Keeth blinked sleepily. "Yes, Cyrus?"

"I was just wondering: did King Alfredo hire you to start that ruckus in the border towns? Or do you just go on rampages for fun?"

Keeth shifted his weight uncomfortably. "There's no simple answer to that question. First off, know that I am not the type to burn Humans' homes just for fun. Second, know also that I am not totally mercenary, or at least not as much as some Dragons I know."

"So which is it, then?" Cyrus looked up into Keeth's amber eyes.

"I can't say, Cyrus. It isn't allowed."

Cyrus grinned. He *knew* he'd been right. "So you can't say whether or not this whole thing was a charade to raise poll numbers for the king, then."

Keeth attempted to look puzzled but ended up looking like an iguana with indigestion. "Pole numbers? What type of pole, and what do its numbers signify?"

Cyrus grimaced. "Forget it, Keeth. Opinion survey numbers. You Dragons don't have to worry about that kind of thing. Dragons have a much simpler form of government than we Humans do."

Keeth looked puzzled again, this time succeeding in the endeavor. "Dragons don't have a government, Cyrus."

"Well, not an official one. But you do take wartime orders from a senior Dragon, right?"

"Mmm. A *Princeps Draconum*. Yes, we do, but what of it?"

"Your *Princeps* is like a wartime-only monarch," Cyrus explained. "Only when really threatening things like the Twenty-Minute War happen does the *Princeps* take charge, and then the cooperation is entirely voluntary. The rest of the time, you pretty much leave each other and us Humans alone. No taxes, no restrictions, nothing."

Keeth smiled, his sharp, pointy teeth a startling spectacle, shining white in the afternoon sun. "You do seem to know a lot about draconic society, young one. But you're not exactly correct. Dragons, while we have no written law code, do have restrictions on our actions. If the actions of a Dragon endanger other Dragons about him, or he causes harm to another, he's either slain or clipped."

"Clipped?"

"His wings are shredded and he is exiled from Dragon territories. It's not death, but it isn't much of a life either."

Cyrus winced. "Ouch. That's harsh . . . "

"Well, where did you think you Humans got the term 'draconian penalties'?" Keeth glanced at the city gate. "But we see that as fair, compared to other punishments. For example, most Dragons would rather fight to the death than give up even a small part of their treasure hoard. I can't imagine giving up pieces of my hoard every year just so people can give me orders."

Cyrus chuckled. "Like taxes, you mean?"

Keeth nodded. "I find many things about Humans strange, but that is the strangest thing of all, to me."

"It is to most Humans, too. But about your hoards— something has bothered me for a long time. They're usually a pretty significant amount of coinage, right?" Cyrus asked.

"Yes, indeed they are," Keeth said. "Mine more than some. Why do you ask?"

Cyrus plucked a small white flower and stuck it in the top of the grass piled on Keeth's tail, making it look as if the grassy fort was surrendering. "Well, I was thinking that the way you Dragons use your hoards isn't very efficient. What do you usually do, sleep on them?"

Keeth nodded.

"Well," Cyrus said, "sleeping on it doesn't make it grow any bigger. If you took some of it out, say about a few thousand gold pieces at a time, it wouldn't be enough to make a significant dent in the hoard, but it sure would make a difference in any market in the world."

"Take it out? What exactly are you saying?" Keeth asked. "As a rule, Dragons don't spend our hoards. A large hoard is a sign of intelligence and courage in a Dragon."

"No, no, not spending it," Cyrus said, "*investing* it. For example, finance an ocean voyage to the Citrus Islands to gather fruit, with maybe two thousand gold. When they come back, they pay you a large percentage of the cargo's value, which, considering the price of fruit these days, would be somewhere in the tens of thousands. Put that in coin, and you've added another five or six feet to your hoard."

Keeth mused for a moment. "Not a bad idea. But impractical. Merchants are unlikely to deal with Dragons, even if large sums of money are involved."

"So you would have to make it a large enough amount to get their attention," Cyrus said. "Or you could do your business through a Human, a middleman. Heck, I would do it if I wasn't a Hero in training."

"Indeed. I would give that some thought, master Solburg," Keeth replied. "It could be a lucrative career if you decide that the Hero business isn't for you, after all."

"And for your meritorious service to the King and people of Filar, We hereby bestow upon you a reward from the people. The gratitude of this kingdom is forever yours." King Alfredo II picked up a small medallion from the table next to him and held it up.

Reginald frowned. "Your Majesty, I don't believe that is the reward we agreed upon."

The pudgy monarch's fake smile disappeared, replaced with a look of annoyance. He glanced at the assorted petty nobles of his court, who obviously waited to see what their monarch was going to do about this Hero. They stood or sat on the cushioned benches that lined both sides of the gaudily over-decorated throne room. "Oh?" the king said. "And what was it that We *did* agree on?"

"I believe it was one hundred gold pieces, your Majesty," Reginald said. He planted both feet squarely on the red carpet of the gilded throne room and wished that petty monarchs weren't so stingy.

King Alfredo pushed his heavy golden crown further up on his greasy black hair, then sighed and gestured for a servant. A burly fellow stepped forward carrying a large, weighty bag.

Reginald took it with his right hand and slung it over his shoulder. The Hero bowed, and the assembled nobles clapped politely. "I thank you, your Majesty," he said, "and may your reign now be peaceful." Reginald bowed again and strode from the room, whistling merrily.

As the doors to the throne room banged shut, the king sighed. He turned to his Chancellor. "Well, then. Now that We're done with that, how do We look in the polls?" he asked, twisting his outrageous black mustache.

"Very good, your Majesty. You're up almost fifteen points!" the Chancellor squeaked, scribbling numbers furiously on his notepad as he talked. "And that's just the initial results. Final numbers from the coastal and plains regions should be in by Tuesday, and—"

"Good, good," the King interrupted. "We got what we paid for. It would have been a bit cheaper, but the Hero didn't slay the Dragon, so we have to pay it as well. Pity."

A minor duke stepped up behind King Alfredo and whispered in his ear. "Excuse me, your Majesty, but perhaps now is the time to capitalize on this good feeling and use it to rig the election."

The king nodded and smiled. As annoyingly self-righteous as Heroes tended to be, they were certainly useful.

Reginald strolled down the cobblestoned main street of Filar Township. His gold pouch was heavy, the sun was shining, and he had done a Good Deed. It was a good day, despite the filthy town.

The gutters alongside the narrow, twisting road contained black sludge, fouling the air with an unpleasant aroma. Many of the houses seemed ready to fall down, simply from neglect and poor design. Even the best-looking house on the street had broken shutters hanging forlornly from their hinges. Dirty children darted in and out of dark alleys, playing games of tag and "slay the Dragon," pausing to watch the Hero stroll by. Some even followed him for a distance, cheering about Reginald's victory over the "vicious Dragon" he had "saved the town" from.

"Excuse me, are you a Hero?"

Reginald turned around to see a small child with something clutched in her hands. She was thin and bony, with a mess of blond hair that would have made her look angelic, if it weren't for the mud in it. Her golden eyes nearly matched her hair.

"Are you, mister?" she asked again.

"Yes, young lady," Reginald replied. He knelt on the dirty street and looked her in the eyes. "I am the Crimson Slash. And who might you be?"

The little girl turned away shyly. "My name's Gloria. You're really a Hero?"

"Of course!"

Gloria bobbed her head, golden curls bouncing. "Can I ask you a favor, mister?"

Reginald smiled. She probably wanted his autograph. "Certainly, miss. Ask away."

The girl held up to Reginald the object she had in her hands. "This necklace belonged to my mommy. She . . . died last year. Her and Daddy got killed by rancha."

Reginald almost fell over. Though the girl's pronunciation was poor, he recognized the creatures she spoke of: Ransha, the ferocious lizard-folk of Centra Mundi's swamplands.

The girl continued. "This is all I have left from Mommy and Daddy. But it's only half the necklace. A bad man from the swamp took the other part when he came with the lizards. Can you find it for me?"

A ray of sunlight cleared the top of the rundown brick buildings, casting radiance across Reginald's armor as he struck a proper Heroic pose. Righteous wrath welled up in his soul. This Villain, whoever he was, and the Ransha would pay for what they had done to little Gloria's parents. Reginald now had a Quest to fulfill.

"I most certainly will help you, young lady. Your parents will be avenged! But first, I will take you home. Where do you live?"

"She lives right here with me." A woman with a kerchief covering most of her black hair said. She stepped out of a nearby doorway. "I'm her aunt. Don't worry about getting her home. I'll take her. But are you sure you want to—"

"Of course! A wrong such as this must be righted. Good day, madam. I am off! Ha *ha!*" Reginald laughed his best Heroic laugh. "Farewell, little Gloria! Your treasure is as good as saved!" he said, and strode out the city's main gate.

The woman ushered the child inside the house, her silver eyes glinting. When the door was closed, she removed her kerchief, revealing pointed ears. "We've started it, then," Nieva said, dropping the simple disguise on the floor. "You may return to your normal form."

The air tensed around little Gloria. Her form blurred, then shifted and began growing. When it solidified, she was a little taller than five feet, and no longer looked like a little girl. Or like a girl at all.

"Excellent work, Lar-kathal," Nieva said. "You were very convincing."

The shifter turned to face the Elf behind him. "Thank you, my lady." The nondescript man was a disturbing sight, even to Nieva's hardened eyes. The shape-changer was clad all in drab grey clothing. He stood just over five feet tall. His face, if one could call it that, was entirely blank. Every feature was "normal," or of average shape and size. It was a face that looked like no one and everyone at the same time. The only discerning features were his hair, which seemed white until you realized it was entirely clear, and his golden eyes, which glinted with honeyed malice.

Nieva smiled thinly and handed over a bag of coins. "Here is your money. But remain close. I feel that I may need your services again."

Accepting the pouch, the shifter nodded. "Yes, milady. But may I request not to mimic a little girl again?"

Nieva laughed. "Very well. But you did make a *very* cute girl."

The shifter grimaced. "Nevertheless. Shape-changing I enjoy. Gender-bending, not at all."

Chapter 6

A-QUESTING WE SHALL GO

In which Cyrus Enjoys his Book and the Party
Fights a Fierce Foe in Feline Form

"THERE HE IS. I was beginning to worry."

Cyrus sat up and rubbed some coagulated sleep out of his eyes. "What now? Reg is back?"

Keeth nodded. "That he is. Hail, Crimson!"

Reginald waved his hand as he approached. When he arrived, he set a pack of goods twice Cyrus's size down next to him and began emptying it of its contents. "Here are the fruits of my labors. For defeating my dire foe," he said, nudging Keeth's scaled flank, "we have acquired two new tunics, a set of Seven-League Horse-Shoes for Wraith in case we need to cover much ground quickly, two flasks of brandy, a new tent, a new breastplate . . . "

Cyrus began finding places for things in the saddlebags as Reginald continued emptying the pack.

" . . . a full week's supply of Chimera jerky for our draconic friend," Reginald said. Upon mention of the smoked meat, drool issued from the Dragon's mouth, and Reginald neatly sidestepped it. "Melvin Darkstar's *Complete Guide to*

Heroics, Volume VII for you, Cyrus, and for me, a fire-proof shield!"

Cyrus groaned. "Please tell me you bought an Elementalist-certified one this time . . . "

"Of course, lad. After that mishap with Keeth here," Reginald elbowed Keeth in the ribs again, and Keeth let out a good-natured puff of smoke. "I needed to be sure about my next magic shield."

Cyrus grinned. "So you made sure there wasn't a 'Not A Fake' sign on this one, right?"

Reginald scowled. "Just for that, lad, you get to pack things up posthaste."

"Huh?" Cyrus paused in the midst of his stowage. "Where are we going?"

Reginald ignored Cyrus and turned to the Dragon. "Keeth, son of Barinol, I would ask for your aid in a perilous Quest."

Keeth extended his hazardous talons and placed his massive foot on the turf in front of Reginald. "Crimson Slash, I hereby offer you my aid and air support in your most worthy Quest, whatever it be."

Reginald clapped his hand onto Keeth's shoulder. "Then it is done! Together, we ride!"

Cyrus coughed gently.

"And you're coming also, Cyrus," Reginald added.

Cyrus's floppy blue hat slid down over his eyes. He frowned and pushed it back up. "What's the quest, Reg?"

"It is a rare thing, Cyrus! I have offered to help a Maiden in Distress. Her precious inheritance, though small, has been stolen by the Ranshan barbarians."

A small groan escaped Cyrus. "Reg, not again! Last time you offered a maiden assistance, she stole my horse and ran off with the Mysterious Swordsman!"

"That's base slander, lad. I *gave* her that horse, and that man was her betrothed."

"Wait, what?" Cyrus said. "That was *my* horse! You just gave it to her?"

"Tsk, tsk, lad. Not good to be stingy when dealing with a lady." Reginald adjusted the belly strap on Wraith's saddle. "Besides, you were a little upset with her when she left, as I recall. It was best that she left, and she needed a mount."

Cyrus looked away quickly and cleared his throat. "Right, right. But why Ransha, Reg? Why do we have to get involved with Ransha again? Didn't we learn our lesson last time?"

As he recalled, their last Ransha encounter had indeed been a disaster. Hero and apprentice had both barely escaped an angry clan of the fearsome lizard-folk, failing the Quest they had been on and earning a black mark in the Guild of Elementalists' record-books.

Reginald scowled as he mounted Wraith. "Squire, that's the first thing about being a Hero: you *never* question a Maiden in Distress. How will you ever become a professional Hero if you can't even keep something as simple as that in your head?"

Cyrus hung his head. "Sorry, sir. I'll do better next time."

"Good." Reginald took up the lead, with Keeth following, and Cyrus and the baggage-laden Toboggan in the rear.

This "proper Hero" business will get us all killed, thought Cyrus. *What if Villains planted that maiden, and this is really some kind of trick quest to get us to provoke the Ransha?* He shook his head. *Nah. Not even Villains would be that dastardly.*

● ● ●

As the group plodded into another forest, this one north of Filar, Cyrus dug a hefty tome out of his saddlebag. The book Reginald had bought him was a worn copy of Melvin Darkstar's *Complete Guide to Heroics, Volume VII.*

The twelve-volume set was a collection of all Heroic lore and tradition, compiled by an ex-Villain who knew both sides of every encounter, and the proper responses from each party to every scenario. Reginald had been teaching Cyrus from the *Complete Guide* for nearly five years now and had told him repeatedly that their entire contents were the first thing every Hero should know.

This particular volume consisted of 650 pages of dos and don'ts for the aspiring Hero, and Reginald had already marked several sections of each volume for his apprentice to commit to memory. Cyrus flipped to the first bookmark and began reading chapter 15, "Proper Methods for Conversing with a Villain."

> Upon first encountering the Villain, be very certain that you Say his Name. This will bring your presence to his attention, ensuring that there is no Advantage of Surprise (for scenarios in which the Advantage of Surprise is acceptable, see Volume III, chapter 7, paragraph ii). The Villain will most likely turn to face you, and Say your Name as well. Now that both parties are aware of one another, you may say "Prepare to Face Justice!" The Villain will begin his Introduction, often Saying his Own Name, and comparing you to Impolite Things, often Deprecating your Abilities as well.

As Witty Dialogue is an important part of any Combat, you must take every opportunity to Taunt the Villain once Combat is engaged. This enjoyable discourse often enrages the Villain, causing him to become sloppy on both the attack and defense. The Taunt can take any form, from your own Deprecations of His Abilities to generic Insults Concerning his Parentage.

When the Villain gains the upper hand, as he likely will, due to his Unsporting Trap (see II, 4, vi for more on Unsporting Traps), he will begin his Primary Monologue (Monologues, see I, 8, i). If you Value your Life, hold your peace. If you interrupt at this stage, you may never learn of his Evil Plan, or how to Foil it.

Suggested Phrases for any encounter include, but are not limited to, the following: "Justice shall Prevail," "Taste my Blade," "[blank] shall be Avenged," (where [blank] is the name of your current employer or a dead friend/relative thereof, or the Ruined Village of your choice), "You shall Never Succeed—"

Brisk bucked, bringing Cyrus's reading to an abrupt halt and almost throwing him off. "Whoa! Easy, girl. What's the matter?"

Brisk snorted and tried to bolt. Cyrus quickly reined the pony in and placed a hand on her neck. "Easy, Brisk!" he whispered. "Furies, what's the matter with you, anyway?" The pony shied off the road, and Cyrus dismounted, attempting to soothe the startled animal.

They hadn't made it far. Just a league or two into the forest on the northeastern side of Filar's border. It was much the same as the forest in which they'd been traveling, with the same kinds of trees and the same wide, packed-dirt path, but hopefully fewer surprise attacks.

"Cyrus!" Keeth bellowed.

Or maybe not.

Cyrus tucked his tome safely back into the saddlebag before sprinting to the head of the party. He squeezed around Keeth's bulk and beheld Reginald in a clearing in the forest, circling with a leopard. They rotated slowly, looking as if each hunted the other. Reginald held only his long hunting knife, for his titanic sword rested in its saddle-sheath, out of reach.

The Dragon looked down at Cyrus. "I'm helpless here, Cyrus. Me trying to help him would be like trying to help a bee fight off a hornet by casting *Kill Flying Insects*."

Cyrus looked askance at Keeth, then at the leopard. It was not a typical predatory cat, that much he knew for certain, for two reasons. First, it seemed too intelligent to try standard carnivore tactics against an armed Hero, and second, it had long, tawny, Human-looking hair on its head, walked on two feet, wore clothing, and wielded a short sword. Perhaps the latter differences should have been listed first.

"The leopard leapt at the Hero at a high angle where the shoulder joint in his armor would not allow him to parry. The Hero dodged sideways, receiving a light slash on the side of the neck as the cat's blade sliced by his head. As an instantaneous counter-attack, he spun and brought his knife down on his foe!"

But this time, Reginald's narration was incorrect. He did bring his knife down on the grassy turf where he expected the cat to be, but it wasn't there. The leopard landed feet first on the trunk of a nearby elm and vaulted off of it, lunging straight for Reginald. Reginald's eyes widened.

"The Hero's knife went flying and sunk into the loamy turf as he crashed into the ground. The leopard brought its arm back, preparing to end the Crimson Slash's illustrious career!"

Every ounce of courage he possessed pumped into Cyrus's legs. He sprinted the short distance and tackled the leopard from behind. A furious ball of cat and Cyrus hit the ground and rolled eight feet. Before the leopard could react, Cyrus twisted around and grabbed it, pinning its front paws to its sides and wrapping his other arm around its neck in *Harold's Holdtight Headlock.* After a brief struggle, the leopard dropped its sword.

Reginald retrieved his knife and sword and walked back over to where Cyrus and the defeated leopard lay. "Excellent work, lad. If I don't miss my mark, you just snuck up on a Katheni! Hmmm . . . Well then, little lady, have you learned your lesson?"

Lady? Cyrus started. *That would mean that my right hand is . . .* Cyrus suddenly let go, his face coloring.

The leopard, or leopardess as it turned out, stood up slowly, first on all fours, then upright. It was indeed female, now that Cyrus got a good look. Her clothing covered not only what a man's would, but also the upper torso, though still leaving visible a large patch of creamy white belly fur. It wasn't just beautiful fur—it was quite soft too. Cyrus blushed again.

"Let me be, Hero!" spat the Katheni. As she spoke she bared her elongated, fang-like teeth.

Reginald sheathed his knife but kept his sword drawn. "Why should we? You attacked me with no provocation."

The Katheni laid her ears back flat, her deep green eyes becoming slits. "Because if you do not, my brother will slay you all!" Her fur stood on end as she regarded the party.

Cyrus knew he was staring. He had never seen a live Katheni anywhere but the occasional slave markets, and this one's fierce demeanor scared him a bit. She looked perfectly at home in the forest, the alternating light and shade playing off her dappled fur. But given the grace and speed with which she had almost killed Reginald, Cyrus was more than a little wary.

Suddenly his hands tingled, and he felt an instinctual warning to dodge left.

He did so—just as a sphere of fire shot by his head and scorched a patch of grass just in front of him.

"Hey, watch those fireballs, Keeth!" Cyrus shouted.

"It wasn't I!" Keeth bellowed. "Beware, Cyrus! Someone else is here!"

Another Katheni stepped into the clearing. This one resembled a black panther and wore deep blue mage's robes. His amber eyes reflected the light of the spectral fire that danced on his paws as he addressed Reginald. "Pray, release my sister, good Hero. She means no harm."

Reginald wiped blood from the slash on his neck. "No harm, sir? Permit me to doubt you."

"I thought as much," the black Katheni sighed. "Very well. Kris, apologize to the gentleman."

"Brother . . . ?" The leopardess looked from Reginald to the black Katheni and back.

"It's all right, little sister," the feline mage said, lowering his paws from their spell-casting position. "They are good people."

"Yes, brother," the female Katheni said with a growl. She dropped from her defensive pose.

The male approached Reginald, his fire spell fading away. "My gratitude for not killing my sister, Hero. She has quite a temper at times. But I forget myself. I am Katana Baravaati, and you've already met my lovely sister, Kris." Katana's voice was a bass rumble with a hint of growl at the back.

Kris stepped forward and made a strange half-bow, half-curtsey. "I apologize for my rash actions, sir." Now that she was not in mortal peril, her fur had lain back down, and her angry growls had calmed to a pleasant, purring contralto.

Reginald smiled and sheathed his sword. "The mistake is mine, miss. I should have watched where I was walking."

Katana embraced his sister. "What were you thinking? Attacking a Hero? Why?"

"I'm sorry," Kris murmured into her brother's robes. "He . . . stepped on my tail."

Katana stifled a feline chuckle. "Yes, well, dear sister, when sleeping, one must be careful that one's tail is not lying across a path."

Reginald clapped Cyrus on the back, nearly knocking him down. "Again you've proven yourself useful, lad. Keep this up and you might make Hero yet!" he boomed.

Cyrus looked up at Reginald. "Yeah . . . thanks."

Reginald caught something in the tone of his apprentice's voice. "What's wrong, lad?"

Cyrus looked at the two Katheni. "Well . . . I just . . . "

"I know exactly what you're thinking, lad."

"You do?" Cyrus asked. "So now I don't have to tell you to be more careful? You scared me there, Reg. I thought you'd had it."

"Well, no, I thought you would be more worried about fighting a female," the Hero replied. "The first thing about being a Hero is that you never strike a lady. It goes against the very moral fiber of any Hero. But don't fear on that account, for the Katheni struck first. And now I suppose you are wondering what one is to do if one is attacked by a female who is *not* a lady?" Reginald asked, then continued before Cyrus could say that he hadn't been wondering that at all. "The definition of a lady is such that she would not attack a man. Thus only females who are not ladies would. So, as in the case of the Black Fox . . . "

Cyrus had heard this sort of thing before. While Reginald told the old legends well, he was *terrible* with recent history. Cyrus sat down to absorb the lecture as a boring but necessary part of his training, while keeping an eye on the two Katheni standing in the clearing with them. They looked strange and exotic, yet seemed Human in their words and actions. Still, they were dangerous foes, predators of the highest rank, and recent political events regarding slavery placed Humans at odds with Katheni. The two would merit watching, at least for now.

As Reginald rambled on, Cyrus found his mind straying to soft belly fur.

Chapter 7

THE TOWER IN THE SWAMP

In which Punishment is Inflicted, a Dark Light Appears, and Plans Change

THOMAS BILBERRY, KNOWN as Thomas Frostbite, staggered as he approached the central room of the Keep.

"You disobeyed us, Frostbite," Nieva said.

Though the Elf stood in a pool of sunlight streaming from the skylight far above the multi-columned circular room, her voice was colder than a blizzard.

"I'm sorry, milady. I didn't know that the squire was a magic user." Frostbite was visibly sweating.

Serimal stepped out from behind a column and grasped the frost mage by his robe, lifting him into the air. "He *isn't* a magic user, you buffoon! He just has a pair of fancy gloves that mimic the ability. Besides, I told you to *observe* the Hero, not attack him!"

"I-guh! I'm sorry, m-milord! I believed I could defeat him!" Frostbite squeaked, shaking.

"I see your attempt was a spectacular success." Serimal dropped the small mage in disgust. "Honestly, I'm unsure why I keep you around. You forget a key rule of Villainy: *always* bring at least enough firepower to annihilate any group of Heroes thrice over. That way, if they have some unseen advantage, you can still destroy them!"

"You do know the punishment for such disobedience, do you not, Thomas Frostbite?" Nieva picked up a heavy sacrificial spear.

The mage sagged. "No, milady . . . Please, no . . . "

Nieva placed the point of the spear on Frostbite's chest. Then, with a strength belied by her slight build, she spun it around and brought the butt of the spear up hard between the mage's legs with a sickening *thud*.

Frostbite crumpled to the floor, wheezing. "Th-that w-was . . . "

"Exactly what you deserved," Nieva said, replacing the spear in its rack. "Had you made a worse mistake, the punishment would have been more severe. No point in wasting a perfectly good mage for a relatively minor mistake. Disobey us again, however, and you lose them."

The mage gulped.

Nieva turned her back to him. "But we can make good use of your mistake. Come back in an hour and I will have more work for you. Leave us for now."

The Lesser Villain obeyed, dragging himself up and limping from the room. Nieva went to Serimal and leaned against his chest.

"Making the punishment fit the offense, I see."

Nieva and Serimal spun at the sound of the new voice. In the corner stood a figure wreathed in shadows.

With a three-fingered gesture, Nieva unleashed a bolt of electricity so powerful that it cracked the wall where it struck. It missed its target, however, and before she could react, the newcomer had a blade extending from his left sleeve to her throat.

"Now, now, Nieva," he said. "No need to be so hasty."

Nieva gasped. She recognized the pale, handsome visage staring down at her. The pointed ears, the raven hair, the softly glowing green eyes, she remembered them all. "Voshtyr?"

Voshtyr smiled. Then he turned his gaze on Serimal. "Hello, brother."

Suddenly Serimal was swinging his two-handed sword at Voshtyr's head. Voshtyr drew his falchion and parried the blow. The ring of steel on steel echoed in the circular chamber.

Voshtyr smiled again. "Good to see you, as always."

"*Half*-brother!" Serimal shouted, holding his blade leveled at Voshtyr. "Why in the Nine Torments did you have to come back?"

Voshtyr's smile disappeared. "That's no way to greet your kin. You never did learn tact, did you, brother?"

Voshtyr swatted the blade aside and slammed his palm into Serimal's exposed stomach, launching him backward. Serimal smashed through one of the pillars. The young Villain struggled to rise, but collapsed.

Voshtyr retracted the blade above his arm, the metal rasping slightly as it slid back into his sleeve.

"Now, what have you two been up to in my absence?" He glared at Nieva. "I went down to pick up my Castle Expense Report and see what had happened to my assets during my stay in Bryath, and I found that they were unfrozen and in use. Would you be so kind as to explain?"

Nieva looked past Voshtyr, to where Serimal had fallen, but Voshtyr grabbed her chin and locked eyes with her. She spoke through clenched teeth. "Milord seeks vengeance on the Crimson Slash for the defeat he suffered at the Battle of Three Streams. We are luring the Hero here with a False Quest."

Voshtyr's eyebrows rose. "Indeed? You seek to bring him here? The Crimson Slash? And with a False Quest, no less?" He smiled slightly. "Very well—you may continue. I've a small score to settle with him, as well." He looked into the center of the room and seemed to replay some scene in his mind. "Oh, yes, a small score, indeed."

"So you two are traveling north also?" Keeth asked, peering down at the Katheni.

"Yes," Katana replied. "We're headed for the desert of Mir. We've kin there."

The entire group walked through the seemingly endless forest northeast of Filar, following the dirt road. It was nearly noon, as Reginald's audience with King Alfredo had been at eight, and the scuffle with the Katheni had slowed them down as well. Fortunately the dim green interior of the forest was much cooler than the fields outside it had been.

Cyrus had abandoned the baggage, leaving it to Toboggan's pedantic care, and now rode alongside the two Katheni, listening to them talk with Reginald and the Dragon.

"Hmmm. I suppose that it would be alright then," Keeth said. "Any objections, Crimson?"

Reginald looked at Keeth with an odd expression on his rugged face. "I suppose they can come with us, if they like. It just strikes me as odd that Katheni would *want* to travel in company with Humans. After all, our species aren't exactly on the best of terms . . . "

Kris stepped up from behind her brother. "I tend to look past quarrels based solely on race, Sir Ogleby. Really, they're only personal quarrels between one or two members of either species, just taken way too far and applied to both species as a whole. They make precious little difference to people who choose to ignore them. Deep-seated grudges should be settled by individuals, not whole people groups."

Cyrus had to agree, but he couldn't reply because he was too busy watching the Katheni girl speak. He'd never spoken with a Katheni before, and the experience was novel. Their mouths moved so differently than anyone else's. Their upper lip, for example, was split in the middle, and revealed pointed teeth every time they pronounced a long *a* sound. Not to mention the unintentional trilling of the *r* in some words, sounding almost like a purr.

There was a lot about them that Cyrus didn't know, but he was learning slowly as he watched them interact with his mentor and the Dragon.

The reader, however, does not have to spend several hours analyzing individual members of the Katheni race to get a general idea of their appearance and behavior. Instead, the Author will provide him or her with a brief summation of these fascinating creatures.

Katheni are Humanoid creatures that look rather like large predatory cats. The variety within the species is quite amazing. Some Katheni resemble lions, complete with mane and tufted tail. Others, like Kris, are closer to leopards. There are also Katheni that resemble tigers, panthers, bobcats, lynx, cheetahs, and jaguars as well.

Their bodies are shaped much like that of Humans, only with more powerful legs and shoulders. Their feet are longer than those of Humans, as they are designed for running. They walk upright, though because they walk on the front portion of their hind paws, they sometimes appear to be walking on tiptoe. When sprinting, they drop to all fours, using the perfect foot design given them by the Creator.

All Katheni—save lionesses—have a large patch of guard-hair on the top of their heads. This patch runs from atop the head, goes between their ears, and continues down the back of their necks. It can be cut to the length of the rest of the fur, but in traditional Katheni culture usually is not. It is more often left to grow, and can be softened, combed, braided, and the like, much like Human hair. But since Katheni have fur on their entire bodies, they typically do not spend as much time taking care of what they term "head-fur."

There is much debate as to whether or not Katheni share the same range of emotions and intellectual abilities as Humans possess. The negative position is popular among Humans who wish to think themselves superior to other Races. These persons tend to disregard the aspects shared by Katheni and Humans, and treat them as animals. Worse, some Humans in this group capture and sell Katheni as intelligent animal slaves. Needless to say, this does not improve the already tense relationship between the two Races.

"It's settled, then," Reginald said, clapping Katana on his furred shoulders. "You may come with us. Welcome to the party of the Crimson Slash." Reginald regarded Katana cannily. "You're an Elementalist, correct? What type of magic do you use?"

Katana shrugged. "It's not like any specific type. My official designation is *Cath Magi*, or Cat Mage. I can use any type of magic that I've been struck with."

They passed by an old and rotten oak that must have once stood beside the road. Or perhaps the tree had gotten in the road's way and been toppled by the irresistible force of Human progress. Either way, the fallen tree had become home to small forest creatures of many types. In particular, one rather cheeky chipmunk decided to pop out of a knothole and chitter angrily at Kris.

The Katheni girl tensed, a predatory gleam in her eyes. Then she leapt from the path and began chasing the chipmunk, which discovered that perhaps taunting a feline predator a hundred times your size is not such a grand idea.

"Struck with?" Reginald asked, ignoring Kris's antics. "You actually *let* yourself be struck with different types of magic? Are you daft?"

The black Katheni chuckled. "It's the fastest and easiest way for me to increase my powers. And it certainly beats studying. I absorb whatever magic that's used against me. And once you get used to absorbing magic, it starts to hurt less. I think I've developed some immunity to it, actually. Any type that's inflicted on me, I begin to resist. Any specific spell used on me, I can immediately cast perfectly. The only real problem is that I can only remember the last ten spells I've absorbed."

Reginald whistled. "You have courage, standing up to magical assault just to learn more about it. Personally, I try not to touch the stuff with a standard-issue ten-foot pole."

Kris couldn't take her eyes off the Dragon's teeth, which seemed particularly wicked when he smiled, which he was doing right now. They made her own teeth feel tiny and blunt by comparison.

"Well," the Dragon said, "I believe that you probably could keep up. But you will undoubtedly tire faster than the horses. How about you and your brother ride on my back?"

Kris took a step back. "Oh, really, Dragon? I've never ridden a Dragon before. Are you sure that would be . . . what is the word . . . good?"

"I believe the word you seek is 'acceptable,' or as Humans tend to put it, 'Oh Kay.'"

Kris smiled, the fur around her mouth dimpling slightly at the corners. "Thank you. Would it be 'Oh Kay' for my brother and I to ride, Dragon?"

"Most certainly. And please, call me Keeth."

"Very well, Keith."

"Two e's in Keeth," the Dragon said good-naturedly.

"Keeith?"

"Lose the i and you'll have it."

Kris shrugged, smiling foolishly. "Keeth it is, then."

"Excellent," Keeth said, giving the Katheni girl another toothy grin. "Really, it is hardly any trouble at all. Dragons have often served as mounts in the past, sometimes for much less noble purposes. In fact, since that debacle with Melcatorix and Descatrion, we refuse to be ridden for combat purposes or while in the air. But giving a friend a casual lift? 'Tis naught." Keeth lowered a wing. "Climb aboard, Miss."

Just then, the apprentice called Cyrus walked around Keeth's side. "Hello, Keeth. Reg wants to know if you . . . " He stopped in mid-sentence.

Kris and Cyrus regarded each other intently. He didn't look that strong to Kris, but the speed and skill with which he had disabled her earlier proved him far more dangerous than he looked. His ice-blue eyes were almost unreadable—since he was probably cowering in fear. All was well then. This Human would be no match for her when she was on her guard.

Cyrus spoke first. "Erm, hi. Sorry about earlier, I was just . . . "

Kris's ears flattened to her head. "*You*. Don't come near me or I will hurt you."

Cyrus flinched backward. "Listen, I just wanted to apologize for, well, um . . . while I was trying to keep you from hurting Reg, I didn't mean to grab . . . "

Kris hissed and bared her fangs.

The apprentice beat a hasty retreat around Keeth's wing, almost losing his hat, and took off up the path to where the Hero and the horses were. "Sorry!" he shouted back.

Kris looked down at the ground. Why is it that I always do that? I need to learn to control my temper.

"You really need to work on controlling your temper, Miss," Keeth said.

Kris started. Was the Dragon reading her mind?

"No, I'm not reading your mind, just your body language." Keeth tilted his head to the side. "You shouldn't snap at people like that. Cyrus is only Human, and he *was* trying to apologize. He's actually rather embarrassed about that fight. Especially the bit about the lock he got you in. He fears that he might have placed his hands somewhere . . . improper."

A blush came to Kris's face, obscured by her fur. "It wasn't that bad. He has nothing to worry about. But two inches higher, and I would have ripped his face off."

"Well, you should tell Cyrus that then," Keeth said. "He really is quite worried about it."

Kris stretched and yawned. "Well, maybe I will. Later."

Chapter 8

EVIL TAKES NO NAPS

In which some Bad Things happen
and a Conflict is Resolved

SERIMAL SAT IN the high-backed oak chair by the window, Nieva sitting beside him at the oaken table. Both of them focused on Voshtyr, the former lord of the keep and Serimal's half-brother. And at the moment, Serimal's brooding thoughts were dark indeed.

"Well, then," Voshtyr said, "if everything goes as planned, all we need to do now is send that ice mage back to lure them in." He toyed with a dagger, flipping it back and forth between the fingers of his left hand. "The mage's inevitable monologue will reveal my presence, and then we will have our Hero. The Crimson Slash will not be able to resist a chance to bring such a foul fellow as myself back to 'face Justice.'" He turned to Serimal. "Where is that dimwit of a mage, brother?"

"Half-brother," Serimal said. "He waits downstairs. I can get him if you like."

"No," Voshtyr said. "Nieva, you go and fetch him. I must have a word in private with my brother."

"*Half*-brother," Serimal muttered.

"Very well, lord. I shall return momentarily." Nieva left the room, stopping by Serimal to whisper in his ear. "Keep safe, my love."

As soon as Nieva closed the door, Voshtyr spun with blurry speed and threw the dagger at Serimal. The dagger pinned Serimal's black velvet doublet to the back of his chair before he could do more than flinch.

"What was that for?"

Voshtyr moved to stand behind Serimal. "Well then, brother, would you care to elucidate why you didn't get me out of prison? Why you instead took over my castle?" Serimal knew that tone. It was the one Voshtyr usually reserved for the interrogation chambers. "I'm *very* interested to know."

Serimal gulped. "I won't lie to you, Voshtyr. I was hoping you were dead. It was only a matter of a year before your execution, so I claimed all legal rights to the castle and the loyalty of the Ransha tribes. I needed them to get my revenge on the Crimson Slash."

Voshtyr paced in front of the table. "Hmm. So you actually do have some spine. And here I was, thinking that you were just weak and didn't care for Villainy. Bravo, brother, bravo."

Serimal attempted to remove the knife from his shirt and chair. "So what will you do now, Voshtyr? Kill me? Take back what was yours? Attempt to plunge the world into chaos once again?"

Voshtyr smiled. "Oh, I will plunge the world into chaos. But kill my own flesh and blood? Come now, brother. What you have done is not worth killing you over."

Serimal began to relax. "So then you'll leave me and the lands be?"

"No." Voshtyr's smile disappeared, and Serimal saw the half-demon that lay underneath. "I have need of the lands and castle. Though yours on paper, they are still mine in fact. You will do with them exactly as I say, brother, or you *will* die. It matters precious little to me who *owns* this mess as long as I *control* it."

Serimal yanked the last half-inch of knife blade out of the chair back and thrust it at his half-brother.

Voshtyr grabbed the knife by its blade. The dagger slashed open the soft black glove, revealing the grey shine of steel beneath it. Serimal gasped. A metal hand?

Voshtyr yanked the weapon from Serimal's hand and crushed it into an unrecognizable lump of mangled metal. He glared at Serimal, green eyes full of frozen venom.

"Try that again, little brother, and I do that to you."

Minutes later, Nieva returned with Thomas Frostbite in tow. Nieva thought Frostbite must have heard of the terrible powers of the half-demon, because he quailed at the sight of Voshtyr. This was really not his day.

"Lord Voshtyr," Nieva said, "here is the mage you requested."

Voshtyr looked the slight mage up and down. Apparently satisfied, he picked up a heavy, leatherbound tome from the table next to him. "You are Thomas Frostbite, correct?"

"Y-yes milord," the mage stuttered.

"Here. This is for you." The Villain handed the book to the timid mage, but did not let go. "It is a genuine Artillery Tome, optimized for users of Ice magic. It contains some of the most powerful and accurate area-effect ice spells ever recorded. I want you to take this and use it to kill the Hero, his apprentice, and the Dragon you assaulted earlier. But before you do," he held on to the book as Frostbite attempted to take it, "you must tell him you serve the Lord of the Swamp. Do not forget that."

"The Lord of the Swamp," Frostbite said. He bowed and took the tome. "I shall succeed, milord."

"You had better. Artillery Tomes are expensive. Fail with that, and your life will become brief and unpleasant."

Frostbite hurried from the room in a cold sweat.

Voshtyr chuckled, an unearthly sound. "The fool. He will serve his purpose and bring the Crimson Slash right into our open arms. However," he said, gathering his black cloak in his fist, "if Frostbite cannot complete this task, he will receive far more than a spear-butt in the *dassak*." He swept from the room, his cloak billowing behind him.

Nieva jumped as the door slammed behind Voshtyr.

Serimal picked up the mangled knife from the table and stared at it. "I believe he means to sacrifice Frostbite like a common Minion, and I cannot stop him. I only pray that you and I survive my half-brother's fury, even if our mage does not."

Nieva ran her hand down the scar on Serimal's face. "He is merely pleased to be out of prison, is he not? He will soon calm down to a manageable level."

"I doubt it," Serimal replied, stabbing what was left of the knife-point into the table. "You did not know him for very long before he was imprisoned, and his stay there has not improved him. He has always been unpredictable, a loose ballista." The young Villain rose from his chair and put his finger through the knife-hole in his doublet, wiggling it at Nieva. "He never learned how to be a proper Villain."

"Despite your father's training?" Nieva asked.

"Yes, despite what Father taught him," Serimal said with a sigh. "It seems he learned more from his mother than our father. And when you learn from a demon, you don't learn Villainy—you learn Evil."

• • •

"That is all the riding I can stomach for one day, my friends," Reginald announced, sliding from Wraith's saddle. "This looks like a decent place to encamp. Cyrus, supper, if you please."

Once they had set up camp in a large clearing beside the forest road, Cyrus began cooking a hearty soup. He first boiled a large pot of water. The water had been easy to find, as it was in a nearby stream. The difficulty was that they didn't have a pot large enough to cook for four plus a Dragon.

Eventually, Katana offered to help. The jaguar-man drew a circle on the ground with one of his claws and drew a picture of a pot on a piece of paper. After placing the paper in the circle, he set the pot caricature on fire and walked thrice clockwise around the circle. With a small bang, a pot appeared in the circle. Cyrus goggled. Katana explained that he'd seen the same spell used to summon monsters, so why not try to summon cookware?

After boiling the water, Cyrus added a large chunk of the Chimera meat that Reginald had bought for Keeth. "I'll make a batch big enough for you to have some as well, Keeth," he explained.

"I suppose that's all right," Keeth grumbled. "I haven't eaten anything cooked in any way other than char-broiled for two months. A soup will be a nice change. Just don't use all of it."

Cyrus added the rest of the potatoes they'd picked up as supplies and found a cluster of benign and tasty mushrooms in the woods. These went into the pot also. Then came the fun part.

Cyrus didn't exactly pride himself on his cooking skills, but he knew a thing or two about soups. As part of his adventuring supplies he carried a pouch with several types of dried cooking herbs. From this pouch came a sprig of rosemary and a palmful of oregano leaves. Finally, he added some amras seeds, a potent fiery spice. Satisfied with his work, Cyrus left the soup to simmer, pulled his floppy hat over his eyes, and dozed off.

Something was messing with his hat.

Cyrus reached up lazily to dislodge whatever it was, but his hand encountered something warm and furry. Cyrus started. Pushing his hat out of his eyes, he saw Kris, who had just pulled her paw back.

"Sorry," the Katheni girl said. "I didn't know you were asleep."

The day had trailed into dusk while Cyrus dozed. Crickets chirped from the woods, and the gentle breeze that had been blowing all day had turned a little chilly. And now, the forest provided trapped warmth rather than shaded cool.

"It's fine," Cyrus said warily. "I was just about to wake up and check the soup anyway." He sat up. "Is something wrong?"

Kris looked down. "No, but something isn't right. I want to apologize for snarling at you earlier."

Cyrus blinked. "It's no big deal, really. Reg yells at me worse than that all the time. And it's really my fault anyway. I should have been more careful where I—"

"No, really, it's 'Oh Kay,'" Kris said. "It was fine. I mean . . . I didn't take it personally."

"Oh, good," Cyrus said. He picked up a ladle from the ground next to the fire and began stirring the soup. "If you *had* taken it personally, I'm sure I'd be in a lot of trouble."

"Mm." Kris nodded, not exactly responding to his comment. "So, do you cook often?"

"I have to, unless I want to eat nothing but trail rations. Jerky, raisins, and hard-tack get old after a while," Cyrus said, making a wry face. "So I work a bit of culinary magic on whatever supplies we have at the moment."

"Culinary Magic? Like *Disguise Flavor*?" Kris wrinkled her nose. "Brother uses that often, but I can taste the magic . . . "

"No, no," Cyrus said, "not actual magic. That's just a . . . I mean, I have a pack of spices I use from time to time."

Kris giggled. "From time to thyme? Like the spice?"

Cyrus snorted. He hung the ladle over the edge of the pot and turned back to Kris. "No, no. Puns are the lowest form of humor. I'd use that sort of seasoning sparingly."

"There's no need to stew over that, Cyrus," Kris replied, giving the apprentice Hero a sharp-toothed grin. She was prettier when she was smiling rather than snarling, Cyrus noted. But the fangs were still rather scary.

Cyrus groaned. "This whole conversation should be taken with a grain of salt . . . "

"Personally," Keeth's voice boomed from overhead, "I think the whole conversation is overdone."

Kris and Cyrus both jumped and looked up. The Dragon stood behind them, neck bent down so his head was not far from theirs.

"I am glad you have evened out your dispute," the Dragon said. "I had begun to worry."

"Curses," Cyrus said with a chuckle. "I had some more *soup*er puns to use."

"Leftovers," Kris added.

Keeth shook his head at the two and looked longingly at the soup-pot. "I'm also beginning to worry about our supper . . . "

"Oh, right, the soup!" Cyrus returned to the pot, Kris in his wake. "Here." He offered the Katheni girl a spoonful of steaming broth. "Try this, tell me if it's any good."

"Mrr?" Kris sniffed the spoon and took a tentative sip. Her eyes lit up and she slurped the rest down rapidly.

"Good, huh?" Cyrus leaned back against a tree, smiling. "Careful, though, it has a bit of kick to it."

"It's alright," Kris replied, licking her lips to catch any of the soup she might have missed. "I'm used to spiciness. My aunt and uncle live in Mir, and they cook the spiciest food you've ever tasted."

"I doubt it," Cyrus said. "I've had some pretty spicy foods. I practically have no sense of 'hot' foods anymore."

Kris grinned, baring the points of her fangs. "And *I* doubt *that*. My uncle's food will light your tongue on fire, Human!"

"If I ever visit your uncle, I'll take you up on that. Nobody has invented a dish yet that can burn *my* mouth!"

"If you two are done boasting, can we eat now?" Reginald said, stepping out from beside Keeth. "It's not the best idea to keep a hungry Hero from his food. Not to mention a Dragon." He smiled and clapped Cyrus on the back. "I'm sure you two will have plenty of time to chat on our way north."

Cyrus looked sheepish, and Kris didn't seem to know *where* to look. Cyrus began dishing the soup into four deep bowls and one appropriately Dragon-sized basin.

After dinner, as everyone retired to his or her sleeping arrangement, Cyrus lay in his tent, staring up at the center ridge.

Well, they seem like nice enough folk, and the girl's sense of humor is fairly Human. It still wouldn't hurt to keep an eye on them, though. Since Reg is never cautious, one *of us should be.*

Chapter 9

REVENGE SERVED COLD

In which the Party Encounters a Foe
and soundly Kicks his Hindmost Part

THE NEXT DAY dawned bright and sunny, though trees obscured the morning sun. The rose colored wisps of cloud streaking the sky above the treetops gave the morning a cheerful atmosphere.

Cyrus was still asleep in his tent. He was having a dream about his hometown on the Citrus Isles, the people there, the food, the bucket of cold streamwater being thrown on him.

The what?

"Gah! I'm awake!" Cyrus yelled, soaking wet.

Reginald laughed, holding a now empty bucket. "It's after dawn, lad. Time to awake and face the day!"

Cyrus crawled out of his sodden tent. "How about I sneak up behind the day and stab it in the back? I get less wet that way."

Reginald chuckled as he handed his apprentice the bucket. "Here, stow this and get moving."

Cyrus grumbled good-naturedly and made a mental note to put something slimy in Reginald's armor.

. . .

The second day of traveling was much the same as the first. Trees lined the path, enveloping the party in shade. The packed-dirt road got neither harder nor softer. And chipper forest creatures still darted about the treetops, chittering and chirping at each other and the party.

Then Cyrus tensed, and the hairs on the back of his neck stood up. Something was about to happen. He didn't know how he could tell, but there was no mistaking it.

He began to slip on his gloves, but a gust of frigid wind blew them out of his hands. A cold wind in midsummer? He knew what that meant.

Cyrus dove off Brisk's back with a shout—just as a cluster of small orbs of snow shot past his head. The magic snowballs exploded harmlessly against a hummock of dirt in a fury of snow and ice. "We're under attack!"

Reginald spun at Cyrus's warning. Keeth turned also, slower due to his size, and the pair of Katheni leapt from his back to the ground, Kris drawing her short sword.

"We meet again, Crimson Slash." The mage's voice carried over the suddenly chilly air. "You may have defeated me last time, but this time I shall be your undoing. Behold my newfound power!"

Cyrus recognized the voice. It was that ice mage again: something-or-other Frostbite.

Frostbite stepped from the trees a few dozen yards away, holding a large, leatherbound book with deep blue runes on its front. "Behold the instrument of your undoing, pathetic Hero. I shall slay thee where thou standest."

Cyrus lay on the ground and chuckled. The Villain had already begun his Primary Monologue. It was time to listen to what he was up to.

The small mage continued his speech. "Yes, fear me now, for I wield far more power than you!"

"A book?" Cyrus called out. "What are you going to do, start a book club and bore us to death?"

Frostbite scowled. "It's a magic book, you dimwit, given to me by the Lord of the Swamp. This book I hold in my hand is all that I need to utterly destroy you. Did I mention that I work for the Lord of the Swamp? Mwahahaha! Today you die!" With a single sweeping gesture, the mage threw forth a gigantic cloud of spinning ice fragments.

Reginald spurred Wraith off the road just in time. The blast blew right by him. Unfortunately, with Reginald out of the way, there was nothing to prevent it from hitting Katana, which it did, square in the chest.

The Katheni mage dropped his spellbook, adopting a strange defensive posture. He stuck his paws straight out as if trying to catch the blizzard. Snow and fragments of ice quickly transformed the Katheni into a prickly snow-cat.

Snow blew around them in an instant blizzard, coating the ground at an unbelievable rate. Cyrus gave up looking for his gloves. They were probably totally buried by now. Drawing his longsword, he rushed at the mage. Kris stepped from behind Katana and ran to catch up with Cyrus.

Frostbite smirked and launched a bolt of supercooled air at Cyrus. Cyrus dodged it and kept coming. Rolling his eyes at the apprentice Hero's foolish tenacity, Frostbite cast *StormWind.* Gale-force winds swirled through the trees, intensifying the blizzard and hurling Cyrus backward into the snowbank.

Cyrus struggled to get up from the snow, but it grew deeper by the second as the icy storm continued to swirl about them. Then a soft hand grabbed his, and Kris pulled him to his feet.

"Come on, Cyrus. You're a Hero—do something about this guy before he kills us!"

Cyrus sprinted forward again. It was slow going, for the wind grew stronger and the drifts grew deeper as Frostbite poured more energy into the spell. He continued tossing more spheres of explosive frost and fragments of incandescent ice.

Cyrus dodged or deflected most of them, taking slash wounds from those he couldn't. Still he pressed his laborious and drawn-out charge, making miniscule but measurable progress.

Frustrated, the mage made an obscure gesture and pointed at Cyrus. The wind dropped abruptly, and a blue glow appeared on the mage's finger. A near-invisible bolt shot from it.

Cyrus sensed it coming and dropped into the snow, just as whatever it was passed over his head. Instead, the attack struck Kris.

Suddenly she stood trapped inside walls of ice.

Kris banged on the ice and tried to say something. Cyrus couldn't hear her, for the ice had grown too thick already. Kris pointed at the mage.

Cyrus turned back to Frostbite. "All right, *ibne serefsiz,* prepare to, uh, Face Justice, or something like that!" He attempted to rush the mage again, but Frostbite put his palms up and raised his fingers. Cyrus's feet froze to the ground and ice began climbing his legs. "What? Why, you . . . *Kahretsin!*" Cyrus yelled in frustration, straining at the solid frost.

"Now, lad, don't get too frustrated," Reginald said, striding up behind the immobile Cyrus. "Time for that move I taught you." With one hand, Reginald grabbed his squire by the collar and yanked him free of the encroaching ice. "Ready, lad?"

"*Thompson's Thrown Tornado?*" Cyrus asked.

"Aye. Get ready!"

Cyrus held his sword perpendicular to his torso. "Ready!"

"*Thompson's Thrown Tornado!*" bellowed the Crimson Slash, throwing Cyrus at the mage. Cyrus focused the muscles in his arms and legs and began rotating rapidly. His sword blade became a blurry circle, and the apprentice Hero became an airborne, spinning projectile.

Frostbite saw his doom coming a moment too late. He began weaving his hands in some mystic pattern, but to no avail. Cyrus slammed into the mage's puny body. The force of the blow knocked Frostbite off his feet, and both went rolling.

"Move, Cyrus!" Keeth bellowed.

Cyrus rolled off the Villain just as a blast of flame scorched the air, striking the prone mage. Frostbite caught fire. Screaming, he leapt up and made two short gestures. The flames dissipated.

However, the delay had been sufficient.

"Revenge is a dish best served cold!" Katana snarled, shaking himself free of the snow and thrusting forth his paws. An ice-storm identical to the one he had just absorbed sprang into existence and smashed into the mage.

"Blinded by the snowstorm, the Villain failed to see the Hero as he leapt into the air, blade glowing a dull red," quoth Reginald, doing exactly that. "With a devastating impact, the Hero smote the frosted mage across the chest, knocking the slim man to the ground!"

Thomas Frostbite slumped as he lay on the ground, bleeding heavily. "You think you've won? Heh heh." A guttural cough racked his frosted frame. "I'm just a small fry. You've wasted enough time on me that my lord Voshtyr's plan is complete." He coughed again, spitting up blood.

"Now, despair, because though you defeated me, you will lose your friend."

Behind the party, Kris was still trapped inside the walls of ice. The walls had continued to thicken, reducing the space inside. Kris frantically scrabbled at the walls with her claws as the ice closed around her, immobilizing and crushing.

"*No!*" Cyrus yelled, running for the cube.

The Crimson Slash placed the point of his enormous sword on Thomas's chest. "Reverse the spell *now,* Villain, or I shall spit you where you lie."

"Heh. Very well, then. I'll say the command word: *teleport!*" He began to vanish in a cloud of frost but was a little too slow. The Crimson Slash jammed his sword into the dematerializing mage, who winced as he faded. Blood stained the sword, and Frostbite disappeared.

Kris had ceased struggling inside the now solidified cube. As soon as Cyrus reached the cube, he began hacking away at it with his sword. "Kris! *Kris!*" he yelled. The ice was regenerating faster than he chipped it away, and within a few moments, his sword froze solidly into the side. He yanked on his blade, but it would not budge.

"Get out of the way!" Keeth bellowed at Cyrus. The Dragon breathed an amazing display of pyrotechnics on the rectangular mass of frozen water. And yet the ice remained. Keeth swore a few choice oaths in the language of Dragons. "It's magic ice! My fire won't melt it!"

Cyrus pressed his forehead against the frigid surface of the cube. "No . . . not now . . . just when we . . . " Cyrus pulled his head from the frozen surface. He stared at Kris's now obscured form, twisted in pain. He glared at the ice, and rage built within him. Pounding his fists on the ice, he shouted at the cube. "Melt! O gods, why? *Melt!*"

With a horrendous crack, small fissures appeared in the surface of the ice. Cyrus started, then placed his hands on either side of the block of ice and concentrated.

The cube began to steam. Rivulets of water began flowing around his boots. Soon, the entire cube dissolved, reducing itself to a watery mess. Cyrus splashed into the puddle and knelt down beside Kris.

"Kris? Can you hear me?" he said, but got no response from the soaked and bedraggled Katheni girl. Cyrus checked her pulse. Weak, but present, yet she wasn't breathing. The apprentice Hero tilted the girl's head back, and began to administer BRP.

Just so the reader is not confused, BRP is not a misspelling of the word *burp*. It is an acronym for Breath Restoring Process. It is a method of restarting the breathing process for someone who currently is not (breathing, that is), by placing one's mouth over the victim's mouth and blowing in air.

BRP's only drawbacks are that (1) it is effective only on those still alive, and (2) given the average state of oral hygiene, some of your intended recipients will likely have unpleasant breath.

Nevertheless, it is an important skill for any apprentice Hero to have and will serve him or her well when healing by magical means is unavailable.

Katana grabbed Cyrus's collar. "What are you doing to my sister?"

"Shut up!" Cyrus snapped between breaths. "I'm saving her life!"

Katana growled softly but placed a paw on his sister's chest. "Here. Perhaps this will mend the damage." A pale white glow spread over his Kris's body. "A cleric of Vertis the Sky god once used this to heal some internal injuries I sustained. I wrote it down so I wouldn't forget it."

The glow faded. Cyrus placed his mouth over Kris's once again and breathed out. After a moment, Kris stirred and opened her eyes.

She promptly swatted Cyrus across the face, claws gouging three deep scores into his cheek.

Cyrus staggered back and fell over. "Ah! Furies! You're alive!" He got up, face bleeding. "Thank the gods!"

Kris looked around, then up at Katana. "What happened, brother? The last thing I saw was Cyrus charging the mage, and then this cold blue light. Then . . . " she looked at Cyrus, then up at Katana. "Why did you let the Human on me like that? What in the Shifting Sands was he trying to do?"

"Save your life," Katana said wryly. "My healing magic simply heals injuries. It cannot restore breath."

Cyrus suddenly felt the need to sit down.

Kris stared at him, her wet fur matted to her body. "You mean he was . . . putting his breath in me?" Kris's green eyes widened.

Katana nodded. "And you clawed him for it. You have a strange way of expressing your gratitude, little sister."

The Katheni girl sprang up from her sodden seat and leapt over to where Cyrus sat. "I'm so sorry, Cyrus. I didn't know you were helping me. I thought you were . . . I mean . . . " her speech petered out.

Cyrus looked at Kris, feeling dizzy. "No, it's okay, really. I should have known that Katheni wouldn't know about BRP."

"But your face . . . "

"What about my face?" Cyrus put a hand to his face, then pulled it away and looked at the blood. "Interesting," he said, and promptly passed out.

"This isn't good," Reginald said.

Katana put a finger to Cyrus's neck "I think he'll be just fine, Crimson. It is nothing to worry about, just a combination of blood loss and the downside of an adrenaline rush."

The ground still squished beneath their feet, and heaps of snow still dotted the woods and road. The air gradually warmed to midsummer heat again, and the melting snow turned the road to mud. Keeth and Kris stood a short distance off, staying out of the mud for the time being. Cyrus lay on the ground with his eyes closed. His face was still pale from the blood loss he'd suffered, but he would certainly survive.

Reginald turned to Katana, chin resting on his gauntlet. "Oh, I do not fear for my apprentice. I was thinking about what the mage said. He mentioned the name 'Voshtyr.'"

"Do you know someone named Voshtyr, this Lord of the Swamp?" Katana asked.

"I once fought and bested an Arch-Villain by that name six years ago, though he had naught to do with swamps," Reginald said. "Voshtyr Demonkin once attempted to assassinate the king of Bryath. I happened to be breaking my fast with the King and was able to hold the Villain until reinforcements could arrive. When the fight was over, I testified against him at the trial. Last I heard, all the legal hogwash was over with, and he was scheduled to be executed. But if this is the same Voshtyr who now serves this 'Lord of the Swamp,' or worse, *is* the Lord of the Swamp . . . "

Kris wandered over from where she'd been standing and sat down next to Cyrus. She looked up at Reginald. "Then that means he's escaped and is trying to get his revenge on you?"

Reginald nodded. "Perhaps. Or perhaps it is merely Fate that I am on this Quest. There is but one swamp nearby large enough to host a tribe or two of Ransha. And it has at its fetid heart an ancient Keep, favored by Villains in years past as a sanctuary. It is more than likely there that Voshtyr has taken up his abode."

Reginald shook his head, then rested his chin on his fist. "The Ransha tribe that has stolen the child's necklace which I seek is in the same direction—nay, the same *location* as this ancient Keep. If Voshtyr is in this swamp, then I may have to fight him once more." He shuddered and picked up his sword from where he'd leaned it against a tree. "I did not relish the fight with him the first time. He is an Arch-Villain, as I said. He has . . . uncanny powers. There are some who say that he's half demon. I did see his eyes glowing a bit red, now that I think about it, but I don't believe that tripe. Still, I'd rather not fight him again."

Kris looked back down at Cyrus's bloodied face. "Then I hope you don't have to. But if he is the same man and he has escaped . . . "

Reginald's face hardened. "Then it is my duty to recapture him."

Katana stood in the rapidly evaporating pool of water left from the magical snowstorm, searching for his dropped spellbook. He found the book readily enough, but something white in the muddied water caught his eye.

It was a soiled silk glove, with a basic Mage's rune on it. Katana picked it up and examined it. Then he frowned and dropped the glove back into the muck and went back to the others.

The rune on the glove had lost its power some time ago.

Chapter 10

THE BOMB OF TICKING TIME

In which Something Unpleasant Happens, Cyrus Dreams,
and Someone finally Notices what is Going On

SERIMAL KICKED OPEN the tall doors to the inner sanctum slammed open and strode in, carrying the bleeding body of Thomas Frostbite. "Nieva! Come quickly!"

Nieva stepped from behind a wicker screen near a dusty, cobwebbed throne and looked at Thomas. "Oh, no. Voshtyr will not be pleased."

"Do you honestly think I give a cracked bucket what pleases Voshtyr?" Serimal said, scowling as large drops of blood spattered the stone floor. He laid the wounded mage on the long-table at the center of the room. "Heal him, quickly."

Nieva moved to a position beside Frostbite's chest.

"Hold." Voshtyr's voice echoed through the sanctum. From somewhere amongst the darkness of the roof beams, he dropped like a cat, landing on his feet, cloak swirling. "He seems to have accomplished his task. Does he still have my Artillery Tome?"

Serimal pried the Tome from Thomas's grasp. Frostbite whimpered and made a choking noise. "Here. Here's your accursed book. You meant for him to nearly be slain?"

Serimal said in disgust, handing the bloodstained tome to Voshtyr.

"Hmm . . . he got blood on it. Oh, well, I expected as much, knowing your soft spot for incompetent henchmen." Voshtyr wiped the bloodied book off on a rich, brocaded tapestry adorning the wall. "And no, I had not expected him to be nearly slain. I had expected him to actually be slain and that I would have to retrieve the tome myself. His return of it is a serendipitous occurrence."

Serimal took a step toward a weapon rack, but Nieva placed her delicate hand on his arm. "Please," she said to Voshtyr, "let me heal him."

"Heal him?" Voshtyr said. "No, he has served his purpose. I shall do this instead." He placed his hand below Frostbite's chin. Instantly, the hand became transparent and passed into the mage's body. Frostbite jerked violently as Voshtyr grabbed hold of something. He withdrew his hand, pulling from his twitching body a full-size, crystalline image of Thomas Frostbite.

"No!" Nieva shrieked. "Not his soul!"

The image glanced around in terror, mouthing silent words.

Voshtyr's eyes changed color, from a soft green to a burning red. He spoke authoritatively, in a language Serimal did not understand.

Serimal cowered backward, Voshtyr's unnatural words striking chords of unreasoning terror in his mind. Nieva cringed away as well, hiding her face in the black velvet of Serimal's doublet.

The outside light darkened, plunging the already dim room into a terrible gloom. Thomas's soul writhed and released a silent scream. With a brilliant flash, it disappeared, leaving a tiny diamond in the palm of Voshtyr's hand.

"There," Voshtyr said pleasantly, the red fading from his eyes. "Problem solved." On the table, the mage's body went limp. "Now the Crimson Slash knows where we are, and we can set up a proper ambush." He held the diamond up to the light. "Healed, an incompetent mage would do me little good. But the pure essence of his magic? That will serve me well indeed."

"Well, it isn't a major problem. Just keep an eye on the others and keep that information away from the pixies. If one pixie knows, all pixies know. And if all pixies know, *everyone* knows."

The Guildmaster sat at the heavy ironwood desk, held the speaking-horn to his ear and scrawled a note about pest control with his free hand. The Guildmaster's private office was an imposing place, with a thick red carpet on the floor and paintings of previous Guildmasters hanging on the walls. Evening sunlight streamed through the tall windows behind the desk, casting into shadows the face of the man sitting at it. A sand-blond boy of eight years sat on the floor with his back against the desk, playing with some miniature knight and Dragon figurines.

"Yes, I will," the Guildmaster said. "Excellent. Good day, Turquoise." He hung up the speaking-horn and pressed a button on his desk. "Saliriana, send Green in, if you please."

A young Hero clad in assorted shades of green entered the spacious office, closing the thick oaken door behind him.

The Guildmaster reached down and tousled the boy's hair before turning to the young Hero. "Yes, Green?" he boomed. "You needed to see me?"

"Message for you, Guardian," Green replied, approaching the desk and depositing the scrap of parchment on the man's desk. "It just came in by Stormcrow from the Bryath Justice Department."

The Guildmaster, also known as Guardian, looked the messenger over. Green wasn't more than thirty, with curly black hair spilling out from under a jaunty green cap. His build was thin and wiry, but he had an air of playful confidence that made him seem at ease no matter where he was, and big, brown, puppy-dog eyes that had saved him from severe reprimands and punishments more than once.

Guardian picked up the paper and scanned it, a frown creasing his brow. "This came in just now?" He leaned back in his high-backed chair as his eyes flickered back and forth across the paper.

"Less than five minutes ago, sir," Green replied. "Why?"

"What is it, Dad?" the boy asked. He put his hands up on the edge of the desk and tried to see the paper.

Guardian glanced at the boy. "News from Bryath, son. Can you take your toys elsewhere? I must speak with the Green Falcon."

The boy nodded. "Okay. Green, did you bring me something?"

"Sure did, Trigger. Check this out." Green handed another figurine to the boy. It was an Araquellus standing with its arms in an *en guard* position. "Press the button on his back."

Trigger did as he was told. Immediately, miniature silver blades sprang out of the figurine's arms. The boy gasped in surprise and delight, then rose and gave Green a hug.

"Psh, get off me, kid. I have to talk to your dad."

Trigger nodded, scooped up his toys, and scampered from the room.

"I hope you paid for that one, Green," Guardian said, glowering at the Green Falcon. "I cannot have my son learning to steal."

Green shifted uncomfortably. "Eh, of course I did. I'm not *always* a thief. So what was in the message?" he asked, changing the subject.

"Disturbing news," Guardian replied. "Combined with what the Turquoise Templar just told me, it could be dire news indeed. He said that someone has stolen the Life Spanner from its resting-place."

The Green Falcon frowned slightly. "Life Spanner? I read about that in a Book of Old Myths. Isn't that one part of an ancient and incredibly dangerous machine? Are you saying it actually exists?"

Guardian nodded sagely, wheeling his chair out from behind his desk. "Myths are true more often than you might think, young man. And, it seems, the older they are, the more likely they are to be true." He winced slightly.

"You okay, Guardian?" Green asked, starting forward.

Guardian waved Green away. "It's nothing, Green. The corruption from that spell just acts up in my legs once in a while. I've become used to it. It takes more than one Necromancer to take down the Swift Justice."

A loud bang on the door echoed through the room, followed by another and then two more. Guardian scowled and picked up the speaking-horn. "Saliriana! What in the Nine Torments is going on out there?"

"A minotaur got a little antsy while waiting, and started punting some Dwarves at the door," Saliriana said cheerfully. "I'll get Purple to herd him out the door until his appointment."

Guardian grumbled and hung the horn back up. "Now, about that Myth," he said to Green. "The one you're thinking of, I believe, concerns the Puissant Lifetime Omnipotence Transfusion device. It harnesses the combined power of all four elements, along with other eldritch magic, to make the recipient completely invincible and catastrophically powerful. Should a Villain ever acquire such a thing . . . "

"Heroes would cease to exist faster than you can say 'contrived plot-hook,'" Green finished. "But what makes this such dire news? The Guild has foiled attempts at its construction before."

Guardian held up the bit of parchment. "This is a notice from the Bryath Justice Department of an unauthorized prisoner release. Apparently, the priest in charge of record-keeping for prisoner sentencing and release dates misfiled this prisoner and got him released. They claim it was 'clerical error,'" Guardian said, rolling his eyes. "How that could have happened with such a dangerous prisoner, they're remarkably close-lipped about. It seems they've 'accidentally' released Voshtyr Demonkin."

The Green Falcon's jaw dropped. "Oh, my, he's the Arch-Villain who slew two thirds of the Bryath Palace Guard and half the Kingsguard in his attempt to get the King's signet, isn't he? Of all the men to have loose again . . . "

"And if you factor in the theft of the Life Spanner, it may well be that Demonkin is attempting to construct the entire device." Guardian looked at the parchment in his hand. "The Justice Department has requested that we dispatch an assassin to slay the Villain before he causes any damage." He sighed. "Thank you, Green. You may return to your post."

Green nodded and left the room, the carved-oak door slamming shut behind him.

Guardian looked at the note for another long moment before turning his gaze back to a shadowed corner of the room. "I suppose you heard all that, then."

A slender figure rose stiffly from a chair in the corner and walked slowly over to Guardian's desk. It was an Elf so incredibly ancient that she looked old by *Human* standards. Both of the woman's eyes were pure white, as if they had never had corneas or pupils. Her clothing floated about her like a shroud, despite the lack of airflow in the room.

"I did," she said, her voice almost inaudible. "Voshtyr Demonkin's line flows with force in the present, and more in the future. His path threatens to destroy the Hero's Guild and all it stands for."

"Then we must dispatch someone immediately," Guardian said. He spoke into the horn on his desk. "Saliriana, contact the Silent Assassin immediately and send him to my office." Turning back to the frail Elf woman, he smiled grimly. "Kerimax has not failed me yet. Demonkin will die ere the fortnight is over."

"Perhaps," she replied. "My sight is only of what may be. It can be altered."

"But what is your opinion, Destiny? Can this man be stopped?"

Destiny lowered her white-haired head. "I cannot say. Nothing is certain save Death."

"And Taxes," Guardian added. He took one of Destiny's frail hands in his hearty one. "Fear not, milady. This threat is taken care of."

The edge of her hood floated across her face. "Perhaps."

Chapter II

The Light at the End of the Tunnel

In which the Party Encounters Cacophonous Vegetation,
Leaves the Forest, and Gets a History Lesson

"WAKE UP, LAD," Reginald said. "I didn't train you to be lazy and sleep half the day."

Cyrus abruptly woke to see Reginald and Kris leaning over him, upside down. He winced as his cheek began to throb. "What . . . ? What happened?"

Kris looked down at him, her bangs falling down over one eye. "Well, after you . . . um . . . saved my life, I kind of scratched you a bit. You lost quite a bit of blood, both from me and that mage. You passed out."

The three of them sat—or in Cyrus's case, lay—at the base of a large tree by the side of the dirt road leading through the forest. A short distance off sat Keeth, sunning himself in a large patch of sunlight that filtered through the tree canopy.

Cyrus scratched his head. "I passed out? What kind of Hero passes out from something as unimportant as blood loss?"

"Any Human one, lad," Reginald said, stepping away from the tent flap. "I've passed out a time or two after a battle from injuries, myself."

Cyrus sat up. "Well then. Let's get going, shall we? That kid can't wait for her necklace forever."

Five minutes later, all the tents were packed and the party had resumed its trek through the forest. Reginald rode Wraith up front, followed by Keeth—Katana and Kris on his back. Cyrus rode Brisk at the rear of the party, next to Toboggan, the pack mule.

The scenery had become boring to Cyrus. It was just trees and more trees. Leaves and piles of leaves. Rocks and more rocks. And the same road that they'd been traveling on for days now. It was almost as if they'd been riding in circles. He began to even wish that some bandits would attack them or something.

Tiring of riding silently, Cyrus spurred Brisk up beside Reginald. "Say, Reg. How long will it take my face to heal up, d'ya think?"

Reginald looked at Cyrus's bandaged face. "Those claw marks are fairly deep. I'd say maybe two days."

"Two *days*?" Cyrus exclaimed, incredulous. "Only two days? But—"

"Keep in mind that you're Hero potential, lad," Reginald said. "That's the first thing about being a Hero. We heal faster than most people. I wouldn't be surprised if those marks were just scars by the day after tomorrow."

"Scars, huh?" Cyrus thought about it. "That's why I see Heroes with so many scars, then. They heal up so quickly that there's more scar tissue than there would be if they healed at regular speed."

"Exactly. On the bright side, women love scars. One time, I—"

"Uh, thanks, Reg. I need to go check on Toboggan now." Cyrus dropped back to the rear of the party again.

Once he'd checked on the mule, Cyrus pulled out the *Complete Guide to Heroics* and quickly became oblivious to the rest of the world as the party continued through the shady forest.

"So what is it like, being apprenticed to a Hero?"

Cyrus started. Kris had walked down Keeth's scaled back and seated herself just above where his massive tail began. The Katheni girl sat there, tail swaying gently behind her as she watched Cyrus.

"Oh! Hi, Kris," Cyrus said. "I didn't see you there. What's up?"

Kris smiled, and Cyrus thought her speckled, tawny fur seemed more radiant than usual. "I asked you what it's like being an apprentice Hero."

Cyrus stowed his book. "Oh, it's not that different from being apprenticed to a blacksmith or cobbler. The pay is terrible, the food's worse—unless I cook it myself—and the hours are horrible."

Kris laughed. "Aren't there any upsides?"

"Sure! There are some pretty exciting moments for any apprentice Hero. It's good for my health too. All the exercises Reg puts me through build some muscle, and with all the sword training he's given me, I'd like to think I'm becoming a pretty fair swordsman. Plus, because I have some Heroic abilities, I can really impress the girls." Cyrus flexed his fairly impressive right bicep. "How many guys do you know that can jump almost a hundred spans into the air, do a quintuple-flip, and land without injury?"

"None," Kris admitted. "In fact, I don't even think you can."

"Oh, really?" Cyrus said. "If we weren't moving, I'd show you right now. On second thought," he paused, looking up into the trees, "I might get caught in those upper branches if I tried it here."

Kris snickered. "That's all right. I guess I will believe you, even if you can't prove it."

"Hey now! Don't knock caution. There are a lot of occupational hazards being a Hero!"

"Like what?"

"Well, roaming bands of unfriendly Orcs, tax collectors, and other strange monsters that appear out of nowhere, princesses, and things like that. Plus, even though Heroes are tough, we aren't invulnerable.

"One time, about four years ago, Reg was teaching me jumping techniques. We were practicing on a pretty tall hill. I mistimed a jump and fell off the far side, a three-hundred-foot drop. Reg saw me fall and jumped after me. He caught me in midair, and when we hit the ground, he rolled, protecting me with his body. He dislocated his shoulder, but aside from that, we were both fine. If he hadn't been right there watching me, I could have died. It may sound kind of stupid, but training is possibly the most dangerous thing we do."

Kris nodded. "I guess so. But what do you do when you aren't training?"

Cyrus smiled. "Lots of things. Fish, read just about anything I can get my hands on, give little kids piggy-back rides while we're in towns, write letters home, that sort of stuff."

"Letters to whom, your family? Or have you a mate at home?" Kris asked. She lay back against the Dragon's scaled hide and stretched.

"Huh? No, of course not. I haven't had time for that sort of thing. Mates—I mean *wives*, I guess—are time-consuming and expensive. I suppose there are perks to having one, but at the moment, I can't think of . . . " he stopped and looked at Kris. "Why do you ask?"

The Katheni girl smiled beatifically. "No reason."

The next day Cyrus opted to ride on Keeth's back with Kris. He let Katana ride Brisk.

It was late morning, and already it was unbearably hot. The number of flies seemed to have increased as well. The forest had begun to thin somewhat, letting in more and more sun, but thankfully more breeze at the same time. And the air smelled slightly different, slightly wetter and less like decomposing leaves. Maybe they were getting closer to the swamp.

As Cyrus and Kris rode together, Cyrus offered to teach her archery. The Katheni girl had never shot a bow before, but Cyrus was an apt and willing teacher. The two sat on Keeth's broad, green-scaled back and shot at things in the trees and alongside the road as the Dragon ambled along. Soon Kris became a passable shot, and Cyrus ran out of arrows.

Then they sat and talked. Cyrus had nearly five years of Apprentice Hero stories to regale Kris with, and the Katheni girl retaliated with the tales of Katheni culture and their peculiar mythology.

Midday, they stopped in a small glade with a crystalline spring bubbling up from the midst of a pile of moss-covered stones. The clearing was large enough for Keeth to unfold his membranous wings to their full span. The Dragon sighed happily as he finally stretched out. His wingtips touched trees on either side of the clearing. The spring burbled cheerfully from its stones, smelling of naught but clean fresh water.

How suspicious.

Before letting even the horses drink from the spring, Reginald produced an all-purpose Water Testing kit. "That's the first thing about being a Hero, lad," he said to Cyrus. "Never go on a Quest without one of these. A kit such as this can save your life. It tests for many magical effects: sleeping spells, love potion effects, amnesia-inducement, or more common things like poison, petrifaction—"

"Fountain of Youth effects, and even 'scientific' things like the mystical 'bacteria,'" Cyrus recited. "I know what they test for, Reg. You gave me one for my last birthday." Cyrus held up two open-topped tubes and a packet of silver-purple powder. "I can even do the test for you, if you like."

"Herm! No thank you, lad, I think I can manage." Reginald strode over to the bubbling spring and was about to dip a beaker into the water, when a terrible, high-pitched, discordant shrieking blasted forth from around the rocks. Reginald dropped his beaker and clapped his hands to his ears. "By the Seven Furies! Pandaemoniums!"

Cyrus stuck his fingers in his ears. "What?" Cyrus shouted.

"I can't hear you with the flowers shrieking like this, lad!"

"I can't hear you with my fingers stuck in my ears! What did you say?"

"Both of you *listen!*" Keeth bellowed. "Look to the Katheni!"

Hero and apprentice turned to look at their newfound acquaintances. Kris and Katana had slid from their mounts and were writhing in pain. Within moments of the auditory assault, Kris passed out, soon followed into unconsciousness by her brother.

Cyrus slid from Keeth's back and knelt next to Kris, wincing at the continuing cacophony. Removing a finger from his ear, he felt the Katheni girl's neck. She was still alive, and aside from being knocked out, there was nothing wrong with her. "I don't get it!" he yelled to Reginald, who had walked up beside him. "There's nothing wrong with her!"

"It's the flowers!" Keeth explained at a high decibel level, his bass roar cutting through the high-pitched shrieking. "Take care of our friends. I shall take care of the noise." With that, the Dragon lumbered over to the spring and inhaled deeply.

Cyrus noticed there were dozens of pink, purple, and red flowers clustered about the base of the rocks. Truly, the sound emanated from these. Each bud emitted a high or medium-pitched shriek while waving tiny green vine-tendrils about.

Keeth breathed out a glorious display of flames that splashed down around the spring, searing the ground and scorching the vegetation. The flowers hissed and whistled as they burned, until the ground was strewn with ash, and blessed silence returned.

"And that," Keeth said with a self-satisfied look on his scaled snout, "is how one deals with a Pandaemonium infestation."

Cyrus and Reginald soon revived the two Katheni by sprinkling them with spring water. As the two sat up and rubbed their furred ears, Cyrus turned back to his mentor. "What were those flowers, Reg? We've been all over, but I haven't seen anything like that before."

"Yes, you have, lad," Reginald replied. "Do you remember those little potted purple flowers of Plainscale's, which sang a G Major chord if you walked by them?"

Cyrus blinked. "Those were the same thing?"

"Aye. Though Plainscale's are the domesticated version, much like a house cat is the domesticated version of a lion. The little ones may be kept for amusement, and some peasants even keep them in their gardens to listen to and to warn if some troublesome brats attempt to make off with pilfered produce. But the wild Pandaemonium is a fearsome plant, possibly the second-most terrifying plant in the world."

Katana leaned wearily against one of Keeth's legs. "I knew of them, but I'd never heard one before. Their proper classification is *Dionea Pandaemonia Cacophona*, a carnivorous plant commonly called the 'Shrieking Bellflower.' I read that they stun their victims with high-pitched, high-volume sound, then use their tendrils to enwrap the prey and dissolve it with a powerful acid. I suppose that due to our more sensitive hearing, my sister and I were more susceptible to their attack." The black-furred cat-mage shuddered. "That wasn't something I really wanted to find out for myself."

"I would imagine not," Cyrus said, looking at the scorched ground near the spring. Abruptly, he leapt up. "Reg! Oh *bok*, Reg, we forgot to test the water!"

Reginald calmly looked at Katana, then at Kris, and finally took a sip from his beaker. "Seems all right to me," he said with a smile.

Cyrus sighed and looked at Kris. "And now you see why my life is so exciting."

Near sunset on their fourth day of travel since meeting the Katheni, Keeth stopped and sniffed the air. "Hmm . . . I can smell the lake. We must be getting close to the edge of the forest."

At the edge of the forest they were indeed. Cyrus could now see open countryside through gaps in the trees. Small songbirds chirruped in the trees, singing lullabies to their hatchlings as night began falling on the forest.

Katana sniffed the air too. "About another seventy yards, I'd say."

Kris sniffed Cyrus's chest. "Your shirt smells like mold."

"Hey, now!" Cyrus protested.

Kris giggled.

The reader may note that the spectacle of a giggling Katheni often scares people. It starts as a twitch at the tip of the tail. Then the ears begin to point straight up. Next, the fur stands on end and the lips part, revealing pointy teeth. The audible giggle occurs only then.

Needless to say, someone *watching* a Katheni giggle may not be amused. It certainly had that effect on Cyrus, who shrank back from Kris as if expecting her to claw him again.

"I'm afraid that I may need to leave your company for a bit," Keeth said. "I feel the need for a good, long soak in the lake."

"By all means, indulge yourself, my draconic friend," Reginald said. "You'll have plenty of time, for we need to re-supply, pay our Guild Dues at the satellite Guild office, and such."

"Not to mention the fact that neither of us has slept in an actual bed for well over two weeks," Cyrus interjected.

Finally, they left the last of the trees behind. Late evening sunshine assailed Cyrus's eyes, forcing him to pull his floppy hat down further to shade his eyes. The forest path gradually faded into a brick-paved road. A fresh breeze blew his worries away as he beheld the fortified sandstone walls of the trading city of Merope.

Cyrus had read his history and knew this city well. Merope was once nothing more than a large farming town and a small fortress atop a hill beside the lake. Then, unlike many surrounding towns and areas, it survived the Twenty-Minute War fairly intact. It had now grown into a bustling trade center. Merchants and businesses flocked to the town after the war, quickly transforming it into a mercantile metropolis. It now had more than ten times its previous population and was the largest city for ninety leagues. Substantial farms surrounded the outskirts of the town for miles. Most were owned by local aristocrats, but lower-class families still ran a goodly number of them.

Cyrus knew that north and east of the town, in the midst of a fetid swamp, lay the Keep of the Falling Stars. The keep had been destroyed in the war, partially rebuilt afterward, and then abandoned. It was to this swamp that he and Reginald journeyed to seek the little girl's lost treasure. Northwest lay Rex Aqui, a large inland body of fresh water. The lake Keeth had smelled on the wind.

The view of the city was magnificent. The setting sun lit up the warm brick of the town's fortified wall in a blaze of red and orange. Multitudinous buildings of varying heights lined the inside of the walls in three tiers, as the fortress had gradually expanded its walls to include and protect layer after layer of urban sprawl. As the sun continued to sink, the light reflected off the lake, casting dancing light across the town's walls.

• • •

The group parted ways at the crossroads between the lake and the rest of the town. Reginald slapped Keeth on his scaled flank. "Well then, Keeth, son of Barinol. Go and have your swim. We shall see you tomorrow at the west side of the lake."

Keeth glanced at the sparkling water of the lake. "Of course, Crimson. Farewell until then." He spread his gigantic wings and leapt into the air, leaving a cloud of dust all around his takeoff point.

Cyrus looked at Katana and Kris. "So where are you two headed?"

"The desert of Mir," Katana said. "It's about another fifty leagues or so northwest," Katana replied, looking in that direction.

"Wow, that's quite the distance," Cyrus said. "We're headed for the swamp around where the old Keep used to be. You want to come with us to town? We can split up later at the swamp."

Katana looked at Kris. "What do you think, sister? Would you like some time in town?"

Kris's eyes lit up. "Of course! I haven't had a real bath in days. And there is a market, right?"

Reginald nodded. "There's not just a market, lass. This place is actually a major crossroads for merchants of everything from spices to silk. It wasn't always that way, but it has grown since the Twenty-Minute War."

"Twenty-Minute War?" Kris said. "A war that lasted only twenty minutes? That's absurd!"

"It isn't when you're dealing with Heroes, Villains, Dragons, magic, and meteors, Miss." Reginald said, dismounting from Wraith. "The most epic battles in the history of the world all took place in the span of less than half an hour."

Cyrus dismounted also, preparing for one of Reginald's recitations of Historic Legends. He knew this legend already, but he didn't mind hearing it again. Learning the great legends was the first thing about being a Hero, after all.

"A thousand years ago, a powerful wizard by the name of Morival came to power in the Council of Highseekers," Reginald began. "He was an intelligent man, but harbored evil deep in his heart. He ruled for two years as the Grand Highseeker. Then one day, he turned on the Council, slaying many. Legends say that he turned their souls into gems, which he used to power his twisted magic.

"With the power he gained from his murderous deeds, he summoned an army of strange and unnatural creatures. He also called all Villains to his side, amassing the most fearsome force of evil the world has ever seen. The world began to plunge into darkness, for Balance had been disrupted.

"Balance is a delicate thing," Reginald explained. "There must always be approximately as many Heroes as Villains, and as many good beasts as evil beasts. If Balance is disrupted one way or other, all things become unstable. Legends say that the Balance must remain—until the End of Time, when the Creator Himself will return and remove the Balance, forever destroying Evil and putting all things in eternal Light.

"But to continue my narrative: when news of the Foul Army and Morival's slaying of the Highseekers reached the Guild of Heroes, the Heroes called forth all reserves. Those Highseekers that remained actually joined the side of Good and called up the Good creatures and animals of nature. The

Dragons also joined the side of Good, under the leadership of Raimarias the Elder. When the five Titans heard that the giants had left their lairs to fight for Evil, they descended to fight against them.

"The war was fought all across the world all at once. The forces of Good assaulted the fortresses of Evil, and the two hosts shed one another's blood. Gryphons, Dragons, basilisks, djinni, harpies, wyverns, and phoenixes fought in the air. Men, Elves, Dwarves, Goblins, Katheni, Ransha, Orcs, and all manner of beasts from hydras to hares struggled on the land and in the sea. It is said that even some of the Great Wyrms and Delvers woke from their slumber and wrestled beneath the ground.

"Then Morival wrought his most terrible magic. His eldritch spell powered by the souls of the vanquished, the dark wizard cast upward to the heavens, and three stars—Anger, Death, and Power—fell flaming from the sky. They bore down on the globe, for to smash it should Good win the day.

"Seeing calamity plummeting from the sky, Saint Michael, Saint Helm, and Saint Greaves prayed to the Creator, pleading that the world not be destroyed so soon after its creation.

"At their prayer, a bright light enveloped the three, and they raised their hands to the heavens. Beams of pure light burst forth from them and shattered the stars of Anger and Death into a rain of a thousand fragments. But the star of Power continued to fall.

"Then it was that St. Michael took the light within himself and used the very energy of his life to change the course of the star. The Star of Power passed safely over the land and plunged into the sea. A wave of immense proportions spread from the impact, destroying all things on the all coasts of all the world—including Morival's keep and what remained of his evil army.

"None know what became of the wizard—nor of St. Michael, who disappeared at the battle's end. Some say that these two titanic warriors will appear again at the End of Time to fight the final battle.

"But personally," Reginald said, breaking out of his Storyteller voice, "I think that is a load of hogwash."

His audience of three sat as if the *Sit Still* spell fixed them to the ground.

"Well," Reginald said, scratching his neck. "We'd best be getting into town, then."

Cyrus abruptly noticed Kris's tail wrapped around behind him. "Um, Kris?"

Kris looked down, started, and instantly lashed her tail away, glaring at Cyrus.

Katana chuckled. "That was a most excellent story, Sir Reginald. Perhaps one day you might tell us what became of the Star of Power."

Reginald paused in mounting Wraith. "That is all there is, Katana. It took the sea five years to clear. When it finally did, no one could find the Star. The Araquellae scoured the sea floor, but never found a trace of it, nor did they find the bodies of St. Michael or Morival."

Chapter 12

A FAMILIAR FACE

In which the Party enters the Town and encounters a Familiar Person

CROWDS GATHERED ALMOST immediately as the Crimson Slash and his companions entered Merope. Reginald still rode Wraith, but Cyrus had dismounted and led Brisk, signifying his lower status as an apprentice. The two Katheni walked in the rear, clinging to Toboggan and glancing cautiously at the crowd as if expecting to be attacked.

Upon spying the Hero, the peddlers cleared their tables of mundane wares and put out everything from the Achilles' Heel-Plate, for protecting vulnerable areas, to Enchanted Helms and Gauntlets of Strength. Some even had "Not A Fake" signs on them. Children flooded the brick-paved streets, cheering and throwing flowers at Reginald.

"The Crimson Slash took the adulation in stride, for Heroes are welcome wherever they go," Reginald narrated. "Cities such as Merope saw more Heroes than some, but still they celebrated his entrance. A young girl offered the Hero a rose, which he graciously took. Thank you, my dear." Reginald bent over in his saddle, took a rose from a peasant girl, and continued riding.

Cyrus smiled and nodded, waving to the merchants as they ran alongside the horses, attempting ride-by-selling. Beautiful peasant girls shrieked with glee as Cyrus waved to them and flexed a bicep. He chuckled. "Hey, Kris," he said, turning back to the Katheni, "this is one of those upsides of being a Hero. Adoration from the crowd. What do you think, eh?"

Kris and Katana looked uncomfortable. Kris glanced up at Cyrus. "It's fine, I suppose . . . "

"Why, what's wrong?" Cyrus asked. "You don't like Merope?"

Kris lowered her green eyes. "No, it's not that. It's just that our last experience with a large, Human-populated town was less than pleasant. We were almost captured by slave trad-ers." The Katheni girl gave some of the merchants alongside the road the evil eye.

"Ooh, that's not so good," Cyrus said sympathetically. "Well, you don't need to worry about that here. Merope's a Free City. They still pay tribute to Bryath, but they set their own laws. And one of those laws abolished slavery almost two centuries ago. You're safe here."

Kris sighed in relief. "Well, that's good to know. We'll sleep easily tonight."

"Speaking of sleep," Reginald interrupted, "it's time for you to go find us an inn, lad. One that takes Katheni as well as Humans. We will also need stables for the horses—"

"And edible food for supper tonight and breakfast tomor-row," Cyrus finished. "I know what to look for, Reg. Give me fifteen minutes, and I'll find one."

• • •

True to his word, Cyrus found a nice inn almost immediately. It was clean, reasonably priced, and had genuine featherbeds for the people and good stables for the horses and mule. The Innkeeper didn't even balk when told that two of his guests would be Katheni. He pointed to a sign above the main door, reading "NO RANSHA. *All other Races welcome.*"

"We tend to have a problem with them around here, what with the swamp and all," he explained. "They drink too much ale, wet on the carpets, break plates, chew on the furniture, and generally make a mess. 'S why I don't serve 'em here anymore. Your cat friends are welcome to stay, though, 's long as they don't shed everywhere."

The interior of the inn was dim but clean. A staircase to the rooms lay to his right, with the common dining room straight ahead. Round tables dotted the large dining room, each surrounded by low-backed chairs. Tendrils of tobacco smoke drifted from the pipes of some laborers who sat about the tables, talking and laughing over their suppers.

Three peasants—farmers, Cyrus guessed by their garb— were singing loudly and drunkenly while throwing daggers at a dartboard. Others sat playing cards and listening to a traveling minstrel tell the tale of the Spectrum Heroes and the Ogres of Highpeak. A boar roasted on a spit over the inn's cookfire, the cooking pork filling the air with its savory aroma. The atmosphere was cheery. Just the thing he and Reginald needed after well over two weeks on the road.

Cyrus grinned and paid the reservation fee. Then, ducking under a poorly aimed dagger, he headed out of the door.

His jaunty step came to an abrupt halt as he bumped into a mail-clad person. "Whoops, excuse me, si . . . ma'am?" He looked into the face of a girl about two years older than himself, and his eyes widened in recognition.

"Hello, Cyrus. Fancy meeting you here!" the girl said.
"Lydia!"

<< Cue Ye Flashback of Blatant Exposition >>

"Oh, come on, Cyrus, come and see me off tomorrow!" Lydia teased, pulling Cyrus's hair.

"Ow, stop it! Of course I'll come. It's just . . ." Cyrus trailed off.

The girl sat down on the grassy turf of the hill beside him, the wind playfully blowing her loose auburn hair about her freckled face. The wind from the ocean was stronger here at the cliffs, and the view from the top was breathtaking. The surf pounded at the rocks far below, a sheer drop from the cliff's edge a mere yard from where they sat. "You . . . don't want me to leave, do you?"

Cyrus glanced up. "Huh? What kind of question is that? Why should I care what some *girl* does?" He shrugged. "You could leave, you could stay here, I don't care!"

Lydia put her hand on Cyrus's hair. "I know you don't mean that. Besides, I think you're just jealous."

"Jealous?" Cyrus said incredulously. "Why would I be jealous of *you*?"

"Because the Hero scouts picked me to be a squire, not you!" she replied. "Apparently, the scouts saw talent in me far superior to anything you have." Lydia grinned maliciously.

Cyrus poked her in the ribs. "You may be superior, but you're still ticklish."

"*Stop* that, Cyrus!" Lydia laughed, slapping Cyrus's hand away.

"When'll I see you again, Lid?" Cyrus asked. "They took Will three years ago, and we haven't seen him since."

Lydia stood up and faced Cyrus. "It might be a long time, Cy. But I promise I'll come back to you. Promise me you'll wait 'til I get back."

Cyrus stood, took her hand, and looked into her deep green eyes. "I promise."

>> *Later, but still not the Present* >>

Cyrus stood in the rain, watching the swordsman and the maiden ride off into the night together on the white horse. Reginald put a hand on his shoulder. "Come inside, lad. We've done our Good Deed for today. No point in catching cold at it."

Cyrus turned his face up to Reginald. "I knew her, Reg. I knew her."

Reginald leaned close to Cyrus's face. "Are you crying, lad?"

Cyrus wiped his eyes. "No."

"You say you knew her?" Reginald said. "The maid? From where?"

"My hometown. We . . . we were childhood sweethearts, I guess. We made a promise to each other that we'd get married when she got back from her training. Then, I was selected as an apprentice also, so we decided to wait 'til we got done with our terms as squires. But now, she . . . " Tears filled his eyes again and he gritted his teeth, not making a sound.

Reginald put his hands on Cyrus's shoulders, turning him around. Cyrus turned his head away from his mentor. "Listen to me, lad," the Hero said. "You cannot expect promises made by children to hold when they grow up. Things change. This maid of yours, she is happy with that man now, and you helped make her that way. Take consolation in that. I see that she has hurt you, but remember: she's not the only girl in the world."

Cyrus sniffed, dragging his sleeve across his eyes. "I'm not hurt. M-my s-stupid eyes are just running. You w-wouldn't happen to have a cure, would you?"

"Aye, lad, that I do."

But instead of pulling out a potion from his saddlebags, Reginald pulled Cyrus close and hugged him. "Heroes don't cry for any physical injury, lad. We're too strong. But there are wounds that go deeper than the flesh. Tears are nature's remedy for them."

>> Back to Ye Present, finally >>

"Well, I'm not!" Kris hissed, stalking back and forth in front of a booth selling colorfully painted lead figurines of renowned Heroes. She'd been looking for one, but Kris hadn't seen the Crimson Slash among them.

"It's not that absurd, sister," Katana said. The black Katheni sat with his back against the sandstone wall of a butcher's shop. "More bizarre things have been known to happen. I personally don't care. I don't even care if you try to deceive everyone about it. I just want you to be honest with me, and with yourself too." Katana licked his paw and used it to smooth down an errant patch of head-fur beside his left ear. "So, if that's not it, what is it then?"

Kris stopped pacing. "I don't know. But it can't be— I mean, we're not . . . "

Katana placed his paw on Kris's shoulder, his golden eyes full of kindness. "Listen to me, sister. You may not know your own mind yet. But I am your brother, and I know you very well. I can see that this is troubling you. My advice is to think it over, pray about it, give it some more time." He squeezed her shoulder. "In the meantime, didn't Sir Ogleby say something about silk and cloth merchants?"

Kris smiled. "What a clever distraction, brother. Let's go see."

Cyrus gaped. He hadn't seen Lydia since she'd run off with the Mysterious Swordsman after a three-Hero Quest almost four years ago. And here she was, auburn hair pulled back in a ponytail, wearing chain-mail, white riding clothes, a silver brooch in the shape of a leaping tiger, and with a broadsword on her hip. Every bit as beautiful as the day he'd fallen in love with her.

"Lydia? Furies! What are you doing here?" Cyrus asked, still not quite believing his eyes. Suddenly he felt like hitting something.

"Good to see you too, Cyrus," Lydia replied sarcastically. "It's been quite a while. You still a squire?"

Cyrus stepped back, letting Lydia out of the brick courtyard and into the Inn. "Uh, yeah. Listen, nice to see you and all, but I have to go."

Lydia scowled. "Oh, no, you don't, Cyrus," she said, barring the door with her arm. "I haven't seen you in three years, and that's all you have to say to me?"

There was a time when he would've taken the opportunity to move in closer to her embrace. Not anymore. "Pretty much," Cyrus replied, ducking under her arm.

"Okay, stop right there," Lydia demanded. "What's eating you? Can't you spare five minutes to talk to a friend?"

Cyrus froze. "Yes. I would. But for you, I have two minutes. What do you want?"

"You're still upset about that Hero, aren't you?" Lydia asked, putting a hand on Cyrus's shoulder.

"No," Cyrus said bluntly, "I'm fine. I'm curious, though, were you really betrothed to him?"

"Who, Ron? The Mysterious Swordsman?" She laughed lightly. It was the sound of cheerful birds playing on the wind. Only the birds were shrikes, and the wind was poisoned. "No, I wasn't. I just needed a reason to be leaving with him, and your master was kind enough to give us a horse. Ron is a most excellent Swordsman, though not very Mysterious, and I needed more training in the sword. He said he was willing to teach me. That was very helpful. But when we finished my training, he told me he wanted to marry me."

Cyrus clenched a fist. "So what did you do?"

Lydia laughed. "Oh, I didn't marry him, if that's what you mean. I was just training, and having a little fun on the side. To get out of that sticky situation, I challenged him to a swordfight. I said that if he won, I would marry him. If I won, he would make me a Hero, Second Class immediately."

"And you won," Cyrus said.

"I cheated. I knew he would avoid hurting me at all costs. Can't be slicing up your bride, right? So I deliberately opened up weak points and threw him off balance. I almost took his sword-arm off when he let his guard down."

Cyrus stared at Lydia. "Wow, Lydia. You never used to be that . . . devious."

She looked away. "Real life changes people, Cyrus. Not everything's as black-and-white as the *Guide to Heroics* makes it seem." She sighed. "So now I'm a full-fledged Hero: the White Tiger. Rawr." Lydia made a scratching motion in the air. "I'm currently looking for work. You wouldn't know where I could find some, do you Cyrus?"

Cyrus slid past Lydia. "Nope. Reg and I have a current Quest, and after that, we're unemployed too. Well, excuse me, Lydia. I've got to get back to Reg and tell him that I found an Inn . . . "

Lydia grabbed Cyrus's collar. "Hang on, dummy, I'll come with you! I haven't seen Sir Old-Fashioned-by in a long time!"

Cyrus sighed and led the way back to where he'd last seen Reginald.

"Well, if it isn't the maiden we helped reunite with her betrothed!" Reginald boomed as Cyrus and Lydia walked up the path. He stood outside a wineseller's booth on the outskirts of the brick-paved main marketplace, helping several peasants toast his good health. "Good to see you again, miss . . . Lydia, was it?"

"Yes, sir," Lydia said. She roughly pushed away a sodden peasant who had tried to offer her a clay cup of wine. Cyrus helped the poor fellow up and accepted the spilled cup. "We haven't been formally introduced, but I believe you are the Crimson Slash? Black told me a lot about you."

Reginald arched his eyebrows. "You know the Black Viper? Wait, are you that squire she had that ran off?"

Lydia stomped her foot, her chainmail jingling slightly. "I beg your pardon, sir. I did *not* 'run off.' I merely changed mentors. I realized I couldn't learn any more from her. She wouldn't teach me the things that men learn for combat."

Reginald glared at her. "There's a reason for that, Miss. A woman cannot fight like a man. If she does, she loses something precious."

"Oh?" Lydia turned. "And what is that?"

"Her status as a lady," Reginald said, looking surprised. "Any woman that talks and acts like a man is no kind of lady at all." He finished his cup of wine and set it back down on the wooden counter of the seller's booth, along with a silver coin.

"What makes you think that I *want* to be a lady? You think I want men to protect me my entire life? I can take care of myself. So, with all due respect, kindly . . . " an obscenity Cyrus had never heard before shot from between Lydia's lips like a poisoned bolt from an Orc's crossbow. " . . . off."

Reginald put his foot down hard, cracking the paving bricks. "That's *enough*! Say one more word, and I may lose my temper and have the Guild reprimand you for conduct unbecoming a Hero!"

Lydia's demeanor instantly changed. She hung her head, auburn ponytail falling onto her left shoulder. "My apologies, Sir. I overstepped myself."

The angry flush faded from Reginald's face. "Very well," he said. "Make sure you don't do so again." The Hero turned back to his equipment.

Lydia looked at Cyrus and winked.

That evening, after Cyrus and Reginald had stowed their belongings in the Inn of the Swaying Branches and settled down for the night, Cyrus came back out to the courtyard to lead Toboggan to his stall. Decorative shrubs lined the walls, providing the Inn's entryway with an almost pleasure-garden feel.

The mule, as it turned out, was nibbling happily on the bark of the mighty oak that dominated the center of the brick-paved courtyard. "Get away from *that!*" Cyrus said, smacking Toboggan gently on his grey-furred flank. The mule gave a startled *hee-haw* and backed away from the tree.

"Hey, Cyrus," Lydia said, rising from a bench on the far side of the courtyard and walking over to him. "I need to talk with you for a moment."

Cyrus sighed. She probably wasn't going to leave him alone until she'd said her piece. "All right, what now?"

Lydia poked Cyrus in the ribs. "Why do you hang around with him, anyway?"

"Who, Reg?" Cyrus said, ignoring the poke. He stared up into the massive oak in the center of the courtyard. "He's my teacher. Everything I know about fighting, I learned from him. More than that, he's a friend." He looked at Lydia pointedly. "He's been there for me when other people abandoned me."

Lydia put her hand on Cyrus's shoulder.

Cyrus shrugged it off.

Lydia put it back on and held it there. "Is that what's been bothering you?" she asked quietly. "Cyrus, I went with Ron because he could teach me how to fight better. The fact that he liked me never came up until later."

Cyrus forcibly removed Lydia's hand from his shoulder. "You don't have a clue, do you?" he asked, turning toward her. "You really tore us all up with that move. You hurt the Black Viper because you left without a word, and you hurt Reg because you hurt Black."

"Don't look at me like that, Cyrus. It's not *my* fault. Jael should have taught me what I wanted to know, and your master should have kept his nose in his own business."

"You mean you just don't care?" Cyrus yelled, clenching his fists.

Toboggan, made uneasy by the arguing, backed up toward the stables.

"You don't care that you hurt people who cared about you?" Cyrus continued. "You've changed, and not for the better. *That's* what's bothering me!"

"I . . . I'm sorry, Cyrus. Not everything's changed, I still have feelings for you . . . "

Cyrus shrugged. "The same kind of 'sorry' you were to Reg earlier, I'm sure. And feelings? Like what, the feeling that you need to steal my horse again?"

Lydia glared at Cyrus. "Why, you . . . " Rather than finishing her sentence, she drew her broadsword.

Cyrus looked at her. "Oh, so now you want to settle it with action, not words. Fine." He turned back to the mule, swapping his floppy hat for his sword, then pointed the blade at Lydia.

Lydia's face twisted in a fearsome smile, and she lashed out at her onetime friend.

"This goes with my fur, right, brother?" Kris asked, holding a bolt of dark green cloth up next to her head. "I like it a lot."

Katana put down the scroll he was perusing and turned his head to regard his sister. "Hmm. It matches your eyes quite nicely. It brings out your spots too," he said, raising his voice in order to be heard above the din of the marketplace.

There was a lot of noise, Katana noted. The twisting brick streets of Merope were crowded with tents and tables, where merchants sold everything from spices to stun wands. Each merchant hawked his wares at the top of his lungs, the various advertisements blending together: "Get a bolt of our finest . . . oregano with your purchase of . . . one pint of . . . fresh clams!"

"I think I'll buy it," Kris said, twirling the fabric around. "Do you think—" she stopped abruptly and looked at the ground.

"Yes, I think he'll like it." Katana smiled. "In fact, I think that if you take this fabric over to that booth over there, you can have it made into an outfit right away."

"Really?" Kris asked, green eyes dancing again.

Katana looked away, brow furrowed in thought.

"What?" Kris asked.

"Oh, nothing. Just thinking of something I must do."

Cyrus dodged the sweeping blow, and Lydia's broadsword bit deep into the turf. He vaulted off the ground, bringing his longsword down on the girl. She interposed the buckler on her left arm. The small shield cracked under the impact of Cyrus's blade, but held.

Lydia dislodged her blade from the grass and began spinning rapidly, blade becoming a deadly disk. She lowered her variation on the basic *Tornado* attack to come at Cyrus from a new angle.

Cyrus leapt over the blade, slamming both feet into Lydia's chest. The spin broke, and she staggered. Cyrus backflipped, landed on his feet, and pointed his sword in Lydia's face.

He noted peasants poking their heads out of the Inn windows to look at him and Lydia. One even stood in the doorway, bearing a torch to light the dimming courtyard. They'd probably heard the commotion and become spectators. It seemed this little quarrel was becoming quite the spectacle. Toboggan seemed to have disappeared entirely. The experience that came from years of staying out of Reginald's fights served the mule well.

"Nice try," Lydia taunted, "but it'll take more than that!" She leapt into the air, and Cyrus followed.

Steel rang against steel as Lydia swung at Cyrus's torso in midair and he blocked the blow. He had barely got his defense up in time, so the impact of the attack sent him hurtling down into a nearby wall, shattering bricks and knocking a large chunk out of the building's corner. More peasants, hearing the commotion, began poking their heads out of nearby windows to watch the fight.

Lydia landed on her feet and plucked up a loose brick from the courtyard pavement. She slung it at Cyrus.

Cyrus shattered the brick midair with a left-handed punch and dodged right as Lydia used his brief distraction to charge at him. He threw a precise cut at the center of her mass, but Lydia performed a single-handed backward handspring, landing on her feet, weapon at the ready.

"Still mad?" Cyrus asked. "Come on!" He beckoned with his hand. "Try and beat me! Just try!" Cyrus flung his cloak off, removing all encumbrance except his chainmail shirt.

Lydia sprang like the white tiger that was her Heroic namesake. She landed right on top of Cyrus and slammed her gauntleted fist into his face.

Though stunned by the blow, Cyrus had enough presence of mind to ward off the second blow and launch Lydia off him with his legs.

She hit the wall and cracked it, sliding down into the shrubbery. A low moan drifted from behind the hedge.

Cyrus got up and ran over to the shrub. "Lydia? You okay?"

A metal-clad foot slammed into his left knee. Cyrus howled in pain, and Lydia rushed from the shrub, slamming into him and knocking him down again. Before he could rise, Lydia knelt over him, sword pointed at his throat.

She grinned. "Yield."

Cyrus scowled and dropped his sword. "Kahrestin, Lydia, you fight like a Villain."

"What?" Lydia said. "I do not!"

"Then what do you call exploiting my caring if I hurt you?" Cyrus demanded.

"Tactics," Lydia said. Without warning, she bent down and kissed him. "Good fight, Cy."

"Wha . . . buh . . . guh . . . " Cyrus sputtered incoherently.

Lydia grinned. "My victory prize."

Kris and Katana left the marketplace, Kris wearing a new blouse and skirt of a deep forest green. The long skirt seemed impractical for a feline, until one got a closer look at it. Slits ran up both sides, almost to mid-thigh for freedom of movement, in the style of traditional Katheni female garments.

Katana carried a large satchel, full of strange odds and ends, some heavy books, and bottles of mysterious liquids. He also had purchased a chewy-mouse toy made from the sap of a spring-tree, but he kept it well hidden.

They walked around the corner of the inn just in time to hear Cyrus emit some startled, incoherent syllables. He was flat on his back, his sword drawn, and in obvious pain. An armored warrior stood over him, apparently gloating over her victory.

Katana wasn't quite sure what to make of the situation, but before he could stop her, Kris leapt into action. The leopard-spotted girl sprang over the shrub and pounced on the hostile Human female.

The woman fell backward under the feline onslaught, knocked topsy-turvy by a furious flash of feline fur. She grabbed at Kris, but his sister was too fast.

Kris pounded the woman with both paws and slammed a foot-paw into her chest. A whoosh of air escaped the Heroine's lungs in a startled "Ooof!" The chainmail she wore did not protect her against blunt impact, it seemed.

Cyrus picked himself up from the ground and grabbed Kris, pinning her shoulders and yanking her off of the woman. "Stop! Stop already!" he said. "She's not an enemy, Kris! Calm down!"

Kris struggled for a second, then twisted her speckled head and looked at Cyrus. "She . . . isn't?"

"Her name is Lydia. She's not my enemy. Though," he glanced at the woman, who bore a murderous expression on her battered face as she rose, "she might be yours."

"Where," Lydia spat, "did you find *that* thing? In an alley?" Kris hissed.

Cyrus glared at Lydia, letting go of Kris. "That was uncalled for, Lydia. This is Kris, one of Reg and mine's traveling companions. You should apologize for that insult."

Lydia and Kris stared each other down. "I will not. The cat started it. Besides, I don't apologize to *animals*."

Kris sprang at Lydia again, but an invisible wall of gentle force pushed her back.

Tired of the bickering, Katana had interposed a *Wall of Force* spell between the arguing girls. "I hate to say this," he said, "but if you are telling the truth, Cyrus, then my sister is partially to blame. But you must understand our confusion. Why were you two fighting?"

Cyrus scratched his head. "Well, it's kind of complicated. You see, Lydia and I know each other from way back when we were kids. Whenever we'd get into any kind of argument, one or the other of us would get our feelings hurt."

Katana nodded. "So my sister did intrude on a private quarrel. Sister? Apologize to them."

Kris's eyes narrowed. "I'm sorry I intruded." She turned to Katana. "Well?"

Katana ignored her and spoke to Lydia. "Now, perhaps you'll apologize for that insult, then?"

Lydia's face was a mask. "No. As I said, I don't apologize to—"

"Very well," Katana said. "If you can't say something nice, don't say anything at all." He made a weaving motion with his paws, then slammed the palms together.

Lydia continued moving her mouth, but no sound came out. She stopped, felt her throat, moved her mouth again, and shut it, glaring at Katana and Kris.

Katana smiled. Another judicious application of the blessed *Shut Up* spell.

Kris and Cyrus walked down the main hall of the inn. Paintings of idyllic pastures and idealized farms hung on the walls, and the rush mats that ran the length of the hallways were fresh, still smelling of their native plants. A cheerfully tipsy peasant tipped his straw hat at the two as they passed him. The revelry in the Inn's lower level had gotten noisier, with louder and more slurred requests for more ale, but it was the wholesome sound of hardworking people relaxing after a day's toil.

"Why did you do that, Cyrus?" Kris asked.

"Do what?"

"Keep me from hurting that female." Kris traced the spiral woodwork on the walls with a furred finger. "I could have beaten her. She was only Human."

Cyrus sighed. "I stopped you to protect you. She isn't just Human, she's a full-fledged Hero. If you got yourself killed because of me, well, I would . . . I mean, that would be rather pointless. Besides, I can handle my own fights. What kind of Hero would I be if I let a girl do all my fighting for me?"

"Hmm. So why *do* you fight, then?" Kris asked.

"What do you mean?" Cyrus opened the door that separated the Inn's noisy public room from the rented sleeping quarters and gestured for Kris to enter. Kris obliged, and he pulled the door closed behind them. "I fight all the time, for all kinds of reasons."

"But to solve disputes?" Kris asked. "Why not reason with your opponents? Surely most would listen to a Hero."

Cyrus scratched his head. "Not as many as you might think. It's amazing how many people refuse to listen to reason. Reg says it's best not to even bother. 'The first thing about being a Hero is knowing that any problem can be solved by the judicious application of Violence,'" Cyrus said, doing a rather good impression of his mentor's pompous pontification.

Kris giggled, attempting to suppress the disconcerting appearance of the action. "So every problem can be solved by violence?"

Cyrus shrugged as they climbed the staircase to the second floor. "I guess so. Name a problem, any problem."

Kris thought a moment. "Hunger. Can you solve the problem of a starving village by violence?"

"Of course!" Cyrus said. "Find a beast or beasts big enough, attack and kill them, and give the meat to the villagers. Problem solved! Simply talking about food wouldn't do them any good."

"But if they're . . . um . . . herbivores," Kris said, not knowing the Common word for an intelligent creature that ate only plants. There wasn't one in the Katheni language. "What would you do?"

Cyrus tripped over the top step, caught himself, and looked at Kris strangely. "Vegetarians? What if a group of vegetarians was starving to death?"

Kris nodded.

"Then they need to learn to eat meat, or die. I've little sympathy for any animal meant to be omnivorous that won't eat meat," Cyrus said with a grin. "I've a feeling you agree."

Kris realized that her spotted tail had begun swaying gently back and forth. She abruptly stilled it.

"Actually," Cyrus continued, "that's not a bad motto: 'I Solve my Problems by Violence.' Has a nice ring to it."

Kris stomped on Cyrus's foot.

"Ouch!" He hopped on one foot. "See! You solve problems the same way! To say you should do things any other way is hypocritical!"

Kris smiled again. "I suppose when you pick your Hero name, it will be something like the Senseless Violence, then?"

"Oh, no, of course not," Cyrus amended. "Reg says that violence should never be used in a senseless fashion. It should be considered in light of other options, then chosen because it's the easiest one."

Kris sighed. For Humans, Reginald and Cyrus certainly thought a lot like Katheni males.

"Nice dress, by the way," Cyrus said. "Goes well with your eyes." Then he stepped into his room and closed the door.

Chapter 13

THE TRIANGLE PLOT

In which the Villains Hatch a Plan to Destroy the Party
and much Philosophizing is Done

IGHT FELL ON Merope. Which was rather painful. Night picked himself up, swearing under his breath about the buildings being taller than they used to be, and continued on his way.

The tiered sandstone city, normally a hive of Human activity, began to slowly wind down. The darkness and rise of the full moon ushered in the sounds and smells of dinner being prepared, revelers in the taverns, the spice merchants in the market packing up their wares for the night, and fading sunlight glinting off bells as they rang in the tower of the Church of the True Faith.

Cyrus stood on the balcony of the suite he shared with Reginald and Katana, listening to the bells and watching the flickering of torches borne by the few people left in the dark streets. If only all of life could be as nice as this night, he thought. Fighting is nice, but I think peace is much nicer. If everyone could have this experience, maybe there wouldn't be any more wars. Cyrus shook his head. Ha! Who am I kidding? People are freaks, psychopaths, racists, and just plain jerks.

Simple things like a beautiful night in a peaceful city couldn't possibly change them that much. They'll still need to be kept in check. Which is why I want to be a Hero, I guess . . .

"What are you thinking about, Cyrus?" Katana said from a corner of the balcony.

Cyrus jumped. "Yipe! Oh, Katana. I didn't see you there."

Katana smiled a toothy smile. "I have black fur. I'm a bit difficult to see in the dim and dark. Sorry I surprised you."

"It's fine." Cyrus leaned more weight on the balcony railing. "I was just thinking about some random stuff . . . "

"What? I'm curious to know, because there's something I was thinking about, too." Katana rose and walked to the edge of the balcony where Cyrus stood.

"What were you thinking about, Katana?" Cyrus asked.

Katana smiled. "I asked you first."

"Oh, I guess you did. Heh heh." Cyrus ran his hands through his hair. "Well, it's actually kind of embarrassing."

Katana's fur bristled. "Explain yourself."

"Well," Cyrus began, "here I am, standing out on this balcony, thinking what a nice night it is. Then I started thinking about . . . other people, and things that won't change."

"How do you mean?"

Cyrus looked back into the suite for sign of Reginald. "Promise me you won't tell anyone?"

Katana's ears laid back, but he nodded.

"Heroes can't be pacifists, Katana," Cyrus said with a sigh. "I was out here thinking of how to stop war. You know, all war in general. If you could change people by putting into them some of the peace that I feel in this city, would they stop fighting? But then I got depressed because it occurred to me that some basic things about Human nature won't ever change. Not even a night as beautiful as this one would make any difference to someone that had already made up their mind to kill people. Like I said, random stuff."

Katana's expression changed and he tore loose in a fit of laughter. He put his furred head in his palm and laughed, rocking back and forth on his heels as tears streamed from his pale almond eyes.

Cyrus scowled. He didn't get what was so funny. "Hey, now! I tell you something in confidence, and you laugh at me? That's just wrong!"

"I'm . . . sorry . . . ha! I'm not making—heh heh—fun of you," Katana said, all but wheezing.

Cyrus gently punched Katana in the shoulder. "Well, it sure sounds like it. Don't tell Reg, okay? He's always gung-ho about wars and such. I wouldn't want to be disappointing to him."

Katana sat up, beginning to catch his breath. "I won't. I promise."

Cyrus looked back out over the town. He wrinkled his nose as a breeze from the lake brought him a whiff of the malodorous swamp to the northeast. "So what was on your mind, Katana?"

"It's nothing that can't wait until later," Katana said, getting up off the floor. "Good talking to you, Cyrus, but I'm going to sleep. I haven't slept in a real bed since we left Salvinsel." He turned and went inside.

Cyrus stared at the town. That was weird. Then he went to bed, too.

That night, evil was afoot in the Keep of the Falling Stars. It was also ahand, akneecap, and alowertorso.

In the Great Hall of the bleak, half-ruined edifice, Nieva and Serimal took their seats around the table that dominated the center of the room. A fortified set of double-doors in the far wall was the only means of entry or exit.

There were six other people and non-Humans in the hall, seated around the ancient ironwood banquet table. Moonlight from the full moon streamed in through the black-tinted glass windows, lighting the room with an eerie twilight and blending with the guttering torches on the walls.

It was the perfect atmosphere in which to plan Diabolical Deeds.

The grey stone walls bore the banners of several important Villains. Serimal recognized the banners as belonging to old-time allies and acquaintances of Voshtyr. There must have been some important business afoot, or Voshtyr would not have assembled so many of his former compatriots. Also present was Torval, the Purveyor of Evil Products, who kept his distance from the table. The men and creatures had been arriving at the Keep since mid-morning.

One of the men Serimal did recognize, a burly, red-headed fellow with a dusky orange beard who sat across the table from Nieva and kept winking at her.

"That's Sir Anthony the Mace," Serimal whispered to Nieva. "He was once a Hero—the Silver Talon—but was cast out of the Guild of Heroes for betraying another Hero, murder, and meting out sadistic punishments for alleged crimes. I heard he was working for my half-brother before Voshtyr was put in prison."

Nieva shrank closer to Serimal. "I don't care who he is, he scares me. Can you make him stop winking like that?"

"I doubt it," Serimal said with a scowl.

She turned her body sideways in her chair. "Why did your brother call this meeting, anyway?"

"Half-brother," Serimal corrected. "I've no clue. It must have something to do with the Crimson Slash. Crimson is the one who arrested Voshtyr six years ago and testified against him, getting him convicted of High Treason. Not to mention that arm . . . ." Serimal clenched his fist on the arm of his velvet-seated chair. "Voshtyr has quite the grudge against him for more than one reason."

At that moment, the large double-doors swung open with a majestic *bang.* Voshtyr stepped through the door, flanked by a pair of heavily muscled Henchmen.

The Henchmen left Voshtyr's side and went to stand on either side of the throne at the head of the table. They sneered at the Expendable Minions scattered along the dining-hall walls.

Expendable Minions, or simply Minions, are one of the most useful tools at a Villain's disposal. It is the lot of Expendable Minions to die for little or no reason, and to do so cheerfully. They are cheap to buy, cost little or nothing to feed, and fight loyally to the death for their Villain.

They are usually weedy, sneaky-looking little creatures with large eyes and a fawning demeanor. They come standard with a chainmail shirt, black cloak, short-sword, and serial number.

Minions are the second-most plentiful and third-cheapest manpower resource available to the typical Villain. These creatures are average in almost all respects, making them ideally suited for jobs that require neither extreme intelligence nor overwhelming strength.

For high-end work, be it of brain or brawn, the discerning Villain is well-served to forgo Minions and step up to Toadies or Henchmen.

Toadies—frail, spindly Humanoids wrapped in black robes, with deep colorless black eyes and diabolically sharp minds—make good Counselors, Viziers, and Tax Collectors. If you need to brainstorm for your new nefarious plan, a Toady is for you. However, they lack even a vestige of physical strength.

Your foul plotting completed, your next step is to turn to Henchmen for the execution of your plans—and your (lesser) enemies. These troll-like creatures are far larger than Minions, usually standing head and shoulders above any Human, and possessing more bulging muscles than any team of oxen have a right to. Their squinting eyes are usually shot with red from a perpetual bloodlust. Henchmen have brute strength in abundance and are able to rend villagers apart in a single snap. Henchmen make excellent Bodyguards and/or general-purpose Thugs. But they have the brains of a brick.

At the exact center of the spectrum between Toadies and Henchmen is the Expendable Minion. As their name implies, they are eminently disposable. They are often slain as therapeutic stress relief or, with the optional Cannon Fodder accessories, can be sent by the handful to soften up a Hero before the Villain takes a crack at defeating him. It is common knowledge that the easiest way to defeat a Hero who fights like a hundred men is to send a hundred and one Minions at him.

Any Villain serious about his sinister machinations will command an array of Toadies, Henchmen, and Expendable Minions in whatever ratios suit his style.

One can acquire a pack of a dozen Expendable Minions for five hundred gold pieces at any Complete Villain Emporium in the Hereditary Evil Empire, Landeralt. Also available: the 101 Expendable Minions package.

• • •

The half-demon wore black armor, a blood-red cape, and a strangely cut tunic missing one sleeve. The dim light glinted off his now-uncovered left arm.

Beginning somewhere on the shoulder and extending to his fingertips, his entire arm was gleaming steel. The gentle whirring of well-oiled gears emanated from the elbow and wrist joints as it hung at his side, moving just like an arm of flesh would.

Serimal blinked. He had been completely fooled by the construct. Until Voshtyr had parried and crushed his dagger, that is. Now, from the whispers of those around him, he gathered that the Crimson Slash was indeed responsible the loss of Voshtyr's original arm.

The steel arm was very finely crafted indeed. It was entirely proportionate. Had it not been shining steel with a few grooves and pivots, it would have looked just like an arm of flesh. Each finger was rounded off and capped at varying lengths, just like a normal hand. And the range and ease of motion he seemed to have with it were extraordinary. Only scars of what appeared to be battle damage marred the mechanical work of art that served Voshtyr as an arm.

Voshtyr strode to the head of the table. The assembled Villains arose.

"Friends and allies, welcome," he said. "Thank you all for coming. Please, be seated."

Everyone sat. Voshtyr alone remained standing. He began to circle the table.

"I have called you together today for purposes of evil deeds, black Villainy, and sweet revenge."

A cheer rose from somewhere down the table, though it quickly died out.

"I will begin by going around the room and introducing everyone," Voshtyr said, stopping first between Serimal and Nieva's chairs. "Some of you already know my brother Serimal and his lovely fiancée, Nieva."

"*Half*-brother," Serimal muttered.

"Next, this fine figure of an Araquellus is Lord Roger Farella of Deep Keep, my friend and accountant."

A short, fishlike man with blue skin and iridescent scales nodded his tri-finned head in a dignified fashion. Serimal knew him as Roger Farella, Lord of the Deep Keep, an Araquellus and a dangerous man. Voshtyr had acquired most of his Minions, Mythological Creatures, and weaponry through this ruthless merchant. Lord Farella made Torval seem like a mewling kitten by comparison.

The Araquellus's retractable organic blade ridges were hidden beneath the blue-scaled skin of his arms. That was good, Serimal thought. Were they extended, Lord Farella most likely would be considering this meeting a war council. And a member of the Araquellan nobility, the current Neptarch's cousin, no less, in a war council? Well, that wasn't something he really wanted to think about at the moment.

Voshtyr moved on, and at the next chair, a low, leather-covered bench, he stopped and ran his metallic left hand down the feathered head and neck of the heavily scarred gryphon who occupied the bench. "This is my companion, Slashback Ricor, a useful ally who has yet to fail me."

Slashback the Gryphon sat on her low bench, but still towered over most of the assembled Villains. Her brown feathers and white wings marked her as a Cliff Gryphon, the largest and hardiest breed still in existence. From sharp beak to feathered tail, from feather-tufted ears to razor talons and hind paws, Slashback was the epitome of a healthy, though aging, female gryphon. Her brown head-feathers faded nearly seamlessly into her tawny, lion-fur coat. The white wings dominating her back were folded while at the table, but when stretched out, probably measured well over fifteen feet.

Scars marred the fur on Slashback's torso and hindquarters, and there were a few on her wings, neck, and head as well. But the most impressive scar ran from the top of her head to where her beak joined her face, cutting across her eye in the process. One eye was blue. The other, beneath the scarred eyelid, was cloudy—a sightless misty-grey.

Slashback nodded softly as Voshtyr's hand traced the scar on her head, her feathers ruffling up as he stroked her.

"This here," he said, moving on to a plainly dressed Human male with mud-brown hair and crooked teeth, "is Victor Kelpy. He has failed me numerous times in the past, and I cannot think for the life of me what he is doing here. Get out of my sight, you vapid waste of fleshy matter."

"But milord, I—" Victor started, but stopped on seeing Voshtyr's expression. Fuming, he rose from the table and stalked toward the door, stopping briefly to slaughter one of his Expendable Minions in a fit of temper.

Victor's remaining Minions dragged the corpse of their fellow from the room and followed after their master.

"Across the table from me," Voshtyr continued as if nothing had happened, "is Tyler Greenfield, also called Tyler Nightraid. Nightraid has just graduated—with dishonors—from the Villain Academy in Landeralt, with demerit badges for Deceit, Treachery, Murder, and Moral Turpitude."

A young man with perfectly groomed, greased-back hair beamed and flipped his cloak back to reveal his row of demerit badges. He didn't look to be more than twenty years of age. His regulation black leather coat, trousers, and cloak were spotless, as if he hadn't worn them since his graduation day.

The brawny man who had been winking at Nieva snorted. There was a kernel of corn in his thick, red beard, and his scratched silver platemail was dinged and battered. Apparently he did not take quite the pains about his appearance as Nightraid did.

Voshtyr moved on to him next. "And this is Sir Anthony Flannels, also known as Anthony the Mace, a Villain in good standing and a long-time associate of mine."

Sir Anthony belched and raised a gauntleted hand.

Voshtyr nodded. "A question, Anthony?"

"Can we get on with it?" Anthony asked, scratching his red beard. "Dinner's in less than an hour, and I hear your cook here is a genius with scrapple and sausage."

Voshtyr sighed. "Yes, yes, he is indeed competent with sausage. But you will have to wait. Dinner is *not* the reason I called you all here." He turned to the woman beside Anthony. "Finally, the lovely lady on my left is Mistress Salvatia Malice, a woman of unusual talents."

Serimal felt chilled by the woman's sinister beauty. She appeared to be in her mid-thirties, but her red eyes, pale skin, and barely concealed fangs marked her as a vampirine.

Salvatia smiled, her eyes becoming crescents, and nodded.

"Well, then," Voshtyr said, "now that you all know each other, we can get down to business." He went to the throne at the end of the table. "Headed straight for this very keep is the Crimson Slash, a known champion of Truth and Justice."

Anthony the Mace booed loudly. The others around the table seemed quite affected by Voshtyr's announcement, Serimal noted.

"Now you know why I have called you here," Voshtyr continued. "Every one of us has been defeated by the Crimson Slash or one of his close friends at one time or another. But we were each alone, and he had a squire with him many of those times. Today, I have a plan for the capture of the Crimson Slash, that we may do as we please with him."

Slashback the Gryphon gave a raucous squawk, which Nightraid echoed as a cheer.

Voshtyr began pacing the length of the table. "There are several problems that must be dealt with before we take him. First, Crimson is currently traveling with a green Dragon, whom we have identified as Keeth, son of Barinol. Someone must deal with this interfering Wyrm. Any volunteers?"

Sir Anthony winked at Nieva again, then stood and bellowed "I volunteer! You know how much I hate Dragons, so let me at him!"

"My thanks, Anthony." Voshtyr inspected his metal fingertips. "Next, there are two Katheni with Crimson and his squire. The male Katheni is a magic user who assisted in the slaughter of Thomas Frostbite. Does anyone here think he or she can best him?"

The vampirine stood. "I can and will, Voshtyr. No magic user can stand up to my powers."

"Very well, Salvatia, Lady of the Dark—I leave the task to you."

"What of the female Katheni?" Roger asked, raising a blue-scaled hand as he leaned against his high-backed chair.

"I'd be happy to take care of her," Nightraid said with a snigger. "I'll take care of her . . . all night long."

"Point of order," Roger said, scowling at the Villain novice. "Tyler neither stood nor raised his hand."

"Uh, I forgot to," Nightraid said sheepishly.

"No contributing to Diabolical Plots if you haven't raised your hand," Roger said. "Honestly, what are they teaching at the Academy anymore? Now be silent and let your betters decide what to do."

Nightraid grumbled, but slouched in his chair and remained silent.

Voshtyr spoke again. "I will take care of the female Katheni. You see, Crimson's squire, one Cyrus Solburg, was childhood friends with one Lydia Weatherblade, now the Heroine known as the White Tiger. Weatherblade just happens to have arrived in Merope this very evening. The female Katheni, as far as my spies can tell, appears to have feelings for young Cyrus. I propose to you assembled Villains that we employ . . . " he paused dramatically . . . "the *Love Triangle* to drive the party apart."

Several Villains began clapping, and the gryphon squawked again. Even Serimal had to clap. His half-brother's plan was perfect. A *Love Triangle* would not only effectively destroy any teamwork within the Crimson Slash's party, it might even cause them to split up into easily defeatable groups.

Voshtyr basked in the adulation. Finally he raised his hand and the applause stopped. "If they leave Merope tomorrow morning, we have two days until they reach the swamp. They will most certainly come, for my brother," he pointed at Serimal, "had the foresight to lure Crimson here with a *False Quest*."

The vampirine and Nightraid glanced at Serimal with newfound admiration.

"Half-brother," Serimal muttered.

"Those of you who have not chosen a specific duty will remain here to assist Roger and myself in assembling a device." His voice swelled in a Villainous fury, his eyes taking on their flaring red hue. "A device of such power that the Guild of Heroes will quake on its very foundation when they learn it is in my hands. They shall quiver and quail, I tell you. And then they shall die."

He stared off into the void, far beyond the limited scope of the four walls of the Great Hall. "I shall crush the Heroes and their pitiful Guild. I shall extinguish their pathetic light and cast the world into shadow." His eyes snapped back into focus, and he glared at the Villains around him. "There are pieces that I yet need to construct this Device, and you will help me acquire them.

"So tonight, we begin our preparations. Tomorrow we shall kill the squire and take Crimson alive. Who is with me?"

The Villains rose and shouted with one voice. The Minions along the walls sent up a shriek of evil glee and the Henchmen roared their approval. Even Serimal and Nieva joined the cheer that filled the hall.

Cyrus sat up. It was no use—he just couldn't sleep. He got up and walked to the balcony again. At home, when he couldn't sleep, he used to walk out onto the docks and look at the stars and the ocean. Well, he thought, it's worth a try here too, I guess.

He craned his neck to look at the sky. The stars were beautiful, but the massive oak planted in the center of the courtyard blocked a large swath of Cyrus's view. So he stepped up onto the balcony railing and leapt into the tree. He climbed up it, then jumped onto the roof of the Inn.

The red roof-tiles still retained heat from the day's sun. Ah, this was much better. Cyrus braced his feet against the gutter and laid back on the warm surface, staring up at the stars. He could see more of them from here, without the tree in the way. In fact, he could pick out many major constellations: the Orc, the Five Heroes, the Stellar Serp—

Something made a noise behind him. He turned his head and looked back up the roof. There was Kris! She was carefully padding her way on all fours across the ridgeline of the roof. She didn't seem to have seen Cyrus. She wore a long shirt and short pants made of another green material, different from that of the dress she had worn earlier.

"Welcome to the party," Cyrus said.

Kris turned and gave a startled mew. "Oh, it's you." She slid down and sat next to Cyrus, perched warily next to him. "There's a party?"

"Now there is. It's not a party unless there's at least two people." Cyrus lay back down and regarded the stars once again. "Couldn't sleep, huh?"

Kris shook her head. "Too many thoughts. At home, whenever I needed to relax at night, I would lay and look at the stars."

Cyrus smiled. "I guess looking at so much grandeur makes your problems seem insignificant by comparison."

Kris lay back on the tiles. "It's not that. When I look up at all that, I remember that the Creator who made all of that made me also. If He can keep it all in the sky, I'm sure He can keep me safe."

Cyrus turned his head, regarding Kris's furry face. "Creator? I don't know about that. I've seen too much strife, too much death, too many horrible things to believe that any Creator could have made the world—not a *good* Creator, anyway. If it's a choice between an evil Creator or none at all, I pick the latter."

Kris stared right into Cyrus's eyes and smiled. "You're a Hero."

"Apprentice Hero—"

"Oh Kay, but my point is that you live in constant contact with evil. It's probably tainted your view. In your travels, don't you see many wonderful things too? Many good things?"

Cyrus frowned and thought of his travels. "Yes, I do, but they just seem like people trying to make the best of a bad world. I see the joy of a newborn baby, but I've seen far too many funerals. The collected wisdom of Dragons leaves me in awe, but it pales in comparison with the base ignorance and superstition of the masses. Even the good in people is overshadowed by their inherent evil qualities. I've never seen perfection, and not much that you could call 'good.'" He looked back up at the stars. "I don't know if there's a Creator or not, but if the creation I've seen reflects what He's like, He can't be good."

Kris closed her eyes. Her face was thoughtful, and the moonlight cast delicate patterns on her dappled fur.

"That's a disappointment, Kris," Cyrus said. "My mother used to talk like you do about the Creator. She talked about the Being that had created everything in the entire world like He was her best friend. It was nice to believe that for a while, but when she died of the fever . . . " He shook his head. "I stopped believing in happy endings, especially fairy-tales about a loving and good Creator."

Kris nuzzled Cyrus's arm with the bridge of her nose. "They're not fairy-tales, Cyrus. Besides, fairies don't believe in the Creator. I don't know. To me it sounds like your mother was a smart woman. Did your father believe the same thing?"

Cyrus put his arms behind his head. "I don't know. The only memories I have of Dad are happy ones, like fishing trips, strange exotic presents, games of 'Deer Hunter,' and wrestling with him and my cousin Marco. He was a Hero, the Bronze Gryphon, so he was always off on Quests; we didn't see much of him. When he came home, everybody was happy for a few weeks, and then he would have to leave again."

Cyrus sat up and rested his chin on his knees. "Dad was killed when I was ten, in one of those stupid, pointless border wars. I didn't take it too well, but Mom took it worse. She started doing anything and everything to keep busy so she wouldn't have to think. She lasted almost a whole year, then contracted a nasty fever in our local infirmary where she had volunteered. It was over in a week."

Kris sat up and placed a paw on Cyrus's arm. "I'm sorry . . ."

Cyrus shrugged. "Like I said, that's when I stopped believing in a good Creator. If there was a good Creator, wouldn't He have saved someone who loved Him so much? But Mom died anyway. Fortunately for me, I wasn't the only Solburg left on Starspeak. My Uncle Jacob and Aunt Catherine took me in, and I lived with them and my cousin Marco until I turned fourteen. I wrote a letter to the Guild of Heroes, trying to get in. Wanted to follow in Dad's footsteps, I guess. Didn't know what else to do, except that I didn't want to live on Starspeak anymore. Finally the scouts for the Guild of Heroes found me, and I've been apprenticed to Reg ever since."

Kris looked at him kindly. "I'm glad you had your aunt and uncle. It would be terrible to have no family left . . . "

Cyrus smiled halfheartedly. "Yeah, I suppose it would be. So what about you, Kris? Why are you headed for Mir?"

Kris frowned. "We . . . had some difficulties where we used to live in Sur Palma, on Salvinsel."

"Difficulties? You mean like crop failures?"

"No, like Humans who got tired of our tribe and started rounding us up as slaves. Our males decided to stay and fight, sending the females as far away as we could get. A few males came with us for protection. Those males were chosen by lot—

except for my brother. Our father sent him with us instead of letting him stay and fight. Even so, we were harassed and attacked on our way. We were too big a target when we were all together. So the group split up into five parties and dispersed, heading for Mir."

Kris scratched one of the roof-tiles as she clenched a fist. She retracted her claws and sighed. "Many members of our tribe have relatives there. Mir is the only region left in the world that's still officially a Katheni-controlled country."

Cyrus shook his head. "That's rough. Why do Humans have to be so thoughtless? Honestly, sometimes I'm ashamed to be one." He sighed and lay back down.

"Don't put yourself in the same category," Kris said. "You aren't like most Humans, Cyrus. You treat my brother and I like we were Human ourselves. Not many people do that."

Cyrus smiled. "To me, biology is the only difference between Katheni and Humans. Just physical differences—only skin and fur deep." He watched a gentle night breeze rustle the leaves atop the oak tree. "You said you and Katana broke off with one of the groups. Was it just the two of you in that group, or were there more?"

Kris looked up at the stars again, a troubled expression on her feline countenance. "We started with five, including brother and I. There were two other females and a cub. We lost the older female to a Roc. It caught her while she was hunting and flew off with her.

"Slavers grabbed the younger female and her cub in one of the Human towns we passed through. Katana tried to stop them, and they almost captured him, too, but we managed to get away. We saw them the next day, being sold in the slave markets. Katana would have purchased them back, but we had no money. Fortunately, they were both bought by the same person, a kind-looking old man and his family. We prayed for them and went on. We have to get to Mir, if only to tell their family where they are so maybe they can buy them back."

Cyrus placed his hand on Kris's head, feeling the softness of her head-fur. "I'm sure you'll get there, soon. After all, if what you believe about the Creator is true, then He is watching out for you two, right? If He's on your side, you can't lose."

Kris smiled. "Thank you, Cyrus." She curled up into a ball and laid her head on Cyrus's arm. "Your face is all healed," she said, tracing the parallel scars on his cheek. "I'm glad I didn't do any lasting damage to this face of yours."

Cyrus chuckled. "Yeah, I like it undamaged." He took Kris's hand in his. "Takes more than a little scratch like this to damage a Hero. Plus, this looks really cool. Like I survived a fight with a cheetaur or something. I'd rather thank you than blame you for it."

"That is good," Kris said, smiling. "I hope you can get to sleep soon. I'm staying up here a bit longer."

"So am I," Cyrus said, instantly deciding to do so. "So am I."

Kris's soft breathing became regular as Cyrus continued to stare at the stars. He smiled briefly, but soon dark thoughts clouded his expression.

Why did I say that about the Creator being on her side? he thought. I don't believe that the Creator, if there is one, is on anybody's side but His own. If He exists, then He must take some perverse pleasure in watching the suffering of innocent people. Either that or He doesn't care, and I can't decide which is worse. At least if He's evil, then I can hate Him without feeling guilty.

Kris shifted slightly and a small smile pulled at the corners of her mouth. She burrowed her head into Cyrus's shoulder and continued sleeping.

Cyrus's somber thoughts drifted away as he looked at her. So peaceful. *I guess her simple beliefs let her sleep without worries. To her, the Creator is like a father or a big brother, somebody who cares about what happens to her. If only things were really that simple . . .* He looked at the stars once again and let his mind wander. Kris's breathing was soothing, and she was warm and soft. The breeze rustled the leaves and a symphony of crickets sang him a lullaby. Cyrus's eyes slowly closed and stayed that way.

Chapter 14

ALL GOOD THINGS
MUST COME TO AN END

*In which there is a Lecture, Diabolical Plotting,
and Unkindness to a Dragon*

ROGER FARELLA WALKED down the dank, chill outer hall of the swamp tower that served as Voshtyr's base of operations. The Araquellus shivered in the damp air as he walked. It was just wet enough to suck away his precious body heat, but not wet enough to be comfortable for his Race. This *serefsiz* tower was going to be the death of him.

In the gaps between the columns of the outer walk, the grey of early morning had just begun to lighten the foggy eastern sky. Roger turned the handle of a thick wooden door and entered Voshtyr's study.

"Voshtyr, the contractors are here. They want to know where to put the lava . . . " he said, but trailed off.

What met his scaled eyes was not pleasant. Voshtyr sat with one knee in the back of a bound and bloodied man on the floor, slowly sawing off the man's index finger with a serrated combat knife.

The half-demon looked up at Roger's entrance and smiled. "Roger, what a pleasant surprise. Come in, I was just dealing with an unexpected guest of a less amiable sort. Heroes—I can't abide them. As for the lava, they can put it in that old fountain in the courtyard. A lava-fountain would warm this damp place up considerably, don't you think?"

The bound, black-garbed man grunted as Voshtyr finished removing his digit, but otherwise made no sound.

Roger shuddered. "For the love of seaweed, Voshtyr! You have a perfectly good torture chamber for such things! Why make a mess in public?"

"Don't meddle, Farella," Voshtyr snapped. "I've just spent the last seven hours clearing my next few actions with the bureaucratic hegemony of the Brotherhood of the Black Hand. And I've had it up to here with these rules and regulations." He drew an imaginary line across his head at eye-height with his metal hand. "If there's one thing I hate worse than Heroes, it's bureaucrats."

"But in your study—"

"When I got back to my study, this buffoon of a Hero jumped me." Voshtyr wiped the bloodied knife-blade on his black trousers. "As you can see, he was not the victor. I was in need of some stress relief, so here we are."

Roger wrinkled his nose-slits. "Still, Voshtyr, it is in poor taste to do such things in public. It's a bit out of character for you."

Voshtyr shrugged. He kicked the prone man on the floor. "I do what I must. Now, did you just come to tell me about the contractors, or was there something else?"

"I also have a report for you," Roger said, deciding to ignore the bound man's plight. He had attacked a half-demon, after all, and deserved his fate. "Anthony the Mace and Salvatia Malice have acquired the Pendulum of Puissance in a daring raid on the armory of the Army of Darkness™ a few hours ago. They will be arriving today with the item."

"Excellent," Voshtyr said, rising and clapping the Araquellus on the shoulder. "Three parts left to go for the Device. Then we secure the power sources. We'll have the—"

Roger reached up and clapped a scaly blue hand over Voshtyr's mouth. "*Kes seseni*, Voshtyr! Don't forget you've got a Hero lying on the floor! If you reveal your plan in front of him, he's sure to survive and take news to his friends!" He began floating a few inches off the floor as he became more upset. "I am *not* going to be exiled from the Deep Realm again because of one of your foolish mistakes. Heroes escape all the time, and I know what they report to their superiors when they do! I read it in that ridiculous book they call the *Complete Guide to Heroics!*"

Voshtyr frowned and placed his hands on Roger's shoulders, pushing him back down to contact with the floor. "Calm down, old friend. You are most likely right. Give me a moment, and I shall deal with him." He turned his attention back to the bound man. "So, Hero, you're been remarkably recalcitrant in revealing your motives or who sent you to kill me. I know you, though. The Silent Assassin—that's your name now, isn't it?" Voshtyr smiled in a decidedly evil fashion. "You worked for my father many years ago in Landeralt, did you not? But then you went by the name Kerimax Nightstrike."

The Hero's eyes widened, but he said nothing.

"I was naught but a lad at the time," Voshtyr said, "but I remember you bringing in the severed head of a beautiful young woman while we were at supper once. One of the lasses that refused to sleep with Father, I would imagine." Voshtyr glared down at his captive. "And you call yourself a Hero now. What hypocrisy, to pretend to uphold truth and justice when such copious quantities of innocent blood stain your hands."

The Silent Assassin hung his battered head.

"So I want you to think of that girl's face as you die," Voshtyr said, a hideous smile creeping up the corners of his mouth as he watched tears stream from the Hero's eyes. "And may her spirit haunt you in the afterlife."

With that, the Villain dragged his knife across the Hero's throat. The Assassin gave a muted cough and slumped to the floor.

Roger turned away. It wasn't that the sight of blood upset him, it was simply the distasteful manner in which it had been spilled. Poor taste. Poor taste indeed.

"As I was saying," Voshtyr said, standing and wiping the blood from his knife with a dark cloth, "we'll have the machine assembled in less than a fortnight."

The Araquellus nodded. "Sooner than that, I would imagine. Tyler Nightraid is well on his way to acquiring the Infinity Inducer from his black-market contacts. He promises delivery by next week. Apparently those Academy friends of his that the boy is so proud of are good for something, after all."

"Excellent," Voshtyr replied, his eyes glowing with an eerie and intense light. "I'm sorry, old friend, but would you allow me some maniacal laughter?"

Roger rolled his eyes and shrugged. "Do what you like. There are no Heroes about to slay you as you do so, and you're not liable to fall off any ledges, given your current footing."

"Thank you." The half-demon cleared his throat and planted both feet firmly on the floor. Head back and palms upraised, fingers curled into claws, he emitted a deep and throaty laugh, sending chills down the collective spines of every sentient creature in a three-mile radius.

"MWAHAHAHAHA!"

• • •

Cyrus woke up cold on one side and warm on the other. He squinted his eyes against the light of the invading dawn and realized that he was still on the roof. Then he realized something else.

Kris was snuggled up against his right side, breathing gently. Cyrus noticed that at some point during the night, he must have put his arm around her. He started to panic, but she was still asleep, so he smiled instead. She was warm and soft, like a heated, furry body pillow.

"Wake up, Kris," he said gently. "It's dawn. We'll be leaving soon."

"Mrr?" Kris stretched and yawned. Cyrus pulled his head back a bit. She certainly had a *lot* of pointy teeth. She opened her eyes a bit, then all the way. "What . . . ? Did we . . . spend all night up here?"

"Yeah," Cyrus said. "We did. We'd better get down now. We're leaving shortly."

Kris nodded. She got up and stretched again, back arching as she did so. Cyrus attempted not to stare. They split up, Kris walking the ridgeline back to her room, Cyrus climbing back down the tree, and jumping down to the balcony.

He landed right in front of Katana.

Cyrus stepped back, seeing the fury in the Katheni's pale eyes. "What's wrong, Katana? Did something happen?"

"You would know," Katana hissed. He grabbed Cyrus by his shirt front and pushed him up against the balcony wall. "Where were you last night? Did you sleep with my sister?"

Cyrus winced as Katana's claws penetrated the thin shirt and dug into the skin on his chest. "Did I *what?* No! I was on the roof, looking at the stars! Calm down, Katana," he snapped. "I didn't do anything to your sister."

Katana retained his hold, still glaring at Cyrus. "Really? Explain."

"I went up there to look at stars last night. I do that. But apparently Kris does too. You should know how she looks at stars to calm down. So she came up to look at them too." Cyrus could feel blood oozing down his chest. "We talked a while, and then I guess we both kind of dozed off. But I swear I didn't touch her. That kind of thing never even crossed my mind. Now let go of me." Cyrus grabbed Katana's wrist with a Crushing Grasp, forcing the release of his shirt, and began to stalk inside.

"Wait, Cyrus," Katana said, rubbing his wrist. Cyrus stopped, but didn't turn around. "Hear me out. I know that you are a good person. You are, however, Human, and my sister is not."

"Your point?" Cyrus replied, turning around.

Katana faced Cyrus. "I've been taking care of my little sister since our parents were killed and our tribe scattered. I've protected her as best I could from the elements, from hunger, and from all kinds of physical harm. But try as I may, I cannot protect her from emotional harm, and it frightens me. Though you may not know it, you are in grave danger of wounding my little sister, and I mean to keep that from happening."

"What are you talking about?" Cyrus paused. "Are you saying . . ."

Katana slumped down against the balcony. "She's quite taken with you. I couldn't decide which would be worse, finding that you thought the same of her, or that you *didn't.* You must tell her how it really is, Cyrus. Don't leave her believing a lie for too long, or learning the truth will destroy her."

Cyrus looked down. "I . . . Well, I hadn't thought about that. I've been too busy expecting her to kill me in my sleep. She's different from anyone I've ever known, probably because I don't have a lot of non-Human friends. To be honest, she still scares me. But she has some redeeming qualities. And I don't mean just physical ones," he added as Katana glared at him again. "Romance is the last thing on my mind. Or it would be the last thing if it were there at all, which it isn't. So, if you'd be so kind as to get out of my face about it, I have to pack."

Cyrus stomped back into the inn to begin packing for the day's journey. "Oh, by the way," he said over his shoulder, "I just realized that technically I did sleep with your sister. But it was a chaste night."

Katana chuckled. "That was very integrous of you, Cyrus."

"Int-what?" Cyrus stopped and turned around.

"Integrous. You have integrity. I meant it as a compliment."

"That's not a word, Katana, not in Central. There is no adjective for 'having integrity.'"

"Well, it should be," Katana countered. "Besides, it's a word now—it's in print."

Cyrus wondered what that meant, but just sighed and walked back into the Inn, shaking his head. What strange folk these Katheni were.

• • •

Keeth waded out of the shallow water at the northern end of Lake Aqui. He had been soaking in it for nearly twelve hours. With all the flying and fire-breathing that Dragons do, they tend to enjoy soaking in water. Since bodies of fresh water large and deep enough for a Dragon to bathe in are few and far between, Dragons have the bad habit of staying in them for excessive amounts of time when they find one.

Keeth was no different. He shook his membranous wings free of excess moisture and folded them to his sides. Now, to find something to eat.

Ten minutes later, Keeth chewed the bones of a suddenly deceased sheep. Belly full, he lay down on the sandy shore of the inland sea and drifted into a doze in the warm sunshine.

Some time later he awoke with a start, heavy coughs racking his enormous lungs.

A pale purple smoke drifted around him in a malevolent cloud. The Dragon reared up out of the smoke, every joint in his body feeling swollen and old. Keeth began to panic. His father Barinol had told him of these effects. They were commonly produced by an herb that was deadly to Dragons.

"Dragonsbane!" a man's voice boomed.

Keeth spun dizzily around and saw a brawny man in silver armor, standing on the shore and carrying an enormous mace.

"The perfect trap ingredient to trap a Dragon!" he shouted.

Keeth's vision blurred. His scales turned a pasty grey. He breathed a half-hearted flame in the direction of his foe but missed miserably.

"I am Sir Anthony the Mace! Men know and fear my name, and thousands have fallen beneath my blade."

"That's a mace," Keeth said, shaking his head to clear the smoke from it.

"Why does everyone *always* point that out?" the man growled. "It matters not. I shall crush you, Keith, son of Barinol!" He leapt over the weakened Keeth, slamming his mace down between Keeth's wing joints.

"It's KEETH!" Keeth bellowed. "Two *e*'s!" He swung his tail at the mace-wielding Villain, but Anthony slammed his mace down on top of it in mid-swing. Bones crunched.

Keeth swung his neck and bashed the Villain with his head, knocking him into the lake. Keeth limped away as fast as his injured tail and unsteady legs would allow.

Anthony the Mace burst out of the water with a flying leap, landing right in front of the staggering Dragon. One swift blow of his giant mace spun Keeth three times in the air, landing the Dragon in a heavy heap. Keeth groaned.

Sir Anthony put a heavy metal boot on Keeth's neck. "Well then, Dragon. Not so mighty anymore, are you?"

Keeth rolled an eyeball up and looked at the man standing on his neck. "I didn't claim to be mighty. What have I done to you? Why do you attack me?"

"Silence, lizard!" Anthony pressed his boot deeper onto Keeth's neck. "I despise your entire species. Once, I was a respectable Hero, and I dispensed true justice. Then, when faced with an impossible scenario, I chose to do what was necessary to survive. This displeased the high-and-mighty Guild, and they sent another Hero to catch me. He never would have, had it not been for the three young Dragons helping him. They found me out and led the Hero to me.

"You scaled beasts think you're superior, but I, Anthony the Mace, have defeated you single-handedly." He attempted a maniacal laugh, but inhaled a lungful of Dragonsbane smoke. He coughed, totally throwing off the laugh. He cursed and cleared his throat. "However, today I am here not because I like to slay Dragons, though I do, but at the behest of my master: Lord Voshtyr. You are an impediment to his plans, Wyrm, and will soon become ingredients for his spells. Now, sleep a sleep of pain!"

The mace came down on Keeth's skull, and a crushing blackness stole his mind away.

Cyrus and the rest of the party arrived at the far side of the lake by mid-afternoon. The sunlight shone off the rippling water, casting waves of light upon the walls of Merope, and a gentle breeze mediated the heat. Two Humans, two Katheni, two horses, and a mule stood ready to leave.

Keeth was conspicuously absent.

The long grass outside the sandstone walls waved and rustled in the wind. The sandy shore bore heavy draconic footprints, but otherwise, the lake seemed completely Dragon-free.

"So, what do we do?" Katana asked Reginald.

The Hero shrugged. "We wait, I suppose. Dragons keep their word, and he agreed to meet us here. Perhaps if we waited a little further up the shore."

Cyrus scanned the surface of the lake. There was certainly no sign of Keeth anywhere along the shoreline. So unless the Dragon had taken to burying himself on the lake-bottom . . . He turned to say something to Kris.

She was looking right at him, but turned away as soon as their eyes met. Her tail lashed as if she were angry about something.

Cyrus blinked. What was that all about?

"Cyrus!"

Cyrus snapped to attention. "Yes, sir?"

"Scout the shoreline a mile each direction and tell me if you see any evidence of our scaled friend."

Cyrus nodded and sped off on Brisk.

Katana's ears twitched, dislodging an unwelcome fly from the tip of one. "Well, if we've some time before we move again, shall Kris and I find some fresh game for our supper?"

"I suppose," Reginald replied. "Fresh meat is better than dried. If you can scare up some partridges or a small deer, Cyrus can—" At that moment, Reginald's pocket began to buzz. He reached in and drew out a small leather bag. It jingled slightly as it buzzed again. "If you'll excuse me for a moment, Katana, I have to take this."

"Take your time, Reginald. Kris and I shall return before the hour is out." The black Katheni made for the taller grass.

Reginald walked a short distance away and removed a large silver coin from the pouch. "This is the Crimson Slash. What can I . . . " His voice trailed off. "Oh, it's you . . . Is aught amiss?"

Cyrus scouted south, finding only a deep depression that had been dug out larger, possibly to accommodate a large Dragon. A confusing combination of Human footprints mingled with the tracks of a Dragon.

He dismounted to kneel down and examine the footprints. Whoever had left these had been Human: the tracks were too deep to be an Elf, too narrow for a Dwarf, and too shallow for an Orc. And none of the other Races could comfortably wear any kind of Human footwear, much less plate-armor boots. A Minion? No, a Henchman at least. Next he saw the grass. It was wildly bent and broken in several places along the shore, as if crushed by the shuffling feet of a giant.

Cyrus moved on.

And then he discovered something by accident that tied all the rest together.

Tiring of overwarm feet he took off his boots and the inner cotton wrappings around his feet, and dug his toes into the damp sand and gravel around the lakeshore. When he took his next step, he saw that his toes were coated with the black grime of charred vegetation.

Cyrus turned around. His toes had uncovered burned plants of some kind, which had had sand thrown over them to cover them up. He knelt down, putting his hand over the blackened mess. No heat.

Cyrus sucked in a sharp breath. One of the charred plants had not fully burnt, and he picked it up. It was a stiff, serrated-edged plant of a venomous green color, edged in purple. He stood and hastily slung his boots over his shoulder.

"*Reg!*" he yelled, taking off at a dead run. "*Reg! George Rampant!*"

Once Upon a Time there was a Knight in Shining Armor who loved a beautiful Princess, the youngest daughter of a kindly Old King. The Knight bore the name of George Ryveroake and was the most skilled swordsman for leagues around. The Knight dreamed to wed the Princess and was planning to approach the King about the matter.

One day, when the Princess was strolling in her garden with her ladies-in-waiting, a Dragon swooped down from the sky and plucked her away as a farmer plucks fruit from a tree.

This angered the Knight greatly, and he vowed to slay the Dragon who had kidnapped his love.

The Old King told him to shut up and sit down, for he had planned for the Handsome Prince of a neighboring kingdom to come rescue his daughter from the Dragon. The rewards, of course, were both simple and rich. For the Prince, a Bride and Half the Kingdom, and for the Dragon, a hundred thousand pieces of gold for his hoard, and two vats of distilled Fire Poppy juice to quench his thirst. It was, the King assured him, all arranged.

But the Knight did not listen to the Old King. Instead, he spent a day and a night brewing the Flowers of Dragon's Bane into a dark and toxic slime. With this he coated his sword, and rode forth to do battle with the Dragon.

The Knight struggled to climb Mount Fyre, and at the top, he did battle with the Three Riddling Gryphons, finally winning entry into the Abandoned Keep of the Iron Skull. A single light shone from the highest room in the tallest tower, and toward the light the Knight made his way.

But the Dragon did spy his unwelcome visitor, and confronted him terrifyingly in the courtyard. The great creature demanded that the Knight leave at once, lest he upset the Old King's careful planning.

Alas, the Knight did not listen to the Dragon. He spurred his charger, and did tilt at the Dragon. The Dragon did sigh, and swatted the lance from the Knight's grasp as a petulant child swats away a spoonful of unwanted vegetables.

The Knight cared little for the loss of his lance, for 'twas his sword that was the most dangerous. As he rode past the Dragon, the Knight opened a gash in the Dragon's side with his blade.

The Dragon groaned as it felt the poison seep through its blood. With its dying breath, it gave a great cry to the heavens, and fell dead on the stones of the courtyard.

Flushed with his victory, the Knight turned to the tower, only to behold the Princess run weeping to the dead Dragon. She berated the Knight for spoiling her father's plans, and told him that his rash actions had most likely ruined any hope of her marriage to the Handsome Prince.

The Knight protested and began to tell the Princess of his love for her, but she did shun him, and got a ride back to her Father's castle from one of the Riddling Gryphons.

Saddened by this rejection, the Knight returned to his post. But no sooner did he arrive, than the Lawyer of the Dragon whom he had slain did arrive as well, and did press charges against the Knight for the Murder of an Elder Creature. The Old King, furious at having his plans ruined by such rashness and disobedience, did not shelter the Knight from litigation.

The Court did find the Knight guilty of Murder of an Elder Creature, as well as willful disobedience of a military order, and did award his estate and monies to the Dragon's next of kin as Punitive Damages. The Old King stripped Sir George of his title and Knighthood, and banished him from the Kingdom forever.

Enraged at what had happened to him, George Ryveroake did place the blame on Dragons, and vowed to kill them until either they had all perished as a race or he himself was killed. And thus began a time of difficulty for the Dragons, as it took several years for them to track down and dispatch the wayward George, who did thenceforth take the name George Rampant.

His dire legacy lives on. To this day, any man who has slain or attempted to slay a Dragon without due provocation is referred to as a "George Rampant," and is prosecuted to the full extent of Bryath Law.

• • •

Reginald sat on a small hillock, looking out at the shining surface of the lake as he thought. Why could the Guild never contact him with *good* news? He ran his fingers along the edges of a token with an eye containing an hourglass emblazoned on it, and scowled.

Then Cyrus's shouting reached his ears. Reginald deposited the token in his pouch and looked up to his returning apprentice. "What, lad? What do you mean?"

Cyrus, breathing fairly heavily, waved his hand back in the direction he'd come. "Footprints and . . . signs of a scuffle. And, I found . . . Dragonsbane." He held out the scorched leaf to Reginald.

The Hero took the plant and scowled. "A George Rampant indeed. I can only hope our draconic friend is not slain." He crushed the Dragonsbane in his fist.

"Listen, Reg," Cyrus said, straightening up. "The mess over there can't be more than a few hours old. If we follow now, we can find out what happened to Keeth."

"We can go nowhere," Reginald replied, frowning again. "I have just received word from the Guild that all unassigned Heroes are to scout for information concerning the theft of several important Magical Devices. Much as I would love to search for our missing friend—"

"Our orders prevent it," Cyrus finished. "I get it. The Guild thinks theft of magic objects is more important than finding out where a single Dragon is." The apprentice sat down on the turf and stared out at the lake. "Well, he's a Dragon. He can probably take care of himself. Still, it's a pain that we have to take off on some Guild busywork instead of risking our necks against a bunch of violence-prone lizards to find some girl's stupid necklace."

"'Tisn't the only pain, lad," Reginald said. "There is another Hero en route to join forces with us, and we're to wait here until he arrives."

Cyrus shrugged. "Eh, could be worse. I could be sweating to death in the sun here, and overheated from a long run, without any hope of swimming in yonder lake." Cyrus gave Reginald a boyish grin over his shoulder.

"All right, lad, go and take your swim," Reginald said with a half-smile.

"Thanks, Reg, 'preciate it." Cyrus dashed down to the shore, stripping off his shirts, both silver chain and blue-dyed cotton, and dove into the sparkling lake.

Kris watched Cyrus run by in a blur and dive into the lake with a clumsy splash. She giggled, dropping the roe deer she had just caught. "Looks like he was in a hurry. Hmm . . . " She looked down at the reddish-gold deer, then back to the water. "Oh, dear brother of mine," Kris began, putting an arm around Katana's shoulder.

Katana chuckled and pushed Kris's arm from his shoulders. "All right, what is it you want now?"

"I was thinking about joining Cyrus for a swim. Can you take care of the prey for me?"

"Certainly, after I have a word with Reginald," Katana replied. "I don't mind, and Cyrus will most likely appreciate the company. But," he said, "I don't think he would appreciate traditional Katheni swimming garb, either."

Kris grinned and ducked into the grass. She bounded back out in her shorts instead of the dress and sprang into the water.

• • •

Cyrus started as something brushed by his leg underwater. Freshwater Sylph?

Kris breached the surface and splashed Cyrus in the face.

"You!" Cyrus retaliated, sending sheet after sheet of water over the Katheni girl. "I thought cats didn't like water!"

Kris grinned. "Cats don't. *Katheni* take swims and baths whenever we can get them!"

Cyrus laughed, getting a mouthful of water as Kris splashed him again.

"I thought you'd learned not to attack a Hero without provocation!" Cyrus reached behind him and flung a larger sheet of water at Kris.

"Full Heroes, yes. Apprentices, no." Kris crouched lower in the water and cupped her paws to form a more directly amiable splash. She got Cyrus in the eyes with it.

Cyrus wiped the lake water from his eyes. "All right, so you need to learn this lesson too. It's the first thing about traveling with a Hero: do *not* attack the apprentice, for he is undoubtedly almost as strong as his master."

"You're making that up."

"Probably. Have at you!" Cyrus threw both hands forward to splash Kris.

But something unexpected happened when he did. Instead of a mere splash of water, many gallons burst forth from his palms. Twin high-pressure beams of fresh water blasted Kris's torso, knocking her over into the lake.

"*Bok!*" Cyrus said. "Oh, what in the— Kris? You alright?" He slogged forward to help the Katheni girl.

Kris poked her head out of the water and scowled at Cyrus. "Magic's cheating! I thought just my brother cheated at water fights. But you, of all people!"

"Magic?" Cyrus frowned. He looked at his hands. No gloves. "That was magic?"

Kris punched him in the shoulder on her way back up to shore. "Yes, it was. And that takes all the fun out of it. Unless you teach me how to do it too."

"I don't know how to do magic!" Cyrus protested.

Kris shrugged. "Suit yourself. I'm done playing."

"No, here," Cyrus said, holding his arms like he had before. "All you do is try and splash someone, then push the water harder than normal. That's all I did."

"Like this?" Kris splashed Cyrus in the face again. No high-pressure cylinder shot from her paws, but it still blinded Cyrus long enough for her to pounce him backward into the water.

Reginald stood with his back to the lake watching the wind blow through the expanse of tall grass, like waves in the ocean. He lowered his head, thinking about the dire news he had just received. He was not one to back down from a challenge, certainly, but for the first time in five years fear was rearing its ugly head within the Hero's head.

Not that Fear's beautiful head looked much better than its ugly one. The beautiful head was currently in the shop, getting some fire damage repaired. Apparently Infernis the Fire god did not scare as easily as Fear had thought he would.

Fear started to whisper something in Reginald's ear, but ducked the aforementioned ugly head back beneath the surface of his thoughts as Reginald felt a soft paw on his shoulder. He turned to face Katana, who bore a concerned expression on his face.

"What's troubling you, Reginald?" the Katheni asked.

"What? How did you know I was worried?"

The black Katheni stood and watched the billowing grass with him. "I can sense trouble sometimes. So what's wrong?"

"I just received news from the Guild that someone has been stealing parts needed to assemble a Weapon of Legend."

The cat-mage frowned, the black fur on his brow creasing into soft wrinkles. "That is a problem? I thought Villains were attempting to assemble Doomsday Devices every day. How is this one different?"

"It wouldn't be, but since that frosty mage mentioned Voshtyr Demonkin . . . "

"I see," Katana said, nodding. "You believe it is he who is doing this."

"I would stake my life on it. And, given what a dangerous foe he is, my *life* is exactly what is in danger. In fact, I may just— Hst! Someone approaches!"

Reginald recognized the approaching rider. It was Lydia, her chainmail glinting in the sun, a silver brooch of a leaping tiger firmly attached to the front.

"Good afternoon, gentlemen," she said, swinging down from her saddle. "The Hero's Guild sent me along as reinforcements for you. So, we're after some stolen weapon parts? I guess the Guild thought you could use another sword."

"We always can," Reginald replied warily.

"Even if we don't choose who wields them," Katana muttered.

Lydia glared at the Katheni. "You're not my ideal choice of traveling companion, either, cat. But I do as the Guild says, even if they're a bit stupid sometimes." She turned back to Reginald, her expression changing abruptly to a sunny smile. "Would you be so kind as to direct me to Cyrus?"

Reginald pointed at the lake.

Katana merely glared at the girl.

Lydia bobbed her head and remounted. "Thank you," she said, and nudged her white horse's flanks. The animal began walking down to the beach.

Katana turned back to Reginald. "What were you thinking?"

"What do you mean?" Reginald asked.

"Telling that girl where Cyrus is! Haven't you noticed certain things recently?"

The Hero raised an eyebrow and scanned the horizon. "What kind of things?"

Katana rolled his golden eyes. "Forget it. I just think it's a good idea to keep that female away from Cyrus, that's all."

Reginald gave Katana a sideways look. "Hmm. I agree. However, my reasons and yours may be quite different."

"Cyrus!"

Kris glanced up from her splashing of Cyrus to see where the shout had come from. That blasted Human Heroine was back again.

"Come out!" the woman shouted. "We need to talk!"

Cyrus had glanced up as well. "Huh. She's back." To Kris, his voice sounded a little odd. "I thought I told Lydia that . . . " He sighed and looked at Kris. "Bah. That was fun, but we'd probably better get up there before she gets mad. Wouldn't want to have to fight her again, would we?"

Kris shook her head. "No, I don't wish that. Perhaps she can find it in herself to be civil this time."

Cyrus snorted. "Don't count on it. Come on," he said, and the two waded out of the water to greet the Heroine.

Upon their arrival at the shore, Lydia looked disdainfully at Kris, who had water streaming from her fur. Then she turned her attention to Cyrus, looking him up and down approvingly. "Hello, Cyrus," she said. "I'm headed north a ways, so I'm joining your party."

"Did someone say you could?" Kris asked cautiously.

"I don't need to ask permission. And even if I did, I'd have it anyway because the Guild sent me. I'm a Hero," Lydia replied, scowling at Kris, "and I don't need to explain myself to an animal."

"Lydia!" Cyrus interjected. "Will you just stop it with the insults! If we're going to work together, you can't go starting squabbles like that!"

"Me?" Lydia said, taking Cyrus's arm and turning to look at Kris. "I didn't start anything. Besides, you act like she has Human feelings. She doesn't, really, or just a few. I'm just calling her what she is." Lydia tossed her hair. "As I recall, you were always in favor of plain speech, right, Cyrus?"

Cyrus sighed. "Listen. It's fine by me if you join the party. We can always use another sword. But stop causing strife, okay?" He pulled his arm from Lydia's.

Lydia pouted at Cyrus. "All right, Cyrus. If you insist." She began walking back toward Reginald, giving Kris a death glare over her shoulder.

Kris growled softly in the back of her throat. "If it's her sword we need, why can't she just leave it with us and then go bother someone else?"

"Don't take it personally," Cyrus said with a chuckle. "She's been like that since we were kids."

Kris blinked in surprise. "You lived together?"

"No, not . . . I mean . . . well . . . we lived in the same village," Cyrus stammered, looking down and scuffing the sand with his bare feet.

Kris tilted her head. "What did you think I meant?"

"Uh, nothing. I've just . . . " he swallowed . . . "known her for a long time, and she's always been that way about any Race that has fur, feathers, or scales. So don't take it personally."

I don't know, Kris thought. She seems like she's being awfully personal about it to me. She's like a female in heat . . . Oh no, maybe she's—

"But anyway," Cyrus said, "I think Reg is calling us. Come on, Kris!" He ran up the beach, collecting his shirts on the way.

Kris followed more slowly, thinking hard.

Voshtyr set down his glass of wine and motioned for the steward to fill Roger and Sir Anthony's glasses as well. "That takes care of the Dragon. Now to tear the remaining party apart."

Five people sat in the small reception room: Voshtyr, Nieva, Anthony the Mace, Roger Farella, and Torval, the Purveyor of Evil Products. The steward, as a servant, did not count in the total, though he was there nonetheless.

The room had drastically changed from the Spartan fashion in which Nieva had kept it. Now a brocaded tapestry of a unicorn hunt dominated a wall, and plush red carpeting covered the stone floor. A pair of copper brazier the size of bathtubs rested on tripods in the far corner of the room, lighting the now-cozy room with their burning contents.

Anthony lounged on a black velvet couch, eating a long loaf of bread stuffed with sausage and spicy sauce. Nieva and Roger occupied gilt-framed, high-backed armchairs, while Voshtyr sat behind the heavy ironwood desk in a red plush chair with skulls on its headrest and armrests. Torval, as neither a Villain nor a particularly respectable member of the meeting, stood near the doorway.

Voshtyr turned to Nieva. Such a beautiful woman. Whatever did she see in Serimal? He rested his elbow on the table and his head on his fist. "Where's that Shifter of yours gotten around to, Nievalarai?"

Nieva looked puzzled. "I haven't dismissed him yet. Why? Do you need him?"

Voshtyr smiled again. "Which is more painful, Nieva? Merely thinking that the man you love may not love you, or having him tell you outright that he simply cannot abide your company?"

Nieva winced. "So that's your plan for the Triangle?"

"As soon as possible, send the shifter here, if you please."

Nieva stood, curtseyed, and left the sanctum.

Sir Anthony groaned. "Ah don umdmershan wha-"

"For the love of sharp objects," Roger snapped, "would you be so kind as to swallow what you have in your mouth before speaking?"

Anthony grinned and showed Roger his mouthful of chewed bread and meat before swallowing. "I don't understand why we can't just capture the Crimson Slash, his party be doomed. I can take any squire, any day!"

Voshtyr turned his gaze on the Mace. "I doubt it. His apprentice, Cyrus Solburg, is overdue to become a Hero, Second Class. To add to that, the boy seems to be manifesting some magical powers that we had not foreseen. For some reason, ley-lines in his general vicinity have been getting tweaked somehow. We must use utmost caution."

He took a sip of his wine, then placed the glass back on the desk. "Of course, if the Triangle fails, we'll have to kill him, whether he's alone or not. It's a cardinal rule that you never let a faithful squire live when you jail his master. If you do, the results are invariably bad. Especially with this squire.

"Take, for example, Venmar Crystalline. He was killed last summer by the same two that we're up against now. Crystalline had captured Crimson, but failed to kill Cyrus. Cyrus sprang Crimson from the cell, and together they killed the old wizard. *Always* kill the squire when you have the chance."

Roger coughed gently, covering his mouth with a scaled hand.

"Oh, Roger," Voshtyr said, turning to him. "Your task is fairly easy." He pulled a small pouch out of his tunic pocket. "Here. Take this, but do not breathe it. It is a special type of flower pollen that has an . . . interesting effect on the sentient mind. Your task is to make the female Hero, one Lydia Weatherblade, breathe it in."

"Is that all you wish of me?" Roger cocked his scaled head. "What will it do, then?"

Voshtyr turned to the flabby Purveyor of Evil Products. "Torval, please explain the effects of this pollen would have on, say, a twenty-two-year-old Human female."

Torval snickered. "Oh, it makes things *very* interesting for her. In the first stage, it puts her in a trance. Secondly, it excites all the areas of the brain used for emotions pertaining to, shall we say, amorous behavior. Thus, she is rendered very receptive to certain types of suggestions . . . "

Roger recoiled, his nose-sits closed, obviously disgusted by Torval's beery breath and perverted ideas.

"In other words," the merchant continued, "it works like a standard love potion, except with only temporary effects, so you don't have to deal with the girl later. I once sold almost fifty pounds of the stuff to a Sheik for a harem party he was—"

"That will do, Torval," Voshtyr said.

"Let's just say that it will make things quite interesting for this Lydia Weatherblade and the squire." Torval snickered again. "It lasts just long enough to get someone in very deep trouble."

Roger looked ill.

Someone timidly knocked on the door. "Come in!" Voshtyr shouted.

Nieva entered the room, alone.

"Where is the shifter?" Voshtyr asked.

Nieva hung her head. "I could not find him. He appears to have left."

"Left?" Voshtyr said, rising from his chair. "Well, see if you can get him back. I need . . . Wait a moment. Come here."

Nieva stepped forward.

Voshtyr examined her. "Look at me," he commanded.

Nieva looked up, tears streaming from her golden eyes.

Voshtyr chuckled, an unearthly sound. "Very, very good, shifter. You almost had me fooled."

Nieva's form blurred and re-solidified, this time as the shifter. His golden eyes danced with mischief. "Thank you, my lord. How can I be of assistance?"

"I have another person for you to imitate, and more fell Villainy to wreak. What say you?" Voshtyr locked eyes with the shifter, and he saw the glow of his own eyes reflecting in the shifter's malicious golden gaze.

The shifter smiled, revealing his pointed teeth, and licked his lips.

Shape-shifters may be the most dangerous creatures in Centra Mundi. They are Humans who have fallen into the possession of fell Demons. A shifter, once bent and controlled by a demon, absorbs the demon's shape-changing abilities and can partially imitate any person he has seen, touched, or had described to him.

While this may seem impressive, it has its limits. A shifter cannot mimic anything more than twice his original size, or anything less than half.

When not mimicking another, shifters all have the same type of face. That is, they present the type of face that is totally unremarkable, with no distinctive features save eye color. All shifters have metallic eyes, of shades ranging from bright gold to dark steel. Aside from that, shifters are the only creatures with truly "blank" faces. Not a single shifter remembers his or her original face, though Ancient Myths suggest that if one does, the demon inside him will flee.

Not all shifters are equally talented. Many cannot manage more than imitating other Humans, but some are capable of copying any individual from any Race, down to the fur, fang, or feather. This type of mastery requires intense concentration, and if it is not held properly, the eyes will show their true color.

Shifters trust—and are trusted by—no one. They have no society of their own and no traffic with each other. Some work for various governments as assassins or spies, but most, Larkathal included, work for Villains, causing mayhem with their abilities. Working with Villains provides the perfect outlet for the demon's mischief.

And some of this mischief would soon befall Cyrus and his friends.

Chapter 15

FROM BAD TO WORSE

In which Several Bad Things happen at Night, and Reginald has a Vision

THE ENTIRE DAY elapsed with still no sign of Keeth. Frustrated, Reginald ordered that the Party make camp a bit farther to the north in a stand of trees. Cyrus set the tents up quickly and began cooking the small deer that Kris had caught. They made an excellent meal of it.

Dusk dropped on the land like a hawk on a rabbit. Everyone went to bed early, in preparation for leaving early the following morning. Reginald, Lydia, Cyrus, and Katana, all having years of practice, fell asleep instantly. Kris, on the other hand, found herself unable to sleep for the second night in a row. She rose from the grassy nest she had made and walked out to the edge of the trees.

The stars were shining brightly, just as they had the previous night. She stared at them for a moment, then, hearing something, whirled around. Cyrus stood at the edge of the treeline, floppy hat pulled over his eyes. "Oh, Cyrus! Couldn't sleep again?"

Cyrus shook his head. "Not really. I was thinking about some things about the last few days. You, in particular."

Kris blushed. Times like these made her glad she wasn't Human, with no fur to hide the red flush. "That's . . . nice. What were you thinking?"

Cyrus turned away. "It won't work."

"What won't work?"

"You and me. It won't happen. I don't know why you thought it would. I'm Human and you're not."

Kris started, heart sinking. "But . . . you . . . "

"Look, I can tell you like me," Cyrus said. "I've known for quite a while. But frankly, the thought disgusts me. Me, with an animal? Revolting."

Tears sprang to Kris's eyes. She ground her fangs. "What? Animal . . . You . . . Then why . . . ?"

Cyrus looked out at the rippling grass for a moment, then up at the stars. He scowled. "Oh, you know. Every Hero needs a cat-girl to fall in love with him so she can die heroically protecting him at some climactic moment." He pointed at her. "Now I've got one. But love? Never. Why did you think I was so glad to see Lydia? Finally, a real girl, one that I could have a future with. That's why I want her to join the party. I hoped that her appearance might give you a clue, but I guess not. How much longer are you going to string yourself along?"

Kris hissed in pain and anger, tears soaking the fur below her eyes. "Shut up! You led me on about the dress, about the stars, and everything?"

Cyrus shrugged. "I certainly meant nothing other than what I said. It's your fault if you took those episodes to mean more than they did."

Kris could think of nothing else to say. She slumped to the ground, weeping.

Cyrus sighed and walked back into the woods.

• • •

Reginald tossed and turned on his thin bedroll. Sleep had come, but was uneasy in its presence. A scene formed in his mind's eye as he slept.

He stood upon a frozen sea, atop unmoving waves
And on that water stood the Man, the Shining Man who Saves.
Surrounded by four colored flames, to Reginald did motion:
"O come with me
And you will see
The Secret of this Ocean."

The Man in White a Path did tread across the water's top
The Hero followed in His wake, with neither pause nor stop.
When stop they did, beheld the two a dark and ancient tower
And on its crest
Flew to their rest
The glowing Flames of Power.

"What means this dream?" the Hero cried,
"And why speak I in rhyme?"
But as response received no words but, "Now is not the time."
"Your journey now has purpose, for you and for this Land.
But do make haste
And no time waste
For My Return is Planned."

The waves resumed their movement, and dragged the Hero down
And in that raging ocean, he feared that he would drown.
"Fear not," rang voice through fearsome storm,
"For when a breath you take

> The Dream will End
> And You I Send
> To Quest when you Awake."

Reginald bolted upright, gasping. He looked around his tent as if for signs of the man he had seen in his dream. It had seemed so real. Like a Sign from the Creator himself . . .

Realization dawned on him: his Quest had just been Blessed.

He chuckled to himself and lay back down. His very own Blessed Quest. Now *that* was something he could gloat about when he got back to the Heroes' Guild. Rolling over, Reginald drifted back to sleep, a satisfied smile on his face.

Lydia crept across the forest loam, feeling dizzy but quite sure of herself. After all, the scaled blue man in her dream couldn't possibly have been wrong.

Cyrus was in love with her, and she knew it. Now she had to prove that she loved him too.

She made her way across the camp to Cyrus's tent and pulled the flap aside.

Cyrus stirred and blinked sleepily, peering at the obscured tent entrance. "Reg . . . ? It's not morning yet. What's—oof!" His sentence was abruptly shortened as Lydia fell on top of him, kissing him.

"I love you, Cyrus, I love you. Let's spend tonight together."

Cyrus, now fully awake, scrambled backward. "What's the matter with you, Lydia? What do you think you're doing?" he shouted. "Are you drunk or something?"

"No," Lydia murmured, tearing at the laces of her clothing. "I'm sober for the first time. Cyrus, take me into your arms!"

Kris wiped the tears from her eyes and stood up. Now she knew what to say to Cyrus. It had just taken her mind a few moments to recover from the shock. If she could talk to him now, everything would work out fine.

She padded into the woods toward the Heroes' campsite. There was movement in one of the tents. Perhaps Cyrus was still awake. All the better, then.

Wait, there were two people in the tent . . .

The Human female who had treated her so poorly was embracing Cyrus, stripping off her clothing as she did so.

The tears flooded back into her eyes. Kris spun and dashed off into the grasslands, sobbing as she ran.

With a beautiful woman tearing off her clothes and throwing herself at him, Cyrus did what any sensible young man in his position would do. He jumped out of his tent and yelled at the top of his lungs. "Reg! Something's wrong with Lydia!"

Well, what were *you* expecting him to do? Honestly.

Reginald came barreling out of his tent, sword drawn and shirt absent. "Where are you, lad?"

"By my tent!" Cyrus hollered back. "I think she's spelled or something!"

Katana, roused from his sleep by the shouting, rushed over to assist Cyrus. He attempted to pry Lydia off, without success.

Lydia was still attempting to tackle Cyrus to the ground. She was, after all, a Hero, and nearly matched Cyrus for strength. He succeeded in getting out of her grasp, but only by leaving his shirt in her hand. She reattached herself to his pant leg.

Upon arrival, Reginald grabbed Lydia by both shoulders and gently pulled her off, setting her down next to a skinny tree.

Lydia sat still for ten seconds, then shook her head violently and looked around. "Huh?" she mumbled. "What's going on?"

Reginald looked from Lydia to Cyrus, then back again. "I think you were under a spell. You seem to have attacked Cyrus, my girl. And, it appears, with . . . impure intentions."

Cyrus started putting his shirt back on. "I was asleep, minding my own business, and you came in my tent, and . . . um . . . got really friendly."

Reginald glared at Cyrus. "Cyrus Solburg, you didn't take advantage of her state, did you?"

Lydia looked up from retying the laces of her shirt and smiled. "Did you, Cyrus?"

Cyrus pulled the shirt the rest of the way on, revealing a startled face. "No! Of course not! C'mon, Reg! You taught me better than that!"

"I did indeed." Reginald turned to Lydia. "Now, tell me what you were doing, invading my squire's tent like that?"

"What are you implying?" Lydia demanded. "I am perfectly innocent of any wrongdoing!"

Katana stepped out from behind the tent, gently swishing a thin reed wand back and forth. "I don't detect any magic. What *were* you doing?"

"Mind your own business, furball!" Lydia yelled at him.

• • •

In the morning, with tempers high and egos bruised, the party began to pack up. It took Cyrus almost three whole minutes to notice the absence of Kris. "Katana?" he said. "Where's your sister?"

Katana looked around. "I've no idea. She was bedded down off in the grass just outside the woods over there. Go and wake her up, will you?"

Cyrus nodded and walked into the woods. He quickly found the grassy nest Kris had made, but she wasn't in it. Noticing feline footprints, he followed them to the edge of the woods. Reading the tracks, he saw that Kris's prints became intermixed with what looked like his own footprints, which was odd. Odder still, his prints seemed to transform into a set of strange prints the likes of which he'd never seen before.

Katana padded up behind him. "Where's Kris?"

"Look at these prints, Katana," Cyrus said, pointing out the tracks that looked like his. "It looks like I was standing here for a while, but I've never even been over here until right now. There's some strange prints that lead back a ways along the road, and they are mixed in with the ones that look like mine right here. Kris's tracks look fine until here. She seems to have sat down, then got up again, stepped into the woods, then run off in that direction." He looked up from the tracks and pointed southwest.

Katana sniffed the air. His nose wrinkled, and his eyes widened. "A shifter!" he said in alarm.

"Huh?" Cyrus said. "A shape-changer? What would— Oh, no!" He looked at Katana. "It must have copied one of us . . . No, it copied *me*, and maybe did something to her. *Orsobu pitchci* . . . And now she's run off!"

229

"It teleported in over there so I wouldn't sense the spell," Katana stated, pointing at the road, "then walked down here and— Where are you going?"

Cyrus ran back to camp, snatching up his chain shirt and longsword. He mounted Brisk and spurred her to a gallop.

"Cyrus!" Reginald shouted. "Catch!"

The Hero hefted something resembling a money pouch into the air. Cyrus caught it with his left hand on his way by. He shot out of the woods, nearly bowling Katana over, and galloped southwest.

"Wait!" Katana yelled, but Cyrus continued his mad dash down the path.

Reginald walked up beside Katana. "He's gone on a Spontaneous Quest of his own. He's becoming a Hero right before my eyes . . . "

"But my sister . . . "

"Don't worry about her. Cyrus will keep her safe. If he gets in trouble, he can call for help. Besides, I don't know if I should tell you this, but," Reginald leaned close to Katana, who swiveled an ear back. "I think he's taken with the lass."

Katana sighed. "I hadn't noticed . . . "

Chapter 16

DIVIDED AND CONQUERED

*In which the Party, now divided, Suffers Capture and
Betrayal, and Cyrus Does Something Inexplicable*

"WE ATTACK NOW."

Voshtyr picked up his falchion. It was an evil-looking blade, cut from a stone that seemed to absorb what little light filtered through the growing storm clouds above the keep's outer courtyard.

He swung the weapon to point straight up.

"The Dragon is removed. The Love Triangle has worked its magic. The Katheni are split, and the squire is no longer at the Hero's side. Today we extract our revenge! Take the Crimson Slash alive, if feasible. If not, kill him!"

A roar of assent came from the assembled Minions. The creatures—in service to Voshtyr, Sir Anthony, and Salvatia Malice—all wore black armor. They had discarded the generic chainmail and been issued new armor emblazoned with an emblem of a severed diabolical hand clutching a crystal.

Mingled among them were Henchmen, some magic-trained Toadies, and several other lesser Villains, too petty to have many Minions of their own, but each with some kind of grudge or blood feud against the Crimson Slash.

Doom was about to fall on Reginald and company.

Reginald and Lydia rode along the northern road while Katana scouted ahead, checking for sign of Kris, Cyrus, and Keeth. After two hours, they stopped at a crossroads. One road ran north toward the desert. The other headed northeast, where lay the fetid swamp.

Katana flopped down in the grass. "I'd like to take a quick breather if you don't mind, Crimson." He wasn't used to trying to keep up with horses for hours at a time. Good food and his scholarly lifestyle seemed to have decreased his tolerance for cross-country travel, he thought ruefully.

Reginald nodded. "There's naught to be in a hurry about," he said. "Besides, I thought we should first investigate the swamp. An abandoned keep lies at its center, an excellent place for a Villain to store pilfered goods undetected." He drew his titanic sword from its saddle-sheath and attached it to the back of his armor. "Besides, perhaps I might find a lead on the girl's treasure there. Perform two Quests at the same time, if you will."

Lydia dismounted. She retrieved a hairbrush from her saddlebag, then took a clip out of her hair and began brushing out her auburn locks.

Reginald opened his spyglass and looked northeast. "The Keep of Falling Stars. It is in far better shape than I had thought. Look how well repaired it is!" he said, offering the glass to Katana.

Katana waved it away. He was jotting down the frost-storm spell that Thomas Frostbite had inflicted on him, recording it in one of his heavy books. The curse of being a Cat Mage was that though he could learn how to use spells just by being struck with them, he couldn't remember more than ten at a time. Katana remedied this by purchasing spell-books and recording the most interesting ones he learned. He tried to keep fresh in his mind the ten spells he thought he might need at a moment's notice.

The fur on Katana's back and neck stood up. A large, area-effect spell was being cast less than seventy yards away. It bore all of the signatures of a *teleport* spell, but to be this large it would have to be carrying a small army . . .

"Reginald! Arm yourself!"

A moment later, the air exploded, and a large group of armed and armored people materialized almost on top of them. They were sixty strong, clad in black, and bore a banner with a Demon's hand clutching some kind of gemstone.

Reginald drew his gigantic sword and snatched his shield. "What ho? An ambush? Katana! Lydia, er, White Tiger! To me!"

It is interesting to note that for some reason, Villains tend to favor the color black. They seldom wear any other color, and this makes them rather noticeable. For example, a Hero can easily pick out the man who is wearing black armor and shoving his way through a crowd as a Villain, first because it is rude to shove, and second because he is wearing black.

The choice of black as a primary uniform color is a strange one. Black is not a particularly useful color, except for sneaking around at night and peering into the windows of unsuspecting people. Like white, it shows much of the dirt it collects on any given day. It absorbs and retains heat, making journeys in the spring or summer uncomfortable. Finally, it is almost useless as camouflage, as it shows up well against most backgrounds. Perhaps its only value is that of inspiring fear, since black is traditionally associated with death.

Black also hides bloodstains very well.

Reginald stared down the assembled mob of black-clad, armed people advancing on their position. "Hold! What business have you with the Crimson Slash?"

An imposing male Human in black armor and a helm with sweeping demon-horns pointed at Reginald. Green light glowed from inside the helm, making the man appear a ghost or phantom of a long-dead warrior. "We seek your life, Crimson Slash!" His voice was the type one would expect the statue of a long-dead king to use, should one come to life: sepulchral, powerful, and authoritative. "Our business is pain, our trade death! Prepare to Meet your Doom!"

"Oh, just Villains," Lydia said, sounding disappointed. "Standard combat greeting. So, are we going to take them on?"

Reginald stood rooted to the ground. That helm, those glowing eyes—it had to be . . . Suddenly he was back in Bryath Castle, five years ago, feeling the life drain from him as metal-clad fingers closed around his throat. Courageous as he was, Reginald suddenly wanted nothing more than to get away from the half-demon. But his Heroic sense got the better of his common sense, and he leveled his titanic sword at the Arch-Villain. "Voshtyr Demonkin!" he boomed. "I hope you enjoyed your stay in prison, for today you return!"

"I'll take that as a yes," Lydia said, running to her horse, swinging up onto it, and drawing her broadsword.

Katana yanked a large, leatherbound book from his satchel. "I'll provide magic support. Go!" he shouted, leafing through the pages.

Reginald leapt onto Wraith and spurred the charger toward the mob, catching up with Lydia almost immediately.

"The two Heroes charged the ranks of their foes, striking like twin thunderbolts, throwing Minions to both sides. The Hero's sword became a five-foot, shimmering arc of death, while the Heroine beside him fought like a Fury, slashing any who stood in her path!"

"Crimson! What in the Nine Torments are you doing?" Lydia demanded as she decapitated a foot soldier.

"Narrating!" Reginald shouted, grinning. "What is an epic battle with no narration?"

Lydia sighed and parried a vicious cut from a halberd. It took her some moments to defeat the foe in question, as he was a Villain and thus more skilled than his Minions, during which Reginald continued narrating.

The Heroine lost her patience. "Button it, Crimson!" she yelled. "This is a battle, not a poetry reading!"

Reginald shrugged, laying about him with his titanic blade, and continued his narration, though at a lower volume.

Three ranks in, a Toady in a pale green robe made two broad hand motions and pointed at Crimson's and White's mounts. It muttered something to the effect of *"Equus Trucida,"* and both horses fell to the ground, laid low by the unsporting *Slay Horse* spell.

The Crimson Slash launched himself from the falling Wraith and landed on his feet, bisecting a pale-skinned man holding a spiked club in the process. The White Tiger hit the ground rolling and came up with her sword-point through the creature in green.

"Back to back, White!" Reginald yelled. Lydia spun into a defensive position behind him. "Wave after wave of infantry washed over the Heroes, breaking and scattering beneath the fury of their blows."

Lydia gasped as a pole-axe caught her in the gut, her chain-mail just barely protecting her from lethal harm. "Crimson! Less talking, more fighting!" She lopped the head off the pole-axe, then planted her sword point into the wielder's eye.

"Despite their combat prowess, they still took wounds. White took a grievous blow from a pole-arm, and Crimson suffered a javelin to the shoulder." Reginald reached down to yank the offending javelin from his flesh. "And still they fought on."

Back on the hillock from which Reginald and Lydia had charged, Katana began weaving his paws in the motions for *Shield of Force*. If they were going in to fight thirty-to-one odds, they would need magical assistance. He had almost finished casting the strengthening spell, when someone grabbed him from behind.

Sharp teeth sunk into one side of his neck.

Katana broke free and spun around. He found himself facing a pale woman, blood dripping from her pointed teeth. "A vampirine!" he yelled, backing up. "No!"

The woman smiled. She pointed a hand at Katana, closing her fingers together. A ray resembling a spider web shot from her fingers, coating Katana in a sticky, rope-like substance.

He struggled to counterspell it, but the side of his neck throbbed painfully, rendering him unable to concentrate.

The woman stepped over the Katheni as he fell, making a sign over his eyelids. Katana suddenly became very sleepy.

He struggled to stay awake, but the lid of his consciousness slammed closed.

Reginald and Lydia were tiring and bleeding from multiple wounds, but were still more than holding their own.

Then the ranks ceased rushing them. The Minions, Henchmen, and lesser Villains backed away.

Reginald let the tip of his massive sword rest on the ground and he inspected the gash in his shoulder. "Prepare yourself, White Tiger," he said. "This pause is an ill omen, methinks."

Lydia tied a quick tourniquet around her leg. "Whatever, Crimson."

Three men stepped out of the black army: a very large man with a mace, a man of medium height with raven hair and a calm face, and the demon-helmed man with pointed ears and faintly glowing green eyes.

Reginald recognized Voshtyr and the one wielding the mace.

"Well, I thought this was certainly a cowardly act, sending an army to deal with three people. But I honestly expected more from you, Sir Anthony."

Sir Anthony shifted in his armor. "Listen, Crimson," he bellowed, "I'm just getting my revenge on you. But cowardice? Never! Merely proper planning on the part of Voshtyr, here."

Voshtyr stepped forward, his face now visible inside the darkness of his horrific horned helmet. "It's been over five years, Crimson. Remember?"

"I remember, you soul-stealing abomination," Reginald said, and spat on the ground in front of him.

The third man—of medium height and raven hair—drew his sword. "Time to taste defeat, Crimson. I, Serimal Voidstar, will defeat you on this very spot."

Lydia turned to Reginald, panic etched on her face. "You know these people, Crimson?"

"That I do," Reginald replied, turning his head. "They are Villains most foul. At one time or another, I have defeated all of them. Save for Serimal . . . I'm afraid I don't recognize him. Well, I've been a Hero long enough to make enemies I do not remember, I suppose. This whole attack must be to settle old grudges."

"Then this isn't my fight!" Lydia protested. "I have nothing to do with these people!" She began stepping away from Reginald.

Reginald grabbed Lydia's shoulder, staring into her eyes. "You aren't deserting me, are you? You are a Heroine! You couldn't possibly do something so cowardly!"

Lydia yanked herself free. "It isn't cowardice—it's self-preservation. If I die in your fight, I won't be able to fight my own."

"Justify it however you like. It still remains cowardice. So be it. If I survive, I will report you to the Brotherhood as Unfit for Hero Status." Reginald turned back to the Villains and hoisted his sword. "If you're leaving, then get out of my way."

Lydia stepped away from Reginald. "I'm . . . sorry, Crimson."

Reginald ignored her, switching his sword and shield to *Impossible Odds Position Omega*.

Lydia moved to exit the ring of Villains, but the burly Sir Anthony grabbed her as she tried to pass by him.

"Well, then, missy," he said with a leer, "you've two options now that you've deserted your friend. First, since you made our job a bit easier, you can join us. We won't make you kill him, but you will become a Villain and join us. Or you can die here." He lifted his enormous mace and placed one of its flanges on Lydia's forehead. "Which'll it be?"

Lydia looked down. "If I join you, will you promise not to kill him?"

"No," Voshtyr said offhandedly, his voice echoing inside his freakish helm. "I could promise, but I'd be breaking it as soon as we finished torturing him. On the other hand, we will promise not to kill *you*."

Lydia stared into Voshtyr's glowing eyes. "As a Villain, would I be allowed to still pursue my own goals?"

Reginald glanced between the two. Abandoning him was one thing. Voluntarily joining Villains was another matter entirely. "Don't do it, White! You can never trust a Villain. They will stab you in the back at the first opportunity!"

"Funny, I hold the same to be true about Heroes," Voshtyr said. "Except they stab you in the front. Now, stop your self-righteous blather. I've business to attend to." The half-demon turned his luminescent gaze back to Lydia. "As for your question, it depends on the goal, but in general, I'd say that you could. As long as it isn't something sappy and Heroic like 'the destruction of all Evil from within Evil's own ranks' or something inane like that."

"Then I'm in," Lydia said, sheathing her sword.

"Good. Welcome to the Brotherhood of the Black Hand." Anthony took Lydia's hand and kissed it. "I hope you enjoy your time with us."

Voshtyr turned to Serimal. "Take Crimson out, brother."

"Half-brother," Serimal muttered, and turned to the Crimson Slash.

Reginald was furious. That woman had betrayed him, and by so doing, had forsworn all her Heroic oaths. Now he faced a fight against over a score of assorted Minions and at least three

Greater Villains—not to mention Voshtyr Demonkin—all by himself. He straightened his shield and armor. If he was going to die here, he would go out in style, taking as many of them with him as he could.

This would go down in history as the Last Stand of the Crimson Slash.

Cyrus and Brisk pelted through the dense underbrush. He'd been riding search patterns in the forest nonstop since he'd lost Kris's trail, and now it had begun to rain. Fat, heavy drops began pounding down, drenching his floppy hat and penetrating his thin cotton shirt, soaking his skin and making his chainmail chafe under his armpits. But he hardly noticed the rain. He had to find Kris.

A bright flash of lightning illuminated the interior of the forest, and dense forest. Unlike the one they had traveled earlier, this place was unkempt, with fallen logs and dense brush everywhere. And it was dark as a tax collector's soul, save for when it was lit by the intermittent flashes from the storm.

Another flash of lightning. This time, for a moment, Cyrus thought he saw two figures in the woods, one Human-sized and one much, much larger. He urged Brisk through the dense brush toward what he had seen.

"Kris! Where are you?" Cyrus yelled.

Someone screamed, an inhuman, feline scream.

Cyrus's eyes widened. "*Kris!*" He spurred Brisk onward even faster.

The pony jumped a fallen tree trunk and Cyrus found himself in a small clearing containing a cave, a soaked Katheni girl, and the ugliest ogre Cyrus had ever seen.

• • •

"Well, what are you waiting for, Serimal?" Voshtyr yelled. "Attack!"

Reginald blinked. Wait, he *had* heard that name before. It was years and years ago, but he knew the name. But from where?

The man called Serimal strode forward and saluted Reginald with his sword. "Greetings, Crimson Slash. My name is Serimal Voidstar, as I said. I am Voshtyr's half-brother. You and I have met before, though I doubt you remember. You defeated me at the battle of the Three Streams. I was only a youth at the time, and you spared my life." He stepped into the light. "But I came away with this," he said, tracing the scar on his face and neck, "and I vowed revenge."

"Very well, Serimal," Reginald said. "Well met."

Voshtyr cursed. "Get on with it already."

Serimal charged Reginald, his sword coming down in a mighty arc. Blade rang off shield as Reginald parried the attack, countering with a sweeping blow of his five-foot sword.

"The Hero's sword slammed into the young, raven-haired Villain's breastplate, knocking him to his back ten feet away and nearly splitting the plate nearly in half!"

Serimal collected his wits and sat up. "What in the name of Strife are you doing narrating at a time like this?"

Reginald smiled grimly. "If I'm to die here, I may as well make a ballad of it while I do."

Serimal chuckled and got up. "You have a rare sense of humor, Hero. Sadly, your ballad dies with you." He rushed Reginald again, this time dodging the sweeping blow and throwing one of his own back at Reginald.

Anthony the Mace joined the battle suddenly, raining furious blows on the Hero's shield. Reginald staggered back and spun to parry yet another attack, this one by Voshtyr, who had come up from behind him and attempted to cut him across the back with a black falchion.

Cursing at being parried, Voshtyr twisted his left arm and a blade sprang out above his hand. He leapt at Reginald, only to get bashed with the shield and tossed away.

"The Crimson Slash stood alone against three treacherous Villains, each trying to outdo the other in unsportsmanlike attacks. The valiant Hero leapt into the air and flipped backward, gathering momentum, then slammed into the ground. A rippling shockwave sprang from the earth, knocking many of the remaining Minions off their feet!"

"Aha," Serimal said, "but the Hero had underestimated his opponents, who recovered more quickly than he had anticipated, and now stood behind the beleaguered Hero."

Reginald spun to face his opponents a moment too late. Sir Anthony slammed his mace into Reginald's chest, knocking him back twenty feet and making him trip over a fallen Minion.

"Ha! Getting a little slow in your old age, Crimson?" the brawny Villain taunted. "Better to give up now and save yourself the pain!"

Reginald spat blood and wiped it from his chin. "You dogs will Face Justice. In the meantime, Taste my Blade!" Reginald sprang up from the ground in a blur of red and steel. In the space of three seconds, he struck Anthony the Mace twenty-seven consecutive times, sending him sprawling in the grass. The Crimson Slash had delivered his signature *Blade of Fury* attack. Reginald was unable to finish with Anthony, for he was immediately attacked by Voshtyr and Serimal working in concert.

Serimal aimed a blow at Reginald's head, while Voshtyr scissored his legs with two blades.

"Crimson jumped, rolling in midair between the two attacks, landing on his feet and delivering a grievous blow to the side of Demonkin's falchion! The black blade exploded, and the dastardly erstwhile assassin was sent reeling!" Reginald bellowed, a triumphant smile on his face as he fought off three Villains, single-handedly.

"Someone shut that Hero up, *now!*" Voshtyr yelled as the shattered pieces of his falchion evaporated in a cloud of foul black smoke.

Pain shot through Reginald's body as an infantry pikeman stabbed him in the small of the back, just where his breastplate ended. He ceased his narration and whirled, sword first, decapitating the offending pikeman, slashing at Serimal on the return.

The young Villain jumped back, countering with a throwing-knife, which stuck in Reginald's shield, quivering slightly. Reginald advanced, bringing his blade down on Serimal.

Serimal braced his sword with his other hand and blocked the blow. Shards of metal went flying as Serimal's blade cracked. He threw it at Reginald, who swatted it away and lunged for the kill.

The air seemed to thicken, and Reginald felt his movements impeded. The world slowed down and turned unusual colors. He feebly blocked two blows from the newly risen Anthony the Mace, tripped, and fell down.

He had just enough time to notice the woman standing on the hill, staff pointed at him glowing in a myriad of colors, before Serimal's gauntleted fist slammed into his vision, and all the colors suddenly disappeared, replaced by silent blackness.

• • •

Lydia turned away. The Crimson Slash had fought well.

What if I had stayed? Would we have won? Could we have carried the day? No, it would have been the same, only I would be on the ground too and would now be subjected to unpleasant treatment. Fare well, Crimson. I will tell the ballad of your final battle to others, though I will never see you again . . .

She walked off into the grass, in the direction of the swamp.

"Cyrus!" Kris screamed. "*Help me!*"

The ogre grabbed Kris and pulled her from her hiding place between two rocks.

Cyrus yelled a battle cry and spurred Brisk into the clearing. As he passed the ogre, he hacked at its legs with his sword. It grunted, dropped Kris, and turned to face Cyrus.

The creature's beady eyes glowed with anger and hunger. It was an ugly beast, well over twelve feet tall, its begrimed green skin covered with warts and scars. Its snout twitched constantly, the two pig-like nostrils sniffing at its prospective prey. The rain pelted its hide, making the monster glisten like a frog on a sunny day.

Cyrus felt rage rising inside him. "*Don't touch her!*" He swung his blade at the monster.

In mid-swing, the sword caught on fire.

Surprised by the flames, the ogre put a hand up to block the light, leaving his side wide open. The sword bit deep into the ogre's tough hide, lighting it on fire. It howled in pain and swung its huge club at Cyrus.

Full of wrath, Cyrus swung his own weapon to parry the club. The club exploded in a flash of sparks and ash. Cyrus eyes widened. He looked at his hands.

He was still not wearing his gloves.

In fact, they weren't even in his pocket. They weren't even in his saddlebag.

The ogre took advantage of Cyrus's momentary distraction, kicking him off Brisk and across the clearing into a tree. Cyrus emitted a gasp of pain and slid to the ground. Brisk whinnied in fear and bolted into the forest.

Kris leapt to Cyrus's defense. She jumped onto the creature's neck, biting it and raking it with her hind feet.

The ogre was quite put out. It staggered backward, reaching for Kris. The rain made the ground slick for them all.

Kris dropped off and sprinted across the clearing to where Cyrus lay. "Get up! It's coming back!"

Cyrus stood and picked up his guttering sword. "Stay back, Kris. I don't want you to get hurt."

"But you—"

"Just stay back. I'll take care of this."

Cyrus placed himself between Kris and the advancing ogre. It lumbered close and swatted at him, but he jumped over the huge hand and brought his sword down on its head, staggering it. He pointed at the ogre with his palm. "Burn and die, *saf kopek!*"

A beam of flames thicker than Cyrus's arm shot from his palm, splashing over the ogre in wave after wave of white fire.

It gargled as it charcoaled, despite the cloudburst. Then it slumped over, dead.

Cyrus sank to one knee, dropping his cherry-red sword, which had become uncomfortably warm. The rain quickly put the fires out and hissed against Cyrus's superheated blade.

Kris ran up to Cyrus and knelt by his side. "Are you all right? What was that fire? Where are you hurt?"

Cyrus slowly got up, looking incredulously at the ogre's smoking corpse. Finally he placed a hand on Kris's shoulder and looked into her eyes. "I'm fine, Kris. I'm more worried about you."

Tears sprang to Kris's eyes, adding more dampness to the heavy rain. "Do you actually care, or are you pretending again?"

"Pretending? I've always been honest with you, Kris. What do you . . . Oh." Cyrus put the last piece of the puzzle where it went. "That wasn't me, Kris. It was a shape-shifter. Whatever it said, it was wrong."

Kris swallowed. "A . . . what?"

"A shifter. I found its tracks with yours over by the edge of the trees. They looked just like mine, but then they turned into something strange. I thought a shifter must've appeared to you, looking like me, and said something that made you run off."

Kris blinked at him. "Really?"

Cyrus nodded. "I'm sorry if it hurt you. I would *never* do anything to hurt you, Kris. Now, let's get out of this rain. I think this cave could serve as a shel—*Oof!*"

Kris pounced on him and buried her head in his chest, weeping tears of joy.

They walked together into the cave, and the rain continued to pound down.

Chapter 17

RECONCILIATION AND RETRIBUTION

In which Cyrus and Kris Reunite and Learn of the Fate of their Companions

"COME ON IN, Brisk."

Cyrus led his bedraggled horse into the cave and led her behind the small fire he had started in the cave's mouth. He looked over at Kris, who was huddled next to the fire. She was shivering miserably. Her green shorts and top had turned darker from being waterlogged. Cyrus pulled an armful of blankets from Brisk's saddlebags and brought them to Kris.

"Here, Kris. Let me dry you off. You must be miserable with your fur all wet like that."

"No, I'm fine," she said, then suddenly sneezed. "Well, if you think so . . . "

Cyrus grabbed the smaller of the blankets and began rubbing Kris's shoulders, wiping away the water and restoring circulation.

The cave was, with the exception of the various partially eaten Human and animal corpses against the far wall, quite a nice place, Cyrus thought. The fire threw some creepy shadows from the stalactites, sure, but it was warming up nicely and had proven satisfactorily waterproof.

Kris received his ministrations a moment, then removed her top.

He all but fell over. "Hey, wait! What are you doing?"

She looked at him. "I'm a Katheni, silly. Fur is natural clothing. We usually only wear clothing when we're around Humans. Or because we have a beautiful outfit." She pulled her knees up to her chest and bent forward. "Humans are the only race born without any natural covering, and they just can't seem to handle it when any other race isn't wearing an artificial covering." She shrugged. "It's usually easier to just put something on than to explain it. But right now, this thing is just in the way. So," she said, looking at his blanket, "are you going to finish?"

Cyrus knew his face had flushed deeply. He took a deep breath. She'd just said it was okay. *It's not really improper for a Katheni, I guess, so* stop *with the blushing already.* He continued to rub Kris down.

Then something odd happened.

"Kris? Are you . . . purring?"

"Mmm. Mrr? What?" Kris looked back at Cyrus. "Was I what?"

"Purring like a house cat. Do you do that often?"

Kris giggled. "Only when I'm having lots of fun."

"Well, then." Cyrus shifted the blanket and began rubbing Kris's head and ears. Her ears, he noticed, had small spots on them too. Kris's purr filled the cave with its warm, mellow sound. Cyrus did a thorough job.

When he finished, he took off his shirt and Kris rubbed him down. He drew the line at the pants, though. Kris giggled again.

Once the fire was blazing with a cheerful fury, Cyrus stepped outside for a moment. He sliced a couple of chunks of meat from the ogre. He didn't eat monsters, as a rule, but this one was already cooked and readily available. Finally finding some that wasn't too scorched, he cut it off and walked back into the cave.

In his absence, Kris had taken out the last three blankets from Brisk's saddlebags and laid them out as beds and covers. The blankets sat near the fire, folded in half for extra padding.

"Here," Cyrus said, offering Kris an ogre steak. "It's a little overdone. I guess I still need some work on that blast furnace impression of mine."

Kris took the questionable grey meat and ripped a piece off it with her sharp teeth. "Mmm. Interesting." She licked her lips, then licked again.

"Greasy?" Cyrus asked.

Kris nodded. She swallowed the piece and looked curiously at him. "About the fire . . . how did you do that? I thought you didn't do magic."

Cyrus shrugged. "I don't. Ever. Reginald says that the first thing about being a Hero is knowing that there are times for magic and there are times for might. And the other first thing is that a blade beats a fireball at close range." He sat down next to Kris and leaned back against a stalagmite. "He's not terribly fond of magic, so I never learned any."

"So what was that, then?"

Cyrus looked out into the pouring rain. It was getting dark again. He'd spent the entire day searching for Kris, and when he'd found her he'd done something that disturbed him. "Could have been magic, I guess. Like I said, I don't know how to use it."

"Maybe my brother could tell you," Kris said. She scooted closer and leaned her speckled head on his shoulder. "He started accidentally doing magic at the age of four. Scared our father to no end." She smiled as she chewed on the meat. "This really isn't bad, for monster. I've never eaten ogre before. Try it."

Cyrus took a bite of his own piece. It was very greasy, rubbery, and tasted like a cross between nutmeg and curry. It was strange, but not inedible. "Mmm."

"That's what I thought," Kris said, nodding.

"Doesn't help that I'm smelling wet pony at the same time," Cyrus said with a chuckle.

They finished their meat in silence, listening to the rain beat on the ground outside. When he finished, Cyrus picked up one of the folded blankets and moved it to the other side of the fire.

Kris picked hers up and moved it as well, putting it down right next to Cyrus's. She looked at him as if daring him to tell her to move it.

Cyrus didn't. He just lay down on his blanket and stared at the fire.

Kris threw the third blanket over the two of them and lay down next to him. She snuggled up, purring gently.

Cyurs smiled. Kris smelled faintly of almonds and dried hay. He put his arm around her as he pulled the other blanket on top of them. Kris's tail curled itself around Cyrus's left leg, and her head rested on his shoulder. Both content with the arrangement, they stared at the fire until they dozed off.

● ● ●

They woke early the next morning. Cyrus, not entirely sure how Kris would take it, experimentally scratched her behind one of her ears. She sighed happily and stretched.

"Good morning, Kris," Cyrus said. "Time to get going, I think. The rain's stopped."

He got up and stepped out of the cave into the chilly morning air. He shivered momentarily, then was suddenly warmed by the Katheni girl's furred form pressing against his back.

"Here," she said, extending one arm from behind him, holding his shirt. "You forgot your fur."

Cyrus smiled. He'd been awake only two minutes and it was already a great day.

They were soon on their way. Cyrus walked, letting Kris ride Brisk. The pony had bucked and snorted a bit as the Katheni mounted, probably uncomfortable with having a predatory feline riding on her. But she was well trained and carried her burden without further complaint.

They arrived at the crossroads in the early afternoon. Kris happily munched a piece of Keeth's jerky while Cyrus examined the plethora of footprints, small piles of ichor-soaked black clothing, and hacked-up bits of equipment.

He returned, not at all happy with the results of his study. "Kris," he said, "something bad has happened to Reg and your brother."

Kris stopped eating and looked at the apprentice Hero. "What do you mean?"

"It looks like they were attacked by a large group of people. Your brother's prints are over there, but it looks like he hit the ground pretty hard at some point. I really can't tell exactly what went on because of the rain, but it looks like there was quite a battle.

He picked up a slimed black garment. "This is what's left when you've killed a Minion and then left it out in the rain. They biodegrade pretty quick once they're dead. And there's easily forty or so piles scattered about here. It must have been a pretty big fight. I don't see Lydia's prints anywhere, and if Reg had won he would still be here waiting . . . "

"So they . . . They were . . . ?"

"No, I don't think so," Cyrus quickly amended. "It looks like the fight ranged all over here, then what was left of the group left, headed . . . northeast. Looks like that's where I'm headed." He looked at Kris. "You were headed north*west*, though, right?"

She shook her head. "Not anymore. I'm going with you. I can't just leave my brother!"

Cyrus nodded. "Right. Let's get going, then."

"What do you mean, you couldn't find the squire?" Serimal yelled. "He's probably still alive, and if the Katheni girl survived they're more than likely to assault the Keep! Don't you remember what happened to Venmar Crystalline? Is that what you want, Voshtyr?"

In the banquet hall in which he stood and Voshtyr lounged, a celebratory feast was already well underway. Carpet runners decked the floor on either side of the large central table. The eating couches were all cleaned and set around the table and occupied by assorted Villains as they stuffed their bellies with roast boar, partridge, and venison. Incense burned in the braziers at either end of the room, adding a vaguely fruity smoke to the smells of roasted meat and overpriced colognes. The Villains feasted in style.

"Please, brother, you're spoiling my flawless victory. Here, have some wine." Voshtyr gestured toward a decanter on the table.

He's too prideful and lazy to pour some for his brother, Serimal thought. Half-brother, he corrected himself. He gave Voshtyr a disgusted look. Pride and laziness—he'd acquired those personality traits from their late father, along with a love of the good life.

Serimal had none of those failings.

For example, Serimal's decorating scheme had been sparse and functional before Voshtyr's arrival. Now, gone were the simple hardwood chairs, replaced with luxurious, gold-trimmed eating couches. Tapestries, statuary, and paintings in the room made it seem warmer and less drafty, yes, but also betrayed Voshtyr's love of decadence.

"Relax, brother," Voshtyr said. "We have Crimson in our grasp, and this fortress is well defended. We have more than enough Henchmen, Minions, and lesser Villains here should anything happen." He gestured behind him, toward the hall full of feasting Villains and soldiers, celebrating their defeat of the Crimson Slash. "If you need to calm your mind, go ahead and check castle security."

"I will," Serimal said, "because I think you're foolish to rejoice so soon. Squires have a nasty tendency to show up at just the wrong time and rescue their masters. As you said, this squire has already done it once."

Voshtyr snorted. "While you have a point, I'm not particularly concerned. Since *you* apparently are, find something constructive to do about it instead of bothering me."

Serimal turned on his heel and began to leave. He stopped briefly to turn the heel back off, and walked out of the room.

Immediately through the large doors he grabbed a passing Minion. "Listen, I want all the gates and windows shut and fortified, all ventilation shafts big enough to crawl through sealed off, and every secret passage lethally booby-trapped. Understand?"

The Minion nodded and ran off down the corridor.

You are too cocky, Voshtyr, Serimal thought. *If you even once bothered listening to me, we would have fewer problems.*

Reginald slowly regained consciousness, then quickly wished he hadn't. Every muscle in his body screamed in pain, and his head ached from all the screaming.

He was manacled to some sort of table. He twisted his head around to get a glimpse of his surroundings. He was locked in a cage in the back corner of a small, noisome dungeon. It couldn't have been more than a thousand square feet, total. There were perhaps six cells like his crammed against the walls, with rusted iron bars. Given the state of the bars, he could easily have broken right out if he wasn't chained to the table.

Water dripped from miniscule cracks in the ceiling, breeding mold and slime across the rough stone floor and walls. The only illumination sprang from guttering torches at the entryway and inside Reginald's cage.

"Hello, Reginald," echoed a deep, melancholy voice from across the dungeon. "Woke up, I see. Well, you'll soon regret it."

Reginald knew that voice. "Keeth!"

He swiveled his head looking for his draconic friend. He finally spotted Keeth. The Dragon occupied a larger, glowing cage across the room from Reginald's cell.

"Well! You are a sight for sore eyes, Keeth! So you were captured too . . . " Reginald craned his neck in a fruitless attempt to see more of the room.

Keeth sounded tired. "I don't know why they're keeping you alive. For unpleasant purposes, I would think. They're using me for . . . ingredients."

Reginald stared at Keeth. "What do you mean? They haven't . . . ?"

The Dragon slowly shook his scaled head. "No, they haven't cut anything off yet, but they have taken a few scales and two or three pints of blood. I think their idea is that the longer they keep me alive, the fresher the ingredients will be when they need to . . . harvest them."

"The fiends!" Reginald said, clenching his fists. "Is there nothing so low that they won't stoop to it?"

"I doubt it," Keeth said, shifting his weight. "They *are* Villains, after all."

Cyrus and Kris stood looking at the massive keep that lay at the center of the swamp.

It was an impressive structure, with large, thick, turreted walls. An unfinished tower in the center soared above the rest of the edifice. Despite its position in the midst of the large, fetid swamp, the keep appeared well maintained. The gates were freshly assembled, no moss or slime stained the misty grey walls, and even the siege ballistae looked to be in fearsome working order. As if the defenses of the keep itself were not enough, over a thousand Ransha surrounded it as yet another obstacle.

• • •

Ransha are the second-least Human-looking of the Nine Races. The only similarity lies in the placement of head and limbs in relation to the torso, and the general shape of the torso itself. There, all resemblance ends.

Ransha have broad, wedge-shaped heads dominated by a mouthful of fangs that almost put sharks to shame. Their eyes are most often pale colors and are protected by transparent scales.

There are two distinct breeds of these curious lizard-folk: the swamp-dwelling hunter/gatherers of Centra Mundi and Lorimar, and the coastal ocean-fishers that live scattered around the beaches of all continents, save Novania, which is too frigid for the cold-blooded reptiles. The only differences between the two are that the saltwater Ransha have webbing between their toes and lack hind claws, while the landlocked lizards lack gills but can walk on dry land with much greater ease.

Nor is their physique very Human. None of the vital organs are where you would expect, and their musculature is entirely different, including special muscles designed for grace and speed while swimming, and for their heavy tails, which narrow out to a point for swamp-dwelling Ransha, and terminate in a flared fin for their oceanic cousins.

But above all, the Ransha's greatest strength lies in his scales. The scales of an adult Ransha rival or surpass those of Dragons when comparing toughness and impenetrability, while still remaining supple and flexible. Thus the hardy lizard-folk are more than a little difficult to kill, as a common weapon is of limited use against them. Fortunately for the other Races, most Ransha are uninterested in conquest and tend to stay in their native areas, revering the elderly and their ancestors.

However, due to their beliefs in spirits and deified ances-tors, any Villain with a few basic necromantic spells can dupe large numbers of Ransha into serving him or her. A mere dis-play of a zombie is often enough to terrify them into believing anything the Villain has to say.

And when your keep is protected by over a thousand Ransha, you must have had a good deal to say indeed.

Cyrus sighed and pocketed his spyglass. "I don't think we'll be able to get in by ourselves, Kris. We'll need some backup."

"I can't help there," Kris said. "My relatives are still a hun-dred and fifty leagues away, and they're desert dwellers. They would not enjoy the environment here. Neither do I, for that matter." Kris shook her leg absently, trying to rid her foot-paw of some swampy slime.

Cyrus smiled. "We'll get out of here as soon as possi-ble. We just need to rescue our companions, slay the people responsible for their capture, and get out of this smelly place." He began digging through the pouch Reginald had tossed him earlier. "Anyway, I think I can solve our problem."

"Really? How? What are those?" Kris asked, attempting to see what Cyrus was doing.

"This here is Reg's collection of *Tokens of Summoning*," Cyrus explained. "He threw these to me when I rode off to find you. They're like magical business cards. Every profes-sional Hero has a few of these to give to his friends and allies. Then, they can use them to send him messages or summon him to his aid. They're quite handy, but I can't remember which of these would be best to use."

There were indeed quite a few to choose from. They were small disks of silver with etched, painted emblems on each.

Like coins, but larger. There were all kinds of emblems, from a green bird of prey, to a purple suit of armor, to a plain token with a simple, dark grey square on it.

"Who's this, Cyrus?" Kris asked, picking up the last one and looking at it.

"Hmm?" Cyrus glanced at the token the Katheni girl had chosen. "Oh, that's the Solid Wall, an old friend of Reg's. Wow, haven't seen him in a long time. I wonder if he's still alive? Wait a minute . . . " he stared at the token. "I think he's experienced at both *Castle Storming* and *Swamp Warfare*. He'd be perfect! Thanks, Kris!"

He took the token from Kris's paw, pressed the emblem gently, and stared at it.

"Just one Hero?" Kris said, frowning. "But you have dozens of those tokens in that bag!"

Cyrus smirked. "Oh, trust me. This one is all we need."

The grey square faded, replaced by the floating, translucent image of a man sitting at a desk.

The man turned to face Cyrus. "Who calls the Solid Wall?"

"My name is Cyrus Solburg, squire of the Crimson Slash. We are in need of your aid. My master has been captured by Villains, and I cannot by myself assault the Keep in which he is held."

"Sir Ogleby? I haven't seen him in years! Hmm. Very well. Stand by—I shall be with you in but a moment." The image faded.

A minute later, a sandstone door sprang into existence next to them. A huge man opened it and stepped out.

He was larger than Reginald, almost seven feet tall, with enormously broad shoulders. His hair was sandy-blond, and his grey eyes had a world-weary look to them. The handle of a large and complicated-looking crossbow poked up from behind his right shoulder. The Hero wore no apparent armor. Instead, he wore a leather jacket with several pockets, the shoulder of which bore a plain device resembling a sheet of metal.

"Greetings, Cyrus Solburg," the man said as the door disappeared behind him. "I remember you from when you were but a callow youth. You have grown much since we last met, both physically and in aspects Heroic."

"My thanks, Solid Wall," Cyrus returned. "This is Kris," he said, gesturing to Kris, "a Katheni of Mir."

Kris performed her half-curtsey.

"She and her brother traveled with us," Cyrus said, "but we believe he also has been captured. We request your aid in the rescue of my master and Kris's brother, along with a green Dragon who has been caught up in this. One Keeth, son of Barinol."

"A son of Barinol, you say?" the man mused. "I fought Barinol son of Kisanth once, and a mighty foe he was. I would be honored to free his son as well. To save a friend, a noncombatant, and the son of a worthy foe all at once? A worthy Quest indeed. I shall help you. Where is the main gate?"

"I don't think the main gate is a good idea, sir," Cyrus warned. "They have over a thousand Ransha outside it, and there are bound to be traps."

"I can handle any force the Ransha can throw at me," the Solid Wall said, pulling on a pair of studded, fingerless leather gloves and drawing his sword from its sheath at his left side. "If you feel like being subtle, you can try to sneak in a different way while I make a distraction out front."

"All right," Cyrus said. "We'll attempt to find a back door. Good luck, Solid. And thank you."

"The same to you, young man. Take care of the Katheni girl," he said, looking at Kris. "You wouldn't want beauty like hers damaged."

Kris dipped her head, shyly acknowledging the compliment.

"Oh, don't worry about that," Cyrus said, looking at Kris. "Her safety is more important to me than my own."

Reginald spat blood, intentionally hitting the pale yellow cloak that Roger Farella was wearing.

The Araquellus scowled and tried to wipe the pink spittle off before it could stain the garment. Sir Anthony punched another of Reginald's ribs—and it caused the same wet, cracking noise as before. Reginald's cheek twitched, but he allowed no emotion to show on his face. Voshtyr was here too, as were Serimal and a woman Reginald didn't recognize. The dungeon now seemed crowded with so many people in it.

Reginald saw Keeth watching silently from his cell. The Dragon had bellowed in protest the first few times Anthony had struck Reginald, but Voshtyr had silenced him with an extremely overpowered *Shut Up* spell, and Keeth could do nothing but watch.

"Had enough yet?" Anthony leered. "I could do this all day. It's too bad you have only a limited number of ribs."

Reginald coughed. "Go ahead and hit a defenseless man again, *kopek*. See if it makes you any stronger."

Fury built rapidly in the large man's face. Anthony slammed his meaty fist into Reginald's face twice before Voshtyr yanked him off.

"Stop that," Voshtyr said with a growl. "He's trying to make you kill him quickly. Let the pain sink in for a while, and then we'll see if he's still so brave." He turned to Reginald. "Now, you of course know why you're being punished. You've inflicted much pain and difficulty on each one of us here. We're merely paying you back."

Reginald began to laugh, wincing from the pain. He rolled his head to look at Voshtyr. "You poor, motherless half-breed. You deserved everything you got. You just can't stand justice, that's all. It's useless, by the way. You cannot break me, no matter how you try. If you kill me, I'll laugh all the way to Paradise, and laugh even harder when I see you fall into the Abyss."

Voshtyr's eyes began turning red. "What did you say about my mother?"

Reginald looked into Voshtyr's reddening eyes, unflinching. "You're a misbegotten *pic*. No one even knows for sure who your mother is. Do you?" He feigned an innocent smile.

Voshtyr snapped, plunging his hand into Reginald's chest as he had done to Frostbite. Reginald struggled wildly as the Villain pulled a transparent version of Reginald out into the air.

Voshtyr spoke, his thunderous voice comprehensible to Reginald alone. *"Listen to me, Crimson Slash. I have killed your squire and your pet cats, I will use your Dragon for spare parts, and I hold the key to infernal torments you have never in your worst nightmares dreamed. Now sleep, and dream of demons!"*

Voshtyr slammed the clear Reginald back into the flesh one. Reginald gasped and passed out.

Voshtyr turned and stormed from the room, Roger and Anthony following in his wake.

When they had gone, Serimal stepped forward, Nieva at his side. "I'm sorry, Crimson Slash. My quarrel with you did not merit such things. May you rest peacefully for now." He pressed his hand onto Reginald's forehead, and a pale white glow spread across Reginald's visage.

Serimal turned and faced Nieva. "Let's go. You shouldn't come next time. It won't be pretty."

Nieva embraced Serimal. "I know. But if you are here, I should be too." Serimal started to protest, but she placed a slender finger over his lips. "I do not wish to argue about it. But you are right. We should leave now."

Serimal nodded, and the two left the room, arms around each other.

Chapter 18

TRIAL BY COMBAT

In which the Battle is Joined and Rescue is Attempted

THE SOLID WALL yanked his sword free of the recently departed Ransha and interposed a barely visible wall of force between him and the incoming javelins. They smashed into it, splintering harmlessly.

The corpses of several Ransha lay floating in the swamp, tainting the dark waters red. The intermittently solid ground was littered with destroyed javelins, cleft leather shields, and shattered swords. Many reeds and cattails, once tall swaying plants, were much shorter now, reduced by the swings of a razor-sharp sword.

The javelin throwers turned their scaled tails and ran. The Hero had slain just over a dozen of them, most likely a heavy patrol of some kind, without even breaking a sweat.

Turner Von Kamish, known far and even wide as the Solid Wall, sighed and pulled a large crossbow from its holster on his back. This crossbow had been custom-made by a wizard friend of his and was enchanted to always cock itself immediately after firing. He flipped up the range-finder and inserted a ten-bolt magazine. He locked the magazine in, then found his targets.

Within two seconds and four pulls of the crossbow's trigger, all but one of the Ransha measured their lengths upon the ground. The last one kept running, headed for the keep.

Good, thought the Solid Wall. Now the real fun will begin.

"Every single decent-size shaft or passageway I've found so far has been blocked off or lethally booby-trapped," Cyrus complained. "It's like they're normal people who actually think, instead of typical Villains!"

He and Kris stood outside the back wall of the keep, searching for a way in. The walls and tower soared above their heads, the grey walls thick and impenetrable. Around the base the walls were crusted with mud from the foul-smelling waters surrounding the keep. The air smelled like someone had taken a head of lettuce and boiled it with some overused socks for several hours. The ground, when solid, squished beneath their feet with the slimy feel of decomposing vegetation. And every step let out a disturbing squishing sound that made Kris cringe.

Kris paused in her search of the wall. "Well, we didn't try that door we found a minute ago . . . "

Cyrus looked back at the door. "True, but it's too obvious. The rescue party must *never* get in the back door undetected. They either find a secret way in or walk in the front door and are captured."

"That's a stupid rule," Kris said, bending down to examine a slight crack in the wall. "Why not just go in? If they expect you to find a secret way in, maybe they overlooked the actual back door!"

Cyrus grinned. "You might be right." He walked up onto the small slab of stone that the door let out onto. He focused on his sword blade. If I can just remember how I got this thing to catch on fire, I can do it again, he thought. Cyrus imagined his sword catching fire, but nothing happened. Frustrated, he slammed the door with his boot.

As it turned out, no one had attempted to actually *use* the back door for nearly three hundred years, and it was lacking in basic maintenance requirements. When Cyrus kicked it, the rotten door practically exploded, disintegrating into mushy fragments and falling backward into the keep.

Kris looked at Cyrus with an *I told you so* expression on her furred face.

Cyrus grinned back. "Well then. Forget subtlety. Let's get moving!"

Among all unusual liquids, the blood of a Dragon stands out as noteworthy. Although it has no special chemical properties—excepting a *very* high boiling point—it abounds in fascinating magical properties.

Since Dragons are magical creatures, their blood contains an incredible amount of raw magic. When distilled, it can be used to cure impossible diseases, temporarily bestow Hero-level powers on a normal person, or empower spells of immense magnitude. Villains use this power for more dire purposes, from slaying entire villages to summoning demons.

An interesting side-effect of using a Dragon's blood arises from the fact that the magic is sympathetic. Sympathetic magic is a certain type of magic that relies on the strong connections between different pieces of the same thing. For example, if someone cast a spell on a toenail clipping, making it dance around, the foot from which it was clipped would begin dancing also.

Thus, if you drain a sufficient quantity of blood from a Dragon, and the Dragon lives, it can feel whatever you do to the blood.

Keeth howled and slammed his back into the wall, again and again.

"Cease, son of Barinol!" Reginald cried. "You'll hurt yourself even more!"

Keeth moaned and fell over on his side. "I . . . can take no more. I'm sorry, Crimson. It's . . . so . . . cold . . . "

Reginald knew that someone was doing something nasty to the blood they had drained from Keeth. The poor Dragon could feel things that weren't there, and he was in dire pain.

Keeth shuddered and lay still, breathing shallowly. Reginald strained against the manacles, wincing from the pain in his ribs. He was furious. His friend and companion was being killed before his eyes, and there was nothing he could do to stop it.

"What do you mean 'another Hero'?" Voshtyr yelled.

The lone surviving Ransha scout gulped. Today was not going well. First, the fish he'd been going to eat for breakfast had been stolen. Next, he had accidentally torn the garment of a tribe elder while walking by. Finally, a Hero had massacred his unit.

"Another Hero," the Ransha rasped. "It killed my cohort. It usess wallss of forsss to fight. Our weaponss broke againsst itss shieldss, and it killed uss without merssssy."

Voshtyr put down the glass of wine he'd been drinking. "The Solid Wall? How did he find out that I have the Crimson Slash?"

"You'll have to kill the lizard now," Sir Anthony said from his place at the table, his bass voice coming around either side of an enormous, half-devoured roast pig on the dining-hall's main table.

The Ransha hissed and cringed backward.

"I what?" Voshtyr said, glancing at the cowering lizard-man and then at the other Villain. "What in the Nine Hells would I want to do that for?"

"Come now, my Lord. Surely you know the rules." Anthony shrugged. "It's traditional to slay the bearer of bad news."

Voshtyr stared at the Mace as if the brawny Villain had just sprouted a second head, one with fewer brains in it than the original. "What an incredibly inane tradition. If I were to do that, no one would dare bring me important information such as early warning of unexpected visits from Heroes!"

"Listen, Voshtyr. What's a little information compared to the feeling of complete and total superiority? Shall I lend you my mace?"

"No," Voshtyr said flatly. "The difference is between keeping my ego bloated and my skin unperforated. I will *not* slay a Minion for bringing bad news. Now," he said, turning to the Ransha, "muster all the Ransha in the area. I will send reinforcements shortly."

The Ransha bent his neck and placed a claw over his heart. Then he turned and scampered from the room, glad to have escaped with his scaled life, and began thinking seriously about retiring from the Swamp Scout position and taking up selling life insurance instead.

"Incredibly loyal, those creatures. Incredibly stupid, but loyal," Voshtyr noted. "Sir Anthony! Get off your posterior and help our lizard friends kill that Hero."

Sir Anthony wiped his mouth and belched. "I'd rather not. I'm enjoying this feast!" he said. He certainly was enjoying it, if the wreckage of many different dishes, the stains on his shirt, and the collateral damage to the furniture were any indication.

Voshtyr glared at him. "It wasn't a request, Anthony."

Sir Anthony grumbled and reached for his helmet.

Kris and Cyrus dashed down the narrow stone corridors, footsteps echoing in the nearly deserted keep. Some rooms of the keep looked as if they had not been used in centuries. Others had torches burning in wall sconces and tapestries on the walls. They ignored the abandoned rooms. They had to find Reginald and Katana before anyone noticed the hole where the back door used to be. While the distraction provided by the Solid Wall was most excellent, someone was bound to feel a draft sooner or later.

Kris halted abruptly and ducked into the corner of an open doorway, dragging Cyrus along with her.

"Hey!" Cyrus protested. "What are you—"

"Hst! Someone's coming!" Kris clapped a hand over Cyrus's face.

Moments later, Cyrus heard the clanging footsteps of armored soldiers running down the hallway they'd just been sneaking through. Several men stepped in front of the arch they'd just ducked through. Kris shrank back further into the corner, but Cyrus peeked out to get a better view.

"You three, take the west wing, and I'll take the east," said a greasy-looking young man as he strode down the hall-way. He wore a tailored black uniform with decorations of some sort on the front. Several Minions followed him about and promptly followed his orders, spreading out to cover various side halls.

"Wait, Tyler," a second man said, this one with raven-black hair. "I haven't thanked you for your help on this yet. So . . . thank you."

The younger man chuckled. "Hey, I don't want to get stabbed in the back by unexpected visitors, either. Hard to succeed in your evil plans when you've got six inches of sword protruding from your guts. I got demerit badges in Murder, not Pincushion."

"Indeed. Well, I'll take these two and check the back door," said the second man. "No one's used it in centuries, but it can't hurt to check. Besides, I think I feel a draft."

"And I'll get the top of the perimeter wall. The Minions can sweep the halls and passageways. Meet you in the dining room in fifteen, Serimal." The younger man started to turn and walk away, but the dark-haired man stopped him.

"Tyler . . ." the man named Serimal said, hesitating. "Don't tell Voshtyr I asked, but don't you think he's being a bit erratic? He's wavering back and forth between overcon-fidence, true Villainy, and utter Evil. Doesn't that seem a little . . ."

"A little like an Arch-Villain?" the man named Tyler replied with a smile. "Relax, Serimal. He may be psychotic and temperamental. He may be unpredictable. But that's exactly what Arch-Villains are supposed to be like. Everyone dreams of conquering the world. Only the truly insane ever do it."

Serimal sighed. "True enough. As long as he doesn't get us all killed in the process. Farewell, Tyler."

The two men split up, each with a group of Minions, and moved away from the archway.

Cyrus got up as if to follow, but Kris put a furred hand on his arm.

"Cyrus," she whispered, "come look at this."

Cyrus turned back around to see what Kris was talking about. He stared in stunned silence for several seconds at what he saw.

The doorway into which they had ducked led into a room filled with some kind of disassembled eldritch machine. Or perhaps they were several separate strange machines, and stacks of what looked like armor plating to go over them. There was a pair of large turbines, and some sort of pyramidal structure covered in faintly glowing nodes. Sitting just a short distance away was what appeared to be a coffin with a bundle of tubes and wires sprouting from the bottom.

"What is all this?" Kris asked.

Cyrus shook his head. "I don't know. But I'd bet that this is the stuff the Heroes Guild sent us to find. I have to tell Reg . . . but first we have to find him. Come on," he said, and stepped out of the archway.

"And Katana," Kris said.

"And Katana," Cyrus said with a nod. "And Keeth."

Thankfully, they did not encounter either of the men Cyrus had seen, or the groups of Minions. They moved stealthily down the corridors, looking for some sign of their friends.

And find it they did. Strange sounds and light emanated from underneath a door just down the hallway. Cyrus stopped, motioning Kris to stop also. They padded up to the door and listened. Someone was chanting in a foreign language. Cyrus could feel an intense magic buildup in the room.

"Whatever this is, it can't be good," he whispered to Kris.

"We should go in and stop it," she whispered back. "They might be doing something to my brother!"

Cyrus nodded. He knocked the lock apart with a blow of his sword and kicked the door in.

The mage inside didn't even have time to yell for help before Kris was on top of him, claws at his throat.

"Don't, mage," hissed Kris. "Make one move and it'll be your last."

Cyrus stepped inside, looking around. The room was obviously designed with space economy in mind. Within easy reach of the round central table were diagrams and sigils inlaid in the walls, as well as racks of bottles, beakers, assorted crystals, and magical-looking apparatuses.

He spotted an active device on the table, one containing a beaker of dark red blood. A pale blue glow bathed the beaker, with frost inching up the sides. Small pieces of what looked like rubies were beginning to float to the top.

"What is this?" Cyrus demanded.

The mage was silent.

As motivation, Kris drew blood from the mage's neck.

"Ack! It's . . . it's Dragon blood from the Dragon downstairs! It isn't my fault, I swear!" the mage sputtered. "Torval sold me the distilling equipment, and Lord Voshtyr provided the blood. I was just following orders!"

"The Dragon downstairs? What color is it?" Cyrus demanded again, shutting down the device and removing the beaker.

"*Green!*" the mage shrieked as Kris dug her claws in again.

"Keeth!" Kris and Cyrus said at the same time.

"Please, let me go!" pleaded the mage, fumbling around in his robe. "If you do, I'll give you *this!*" He pulled out a wand crackling with electricity and pointed it at Cyrus.

"*Stop him, Kris!*"

Predatory cats are very efficient killers.

Keeth suddenly sighed and relaxed. Reginald looked at him curiously. Whatever had been torturing the Dragon had abruptly stopped. Wait, he thought. Could it be that Cyrus is . . . ? Reginald shifted his weight, testing the manacles. "Wake up, Keeth!" he hissed. "We're getting out of here!"

"Is that what you think?" A voice echoed from the far wall of the dungeon. "Well, you're right." A young man stepped out of the stairwell.

Reginald recognized him from the battle. The scar on his face was quite distinctive. Its familiarity itched at the back of his brain as if trying to remind him of something. "Serimal?"

"Yes, Crimson. As I told you before, I vowed revenge upon you for your treatment of me at the Battle of the Three Streams. And my revenge would not have been complete without seeing you suffer a little." Serimal shrugged. "It comes with the territory of being a Villain, I suppose.

"But now my revenge is more than complete. If this had been my doing, I would have followed the torture by a mercifully quick murder. I had no intention of involving the

Dragon, nor your squire, wherever he is. But my half-brother's arrival has forced me to change my plans."

Serimal walked farther into the dungeon, where he unlocked the gate to Reginald's cell. "Somehow Voshtyr managed to get out of prison, and he threatens to take from me the birthright that I had so briefly enjoyed. Now, I am going to release you. You can perhaps thwart Voshtyr. But either way, by letting you live, you and I will be even." He unlocked the manacles.

Reginald sat up, wincing from the broken ribs. "My thanks, Serimal. But why would you—"

"*What do you think you're doing, brother?*"

Reginald and Serimal spun. Voshtyr stood at the base of the stairs.

"You aren't betraying me, are you?" Voshtyr said, his eyes glowing a dim red.

"Get your Dragon and go," Serimal said to Reginald, handing him a key. "I'll hold my brother." His stormy grey eyes flashed with intensity.

Reginald put his hand on Serimal's shoulder. "You are too honorable to be a Villain. It's a shame that we couldn't have met again under other circumstances. Good luck, lad."

Reginald ran to Keeth's cell and unlocked it. "Time to go."

Keeth looked at the two Villainous brothers facing off. "Shouldn't we—"

"No. It's their fight, and neither you nor I are in any condition to help," Reginald said. They limped down the wide corridor away from the fight as quickly as they could.

• • •

Serimal drew his damascened saif, a broad-bladed sabre with a hooked pommel. "This ends here, half-brother. Either you die or I do."

"Don't be foolish, brother." Voshtyr said, stepping closer. He stopped abruptly, watching the Crimson Slash scurry away with the Dragon. "Why are you releasing our prisoners?"

"I am righting a wrong," Serimal replied. "I know that's a disgrace to Villainy, but it has to be done."

Voshtyr backed up, throwing off his coat. His metallic left arm glinted in the flickering torchlight. A blade snapped out above the wrist, the scraping ring of spring-loaded metal echoing in the spacious dungeon.

"You pathetic fool," he sneered, drawing an ornate klewang-sabre with his right hand. The klewang had a single, straight-edged blade, rounded toward the back, forming an obtuse angle.

"Disgraces don't bother me," the Arch-Villain said coldly. "Interfering nuisances do. And interfering nuisances must be removed."

Serimal charged Voshtyr, but Voshtyr parried the rush and swung both his blades in a scissor pattern at his half-brother's chest.

Serimal dodged back again and lashed out with his saif in a deadly arc, but it glanced off Voshtyr's metallic arm and bit into the stone floor.

Voshtyr smiled unpleasantly. "Not good enough, brother."

"You're not even fully Human. I will never call you my brother! Now die!" Serimal yanked his blade free of the stone and began slashing at Voshtyr with deft, rapid strokes.

Voshtyr backed up, parrying the devastating blows. "Tsk, tsk, little brother. What would Father say about your betrayal?"

"Don't you speak to me of Father. If he hadn't dallied with that Demoness I would have been the firstborn. If you weren't alive, Thomas Frostbite would still draw breath. The world would be a better place, because it wouldn't contain you!" Serimal brought his saif down hard on Voshtyr's crossed blades, sending the half-demon staggering backward.

"What a disappointment you would have been to him," Voshtyr said, regaining his balance. With catlike grace, the Arch-Villain leapt onto the wall, then sprang off it toward Serimal.

The sudden attack caught Serimal off guard. His knees buckled under the impact of his diabolical half-brother's attack. He fell to the floor but scissored his legs, tripping Voshtyr.

"No," Serimal said through clenched teeth, "*you* would be. I can be evil without demonic assistance, you soul-stealing *vorsch tr'ka pic!*"

Voshtyr's eyes glowed red. "Mistake, little brother. Big mistake."

"Half-brother."

Katana woke up. The side of his neck throbbed, and he felt very, very weak. He found he was on a rich divan. He sat up and stared around the room he was in.

It was not much larger than a room at a nice Inn, but the décor was far different. It was richly decorated, with tapestries on the wall and a deep purple carpet on the floor. He scanned the room slowly, looking for any hostiles. Candles in ornate holders sat on every available surface, providing much light and an uncomfortable amount of heat. A large decorative lamp hung from the ceiling, keeping the room brightly lit and rendering the candles unnecessary. Incense burned in a bowl before a mirror, its spicy scent almost covering up the faint smell of death in the room. And the smell was no wonder. There was an open coffin on a stone shelf at the back of the room, empty.

"Woke up already, my pet?" whispered a silken voice from a back corner of the room.

Katana spun and saw the vampirine who had ambushed him earlier. His ears flattened and he bared his fangs. "You aren't catching me off guard this time, female! You were quite the pain in the neck last time!"

"Now, now. That's no way to talk to a lady. You must be nicer to me if you're to be my consort," she said sweetly, standing up from her deep plush chair.

"Consort?" Katana slid off the divan. "Why would I ever associate with someone like you?"

The vampirine smiled. "Because once I drain you of your blood, you will have no choice. I'm already a third done."

Katana's remaining blood chilled. She was serious. He had to get out of this. "My name is Katana, son of Marcellus Baravaati, chieftain of the Southern Tribes. I will be consort to no vile, undead woman. Now, fight me for my life!"

A cold glare crossed the visage of the vampirine. "So be it," she said in a voice devoid of all emotion. She wove her hands in the netlike pattern again.

Katana, having been struck with the spell once already, recognized and immediately countered it. As she narrowed her hands and pointed toward him, Katana pressed his palms together and turned them parallel, then pointed to the ceiling. The beam of sticky rope shot up in an arc, wrapping itself around the ceiling lamp instead of the Katheni.

Katana sprang backward, grabbing a torch off the wall and holding it between himself and the vampirine.

She glared at Katana through the flickering flames. "I am Salvatia Malice. Innumerable men have fallen to my might, and you will be no exception. You *will* bow to me, Katheni, willingly or no." Her face twisted in a horrible expression of rage, and she launched herself at him.

Katana threw the torch at her and rolled aside, letting her fly right by him. He came up with two pawfuls of pyrotechnic power. Focusing on the vampirine, he spoke a command word, and twin beams of fire shot from his paws.

Salvatia shrieked, running up the wall and across the ceiling. Katana pivoted with her, and the beams traced a path of fiery destruction in her wake. Salvatia dropped from the ceiling, landing in front of the mirror, and ducked.

The cat-mage's eyes widened, and he canceled the spell, dropping to the floor just in time to dodge the reflected fire.

As a historical note, the reader may be interested to know a bit about the Battle of Banburg, one of the most well-known battles of the Twenty-Minute War.

Eight siege engines and a host of ten thousand soldiers, not to mention two cohorts of Villains, were held off for sixteen minutes by seven Heroes, fifty common soldiers, and a wing of Dragons. When the Heroes finally abandoned the city, the Villains flooded in, setting the city aflame. The Burning of Banburg is often depicted in works of art, such as paintings, murals, and tapestries.

Unfortunately, of these art forms, tapestries are the most flammable.

• • •

Fire splashed around Katana as his reflected fire spell turned the tapestry of the Burning of Banburg into the Burning of the Tapestry of the Burning of Banburg. He leapt from behind the divan and onto a desk just as the remains of the flaming tapestry fell from its place on the wall into a smoldering pile, coming to rest where he had been standing.

Taking advantage of his momentary distraction, Salvatia pulled a piece of honeycomb from her pocket and began chanting. A swarm of luminescent green bees appeared around the sticky blob. With a command from the vampirine, the bees shot forward as a line of phosphorescent, explosive projectiles.

Katana brought up a deflective wall of force, and the bees detonated on it with sharp popping sounds. The wall abruptly failed. A counterspell? Katana sprang to the side, dodging the remaining bees, then launched himself from an opposite wall, straight at the vampirine.

The Minion crumpled to the ground, chest perforated.

"There," Cyrus said, removing his blade from the corpse, "we've just lost the element of surprise."

The two were in yet another hall, having had no luck finding any of their companions. Probably because Cyrus was lost. The rough-hewn stone walls all looked the same to him, and there was no way to see their footprints on the grey stone floor. The two Minions they had just run into were the first sign of life they'd seen since they'd left the mage's room.

"The mage said Keeth was in the basement," Cyrus said, "and since Villains always make the mistake of imprisoning Heroes and their companions in the same cell block, Reg should be around there, too."

Kris dropped the second Minion, his neck twisted at an unnatural angle. "What about my brother? Where would he be?"

"Possibly with Reg and Keeth, but I wouldn't bet on it. Magic users are usually treated with more caution. They're usually sealed in a magic-proof room or something. Don't worry—either way, we're not leaving without him."

Kris nodded. "Let's find your friends first. Brother can take care of himself."

Cyrus looked at Kris askance. "Are you implying that Reg and Keeth can't?"

Kris smirked. "I'm sure the Dragon is perfectly competent."

Keeth made an odd face as he swallowed the soldier. It was inconvenient that Minions wore metal armor instead of that nice hide stuff. Metal armor always gave him indigestion.

Reginald, having reacquired his massive sword from a weapons rack conveniently located near the cells, had neatly slain three prison guards, a watchdog, and a giant five-headed snake that was apparently some sort of dungeon keeper. His sides heaved as he coughed up a small amount of blood. He clamped a hand over his ribs and turned to Keeth. "Come on, then. We've got to get out of here and find Cyrus!"

Keeth burped. "Excellent plan, but there is a slight problem. I won't fit up the stairs, and I haven't a clue how I got down here in the first place. Any ideas?"

Reginald scratched his head, which was free of helmet because they hadn't discovered where the Villains had stashed the Hero's armor. "I don't know, Keeth. Perhaps if we removed a wall . . . "

"*Reg!*" a voice shouted.

Keeth swung his neck toward the sound.

Cyrus pelted down the stairs, chainmail jingling, and holding his floppy blue hat onto his head. Kris was right behind him. "Reg! I found you! Let's find Keeth—oh, hello, Keeth—and Katana and get out of here!" Cyrus shook Reginald's hand. "I'm glad you're okay. And Reg, I found some weird machines upstairs that might be the Device the Guild sent us after. We have to get out of here and report this to the Guild."

Keeth sniffed Cyrus. He smelled like the Katheni girl. The Dragon smiled to himself and listened.

"I suppose we cannot take them by ourselves," Reginald replied, looking disappointed. "There is precious little time to lose, and we are hardly in a position to mount a proper assault, even if we were to enlist assistance . . . "

"I already brought the Solid Wall in to provide a distraction," Cyrus said, "so we do have some help already. But we need to move, or they'll find out we're here."

"The Solid Wall?" Reginald's demeanor changed. He squared his shoulders and stood taller. "Perhaps we could make a run at it after all."

Kris put a soft paw on Keeth's shoulder. "Have either of you seen Katana?"

The Dragon shook his head. "He was not imprisoned with us. Perhaps he is upstairs, in a magic proof room."

Cyrus shot the Katheni girl a meaningful glance. Keeth couldn't read Human expressions well enough to tell if it was an *I told you so* glance or something having to do with uncomfortable undergarments. He often got the two confused.

Cyrus turned back to Reginald. "Are you okay, Reg? You look kinda pale."

Reginald snorted. "Broken bones, a concussion, and massive blood loss, lad. I'll be all right by morning. Cyrus, you need to get going. Get Keeth and Kris out of here. I shall attempt to find the Solid Wall, but even if I cannot find him I shall—"

Cyrus shook his head. "No, *you* get going. You can't do this one alone, Reg, not in your condition. You're not invincible, no matter how many years of experience you have. What's the first thing about being a Hero?"

Reginald chuckled. "Never leave your wet socks in a saddlebag."

"No, Reg," Cyrus said. "Never Attempt the Impossible unless there is a reasonable Chance of Survival."

Reginald pointed at Cyrus and nodded. "Of course."

Cyrus adjusted his floppy hat. "Now, you and Keeth get out of here."

Keeth's stomach was complaining about the recent helping of plate armor. Inconsiderate guards. "I hate to remind you again, Reginald, but I can't get out."

Cyrus stared at him. "You can't? Why not?"

"I am apparently of too great a size to exit any of the local doors."

The apprentice Hero grunted. "Let me handle this." He walked over to the wall of the dungeon. Reaching behind him, he grabbed a handful of nothing and hurled it at the wall. Dust and bricks went flying outward with a tremendous explosion.

When the dust settled, there was a Dragon-sized hole in the wall, leading outside.

"There," Cyrus said. "Now you can both get out."

Keeth was fairly certain that Cyrus had never before shown the ability to do what he just did. His suspicion was confirmed by the look of surprise on Reginald's face. *Some* Human expressions were easy enough to read.

"Cyrus," Reginald said, his eyes wide, "where did you learn to do that, lad?"

Cyrus shrugged. "Beats me. Weird stuff's just been happening the last few days. I'm not going to question it until we get out of here."

"That was magic," Reginald said, pointing a finger in Cyrus's face. "Who taught you magic? No squire of mine is going to fool around with that sort of junk! You could have blown yourself up just there!"

"But I didn't, and now there's a Dragon-door in the wall," Cyrus retorted. "Listen, we can argue about this later, but you need to go, *now*. We'll meet up with you once we find Katana. Come on, Kris, let's find your brother."

Reginald nodded and followed Keeth out the hole.

One minute. Two minutes. Five. The Solid Wall had to keep his wall of force raised near-constantly as a protective wall.

Javelins flew in from all directions, shattering to pieces against the invisible field. Still he slew rank after rank of Ransha. Sweat began to bead up on the Hero's brow. Bringing the wall up was not difficult, but maintaining it was.

He knew that, with such effort, tattoo-like marks would soon appear on his face and arms, followed by . . . a problem. He glanced down at his sword arm. Sure enough, the barbed swirls of the markings were beginning to show through his skin. It would not be long now before his wall would no longer be strong enough to deflect the javelins.

• • •

Voshtyr's arm-blade sliced across Serimal's face. Serimal jerked back, avoiding death, but receiving a cut from his right cheekbone across his nose and to his left cheek.

"Not good enough, brother!" Voshtyr taunted. "Your pathetic excuse for mortal flesh is failing you!"

Serimal took a deep breath and wiped the blood from his face with the back of his sleeve. "If I'm getting a little tired it is only because holding back wears me out. You think I'm actually trying to kill you? You think I'd kill my own blood? Father taught us better than that!"

Evil light glimmered in Voshtyr's eyes. "Yes, he did, but Mother taught me much differently!" Faster than a thought, Voshtyr flashed across the distance separating them, releasing a powerful vertical chop on Serimal.

Serimal staggered back and tried to block, but was slashed across the back. Voshtyr was moving too fast. Serimal breathed out slowly, willing a pale blue glow to surround him.

Everything stopped. Voshtyr hung airborne in mid-lunge, his blade inches from Serimal's face. Serimal stepped aside and braced his arm in front of Voshtyr's throat, waiting for the *Halt Time* spell to wear off.

Katana hit the ground hard. Somehow, Salvatia had anticipated his spring and brought her hand down on his back as he flew by. He rolled over, springing to his feet.

"Don't make me hurt you, Katheni," the vampirine said. "I don't want a damaged consort. Now, lie back down like a good kitten and we'll have a drink."

Katana shuddered. "I think not. Unless," he said, raising fingers glowing with fierce blue energy, "you can drink this!"

The floor of the room cracked open, and a geyser of water shot up, blasting the vampirine into the ceiling. Katana yanked from his pocket a small flask marked with a cross and emptied it into the water deepening on the floor of the room. Chanting in an arcane language, he spread his palms over the surface of the water, which began glowing with faint white light.

The vampirine shrieked as her skin began smoking from contact with the water.

The door burst open, and Cyrus and Kris attempted to rush in, only to be knocked backward by the rush of transmuted holy water.

Katana sprang at Salvatia, knocking her flat into the water. Vile, smoky bubbles rose and burst on the surface as he held her under. "Cyrus!" Katana shouted, "It's a vampirine!"

Cyrus's eyes went wide. "Unholy . . . " He grabbed an end table that was floating nearby and chopped a jagged piece off of it with his sword. He handed the sharp piece of wood to Kris.

She nodded.

"Katana!" Cyrus shouted. "Throw her over here!"

Katana heaved the dissolving vampirine at Cyrus, who caught her, pinning her arms and neck.

Kris plunged the sharp impromptu stake into the vampirine's pale chest. A rush of air and a whimper escaped the creature, and her eyes glazed over.

The life went out of Salvatia's body and Cyrus dropped the corpse. "Yuck," he said. "Glad that's done with. Come on, Katana, let's get out of this— Oh. Excuse me."

Katana would have replied, but Kris was holding onto him as if she would never let go—and as if he would never need to breathe.

Chapter 19

COMBAT CONCLUSION

In which the Heroes temporarily Foil the Villains and the Villains, Plans Foiled, Retreat to a Secondary Location

THE WALL OF force dissipated. Instantly, two javelins slammed home. The Solid Wall grunted in pain and tore the javelins from his back.

"Retreat!" someone yelled. The Ransha backed off, parting to reveal a large Villain in heavy armor. "Let me handle him!"

The Solid Wall's eyes narrowed. "The Silver Talon. So very good to see you."

The Villain hefted his mace and chuckled, an irritating sound. "Well, if it isn't the Solid Wall. I've changed my name, though. 'The Silver Talon' sufficed when I was a Hero, though it never really worked for me. But my Villain name is much better, more fitting. Now I go by 'Anthony the Mace.' Good to see you again, old friend."

"I am not your friend, traitor," Solid growled, pointing his sword directly at the Mace. "I'll send you to the Deepest Abyss, where you belong! Prepare to Meet your Doom!" the Solid Wall shouted as he rushed Anthony the Mace.

"Hey, that's my line!" the Villain protested, swinging his mace at the Solid Wall.

Solid ducked under the blow, slamming his sword into his opponent's chest-plate. Sir Anthony grunted and brought his heavy left gauntlet down on Solid's head. Surprisingly, it bounced off of nothing, an inch from his head.

Solid grinned. "It recharges very quickly." Launching into *Claymore Roulette*, the Solid Wall spun out of the Villain's attack range, delivering several blows as he did so.

A commotion broke out in the ranks of the Ransha behind them. Stopping to spare a quick glance, Solid saw Ransha corpses flying and the long neck and head of a Dragon breathing pyrotechnic fury on the hapless lizards.

Then a gigantic sword cleft through the front rank of Ransha. The Crimson Slash stepped through the breach, breathing heavily. "Solid Wall! I have come to your aid!"

The *Halt Time* spell wore off and Voshtyr leapt forward, his throat colliding with Serimal's outstretched arm.

Voshtyr fell backward, choking.

They still stood in the dungeon complex, though the place was much draftier than it had been, thanks to a large hole in the wall two dungeons away. The dungeon in which they stood now was primarily used as a torture room, and various engines designed for that purpose lined the walls: a rack, a forge and hot irons, an Iron Maiden, and a chair connected to several large copper tanks. Needless to say, this was not one of the keep's friendlier rooms.

Serimal pointed his saif at his half-brother's throat. "I could have killed you just now, Voshtyr. But I don't want to. We don't kill family."

"You're wrong, brother. Dead wrong. You should've killed me when you had the chance." Bringing both blades together, Voshtyr snapped the blade from Serimal's saif. As Serimal recoiled, Voshtyr leapt up, slashing madly. Serimal continued to back up, dodging the rapid but inaccurate slashes.

Voshtyr threw his klewang at his brother, who dodged. But in that moment of distraction, the Arch-Villain's eyes glowed red, and he slammed his right fist into Serimal's chest, sending him flying backward into the Iron Maiden.

Spikes penetrated Serimal's back. He screamed.

Voshtyr retrieved his blade and walked up to the spike-lined coffin. "That's it, then. I won't take your soul. I imagine it would leave a bad taste in my mouth if I did. So you can just die quietly instead, traitor brother."

Serimal coughed up blood. "Half . . . brother . . . "

Voshtyr slammed the spiked lid closed with a resounding bang.

Someone sighed from behind Voshtyr. "I don't think that was necessary, Voshtyr."

Voshtyr whirled, his klewang slashing wildly. It rebounded off the organic blade extending from the blue-scaled arm of Roger Farella.

"I don't think *that* was necessary, either," Roger said in an amused tone. "You did know that the Crimson Slash, the Dragon, and the Katheni have all escaped, correct?"

"They got out of the castle?" Voshtyr said in disbelief. "How did they get out?"

"They killed Salvatia and fought their way through those guards you hired," Roger said. "And after all those things you said about incompetent henchmen too. Not to mention the giant hole in the wall. They might have escaped through there." He chuckled.

Voshtyr pointed his klewang at Roger. "I'll have none of your cheek! What of the Hero outside?"

Roger grabbed the tip of Voshtyr's blade and pointed it away. "It's the Solid Wall, all right. He defeated the Mace with the help of Crimson. The Ransha are finished, also. Indeed, the Heroes may be headed here right now."

"Blast!" Voshtyr snarled. "We'll have to abandon everything. Quick, Roger, get that gryphon and whoever else you can find, and head west for the Mountains of the Morning. I've a fortress there where we can meet for the next stage of my plan."

Roger nodded. "I take it you'll want your apparatus, too . . . "

"We don't have time to take the whole thing," Voshtyr said, sheathing his sword and scrawling a quick note, using the rack as a hard surface. "Just get the core and the crystal, they're portable. I'll have someone pick up the other parts. Oh, and make sure that Nightraid delivers his package to this new address," he added, handing the note to Roger. "It would be counterproductive, not to mention a little embarrassing, to have the postman deliver the Infinity Inducer right into the hands of the Heroes instead of to my new base of operations. Now go!"

"What about your brother?" Roger asked, glancing at the blood pooling at the base of the Iron Maiden.

"Leave him. He's dead, or will be soon. Either way, he's none of your concern."

Roger bowed and stalked from the room.

Voshtyr fumed. His plan had been thrown into ruins. He glanced at the Iron Maiden. At least Serimal had been punished for letting the Crimson Slash go. But he would have revenge, oh, yes, he would. The Heroes had escaped, but he would find where they had gone, and that they would be easy to find.

If young Cyrus Solburg kept using magic so haphazardly, he would be easier to track than a phoenix on a clear night. But for now, it was time to leave.

"Weatherblade!" Voshtyr shouted.

In a few moments, Lydia, the Heroine-turned-Villainess, stepped from the adjoining room. "Yes, what is it?"

"You'll be coming with us, just as a precaution," the Villain said. "Get whatever you must, and meet me atop the tower in five minutes."

The girl nodded and left.

She cannot be trusted yet, Voshtyr told himself, *not while that apprentice Hero is still about. Once I have settled my score with Crimson and his squire, and both lie dead,* then *I may trust the girl somewhat.*

"I have to say, I wasn't expecting a *False Quest,*" Reginald said, looking at the half-necklace the little girl had given him back in Filar. "It caught me totally off guard. Was it the shape-shifter, then? Brilliant. And if it weren't for the fact that a *False Quest* requires blatant deception and cowardice, I would have to admire its execution."

Reginald scowled down at the Villain, who knelt before him in the muck. Between himself and the Solid Wall, it had taken less than five minutes to both subdue Anthony the Mace and prove to the Ranshan host that they were no match for two trained Heroes. Acknowledging this fact, the surviving lizard-folk now knelt around the two Heroes in submission. Keeth kept a watchful eye on them.

The orange glow from the setting sun tinged the swamp plants fiery shades and turned the water inky black. It even made the half-ruined keep seem beautiful, as the grey stone took on the color of the sunset, perhaps as its original architect had intended.

"I have to say, the divine vision was an especially nice touch," Reginald said. "You had me quite convinced. I'm a little sad it wasn't real, to tell you the truth. How did you fake that one? More magery, I suppose?"

Anthony the Mace blinked. "The what?"

Reginald shook his head. "You've been defeated already, Anthony. There's no point in denying it anymore. How did you give me that dream?"

"I swear on my mother's grave, Crimson, the only person's dreams we fooled with were those of the White Tiger when we convinced her to try to seduce the squire, and that was mostly harmless, right?"

"Your mother isn't dead yet, is she?" said the Solid Wall, more statement than question.

"No," Anthony replied, unruffled, "but that doesn't change anything. We simply don't have the power or the capacity to fabricate entire dreams. Dreams are beyond the realm of magic. Whatever you dreamed, Crimson, it was from your own mind."

Reginald turned away. "Or from the mind of someone not mortal . . ."

Cyrus, Kris, and Katana rushed out of the dank and dim Keep and into the sunny and malodorous swamp. An unusual sight met Cyrus's eyes.

Two Heroes stood over a Villain, who groveled in the mud. One of the Heroes—he recognized him now as the Solid Wall—lifted his sword as if to decapitate the Villain. Reginald folded his arms grimly. A host of kneeling Ransha surrounded the scene, while a Dragon presided over the whole affair.

Cyrus sloshed through the muck to where they stood, arriving just in time to stop the Solid Wall from separating Anthony from his head.

"Wait! You can't kill him here!"

The Solid Wall lowered his sword. "Why not?"

"Codex Heroic, page 212, paragraph A, subsection 2. 'After a Villain has been defeated, if he or she still lives or has surrendered, he or she must be turned over to the Guild authorities, who will keep custody of him or her until he or she is tried by the Civil Courts for his or her many Crimes,'" Cyrus quoted. "You have to turn him over to the Guild for a trial."

"No," the Solid Wall said petulantly. "I swore long ago that I would kill this man for his many treacheries, and I will do so." He raised his sword again.

"Hear me out," Cyrus pleaded. "Turn him in, but with the request that you be allowed to execute him if he is found guilty. I'm sure the Guild would allow that, considering your Standing and the Oath you took. I have no doubt that they will find him just as guilty as you do."

The Solid Wall blinked. "I . . . suppose that would be acceptable." He sheathed his sword and leaned down next to his pathetic prisoner. "Your life has been spared for now. But it is only a reprieve. You *will* die for your crimes."

• • •

Nieva sat weeping over the punctured and bleeding body of Serimal. She had strained her healing powers to their utmost, yet he wouldn't wake. He lay now in a pool of his own blood on the dungeon floor. Nieva had been unable to carry him far from the Iron Maiden after she'd pulled him from it. And now there was nothing else she could do to help him.

"Serimal," Nieva breathed in his ear. "I love you, and I will forever." She drew a dagger from her belt and placed the point on her breast. "I shall follow you into death."

"I'd rather you didn't," Serimal whispered, and coughed.

"Serimal!" Nieva shrieked, dropping the dagger. "You're alive!"

"Not for much longer, unless we find someone with healing powers greater than yours," he said, smiling faintly.

Nieva ran her hands through Serimal's dark hair. "Then we must go and get far away from your brother."

Serimal coughed and seemed to try to say something.

Nieva nodded and stroked his forehead. "I mean, your half-brother."

Serimal smiled and leaned back.

Slashback the Gryphon and Roger Farella flew side-by-side northwest in the dusky sky. So long as Slashback did not go into any steep dives, the Araquellus could keep up with her himself, rather than ride her. And at this pace, they would meet Voshtyr in his mountain keep in a day or so, providing he survived the ordeal before him now.

How irritating, Roger thought as he tightened his grip on the tarpaulin-covered bundle beneath his arm. *To have an entire Dark Keep of Evil routed like that. To be humiliated— and by whom? Two Heroes and a squire. Thoroughly irritating.*

And to think it could have been prevented by a little foresight on Voshtyr's part.

Slashback squawked and banked west. Roger followed, muttering under his breath. Voshtyr was not paying him enough to deal with this kind of inconvenience. But perhaps when Voshtyr's Device was finally activated, all the trouble would pay off.

There is always Much Ado after a battle between Heroes and Villains. Damages must be paid, reparations made, captives returned, and so forth.

In this case, Katana agreed to transport Anthony the Mace to the local Heroes Guild and place the ex-Hero in Guild custody. The Solid Wall left amidst many thanks, stepping through the sandstone door once more.

There was also the matter of the *False Quest*. The little girl had claimed that the Ransha had slaughtered an unprotected village, taking many lives and much property. But the tribe elder swore to Reginald and Cyrus that their tribe had not attacked anybody south of Merope for at least five years. Cyrus vouched for them, explaining how it had been a shape-shifter who must have sent them on the *False Quest*. The surviving Ransha dispersed, having cleared themselves of any crimes against local families.

When everything had calmed down, Reginald approached Cyrus. "Lad, it is time."

Cyrus looked up. "Time? For what?"

"You have truly proved your worth today," Reginald intoned.

Cyrus perked up. Reginald never intoned unless he was about to say something Extremely Important. A chill ran up his spine.

"Today, Cyrus Solburg, thou hast demonstrated thine courage and strength in combat, as well as thine mental faculties and insight. As your teacher, I can honestly say that I have had no better pupil." Reginald drew his gigantic sword and placed it gently on Cyrus's shoulder. "Thus, by the power vested in me by the International Guild of Heroes, I hereby proclaim you Cyrus Solburg, a Hero, Second Class."

Cyrus felt dizzy. This was the culmination of five years of constant training and experience. Right now virtually all he could think about was not spoiling it by having his knees give out on him. They certainly felt like they were going to.

But instead, Cyrus found the strength to stand tall. "I thank thee, Crimson Slash. Your training has provided me with the skills I will need to excel." He swallowed and scanned the horizon eagerly. "Now all I need is a Quest!"

Tears welled up in Reginald's eyes. Cyrus stood and looked him in the eye. His own eyes weren't exactly dry, either. Reginald extended his hand and Cyrus shook it, for the first time as a fellow Hero.

"I feel as though I haven't taught you anything about being a Hero, lad," Reginald said, hugging his former apprentice. "Not the first *thing*."

Cyrus chuckled. "Yes, you have, Reg. One thousand, eight hundred, and sixty-two times."

PART TWO:

HERO, SECOND CLASS

Chapter 20

ONE HUNDRED AND FIFTY LEAGUES

In which Cyrus, Kris, and Katana Begin their Journey

DAWN, WITH NAILS neatly manicured, spread her rosy fingers into the early morning air, sending gentle beams of sunlight cascading down into the Inn's brick courtyard as Cyrus made the final adjustments to his new horse's saddle.

The big bay charger was a graduation present from Reginald. It was a spirited animal that stood seventeen hands high. The horse, whose name was Driver, had been bred for speed, endurance, and combat—the epitome of a warhorse.

Kris stepped into the courtyard, finally joining Cyrus as he prepared them for immediate departure. He couldn't help but smile when he looked at Kris. She was wearing the green dress she had purchased but had little chance to wear. The neckline swooped low, but the folds of fabric in front and the ankle-length skirt made it appear almost conservative in design. Almost. There were those slits up the sides of the skirt to allow for easy riding and unhindered motion.

Cyrus thought it made her look elegant, as it defined and displayed her figure quite nicely.

Katana followed close behind her, wearing his habitual blue robe, but also with a skin of oiled leather slung over one shoulder in case of bad weather. He looked grouchy, as if he had had either too much wine or too little sleep.

Keeth looked down at the two Katheni from his spot in the center of the courtyard, leaning against the ancient oak from which the Inn of the Swaying Branches derived its name. "Good morning, you two. Are you prepared for departure?"

Kris sighed happily as the sun made a radiant halo of her head fur. "I'm ready, Keeth. How about you, Cyrus?" She gently padded over to Cyrus's side.

Cyrus nodded. "Yep. We'd better get going. You and your brother out of the room?"

Kris glanced over her furred shoulder at her brother. Katana gave the Katheni paw-sign for "all clear." Kris nodded and turned back to Cyrus. "We're ready."

"Well, let's go, then," Cyrus said. "Farewell, Keeth! We're moving out!"

Keeth shifted his green-scaled bulk and stretched his membranous wings. A peasant opened his room's window to greet the morning sun and got a wingtip in the face instead. "Mmm?" the Dragon said. "I see. Well, may fortune smile upon your journey, Cyrus. Whatever your Quest may be, I wish you the best of luck."

Kris and Katana mounted their ponies. Kris rode Brisk, and Katana rode a slightly nervous new purchase named Yurt.

"Well, now," Reginald said, stepping from the doorway of the inn. "I guess you'll be going, then?"

Cyrus turned and faced his erstwhile teacher. "Reg, I want to thank you for all the time you spent training me. I just wish you were coming with us."

Reginald grunted. "No thanks needed, lad. Training the next generation is part of what Heroes do," he said. "And I can't come with you for three reasons. First, a Hero, Second Class has to perform his First Quest with no help from his mentor. Second, the Guild ordered me not to go anywhere near that swamp again until they clean it out and recover the lost devices. And third, I've received Divine Instruction on what to do next. I'm headed for the Keep of Five Flames to see what my Vision was about, and to wait for whatever god sent me that dream."

"The Keep of Five Flames?" Cyrus asked. "You're not going to attempt to enter it, are you?"

"Of course not! What do you think I am, daft?" Reginald laughed. "That place is as full of obscure magics as a jester is full of bad jokes. I wouldn't touch it with a standard-issue ten-foot-pole." He sheathed his sword in Wraith's saddle and regarded Cyrus with a mildly disapproving gaze. "No one who's attempted the Keep has survived—not since the Third Assault seventy-five years ago, and only two out of seven survived *then*. To try it by myself would be suicide, and you know what I think about suicide."

Cyrus scratched the back of his head, further disordering his already uncombed red hair and nearly displacing his floppy hat. "Yeah, I do. Still, I wouldn't put a solo attempt past you."

"Don't worry yourself about it, lad. I'm not that foolish. I'm bringing this scaled lummox with me," Reginald said, nudging the Dragon beside him.

Keeth smiled, his dangerous fangs glinting in the early morning sun. "I will indeed come, but I doubt I could even get to the Keep, much less assault it. Remember, Dragons find the Circle of No Magic very uncomfortable."

Reginald shook his head. "No, don't bother. I was only jesting. If we indeed reach the Keep, I will not ask you to come inside. Are you sure you wouldn't rather accompany Cyrus? My squire can use all the help he can get!"

"Thanks for the vote of confidence, Reg," Cyrus said. "I stick around long enough to say good-bye, and what do I get? Insults!"

Reginald laughed and crushed Cyrus in a massive bear hug. "Here now, none of that. Get going, and good luck to you."

Cyrus struggled to get his wind back as Reginald released him. "Thanks, Reg," he managed. "Be careful, okay? We never did find that Voshtyr guy or his brother at the keep, so be on your guard."

"Don't worry about me, lad," Reginald said. "Just get thee gone and come see me in Velthomen when you get done with your Quest!"

Cyrus gave a crooked Hero's Salute to Reginald. "Can do. See you there or in the Abyss!" He swung up onto Driver and kicked his flanks. Driver reared and thundered into a gallop, Kris and Katana following as quickly as their mounts could manage.

A journey of a hundred and fifty leagues is no mean feat, even on horseback. This is especially true if you have no idea what a league is, or what kind of distance it entails.

Here we are talking about the kind of league in the distance sense, and the reader should not confuse this with other types of league.

It is not, for instance, a group of people joined together for combat, sports, or a spot of tea. It merely measures distance in an ambiguous and confusing way.

For example, the League of Colors is a fighting group, not a rainbow road. The International Fire-Bowling League is a sports event in which players from across the world hold a tournament to see who can destroy wooden pins most accurately with rolled fireballs, not measuring distance at all. The Infernal League of Imported Tea is a guild of Villains dedicated to decreasing the price of teas and other beverages for the Hereditary Evil Empire, and increasing them in others by means of tariffs and other taxes.

None of the aforementioned has anything to do with distance. A league, as a unit of distance, is generally reckoned to be somewhere between one and a half to three miles, or somewhere in the vicinity of 4.8 kilometers. This means that, assuming the average walking speed of a laden equine is between three and six miles per hour, the Hero, Second Class and the Katheni siblings would reach Mir in approximately one week.

Slashback Ricor alit on the flat outcropping on the mountainside and folded her oversized, dusty white wings onto her back. Roger Farella the Araquellus dropped down beside her, landing on two feet and his right hand. In his left hand he carried a bundle wrapped in a tarpaulin.

Gryphon and Araquellus stood on a flat ledge cut into the side of the mountain. Mere feet from where they stood, the flat surface dropped off sharply, down into an unclimbable cliff. But the ledge itself was rather an interesting sight, even to the gryphon's jaded eyes.

The place was decorated with stone benches and basins of assorted polished rocks. Slashback hadn't much experience with such things, but she did not think that the small rock-garden looked like something that would typically be seen decorating the secret fortress of a demon lord. In the center was a large square pad of a different, lighter color of stone. And in the center of that was a darker stone set in the square, carved into the shape of the letter "G" in the Central language. But what Villain would put a gryphon landing-pad on the side of his fortress?

Roger repositioned the bundle in his hand and spoke to the gryphon. "Well then, Slashback. Here we are. Assuming, of course, that 'here' is Voshtyr's fortress. Is it?"

Slashback the Gryphon cocked her head to one side. "I onli follo direktions," she snapped, her beak clipping off the ends of her syllables. "I can fly in dark, in storms, have attack by fire birds, and still be finding any place. What I neffer do is fly to wrong place. If I am wrong, then the direktions are bad, not me."

The reader cannot expect a creature whose main facial feature is a beak to be able to properly pronounce syllables in the Central language. Thus, all gryphons are cursed with a very heavy accent, sometimes so thick as to render their speech incomprehensible.

Roger put up a blue hand. "Now, now, Slashback. I wasn't deprecating your navigational skills. I just asked if this was the place."

"It is," Slashback huffed. "I proof it." She approached a massive stone door embedded in the mountainside and examined it. It did indeed have Voshtyr's personal coat of arms carved into it: a severed hand clutching a crystal. The gryphon raised her clawed forefoot and rapped on the door.

Dust blew from under the door, and it swung open— revealing a seven foot tall misshapen suit of armor.

A dim red glow emanated from inside its helmet, and Slashback's feathered ears picked up faint whirs and clicks coming from behind the breastplate. The suit of armor took two ponderous steps forward, then stopped and stared at the gryphon and Araquellus.

"Grrreetings. You arrrre Miss Slashback and Lrrrd Rrrogerrrr Farrrrella, corrrect?" Its speech was slightly slurred, like that of a person who had drunk three too many glasses of wine and pronounced any *r* with a rapid metallic stutter. "Please step inside," it said, and stepped back into the fortress.

Slashback stood dumbstruck, gaping at the titanic suit of armor that spoke.

Roger rudely pushed past her with his bundle, then looked back. "What's the matter, Slashback? Have you never seen a golem before?"

Slashback shook her head. "Neffer. Is it alife?"

"Not really," Roger said, squeezing past the golem. "It's powered by magic and has rudiments of personality, but nothing more. It's a semi-intelligent machine, like a water-wheel with a brain." Roger looked up at the golem. "Take us to your master, construct."

The golem nodded and began slowly pounding its way down the corridor, its flat metal feet making an echoing din in the stone hallway.

In classic Neo-Dungeonic style, the hallways had been smoothed but left intentionally dim. They were lit only by some flickering oil lamps in wall sconces. The hall was more of a tunnel, carved right through the rock. It was probably of Dwarven design, Slashback thought. Why those creatures always wanted to live in dark places beneath the ground instead of out in the sun, where they could feel the wind on their wings, she could never think. Probably because the wretched things had no wings.

Either way, the animate armor's giant feet made quite a din in the corridor, and there were no wall hangings or the like to dampen the sound. Slashback laid her pointed ears flat against her head to block out some of the sound.

Roger, impatient with the construct's slow pace, walked a good deal ahead of the golem down the narrow hall, carrying the tarpaulin-wrapped package.

Slashback walked just behind the animated suit of armor. "You haff name, kolem?"

"Yes. I am A424 Imperrrvious 3," the golem answered. "The masterrr has given me the use-name Locke. Thank you forrr yourrr interrrest."

Slashback nodded and continued following the metallic construct. *For a water wheel,* she thought, *it seems much like a person.*

Tap tap tap.

Voshtyr looked up from the book he'd been reading, a copy of Tiresian Bloodcurdle's documentary *Five and Twenty: the Five Mistakes of the Twenty-Minute War.* He set the book down on the oak table next to his overstuffed crimson armchair.

Perhaps it was Roger knocking on the door. Voshtyr could certainly do with a bit of good news right about now. "One moment," he said, rising from the chair. His red and black cloak swirled as he rose, rustling against his black silk shirt. Light from the cheery fire in the fireplace glinted off his burnished steel left arm. The Arch-Villain moved a stack of scrolls off the black velvet chair in the other corner of his small reception room, then opened the door.

"Roger!" he said, clasping the Araquellus's right tricep in a traditional Araquellan greeting. "Welcome, welcome. Come in and have a seat."

Roger clasped Voshtyr's arm in return, his burden tucked beneath his left arm. He stalked over and flopped heavily into the black velvet chair opposite Voshtyr's red one. "Remind me again why I go to all this trouble for you, Voshtyr."

Voshtyr closed the door behind him and muttered a spell to silence their conversation, should anyone be so foolish as to eavesdrop on them.

"'Tis a simple thing," he replied. "You served my father for many years, with extraordinary pay and benefits. But he never gave you the one thing you wanted, something I do give you." He pulled a bottle and two glasses out of the drawer in the table next to his chair. "Respect. I respect you, Roger. Given that, and the money, you couldn't possibly deny me a favor or two. Spirits?"

Roger glanced at the bottle and cringed. "What are those: orphans?"

"They're spirits, Roger. The spirits of war orphans, Landeralt campaign of the fifth century," Voshtyr said, holding the bottle up to the light so the swirling misty faces inside the bottle would better catch the firelight. "South Bloodfield, to be exact."

"I'll just have some port," Roger replied, looking rather ill.

Voshtyr chuckled, putting the bottle back in the drawer and retrieving a bottle of port from the table instead. "How was your trip?"

Roger scowled. "Terrible. We were assaulted by a clan of phoenixes, passed right through a thunderstorm, and nearly got lost. You're lucky this is in one piece." He handed the tarpaulin-wrapped bundle to Voshtyr.

"Excellent, Roger. Most excellent." Voshtyr's eyes momentarily glowed brighter. "Thanks to this, and to Nightraid's delivery, I now have all the basic parts. Another associate will shortly be bringing the parts I left behind, and then we can construct it in the tower immediately. After it is built, there will be just six things I need to complete the device."

"And those are?"

"The Five Essence Stones of the Elements," Voshtyr said, clamping his metal hand onto the arm of Roger's chair and staring into Roger's pale yellow eyes. "The refined essences of the most powerful forces in the world, at my beck and call."

Roger shrank further into the chair, looking uncomfortable. "You need all five Essence Stones? Aren't four of them on other continents? And isn't the last one . . . "

"At the top of the Keep of Five Flames? Yes, they are, and it is." Voshtyr said, turning and placing the bundle on the oak table behind him. "Those are hardly insurmountable obstacles, and I don't expect much difficulty in acquiring the first four."

"But the fifth is impossible to acquire, Voshtyr."

"So one would think, but that is what I need the sixth thing for."

Roger tilted his head to the side. "And that is . . . ?"

"The sixth thing is Cyrus Solburg." Voshtyr swept back from the chair and laughed, his sinister chuckle filling the small room. He smiled, and the room darkened as he did so. "His . . . interesting use of magic may be just what I need to acquire the final stone. Just one Hero to do my dirty work for me, and the infernal, unstoppable P.L.O.T. Device will be complete! Mwahahaha!"

Chapter 21

IN A SYCAMORE TREE

In which Cyrus and Company encounter
an Unpleasant Companion

IDMORNING ON THE third day
of their trip, Cyrus dismounted from
Driver and removed his saddle. Kris
and Katana rode up and dismounted
also. They had made good time, having
been delayed only twice, once to bathe in a cold, crystal-clear
stream they had discovered, and once by a tax collector and his
goons, who soon decided that trying to tax an armed Heroic
party was not such a profitable idea, after all.

They had ridden for almost six hours, and it was time for a
break. Cyrus led the horses over to a shaded patch of grass and
clover and left them, while Kris and Katana spread a small
repast out for the three of them beneath a lone sycamore tree
in the midst of the hills of rolling grass. The shade the tree
generated was a welcome relief from the sun as it blazed in the
cloudless cerulean sky.

Katana smiled and lay back in the grass, the gentle breeze
rippling his black fur. He gazed up into the treetops. This
action turned out to be a mistake. The Katheni's fur stood on

end, and he scrabbled backward across the grass, a low growl rumbling from his throat.

"What's the matter, Katana?" Cyrus asked, placing a hand on his sword-hilt.

Katana pointed up into the tree.

A corpse dangled from a rope. It hung from one of the higher branches about a third of the way up the tree. The desiccated body was at least a few months old, and the flesh, where still present, was greying from exposure to weather and in rather bad shape, probably from being pecked apart by crows.

Cyrus took a step back. "Ooh, that's a nasty surprise. Wonder what his story is." He shrugged. "I suppose we should cut it down and bury it."

Katana nodded. "I'll cut it down if you'll start digging."

"Deal," Cyrus said, and walked off to cut some sod.

Katana leapt into the tree and scrambled up it. Drawing a short knife from his robe, he severed the rope from which the weathered corpse hung. It fell and landed with a mushy thud and a sharp crack. Katana slowly climbed back down the tree. For some reason, getting back down a tree was always more difficult for him than climbing it.

When he finally made it back down, Katana knelt in front of the corpse, crossing himself. "O Lord of Light and Dark, Creator and Destroyer, Ruler of the Twelve, hear my plea," he prayed aloud. "Guide this lost one's soul back to Thee, that it may find peace and—"

"Grrruuuuuaaghhhhh . . . "

Katana leapt backward, fur bristling.

The corpse was moving.

"*Cyrus!*" Katana shouted. "*Zombie!*"

• • •

Cyrus dropped the slab of grass he'd just cut and rushed over to the trees.

Katana's ears were laid back flat against his head, and he held a fire spell ignited between his paws. He was staring into the eye-sockets of the corpse, which was now standing almost upright.

"What in the Nine?" Cyrus exclaimed. "Is it necromancy?"

Katana shook his head. "I don't think so. There's no magic aura around it at all. It looks like a zombie, but zombies are most certainly not naturally occurring phenomena."

"Hhhhaaannkkk gooooo," the zombie moaned.

Cyrus readied his sword. "I think it just said something, Katana."

Katana nodded. "It did, but I have no idea what it means."

"Aaaaahhh aahhhhhmmm ghhhaaaakeeehhhhuuuuhhhhh . . . " it gurgled.

The fire faded from Katana's paws. "It doesn't seem to be hostile, and it's unlike any zombie I've ever seen before. It doesn't smell like decomposing flesh, for one thing. It smells more like . . . " Katana sniffed in the general direction of the zombie . . . "moist earth. For another, it seems to be attempting to communicate with us. Most zombies have no minds. They are simply decomposing killing machines, usually controlled by a sorcerer, and third, *Kris, get away from that!*"

Kris had stepped up behind the zombie and loosened the noose that still hung about its neck. "What?"

"It could be dangerous!" Katana said, bringing up another fistful of phantasmal fire and aiming it at the zombie. "Step away from it, sister."

Kris removed the noose and dropped it on the ground. "That's ridiculous. He's not going to hurt anybody."

"What?" Cyrus said, lowering his sword. "How do you . . . ? I mean, what . . . ?"

Kris looked at them as if they didn't have the brains of a pixie between the two of them. "He thanked my brother for cutting him down and introduced himself as Zaccheus. He seems friendly enough to me."

Katana dropped the fire spell and stamped it out. "You understood him?"

"Of course. You just have to take the time to listen. Honestly, males . . . "

Cyrus shrugged. "Okay, whatever you say. Does he want food?"

The zombie slowly shook his head. That head, apparently loosened by his landing on it, abruptly fell off. "Ngoh hhaahk gooo . . . " the head gurgled.

Cyrus and the two Katheni ate in uncomfortable silence as Zaccheus shuffled about, regarding various objects with a blank, eyeless stare.

They were resting uneasily beneath the lone sycamore, their idyllic picnic lunch having been spoiled by the presence of a member of the undead. Flies intermittently landed on the zombie's skull, adding their buzzing to the sounds of rustling grass.

Zaccheus was not exactly nice to look at, but he wasn't disgusting, either. His skin was a dark, weathered grey, and slightly shriveled. A lone tuft of brown hair tenaciously clung to the top of his head. Two empty pits replaced his eyes, which had probably been taken by ravens long ago. Cyrus felt sorry for the creature. It was perhaps the second most unnatural thing he had ever seen, surpassed only by an Orc and Dwarf couple he and Reginald had once met in a tavern.

Zaccheus had attempted to explain why he was still half-alive, but his gargled speech had rendered him near unintelligible. Kris explained that, as near as she could tell, the zombie, when he had still been alive, had been lynched for some unknown crime, even though he was innocent. Instead of dying, however, he somehow remained alive and had spent the last two months fighting off birds and trying to get down from the tree.

After the three finished their lunch, Cyrus gingerly placed a hand on Zaccheus's moldy shoulder. "Good luck," he said, unsure what to say to someone who was already dead. "I hope you find rest soon."

Zaccheus nodded, and his head fell off again. Cyrus picked it up and placed it on the zombie's shoulders.

Cyrus swung up into his saddle atop Driver. "Come on, let's get going. There's a village we can make by tomorrow night if we hurry. I could use a hot meal."

Kris and Katana nodded and leapt onto their mounts also. The three galloped off into the evening, leaving a cloud of dust and a shambling zombie in their wake.

"Guuuuuhhh huuhhyyeee . . ."

Chapter 22

RUINS AND HOPE

In which Cyrus gets some important Questions answered

CYRUS AND THE two Katheni rode in the twilight, headed across the vast grasslands for the small village where Cyrus had said they might find a hot meal. It was nearly dark before they crested the hill that sheltered the village from the strong winds that habitually blew across the plains in this region. When they did, they beheld a terrible sight.

The village was totally destroyed. Burnt to the ground. No smoke rose from the gutted buildings. It did it look as if an errant Fire Elemental or Dragon had blundered through. No, this destruction had been deliberate. Cyrus stared at the wreckage. Had he been here, could he have prevented this? Were people hurt? Killed?

"Well," Katana said, "I guess we're not spending the night here after all."

Cyrus noticed Kris looking into his face.

"Cyrus," she said, "what's wrong? What are you thinking?"

He sighed. "I've seen this kind of thing before. It was probably an Orc war-band. Reg and I bumped into one of their

Hordes just after they had sacked a small city. Everything was gone, every building razed or afire, and every man, woman, and child slain. Orcs hate every other Humanoid, and this kind of wanton destruction," he said, jutting his chin over the ruins of the village, "is their usual handiwork."

Katana surveyed the blackened wreckage. "Are you sure?"

Cyrus drew his sword. "No. I'm just guessing. I don't like jumping to conclusions—the landing is always rough. But right now, I'm going down there to see if there are any survivors. Katana, watch your sister." He spurred Driver and broke off from the group, headed down into the ruins.

It was not, on second thought, much like that city he and Reginald had arrived too late to protect. This time, most of the valuables were still there, and there were no bodies lying about.

Then Cyrus saw the church.

It was a small building with a steeple and what had once been stained-glass windows. Soot from the hulks of nearby buildings had blackened its stone sides, but there was a light in the single unbroken pane of glass. Survivors? Orcs? Cyrus tightened his grip on his sword and strode toward the church.

As he entered the church courtyard he noticed twelve fresh graves, two of them small. Cyrus gritted his teeth and pushed open the door.

The interior of the church was almost entirely undamaged. Certainly, the wooden pews were scattered and broken, and only a single pane of stained glass had survived the heat, but the roof was intact. A pulpit and an altar dominated the front of the room, neither damaged by fire or smoke. A red runner of carpet, very muddy, stretched down the center aisle. Several candles rested on the simple wooden altar at the back of the room, casting flickering light and shadows across the long benches. Those benches had been scattered about, tipped over, and broken. Someone had ransacked the church. And yet, something was odd: who had lit the candles?

"You weren't thinking about bringing a drawn sword into a church, were you, young man?"

Cyrus jumped.

A man dressed in the black and gold garments of a priest of the True Church stepped out of the small confessional stall to the right of the altar. The man was about Cyrus's height, though broader, with thick black hair and a square jaw covered in stubble.

"Sheathe that weapon and come in," the priest said. "It's dark and depressing out there."

Cyrus obeyed, putting away his sword and stepping further into the church. "Sorry, Father. It's just that I thought you might have been an Orc."

The dark-haired priest shook his head. "It wasn't Orcs," he said, his mellow tenor filling the room with a very listenable sound. "Why does everyone assume that Orcs are responsible for every vile act? Humans are hardly any better." He sighed. "No, this was a group of Human mercenaries, working under some half-demon fellow who'd heard of the treasure stored here."

"Half-demon?" Cyrus asked, glancing behind him. "You mean Voshtyr Demonkin?"

"His name matters little," the priest replied, sitting down heavily in a hardwood chair beside a slightly scorched table. "I seldom get directly involved in such things. The treasure was called the Transfusion Token. It's a shining disk the locals kept here as part of a sun-worship ceremony that took place once a year.

"The mercenaries swept in without killing anyone. Well, until they discovered the location of the disk, that is. Then they put everyone to the sword and razed the village to the ground. Everyone who survived headed for the next nearest town, now that their homes have been destroyed." He sighed. "I buried the dead, and I'm going to leave shortly, myself. So, young man, what brings you to this church?"

"My friends and I were planning on spending the night in this village . . . " Cyrus's voice trailed off.

"Bring them here," the priest said. "I'm sure the Creator wouldn't mind some needy travelers borrowing His roof."

"Really?"

"Positive. Go on and get them."

"Thank you, Father, I appreciate it. I'll be right back," Cyrus said, heading for the door.

He was back in five minutes, Kris and Katana in tow. After brief introductions, the priest welcomed them in and showed them to a pair of back rooms.

"They burned almost everything," the priest said. "Some of the sparks even caught my roof afire for a while. But the storage rooms have their roofs yet, and you can sleep here. I hope it suits you."

"Thank you, Father," Kris said, smiling. "This will be fine."

"Beggars can't be choosers," Katana muttered.

Cyrus elbowed the black Katheni in the ribs. "Would you rather sleep outside with the bugs?" he whispered.

The priest smiled. "All right, then. Sleep well." He turned and walked back out into the main room.

The three adventurers laid out their sleeping gear and turned in, Kris to one room, Cyrus and Katana to the other.

• • •

Cyrus turned over again. He sighed. Even after a long day's ride, he couldn't get to sleep.

He got up, careful not to disturb Katana, left the back room, and walked out of the church. The night sky was overcast, not a star to be seen. He checked on the horses, who were sheltered under the roof of one of the few houses that still had one. Satisfied, he returned to the church.

In the sanctuary he found the priest making a pot of tea on a small, portable, magical burner atop the altar. "Well, young man. Why are you up so late?"

"I couldn't sleep," Cyrus said. "It's been happening a lot these days."

The priest gestured to an empty chair. "Have a seat. I find that sometimes people cannot get to sleep because they are mulling over their troubles in their heads. Would you care to share them with me? I am a priest, after all."

Cyrus smiled and sat down, accepting a proffered cup of tea. "Thanks, Father, but I don't really think priests are different from regular people."

"Neither do I," the priest said. "Priests are exactly like anyone else. For example, I tended bar for two years in a tavern on Salvinsel."

Cyrus almost choked on his tea.

The priest laughed. "Sorry, I didn't mean to startle you, but my point is that you are right. Priests are just like everyone else. The only difference is their relationship with the Creator."

"No offense, Father, but I don't really believe in a Creator." Cyrus put his tea down and stared into it. "I don't want to."

The priest shrugged. "What you want has very little bearing on reality, I'm afraid. Why don't you want to believe in a Creator?"

Cyrus looked into the priest's kind face. "Well, I don't want to seem insulting to what you believe in, but if there is a Creator, it seems to me He has to be either evil or neutral. Both are bad, but I can't decide which would be worse."

The priest looked thoughtful for a moment. Then he drew a small flask from inside his robe and poured a dollop of something into his tea. "Well, let's think about it for a moment. An evil god would intentionally be causing more harm, wouldn't he? He wouldn't really have the power to stop evil, because that would be stopping himself." He offered the flask to Cyrus.

Cyrus accepted the proffered beverage additive. "Hmm. Well, what about a neutral god? That seems worse, really, because he would have the power to stop these evil things, but lets them happen anyway. Just standing off when you could fix things is more cowardly and vile than committing the acts in the first place."

The priest put down his tea and stirred it gently. "I notice that you exclude the possibility of a good Creator."

Cyrus frowned and took a sip of his tea. Brandy! The priest had put brandy in their tea! Cyrus swallowed both the surprise and the tea, and continued. "I just can't reconcile the possibility of a good Creator with there being evil in the world. I mean, look at your church, Father! Look at this village. Look at those graves out there. If there is a good God who has power over everything, there wouldn't be evil. He would block it, stop it. But there *is* evil, as you well know, so . . . " He shrugged.

"There wouldn't be evil, you say?" The priest leaned back in his chair and rested his teacup on his chest. "What if people deliberately chose to do evil?"

"Then He should stop them. What's a good God for if not to eliminate evil?" Cyrus said, then blinked. "Wait a minute, what do you mean? You think evil is only in the world because people bring it with them?"

The priest sighed. "All sentient creatures in the world have been given a precious gift: free will. However, such a gift can be misused. The choice to do evil is there, and many choose it." He paused and finished his tea. "If the Creator kept people from doing that evil, then they wouldn't really be free, would they?"

Cyrus was silent for a moment. He stared at a candle guttering on the altar. "I guess not," he finally said. "But that still begs the question of why He created evil in the first place."

"He did *not* create evil!" The priest stood up and thumped his hands onto the table. "Evil is created when free will is misused. To say that the Creator created evil is practically blasphemy!"

Cyrus was taken aback by the priest's angry demeanor, and held up his hands. "Sorry, sorry. But really, why would . . . "

"Because He loves His creations," the priest said gently, sitting back down. "It may be confusing at first, but only until you realize that Love is a far more wonderful and terrible thing than simply kindness. When people are comfortable, they don't feel a need for a Creator. It's only when things go wrong or they're suffering that they cry out to Him. The Creator uses the suffering, lad. Yes, uses it. The very suffering caused by evil acts like His voice-amplification spell, calling people to Him. Without the evils of the world, only the very moral or very lowly would seek Him."

"So then evil is allowed to remain because it's . . . useful?" Cyrus put his teacup down on the edge of the altar.

"Far from it. The Creator merely makes the best possible use of a bad thing." The priest accidentally dribbled some tea down the front of his habit and wiped it off with his free hand. "Eventually, He will destroy it. That is why Heroes are so important. They keep evil from growing too strong, from causing too much suffering. The Creator does not want His creations to suffer needlessly, but only what is good for them."

Cyrus thought for a moment. "Kind of like exercise. It hurts, but in the end, it makes you stronger."

The priest nodded. "Close, but not exactly the same thing. It's more like taking small amounts of a poison to build up your immunities to it. It isn't a good thing at all, but it will strengthen you."

Cyrus shifted in his chair. "I don't know if I accept all of that, but it does help a bit. If there's even a possibility of a good Creator . . . " He fell silent.

The priest waited. The chill night wind whistled through the colored shards of the broken windows, blowing out a few of the candles along the west wall. It also carried in a small black bird, which perched on one of the shattered pews, chirped sadly, and flew out again.

"So," he said at length, "is that what was troubling you, or was there something else?" The priest's gaze was intense from beneath his thick black eyebrows.

Cyrus felt a little uncomfortable, then remembered what he had been thinking about before he went to check on the horses. "Yeah, there is, Father. It's about . . . well . . . it's about Kris, and, well . . . "

"Stop hesitating and spit it out, Cyrus," The priest sat back up in his chair and placed an elbow on the table. "Everything you tell me is kept in strictest confidence. But if you don't say what you need to, I can't help you. Stop beating around the bush and speak."

Cyrus sighed. "Right. Well, Kris and I have been through some pretty rough stuff together. We've been under pressure, fought side by side, and talked under the stars about our beliefs. During all this, something has been happening to me. I don't understand it, but it boils down to this: I think I'm falling in love with her."

"And?" The priest motioned for Cyrus to continue.

"Is that . . . right? I don't know what the Creator would think of it. It seems kind of, well, unnatural. I've heard of Humans who turn to other races only to . . . um . . . "

"To fulfill their lustful desires? No, that would be wrong. Unnatural lust. There's a difference between that and love. Love is your commitment toward the person inside the body, not just attraction to the body itself."

Cyrus frowned. "But how can I be sure that that's what it is? What if I'm just some pervert with an unnatural lust?"

"Let's put it this way," the priest said. "Would you still love her if she was Human?"

"Of course!" Cyrus said.

"What about if she was an Orc?"

Cyrus grimaced. "Hey now, that's not fair!"

The priest chuckled. "I know it isn't, but it does prove a point. How much of this 'love' you think you have for her is based on how she looks?"

"To be honest with you, some of it was," Cyrus said, looking away. "Once she stopped trying to kill me, and I got over being suspicious of her and her brother, I realized that she was beautiful, physically and mentally."

"Despite the fur?" the priest said with a raised eyebrow.

"Fur notwithstanding," Cyrus replied. "If she wasn't, I probably wouldn't have given her a second thought. But once I got to know her, I thought less about what she looked like and more about what kind of person she is, and how much she's like a Human girl."

"An astute observation, young man," said the priest. "The Nine Races are more alike than one would think just by looking at them."

"But what would my family think if I . . . well, if I married her? People would talk behind my back. I don't really mind that myself, but I don't want Kris to get hurt by that sort of talk. I've seen how angry she gets when people refer to her as an animal."

The priest finished his tea and put the teacup down on the saucer with a muted *clink*. "Well, your friends and family won't think anything worse about her than hers will about you. Look at you: no fangs, no claws, no tail, and no real fur to speak of. There's very little about you that *is* like a Katheni. And besides, it isn't like she is inferior in any way, just because she's a Katheni. The Nine Races are equal in the sight of the Creator."

"Equal? Even Orcs?" Cyrus shifted in his chair, scooting it backward across the scarred and muddy floor.

The priest nodded. "Even Orcs. The Creator gave each Race a different gift. To the Ransha, He gave tough scales to defend themselves and strong tails to balance and swim. To Elves He gave long lives and wisdom. Katheni received the gifts of speed and agility. Orcs received great strength and stamina. The Istaka were granted great skill at hunting for their families, warm fur, and a structured society, and so on. But Humans have no natural defenses, no claws or fangs, not even any natural covering.

"Humans would seem the most vulnerable," the priest said, "but their Creator-given gifts are great though less obvious: genius and community. Humans are the most innovative Race, and the only one to build and maintain such large cities. For example, Elves have used the same type of longbow for countless centuries.

"But Humans, once they got a look at the original design, developed the crossbow, twin-curve bow, wheeled bow, and ballista. Human strength lies in this genius, and in the fact that Humans easily band together for a common cause. One or two large Human cities can easily field an army to match any force thrown at them by the fragmented tribal leadership of most Races.

"But I digress. The point is that the Nine Races, though different from each other, are still equal."

Cyrus pondered for a moment, scuffing his toes on the carpet runner. "But still, wouldn't the fact that we're members of different Races make it wrong? Kris and me, I mean."

"Listen," the priest said. "I'll make this as clear as I can. Your souls are the same. They are merely placed in different types of body. Thus, though it is unusual for two members of different races to fall in love, it is not unnatural."

"So the Creator . . . "

"Wouldn't have a problem with it," the priest said with a wink. "The Katheni girl is every bit as 'Human' as you are."

Cyrus gave a sigh of relief. "Well, then. That does clear things up. Thanks, Father. If you would," Cyrus looked down at his shoes for a moment, "tell the Creator I said thanks."

The priest smiled, "You can tell Him yourself. You may not be able to see Him, but He's always around."

Cyrus nodded and headed off to the back room. He lay down and fell asleep almost immediately.

Ten minutes later, the priest heard soft footfalls behind him. He turned to see Kris, who stopped in her tracks.

"I'm sorry," Kris said. "I didn't know anyone was still up."

"If you're thinking about going outside to look at the stars, it's overcast," the priest said.

Kris frowned. "Well, then can I talk to you for a while?"

"Certainly," the priest said, showing Kris to the same chair Cyrus had just been sitting in. "What's troubling you, my dear?"

Kris looked at the floor. "It's about Cyrus . . . "

The priest sighed amiably. It was going to be a long night.

Chapter 23

THE GLOAMING

In which the Villains begin collecting Parts for their
Dastardly Plan, and Slashback has a Flashback

A SINGLE TORCH burned in the dark passageway. It bobbed up and down, weaving its way down the narrow stone corridor, stopping at cross-passages and doors, searching for the correct one.

Finally it arrived at a thick, oak door marked with a *Wizard's Rune of Silence*. The flame went out. Its bearer stepped inside the small room and met a cheery fire and a not-so-cheery Voshtyr.

⬤ ⬤ ⬤

You're late," Voshtyr snapped. "What took you so long?"

"My apologies," the black-robed figure said, setting the extinguished torch down near the door. "I had to travel to this mountain from your other keep, of course, and I had not anticipated encountering an entire regiment of soldiers and Heroes investigating your swamp keep."

"Bah. They are of little import," Voshtyr said with a snort. "I trust you dealt with them?"

"Of course. It would not do to have them know that I was about."

"Survivors?"

"None."

"Good."

This reception room was too small for the rich decorations in it. The chairs were too fancy, too soft, the paintings too risqué and worldly. Even the fire put out more heat than was needed, another sign of this man Voshtyr's weakness. But it mattered not.

Voshtyr indicated a black velvet chair at the small round table, and his guest sat. "And the pieces of my device?" he asked. "You secured them?"

The cloaked figure nodded. "I disassembled it. It is stored within the reach of my arm."

"In one of those storage spheres?"

"Of course." The man removed a small shining ball from a pocket in his voluminous black cloak.

The eldritch brilliance of the sphere cast shadows all around the reception room before dimming to a viewable light level. At first glance, the sphere appeared to be a clear bouncy ball, the type small children played with. However, on second look, it seemed to have extraordinary depth, appearing to contain a miniature sea.

He placed the sphere on the table between himself and Voshtyr. "You are aware, I assume, of how these spheres operate?"

"No," said Voshtyr, picking the sphere up and staring into its stormy depths. "I am not. Though they have fascinated me for a long time, I never did learn how they can store so much in such a small area."

"They do not. They store things in an enormous area, elsewhere."

Voshtyr blinked. "What do you mean?"

The man leaned back in his soft velvet chair and sighed. "Have you ever lost something and then thought, 'Since it is not where it belongs, it must be somewhere else'?"

"A few times, why?" Voshtyr asked.

"As you know, we are aware of two distinct worlds: ours, which for the sake of simplicity we will call *Home*, and the world home to demons and gods, which we call *Another Space*," the man explained. "However, between these two, there is a gap, where a world could perhaps be, but is not. It is hazardous to even look inside this gap, which we call *Somewhere Else*. This sphere," the man said, tapping the effulgent sphere in Voshtyr's palm, "is a direct connection to *Somewhere Else*. We do not fully understand it ourselves, but when you place something in it, that object is slipped in between the layers of existence, somewhere between *Home* and *Another Space*—a shadow world, a place with no name. *Somewhere Else*."

Voshtyr leaned forward in his leather-covered chair. "Interesting. How does one access this area without using one of these spheres?"

The man snatched the crystalline orb from Voshtyr's hand. "One does not," he said in a tone of voice harder than hundredfold steel. "The gods do not, we do not, and you most certainly do not. It is not a place to be trifled with."

Voshtyr clamped his hand on the man's wrist. "I don't intend to do anything with it. Give me back that sphere right now, Keltar."

"*Lemarath karashanti*, Voshtyr. I have already told you not to speak my name aloud. Unhand me at once," Keltar said, staring into Voshtyr's eyes, sending the desired message.

Voshtyr's eyes widened, and Keltar knew that his mind was filling with stark, unreasoning terror and the urgent need to remove his grasp from Keltar's wrist. The moment Voshtyr released his grip on Keltar, Keltar released his grip as well.

Keltar removed his hood, enjoying the effect his pointed ears, silver hair, colorless eyes, and other albino Elven features had on Voshtyr. He placed his face inches from Voshtyr's. "Touch me again," he said softly, "and the wrath of the Citadel will wipe this pathetic mountain keep and your grandiose plans from existence. Do I make myself clear?"

Voshtyr scowled at him. "Inescapably. Now, deliver what is mine."

Keltar focused his attention on the transparent sphere in his palm. He deftly cracked it with a single hand, as a chef cracks an egg. "Voshtyr's device," he said. "To be placed on the top floor, in the space provided. *Merionath hjovar.*"

A small ripple passed through the air, and the sphere glowed brilliantly for a brief moment. Keltar smiled and cupped his left hand over the broken sphere. "Your machine is in its designated place. Now," he said in a businesslike tone, "I believe you owe me two thousand gold pieces."

Voshtyr nodded and handed Keltar a small leather bag. "That contains several dozen assorted magical gemstones. They should more than compensate you—not only for the service rendered and your trouble, but also for the good graces of your people. I hope to one day call the Kinetics my allies."

Keltar smiled a discomforting smile. "It may happen one day, but it will not be soon. Farewell, Voshtyr. We may not meet again, but we shall be watching you intently."

"I would hope so," the Villain replied. "If my plan succeeds, your people will be treated to the sight of the most impressive slaughter seen since the Twenty-Minute War. Tell your Elders to observe the Vale of Dreams closely," he said, extending his hand to the Elf.

Keltar grasped Voshtyr's proffered hand firmly. Then he reached out a pale hand. The torch rose from its place on the floor and floated into the Elf's hand. With that, he left the room, cloak swirling.

A single torch bobbed up and down in the dark passageway, retracing the route it had taken less than an hour earlier. It flickered its way to where daylight could once again strike the bearer's eyes, and went out.

Roger Farella and Slashback Ricor collapsed into a pile of scales and feathers. "Is no use," the gryphon whistled. "Is too heffy. My wings cannot help enough."

The gryphon and Araquellus were working, so far without much success, to move and connect the large and unwieldy device that had recently appeared in the pinnacle of the keep's tallest tower.

Slashback sat up, wriggling violently to shake the dust from her feathers and fur. Done dislodging dust, she looked up at the machine they were having so much difficulty with. It was a monstrosity, a cobbled-together metallic cylindrical mess. The gryphon wasn't even sure that the thing would fit in the room when fully assembled, despite the vaulted ceiling.

Sunlight streamed in through four arrow slits in the walls facing north, south, east, and west, illuminating the round towertop room and the large chunks of machine and stacks of boxes it contained.

"I don't know how Voshtyr expects us to move this thing when it's already partially assembled," Roger said irritably. "It was hard enough getting it set up in the swamp keep—and we were doing it piece by piece then. Now . . . ?" He rubbed a blue hand over his face. "Well, let's give it one more try, and if we can't do it, we'll just have to give up."

"Can I be of assistance?" a metallic voice asked.

Slashback turned to see Locke, the golem who had guided them up to the large circular room in which they now stood.

The animated suit of armor paused briefly at the entryway, then clanged into the room. "Do you rrrequirrre assistance? I am prrroficient in all forrrms of manual labor," the golem said.

Roger indicated the large and unwieldy turbine they had unsuccessfully attempted to move. "That right there," he said, "needs to be moved into the green circle on the floor. Get to work."

"Pliss," Slashback added.

"Of courrrse." Locke stepped up to the bulky piece of machinery and placed both of his flat, four-fingered hands on the turbine. With no apparent strain, the golem shoved the heavy fan into its proper place with the harsh scrape of metal against stone.

Roger eyed the golem admiringly. "Excellent, golem. Are you familiar with the assembly of this machine?"

The interior of the golem's helmet-like head glowed a dim red as he thought. "I have such instrrructions, yes."

"Then finish assembling it. Slashback and I will report to Lord Voshtyr." Roger turned on his heel and strode from the room. He stopped outside the door to turn his heel back off again, and continued down the hall.

Slashback watched Locke effortlessly move several more of the large pieces of equipment, whatever strange devices animated him whirring inside his metal torso. Voshtyr's magical Device rapidly took shape in front of her. Now she could see that it was a miniature version of the Keep of Five Flames, with five slots in the front. The tower was composed of powerful turbines, with thick, insulated cables leading to a coffin-like box against the far wall.

The golem was finally frustrated by being too short to place the top on the tower. He stared up at the machine. As he did so, the visor of the helmet fell open with a hollow clank. Slashback noted that there was absolutely nothing inside the golem's head, save a large garnet, which was somehow fastened to the back of the helm.

He clanged over to where Slashback perched atop a pile of boxes. "I am sorrry, Miss Slashback," the golem said, eye fading until it was barely lit. "I have failed in my task."

"What you mean?" Slashback said. "You haff not failed! See, I show you." She took the crown-piece from the golem's large steel hands and flew to the top of the device. The gryphon had to be extra cautious with the pinnacle, as it appeared to contain some sort of pendulum that crackled dangerously every time it swung near the cap's glass sides. Carefully noting the thread pattern, she screwed the pinnacle onto the tower replica, then returned to her perch and shook her wings. "See? Job iss done. You haff not failed."

"Thank you, Miss Slashback," Locke said. "Yourrr concerrrn is not necessarrry, but apprrreciated."

"Why you say such things?" asked the gryphon. "You talk as if you are to be treatet as object!"

The golem creaked as he tilted his head, regarding Slashback with the fist-sized garnet, which apparently served him as both eye and brain. "That is only prrroperrr, Miss Slashback. I am a parrrt of this castle, a serrrvant to whoever owns it. It is not up to me how I am trrreated, norrr what my orrrderrrs are. It does not concerrrn me. All I am rrrequirrred to do is obey, and I am content with that."

"Hmph," Slashback snorted. "It seems fery unfair to me. Why is one so strong not free?"

"Because it is my purrrpose," Locke replied, locking the clasps on the giant mechanism down into place with a squeak and a bang. "If I do not do what I was designed forrr, then I have no use. To you, it would be much like not flying because you did not like how yourrr wings looked. A grrryphon is meant to fly. I am meant to worrrk. Now," he said, turning back to the gryphon, "shall I show you to yourrr quarrrterrrs?"

"Uf course," Slashback replied, the skin around the corners of her beak turning upwards in the gryphonic equivalent of a smile. "Lead on, Lok."

The mercenary captains stood in a disorderly line in the great central hall of Voshtyr's keep.

It was a grand and ancient room, the columns carved into towering statues of unknown Heroes and Villains. Fading light shone in from the expansive terrace, which was lined with dark green foliage springing from stone planters embedded in the exterior walls. A red carpet ran down the center of the room, terminating at a pair of brass-inlaid double-doors. At the far end of the room was a small table with a single Human skull resting on it. Behind the table sat a high-backed chair. Red plush chairs sat vacant in a corner of the hall, the perfect number to hold all of the mercenary captains.

The aforementioned mercenary captains numbered several dozen. Most were Human, but there were also several Orcs, a handful of Dwarves, and a grizzled Istaka, his lupine features marred by multiple scars. Their assorted uniforms, if they could be called such, ranged to every color from startling yellow to drab and ragged grey.

Emily pulled at her studded-leather armor and violet sash and turned to the man standing next to her. "I can't believe this. This Villain summons the best groups of mercenaries in Centra Mundi, then leaves us waiting."

"I can believe it," the man said. He adjusted his bandolier, which had become just slightly crooked during his wait. "It's a standard tactic of those who would employ mercenaries. They keep you waiting, then make a grand entrance, hoping to impress or frighten you. That done, he will use that leverage to weasel the lowest price possible out of you."

Emily scowled. "Well it isn't going to work on me. I've got more than enough power to back me up, and I can take any man in a fair fight."

"With this many mercenary captains," the impeccably uniformed man said, "I get the impression that this Villain is not the type that enjoys fair fights. I believe he's more likely the type to either stab you in the back or annihilate you with overwhelming odds."

The large, brass-inlaid doors at the back of the room opened slowly and majestically, as large double doors in hidden fortresses are wont to do. From out of it stepped four black-armored foot soldiers, an Araquellus, and a gryphon. They took places at either side of the small table in front of the mercenaries.

Then, with a flourish of unseen trumpets, a raven-haired man in a black and red cloak strode into the room, accompanied by a towering steel golem. The man took a seat in the high-backed chair at the table and motioned for the gryphon and Araquellus to sit also.

"Ladies and gentlemen," the man said grandly, "soldiers and professional cutthroats, mercenaries and murderers, I have a business proposition for you all. Anyone self-righteous enough to have such a useless thing as a conscience, you may as well leave now."

Two men in gold armor stood and left the room. Emily gave them a curious glance. They must have been Paladins, or perhaps ex-Heroes not yet inducted into the Brotherhood of the Black Hand. Good riddance. More money for her group. Still, Emily didn't much like this Villain's tone.

"Also, if you object to killing women and children, you may leave also."

A spiky-haired man in a grey silk robe bowed slightly and stepped from the line. He headed toward the exit, but dipped his head beside Emily's ear. "Emily san, this man's proposition will not please the General-sama."

"I know, Koshiro," Emily replied. "But I'll stick it out and see whether or not he's the thief and what he's up to. Go tell her for me, all right?"

Koshiro nodded and left the room.

"And finally," the Villain said, "if you've any deep attachments to a country or would have problems attacking your homeland, be so kind as to leave as well."

Several Elves left, along with every Dwarf in the room. The rest—Humans and Orcs for the most part, with a smattering of Elves and the lone scarred Istaka—remained.

"Wonderful!" The Villain clapped his hands, the combination of metal and flesh making an unusual ring. "Indeed, now I am addressing the nadir of all Races, and so I can continue. My name is Voshtyr Demonkin. I have need of several objects, the value of which is extraordinary, as only four of them exist."

At this, three mercenary captains turned to leave.

"However," Voshtyr continued quickly, "I do not ask you to lower yourselves to base theft."

This seemed to pacify the captains. They returned to line.

"No, no thievery," Voshtyr said. "All I require of you is to start a war."

A murmur ran through the assembled mercenaries. Emily blinked. Starting a war in this day and age was a difficult task. Not only would Heroes attempt to stop them, but the common people were so sick of wars that they would, with very little provocation, hang anyone who tried to incite them into rebellion.

"Now, please know that I do not start wars for no reason. I need this war to draw attention away from my true design. I will use the distractions provided by your war to acquire the . . . objects. When I have them all, I shall quite literally rule the world."

Voshtyr paused for a halfway decent maniacal laugh. "For assisting me in my rise, you will all be rewarded handsomely. Nor do I expect you to work without advance payment. Therefore I have invited you all here to settle on the proper amount. You, there," he said, pointing at the impeccably dressed man. "Name, rank, and company?"

"Captain Horace Landrus, division commander of the Mandrake Mercenaries," he said, snapping the heels of his well-polished boots together and saluting Voshtyr. "What do you need, sir?"

Voshtyr smiled. "Captain Landrus, follow me. The rest of you, please make yourselves comfortable. If you have any questions, please ask Lord Roger here, or Slashback Ricor." He gestured at the Araquellus and gryphon, then turned and strode from the room, cape billowing, with Captain Landrus following in his wake.

The mercenary captains broke from line and lounged in the Great Hall. Most took seats in the red chairs, but a few milled about impatiently. Slashback the Gryphon remained in her place, while the Araquellus, Lord Roger, sat gingerly in the chair next to her. The guards remained behind the chair, on either side behind Lord Roger.

Emily approached the Araquellus, judging him to be second-in-command of Voshtyr's operation. "Hey, 'Quellus," she said, leaning on the table. "I don't have time to wait around for all these other sods to have their interviews. I need to know the low-down, and I need it now. Can we speed it up a bit?"

The Araquellus glared at Emily. "I wasn't aware they allowed children to be emissaries for important mercenary companies. And what is your name, Miss?" he asked in a bored tone.

"Emily Cartwright, Salvinsel Salamanders," Emily replied, a bit miffed by the Araquellus's response. "And I'm not a child. I'm eighteen this year."

Emily noticed the gryphon swing its head toward her. What had she said?

"As I said," the Araquellus said. "Perhaps your organization is not important if it sends us someone with so little experience, tact, and patience. *Captain* Cartwright, you and your outfit do not qualify for Voshtyr's missions. You wish to hasten this process? Very well, you may leave this very moment. You operate on Lord Voshtyr's timetable or not at all. Good day to you," he said, turning away.

"What?" Emily said, taken aback.

"Voshtyr is not interested in dealing with hasty, impatient children who have no respect for his rules. Go back and tell your outfit that you have not been hired. Good day."

"You can't do that!" Emily placed a hand on the hilt of her colichemarde. The rapier-like blade started out as wide as a shortsword, then stepped down to almost the thinness of a fencing foil, combining good parrying and rapid thrusting abilities.

Air hissed over the instantly extended organic blade-ridge on the blue man's arm as he stepped inside Emily's guard, the edge of his blade coming to rest right across her throat. "Yes, I can," he said in a lazy monotone. "Can and have. Leave now before we throw you out."

Emily carefully removed her hand from her colichemarde hilt. She scowled darkly as she slowly backed away. "You're going to regret that, 'Quellus. Whatever your half-baked plan is, it'll be foiled, and we'll help whoever's foiling you."

A cold smile crept across the Araquellus's face. "Really? How disappointing. Guards, kill this woman."

Emily broke out of her shock when the four black-armored guards stepped forward, pikes leveled at her. Determination quickly replaced shock, and she drew her colichemarde. She lunged at one of the black-clad soldiers. The guard thrust at her with his pike, but Emily's lunge was a feint, quickly followed by another thrust, this one through the narrow gap twixt the soldier's helm and breastplate. He fell heavily to the floor, clutching his throat.

Emily pivoted in time to parry an attack from the soldier behind her, slamming the head of the pike into the floor. As the guard pulled at it, Emily jumped atop his pike, ran up it, and somersaulted over the incredulous soldier, landing behind him and sprinting for the door.

"What are you buffoons waiting for?" the Araquellus yelled. "Chase her down!"

The remaining guards nodded and hastened after Emily.

"Slashback!" Emily heard the Araquellus yell, "if she makes it out of the keep, make sure she doesn't survive!"

The gryphon squawked, bounded to the window, and leapt out.

• • •

Slashback plummeted fifty feet from the tower, spread her wings, caught the air, and began circling the keep and looking for anyone fleeing on foot. Her mind, however, was elsewhere. Emily Cartwright . . . Was that girl perhaps related to . . . ?

<< Flashback of Slashback <<

"Gavin Cartwright! Where are you, you worthless boy?" Mary-Beth yelled.

Gavin kept his eyes on his kite. Of course his sister wouldn't let him have his fun. "Up here, Orc-face!"

Mary-Beth looked up into the fir tree that stood next to her faded red barn. Perched near the top was Gavin, flying his enormous kite.

"Whaddaya want?" Gavin yelled.

"I need you to go down into town and pick up those spells that old man Cornelius was preparing for the Autumn Rise celebration!" Mary-Beth hollered. "Get down here right now!"

Gavin leapt from the tree, using his kite to slow his descent. He landed almost perfectly in front of his sister, his blond bangs shrouding his vision. "Can do. Just let me—oops!"

The kite, having turned in an inappropriate direction to maintain its altitude, had plummeted and now came crashing down on top of the already grouchy Mary-Beth.

"*Gavin!*" Mary-Beth screeched, blindly swinging her broom in the general direction of her brother.

"Yipe! Ha! You can't hit anything with tha—" Gavin's sentence was interrupted by an application of broom to face. "Hey, hey! I'm going already!" he shouted over his shoulder as he began running toward town. His irate, kite-shrouded sister stayed close behind, still swinging the broom.

• • •

Gavin plodded down the dusty street, aimlessly kicking a small piece of granite. Even decorated for the Autumn Rise festival, the drab streets down which he plodded were crowded with the noisome bustle of preparations. Men tacked up faded signs, women rolled out trays of food, and several small children and a large dog romped in a mud puddle outside the baker's shop. Definitely the epitome of excitement in this town.

Gavin was bored: bored with the town, bored with the people living in it, bored with his boring life of boredom. At least coming to town provided a halfway interesting change of scenery. The aforementioned scenery consisted of sandstone and clay buildings, farmers selling their wilted vegetables, a few tired merchants half-heartedly hawking their grimy goods, and packed-dirt streets. Even the preparations and decorations for the Autumn Rise harvest festival failed to excite him. Who wanted to see another pumpkin carved to look like a demon's head or a Dragon's maw?

It was boring, perhaps, but at least different from the scenery of the farm. The only interesting thing on the farm was his giant kite, which he spent any spare time flying, fascinated by its flight and wishing he could fly as well.

He was still thinking these melancholy thoughts when he heard a high-pitched squeak and was knocked off his feet by the impact of something small and furry striking his chest.

Shaking his head to get some of the dust out of his hair, he looked down at his torso. Perched on it was a very young gryphon, barely more than a hatchling, which was about the size of a large house cat. The gryfflet looked at Gavin and squeaked again, attempting to extricate its tiny talons from his rough brown shirt.

"Easy there, little one. I'm not going to hurt you," Gavin said in a soothing voice. He couldn't believe his eyes. A real gryphon, in this boring town? He helped the grywflet get its talons free, stroking its gold-furred wings. From what he had read of gryphons, this one couldn't be more than three weeks old, because by the fourth week, they shed the baby-fuzz from their feathers.

"Hey, you!"

Gavin got up and looked around, cradling the grywflet in the crook of his left arm.

"The boy with the gryphon! Stay where you are!" A man in a purple-tinted suit of plate-armor stepped out of an alley, his labored breathing echoing inside his helmet. "Hand over the gryphon, boy."

Gavin raised an eyebrow as the grywflet squeaked again and attempted to hide in Gavin's shirt. "Is it your gryphon?"

"Well," the man said, "not yet, but I am capturing it for a nobleman. Now, hand it over. I've chased it all the way from Firestorm Peak, and I'm not losing it now."

"Hmmm," Gavin said thoughtfully. "How much does a grywflet sell for?"

"What?" the man exclaimed. "You expect me to pay you for it?"

Gavin smiled. "Of course! I have the animal right here. You can buy it from me for . . . let's say . . . three thousand gold pieces."

"Three thousand?"

"It seems a fair price to me. After all, a gryphon egg usually sells for around twenty-five hundred, and this one's already hatched and partially grown. It's really quite the bargain."

The man removed his helmet, letting a blond ponytail fall free, and scowled at the boy. "Listen here, brat. I don't have time for this idiocy. Give me that gryphon, *now.*"

"Nothing doing." Gavin wasn't about to give up the most exciting thing that had happened to him in years.

The armored man stalked forward, grabbed Gavin by his shirt-front, and lifted the boy from the ground. The gryfflet panicked and crawled through Gavin's shirt, getting behind him. "Boy, I'm taking that gryphon. Whether or not your face remains in one piece when I do is up to you." The purple-armored man drew back a gauntleted fist, prepared to bash the boy's skull. He almost did, and would have, had the townspeople not started whispering around him.

"Is that a Hero or a Villain?"

"I think that's the Purple Paladin . . . "

"What's a Hero doing threatening a child?"

"Shameful. What's this world coming to when a Hero bullies a young boy?"

The knight glanced around him, absorbing the disapproving stares of passerby. Slowly, he lowered Gavin to the ground. "All right, boy. I'll pay you your accursed money," he said, glaring at the boy. "But don't you *dare* move from this spot until I get back, or there will be Hells to pay."

"Y-yes sir," Gavin said, just getting his breath back.

"And don't you go letting it escape, either. I'll be back in ten minutes." The Paladin turned and stalked off.

Gavin watched him go. He had ten minutes to find a good hiding place. As soon as the Hero left the town to search for him and the gryfflet, the boy would have to get as far from this place as possible.

And he did. That very moment Gavin Cartwright ran away from home, gryphon in tow. Although he was not a Hero, he did become a hero. As he grew, his exploits as a mercenary, soldier, and gryphon-rider spread far across the land of Salvinsel. He and his gryphon lived happily and well. His parents eventually sold the farm and moved to Bryath City and opened a farmer's market. Mary-Beth went on to marry a minor duke, and had several children.

Then Gavin's mercenary company was hired to settle a border dispute. A warlord expanding the borders of Kelm, a country on Landeralt's west coast, was attempting to take over the neighboring kingdom of Bedrin to the south. Bedrin's large but poorly trained military made it an easy target for a cunning warlord with a trained army. Realizing that this situation could be easily taken care of without involving his own men, the warlord hired Gavin's company.

But the soldiers of the Bedrin turned out to be much more competent than the warlord had painted them, and Gavin's company was nearly annihilated. Gavin and his gryphon airlifted many of his company to safety, salvaging what remained of his unit.

Unfortunately, two wandering Heroes stumbled across the battle. Knowing the history of the region, they immediately sided with the Bedrin rather than Kelm. Noting the lone gryphon-rider, one of the Heroes climbed to the top of a nearby tower.

Gavin was flying in to pick up the last survivor when the Hero leapt from the tower, five-foot sword glittering in the sun, and struck Gavin and his gryphon out of the air. All three landed heavily in the dirt.

The Hero dusted himself off and began walking away, but he was not the only one who had survived the fall.

The gryphon put her snout to see to Gavin, but he was dead on the ground. The gryphon, full of hate and uncomprehending anger, charged her assailant.

But the Hero was ready.

Thus it was that Slashback Ricor was deprived of the one who had cared for her, and was herself injured to the point of death, by a Hero named the Crimson Slash. She would have died, but a Villain named Voshtyr found her on the battlefield and cared for her until she could once again fly. When the Villain promised to help her get revenge on Crimson, she joined his cause.

>> *End of Slashback's Flashback* >>

Voshtyr no longer helps me seek the Crimson Slash as he once promised, Slashback thought as she circled the Keep, her internal monologue thankfully free of speech impediments. *He seems to have forgotten, and now rides a different wind. If this girl is of Gavin Cartwright's brood, perhaps she will help me gain my revenge.*

Slashback spotted a lone figure leaving one of the side-gates of Voshtyr's mountain Keep. As soon as the girl had put sufficient distance between herself and the keep, Slashback dove.

Emily never knew what hit her. One minute she was running for her life, the next she found herself soaring a thousand feet in the air, strong talons holding her arms securely. She craned her neck and saw she had been snatched by Voshtyr's heavily scarred gryphon.

Well, Emily thought. *I guess there are worse ways to die than to be dropped from a great height. It wasn't how I expected to die, though . . .*

Her morbid thoughts were interrupted by the gryphon. "Emli Catrite! Who is Gaffin Catrite to you?"

"Gavin?" Emily repeated. "My lost uncle Gavin? You know him?"

"He iss your uncle?" the gryphon asked. "You are chilt of Mary-Bet?"

Emily twisted uncomfortably in the avian mammal's claws. "Yes," she yelled over the rushing wind, "but how do you know that?"

A tear welled up in the gryphon's large blue eye, only to be swept away by the wind. "Your uncle was my friend and rider. We haff no time for talk now, but we will. I must drop you so Koshtyr will tink you are deat. Gut-bye, Emli. Do not die."

Slashback released her grip on Emily's arms.

Emily screamed as she plummeted through the air. As she saw the ground rushing up at her, she passed out.

Chapter 24

TROUBLE ON A RAINY DAY

In which it Pays to Listen to the feeling
that Something Bad is going to Happen

CYRUS WOKE WITH a smile on his face. The priest in the church had answered, to one degree or another, a question that had troubled his mind for years. And he'd set Cyrus's mind at ease concerning Kris, as well. It was already a good day, and he hadn't gotten out of bed yet. Cyrus rose, dressed, and checked his equipment.

Katana was still asleep, his black-furred head resting on a spellbook. Cyrus knelt down next to the slumbering Katheni. "Katana."

Katana didn't stir.

"Katana," Cyrus repeated, louder.

Still no response.

"*Vampires!*" Cyrus yelled.

Katana jumped bolt upright, fur standing on end, and phantasmal fire blazing around his paws. "The Fiends! In a church no less! They will— Wait, what are you laughing about?"

Cyrus leaned back against the wall, chuckling. "You're a bit difficult to wake up, y'know that?" he said. "Come on, we'd best get going if we're going to make it to Mir by the end of the week."

"A dirty trick," Katana complained, canceling the spell and attempting to smooth down his bristled fur. "I should lodge a formal complaint with the Guild of Heroes about you. But since you are in such a blasted hurry, let me collect my things and wake my sister. I assume you'll ready the animals?"

"Actually," Cyrus said, "I'll wake Kris up, if you don't mind. Go ahead and get packed. I'll have everything else ready by the time you're ready to leave."

"All right, but be careful. She can be a bit grouchy in the early morning." Katana turned his attention to the pile of spellbooks he had been studying the night before.

Cyrus left the room and crossed the small hallway between the two storage rooms.

Early sunlight streamed in through the sanctuary windows, some of it tinted into beautiful colors by the single remaining pane of stained glass. The priest himself was nowhere to be seen.

Cyrus shrugged and walked over to the other door. "Kris?" he said, knocking gently.

There was no response.

Muttering under his breath about Katheni being heavy sleepers, he gently opened the door. He was almost bowled over by a ball of spotted tawny fur.

Kris pounced Cyrus, knocking the wind out of him. "Good morning, Cyrus," she said, wrapping her arms around him and rubbing her speckled head on his chest.

"Well, good morning to you too, Kris," said Cyrus, putting an arm around her and trying to catch his breath. "You seem to be in a good mood today. Why is that?"

"Oh, no particular reason," Kris said, then tilted her head up and kissed Cyrus.

Cyrus was too startled to say anything at all, not even his usual incoherent monosyllables. He simply stared at the Katheni girl on his chest.

Kris frowned. "Did I do that wrong?"

"Uh . . . um, no, I just wasn't . . . expecting it, that's all. Now that I'm paying attention, though," Cyrus said, a mischievous smile dancing across his face, "want to try it again?"

"Of course!" Kris said, and repeated her last action.

"A-*hem!*" Katana said from the doorway.

Kris and Cyrus immediately broke apart, blushing madly. "Er, right then," Cyrus said. "I, um, need to go get the horses ready."

As Cyrus passed, Katana grabbed his arm. "That didn't look much like 'having everything else ready' to me," he whispered.

Cyrus chuckled. "Well, that didn't seem much like 'a bit grouchy in the early morning,' either," he said, and stepped out the door.

The horses were fine. Cyrus fed them their rations of oats and went back inside the church. Kris and Katana had finished packing up and were chatting with the priest.

"All right, we're ready to leave," Cyrus said. "Thank you for letting us stay here, Father. We really appreciate all you did for us."

The priest smiled. "You're very welcome," he said with a wink at Cyrus.

Kris and Katana thanked the priest also, then followed Cyrus out the door. The priest wished them a safe journey, and they mounted their horses, riding through the ruined village at a brisk pace. Cyrus turned back to wave to the priest.

And received a shock.

The church was gone. Not a shingle, not a stone of it remained. Only the fresh graves marked where the courtyard had been. The party quickly returned to the village. There was no sign that they had been there, and no sign of the priest.

Katana shuddered, his fur bristling. "It wasn't magic," he said. "There's no trace of anything. It's just . . . gone. It's gone, and it scares me. Nothing scares me more than things I don't understand."

"But what was it?" Kris asked.

"Whatever it was, I don't want to think about it," Cyrus said with a look at Kris. "It was a good thing for us, and I'm not about to question the source. If I did, it would only lead to more questions."

With that, they continued on their way, leaving the destroyed village and the mystery behind.

From sunrise to sunset, Cyrus, Kris, and Katana rode through fields of waving grass, punctuated occasionally by small farms and patches of dry wheat. At the horizon during the day, Cyrus could see a vague heat haze. They would soon be in the desert of Mir.

It was an uneventful ride. Well, more or less. For Cyrus, the long day was kept interesting by the fact that when he rode next to Kris she would sneak kisses whenever Katana wasn't looking. And Cyrus was just fine with that.

At the end of the third day they made camp in the lee of a rocky hill. The thick grasses made for soft bedding for the two Katheni, and an easy setup for Cyrus's tent. After lighting a cookfire and setting a pot of water to boil, Cyrus sat down with a map and began studying it by the dancing firelight. Kris lay on the ground next to him, resting her speckled head on his left thigh.

Katana tied the horses to stakes in the ground and sat down to sort some things in his spellbooks. After the sun finished sinking beneath the waves of grass, Katana rose and stretched. "How far, Cyrus?"

Cyrus scanned the map for a moment, tracing their route with his index finger. "I think if we keep up our present rate of travel, we should make it to Mir by midmorning or afternoon tomorrow. The ground's already turning a bit sandy. Once we hit the desert, you two will have to take the lead. I've never been this far north. At least not on Centra Mundi."

"Well, to be honest with you," Katana said, rubbing the back of his furred neck, "I don't know exactly how to get there."

"What?" Cyrus looked up from his map. "You've never been to Mir?"

Katana sat down next to Cyrus. "To Mir, yes, but that was years ago. I've only been to Centra Mundi twice before now. I studied at the Rubic Academy of Magic for three years, then returned home. Kris has only been there once, and aside from that, has never been off of Salvinsel. I'm not sure our kin even know that we're coming."

Cyrus scowled. "Why didn't you tell me that earlier?"

"It wasn't important," Katana said. "We *are* kin, and they know that our tribe was nearly wiped out and that there were survivors. They will think that some of us would be bound to head for Mir. I know that we're welcome, if we can get there. I just don't know if they're expecting us."

"Well, that makes things more difficult," Cyrus said, annoyed. "What am I supposed to do, just dump you at the entrance to Mir and say, 'Here you go, have fun in the desert,' and leave?"

Katana's eyes narrowed. "If you think that is what will be necessary, then yes. If that's all you're capable of, fine. A real Hero would do better."

"Hey, now," Cyrus protested, rolling the map up. "What's that supposed to mean?"

The black Katheni stared into Cyrus's eyes. "If you're afraid of a little sand, then Kris and I can handle the desert by ourselves."

Kris cleared her throat. The two stopped arguing for a moment as she got up and removed the map case from Cyrus's hand and promptly thumped Katana on the head with it. "Honestly," she said, "males. What is your big problem? Katana, Cyrus only offered to get us to Mir, no more. It's his choice whether or not to help us find our kin once we get there. Stop trying to shame him into it, brother. I'm sure he would help if you asked him to."

"I'm sorry, Cyrus," Katana said, hanging his head. "She's right. I was trying to get you to take us further than you'd said. I was afraid we wouldn't make it by ourselves. There are slavers and other monsters in and around Mir that I can't handle by myself."

Cyrus smiled. "Well, why didn't you say it that way in the first place? I'll take you as far as you need me to. I don't care if we have to wander the length and breadth of Mir to find your kin—that just makes it more of a Quest."

"Thank you, Cyrus," Kris said. "Now, I'm very tired, and I'm going to sleep. You males can stay up and argue all you like, as long as you do it *quietly*." She then walked off to a patch of tall grass and bedded down for the night.

Cyrus looked her direction for a few moments, then back at Katana. "She's very good at that, isn't she?"

"Ever since we were cubs," Katana replied, chuckling. "It didn't matter where an argument was, as long as it was within her hearing she would find and defuse it. She could even take most of the sting out of arguments between my father and me."

Cyrus detected a bitter note in Katana's voice. "Argued with your father a lot, did you?"

"Only whenever we spoke to one another," Katana said, staring into the fire. "He wasn't fond of my magic use. He only tolerated it because it was good for the tribe. Our last fight was so violent that he threatened to disinherit me. Had we not been attacked and scattered . . . "

Cyrus placed a hand on Katana's shoulder. "At least you had your dad your whole life. I envy you for that."

"You don't know my father," Katana said, shrugging Cyrus's hand off. "He sent me to Rubic's Academy of Magic to get rid of me for a few years. When there finally came a time to put my magic to use for the good of the tribe, he sent me away with the females. All my life he's either ignored me or tried to get rid of me." Katana absently began tracing a small circle in the ground with one of his toe-claws. "It didn't make for a healthy father-son relationship."

"I'm sure he's proud of you, though."

"I'm sure he's dead!" Katana said with a snarl. "He would have caught up with us by now if he was still alive. He would have found Kris, whether or not it involved finding me also." He paused a moment and slowly let out his breath. "I'm sorry, I didn't mean to snarl at you, it's just a sensitive subject. Now if you'll excuse me, I have some thinking to do." He stalked off into the night.

Cyrus watched him go and sighed. *Even if I hadn't got along with Dad, I wouldn't have given up my time with him for all the gold in a Dragon's hoard. Poor Katana.*

A gentle hand on his shoulder interrupted his thoughts. It was Kris. Cyrus sighed. "I suppose you heard all that?"

"I couldn't help it." Kris sat down next to Cyrus, leaning her head on his shoulder and staring at the fire as it licked hungrily at the blackening wood. The chirping of crickets in the tall grass blended with the wind to create one of nature's lullabies. "My brother is rather loud. It's hard to sleep with all that going on. But it wasn't anything I haven't heard before. Brother and Father never got along well. Just thinking about all the arguments they got into gives me a headache."

"But was it really all that bad?"

Kris leaned back against Cyrus, resting her speckled head on his shoulder. "Not really," she said. "My brother wanted to learn more magic, but Father was against it. It took a while, but Father finally gave in, because he saw how much it meant to my brother. The reason he was sent with a group of females when we were attacked was because we were out of able-bodied males that could be spared. Instead of the three males Father sent with the other groups, he sent Katana, knowing that his magic was strong enough for three regular Katheni."

"So those were really more of compliments than insults?" Cyrus put his arm around Kris and gave her a hug. "I take it he doesn't see it that way."

Kris looked up into Cyrus's face. "No, he doesn't," she said. "Father had a healthy fear of magic, but he loved my brother. He was trying to train him as the future leader of our tribe, but it all fell through after the attack."

"I see," Cyrus said, poking at the campfire with a stick. "So there's nothing we can do. He'll just have to sort it out himself."

Kris sighed. "If he can. It's more difficult with Father gone, but I think he'll figure it out eventually."

Cyrus smiled. "Katana's smart. I'm sure he will. Good night, Kris." He kissed her on top of her head, between her ears.

"Good night, Cyrus," Kris said, nuzzling Cyrus's chin. She got up and padded back to her grassy bed.

Cyrus banked the fire and crawled into his tent. His thoughts did not stray far from the Katheni girl. *I sure hope the priest was right, because I like her more every day . . .*

It was raining.

The day dawned cold and wet, but Cyrus woke up warm. The inside of his tent smelled of almonds and dried hay. He snapped instantly awake. Turning his head, he saw Kris sleeping gently beside him—and promptly panicked.

"Kris!" he said, rapidly scooting out of the tent. "What are you doing in my tent?"

Kris poked her head out of the tent-flaps and giggled. "What's the matter with you, Cyrus? It was wet outside last night. I assumed your tent would be warm, dry, and safe. Would you have not wanted me to stay dry?"

Cyrus scowled. "No, I . . . I mean, yes . . . I, um . . . "

"You're so cute when you get flustered," Kris said. "I'm sorry, Cyrus. I won't do it again."

"No," Cyrus said. "Next time the weather threatens to get bad, come wake me up and I'll give you the tent. Just . . . it's not right for us to share a tent, you see."

"I think so," Kris said, rubbing at her eyes. "It's because we're not mated, right?"

"Married," Cyrus said.

"Same concept, different word," Kris said.

"No, not really. Married is a state of being, whereas mating is, well . . . "

Kris smiled. "Your language has more than one word with two meanings, Cyrus, as does ours. Your word *sex* can refer to gender or an act. It's the same in Katheni. *Mated* is the same as your *marriage*."

Cyrus picked his shirt up and put it on. "I guess so. Either way, I was taught certain things by my parents . . . "

"As was I," said Kris, crawling out of the tent and indulging in a luxurious stretch.

"And we agree that things such as spending nights together are wrong until marriage?" Cyrus concentrated on donning his boots.

"If you want to call it that."

"Then we understand each other?"

"Completely."

"Good," Cyrus said. "Now, where's your brother?"

"Over here," Katana said miserably from his seat on the horse-blankets.

Kris and Cyrus took one look at the soaked black Katheni and nearly fell over laughing.

They rode in the unrelenting rain, growing more soaked by the mile. The grassland gradually thinned out as the ground beneath them acquired a more sandy texture. To their left, Cyrus could see sand dunes off in the distance. The road, such as it was, was the dividing line between desert to the north and solid ground to the south. At least they were headed in the right direction. Despite that, Cyrus kept glancing over his shoulder.

"Why do you keep doing that, Cyrus?" Kris asked. "Are you worried about something?"

"Huh?" Cyrus said, starting. "Well, yes, actually. You know how bad things usually happen when it's raining? I can't shake the feeling that something's about to happen."

"That's not very scientific, Cyrus," Katana said, shaking to remove excess water from his fur. "Rain is a natural part of the water cycle. It has no sinister connotations."

"'Not very scientific,' says the one who uses magic," Cyrus said. "If I wanted scientific nonsense, I would ask an alchemist."

Katana sniffed. "That has nothing to with the topic at hand. Why have you got the impression that rain is a harbinger of bad things?"

Cyrus pushed his floppy hat back on his head, sending a cascade of collected rainwater down the gap between his oiled-leather raincloak and his shirt, and jumped in his saddle.

Kris giggled.

Upon recovering everything but his dignity and dry garments, Cyrus turned back to Katana. "It's just that bad things that happen to Heroes during their Quests usually happen during a rainstorm. Take our little mishap with the ogre a week ago as an example. I can't count the number of times it has been raining during a crushing defeat, the death of a trusted friend, a betrayal, or the sudden appearance of a tax collector. Most sudden ambushes happen during rainy weather."

As if he'd said the cue words, a volley of crossbow bolts shot from a thicket on a slight hill less than a dozen yards away.

Katana brought up an invisible wall that deflected several bolts.

Kris leapt from Brisk's back as soon as she heard the strings twang, and the unseen archers missed her entirely.

Three of the bolts, however, struck Cyrus, knocking him off Driver. The young Hero hit the ground hard, clutching at the bolts protruding from his side. "See?" He gritted his teeth and yanked out the bolts. Only two had penetrated skin—the other had been deflected by his chainmail, and was merely stuck in his raincloak. He slowly stood and drew his sword. "All right, you *orsobu pitchin*! Show yourselves!"

"Cyrus Solburg! You are hereby advised to stand down!" a voice yelled from the thicket. A man wearing an impeccable blue military uniform with gold trim and banded mail beneath his oiled raincloak stood up out of the thicket. He pointed a cavalry-saber at Cyrus. "All attempts at resistance will only get you injured and your Katheni friends killed."

"Who do you think you are, giving me orders like that?" Cyrus demanded.

Kris stood and began examining Cyrus's quarrel wound. "Cyrus," she said softly, rainwater dripping from her spotted ears, "I think those bolts were poisoned."

Cyrus shook his head. "Doesn't matter. I'll take care of it after I take care of *them*," he said, indicating the regiment of soldiers who had risen from their concealment and now stood next to their captain.

"I am Captain Horace Landrus of the Mandrake Mercenaries," the man said. "I will give you one minute to make up your minds, whether you will come along with us or attempt to resist."

"I appreciate the courtesy," Cyrus said, and stepped behind the horses, turning to whisper to the Katheni. "All right, this is a classic 'Ambush in the Rain' scenario. Bryath's *Complete Guide* says there are three things we can do in this situation: One, we run. That's out if I'm poisoned. Two, we surrender and go with them, then escape at an opportune moment. Not so great for multiple party members. Three, we defy them and kick all manner of *dassak*. What do you think?" he asked Kris and Katana.

Kris merely growled menacingly.

"All right," Katana said to Cyrus. "We resist. But you let me help, understand?"

Cyrus nodded. "Fine. If you're thinking magic support, I could use some kind of speed-boosting spell. Those crossbow-men are a problem, and I'll try to take as many of them down as I can within the first ten seconds."

"And cast *Spectrum Antivenin* on him, while you're at it," Kris added.

Katana frowned. "I don't have either of those memorized at the moment," he said. "Give me thirty seconds and I can come up with one of them. In the meantime, Kris, help Cyrus. I'll use *Limited Invulnerability* on you, but be careful. As the name implies, it isn't perfect."

Kris nodded and drew her short sword. Then she kissed Cyrus, "For luck."

With no further ado, Katana spoke several words in a strange tongue and traced a shield-shape on Kris's forehead, then pulled two spellbooks from his saddlebags and began leafing through one.

Cyrus stepped out from behind the horses, sword drawn. Kris was at his side. "We have decided that we will resist you!" Cyrus shouted.

"Very well," Landrus said. "Men, fire when ready!" At Landrus's signal, a volley of crossbow quarrels streaked through the rain like a swarm of angry, poisonous bees.

Cyrus ran right through the thick of them, deflecting all but one with a modified *Tornado* spin, swatting the enven-omed bolts aside.

The final bolt struck Kris on the shoulder—and glanced off of her shimmering fur. Imperfect though it was, the spell *did* provide a measure of invulnerability.

The moment the crossbowmen began reloading, the world slowed around Cyrus. Katana, true to his word, had found a *Hurry Up* spell in his spellbook.

"The Hero walked through the front rank of mercenaries, shoving any aside that got in his way, and began sedately massacring the archers in the back rank." It occurred to Cyrus that something was odd about this moment, but he couldn't put his finger on it "In the Hero's hastened state, all attempts at retaliation were easily deflected by his swift and skillful sword."

Katana watched Cyrus become a blur and begin his slaughter of the archers. He raised an eyebrow at the Hero, Second Class.

What was that high-pitched chattering sound? It sounded like a West Plains Greater Prairie Squirrel, the kind that would berate travelers with high-pitched insults for stepping too near the creatures' dens. But they were nowhere near the West Plains. They weren't even on the same continent.

Could it be the sound of Cyrus . . . narrating? It didn't sound like him. But then, he was moving at such an insane and frenzied pace that it would raise the pitch of his voice if he tried to talk. But surely that couldn't be. Cyrus would allow for no such folly.

Katana shook his head and looked back to his spellbook, searching for *Spectrum Antivenin*. It was a fairly rare medical magic, capable of nullifying any and all poisons from bee stings to the bite of a Skull Asp. He had had it used on him only once, after a run-in with a flying bloat-flower in a marsh outside of Rubic's Academy during a field trip. And for some reason, it was harder to find in his spellbook than he'd anticipated.

Apparently, they'd brought a spellcaster.

Cyrus's surroundings sped back up to normal pace. He wasn't anticipating such an abrupt shift and leapt awkwardly backward to avoid an axe to the face.

"There!" A tall Elf clad in what appeared to be mostly vines was pointing at Cyrus. "He's slowed down! Get him!"

"Oh, *bok*," Cyrus said, realizing that he was totally surrounded by his opponents and no longer had the advantage of speed.

And these men were *skilled*. Not Heroes, mind, but even with his speed and strength Cyrus couldn't dodge all the blows raining down on him, not with the ground as wet as it was. And the rain continued, making the footing progressively worse. An axe bludgeoned him across the chest, and a sword cut a gash through his chainmail.

"The young Hero fought bravely against unnumbered foes, but his skill was proving insufficient against such numbers!"

A fighter drove a spear into Cyrus's side through the rent in his armor. Cyrus gasped and yanked the spear from the man's hand. He tossed it aside and cleft the man's head in two.

"To counter such dire foes, the Hero called upon the unknown magics that had aided him before, summonging fire from the heavens!" Cyrus held up his free hand and pointed it forward at his plethora of foes.

• • •

The spell wasn't in Katana's black leatherbound tome. He reached for his second spellbook and was flipping through it, when suddenly he felt a massive drain building on the ley-lines around him.

No one really knows what force powers magic. It is an unpredictable force, the untrained working of which is nearly as dangerous as eating unidentified mushrooms in an attempt to obtain prophetic visions.

Two millennia ago, a group of wise magicians and sages met in a sacred grove to discuss magic. There they developed rules for using magic and a set of laws that explained many things about it, including the theory of "ley-lines."

These invisible lines supposedly carry pure, unadulterated elemental energy. All magical spells operate by siphoning off minuscule amounts of the elements from these lines.

This theory also explained certain things, like why fire spells were stronger near volcanoes—there were simply more fire ley-lines present. With enough practice, a spell-caster can *feel* the presence of the invisible lines, sometimes well enough to judge their approximate location.

Katana's fangs ached as he felt the nearby air ley-line vibrate rapidly. He'd felt this before. But now it seemed unusually—

To his horror, the ley-line suddenly broke. Ley-lines *cannot* break. But it did, and Katana could almost see it dangling from the storm clouds.

He watched in horror as the *entire line* bent down from the sky and wrapped itself around Cyrus's outstretched hand.

No fire funneled from the sky into Cyrus's hand, as he was hoping. Instead, his hair stood on end and a bolt of lightning arced from the cloudy sky, ran along his arm, and shot from his fingertips. It tore chunks out of the earth and sent a dozen men into screaming convulsions as the bolts danced across their wet metal armor.

"I . . . uh, I mean, calling forth Heaven's Fire!" Cyrus said, looking at his steaming hand.

As soon as the bolt dissipated, Captain Landrus of the Mandrake Mercenaries leapt at Cyrus from behind a bush and threw a vicious slash at Cyrus's throat with his saber.

Cyrus parried the blow and countered with one of his own. It too was turned aside. From what the young Hero could tell, this man was not a Villain, and thus could not match Cyrus's Heroic strength. But he was a master swordsman and proved it by diverting the force of Cyrus's blows in harmless directions at every stroke.

Kris was wreaking havoc among the foot-soldiers. Several fled, screaming about a demon cat with armor-plated fur upon which their weapons broke in their hands. She let them run, focusing only on those who had enough spine to stay and fight against an invulnerable foe.

A burly fellow brought an axe down on Kris's back with all his might, but only knocked the wind out of her.

She turned and faced the man, growling.

All the color drained from the mercenary's face.

Without a second thought, Kris pounced the man, latched her powerful jaws onto his neck, and bit.

At that sight, nearly the entire remainder of the infantry unit fled or laid down their arms.

Cyrus and Landrus dueled back and forth across the small stretch of field, churning the patch of sparse grass into thick mud. Cyrus's blows were slowing, and he clutched his side where he'd been speared. Rather than use brute force, which seemed to be failing, he began trying to find gaps in Landrus's defenses rather than trying to beat the soldier into the ground through sheer power.

"I don't understand why you aren't dead or paralyzed yet," Landrus said as he thrust his sword at Cyrus's torso. "That poison was supposed to act instantaneously."

Cyrus parried the attack with ease, and a half-smile tugged at his lips. "Isn't it obvious, Captain? I'm a Hero. You know, with Heroic abilities? And you expect something like a little poison to take me down? What do you think this is, a bad adventure novel?"

"Well, Hero, I see you're a decent swordsman as well as a magic user," Landrus said, parrying a series of rapid-fire blows Cyrus had thrown at him.

"I'm not a magic user," Cyrus said, launching another attack at the overdressed mercenary captain. "This stuff just keeps happening by accident!"

Landrus diverted Cyrus's blade, which bit deep into the turf. "Very convenient accident, a giant bolt of lighting that strikes you but kills my men instead." He struck at Cyrus once again.

Cyrus ducked under the blow and slashed at Landrus's torso. His blade bit into Landrus's banded armor. "I don't know how it works, but it's there when I need it, and it isn't when I don't." He yanked his sword free and backed off.

"Eh. Then I assume you don't need it right now?" Landrus asked, gingerly holding his side.

"Not particularly," Cyrus said, removing his hat. "I do need this, though, and so do you. Here, catch," he said, throwing the hat at Landrus's face.

Landrus flinched, swatting the hat aside with the flat of his saber. But the distraction was sufficient. In a split second, Cyrus was on top of Landrus. "With one swift stroke, the Hero opened his foe from shoulder to waist! The bright blood burst forth, and darkness shrouded his eyes!"

Landrus crumpled to the ground, his uniform shredded and his mail rent by Cyrus's final blow.

"Sorry, Landrus," quoth Cyrus, "but there is no mercy for a coward who uses poisoned arrows." He retrieved his hat, turned from his dead foe, and made for the remaining mercenaries. It was time to help Kris finish the fight.

It was not Kris, however, who needed the help.

Katana was still staring at Cyrus and the ley-line dangling above his head. He broke out of it only when a twig snapped behind him.

Katana whirled, dodging the axe stroke that had been aimed at the center of his back. A soldier had snuck up on him. Katana snatched up a twig and ran his furred finger along its short length, muttering in an ancient tongue. The twig grew and changed shape, becoming a finely crafted wooden katar.

The katar is a traditional weapon of the Katheni. The blade is just over a foot and a half long and is affixed to the front of a pair of flared guards on the right and left side of the handle. The handle itself runs parallel to the base of the blade, and thus one forms a fist around the handle when using it. Hence the blade's other name: "punch-dagger."

Most Katheni who chose this weapon wielded two at once, the better to parry with. Katana's other paw carried a spellbook, so he used only one. Either way, it was an ideal weapon for a Katheni, whose natural agility made rapid, repeated thrusts and slashes nearly impossible for foes to avoid.

But the mercenary was on the attack, not the defense. He laughed and chopped at Katana again.

"*Maryah mefaturaie,*" Katana said. His wooden katar began to glow with an eerie green light, stopping the mercenary in his steps and making it Katana's turn to advance. The crackling katar ionized the air as Katana thrust and slashed.

The mercenary tripped and fell backward onto the damp sandy ground on the western side of the path. He scooped up a handful of gritty earth and flung it into the Katheni's eyes.

Katana hissed, staggering back. The mercenary leapt up, swung his axe at the blinded Katheni—

And died.

"That was a dirty trick," Cyrus said, wiping the mercenary's blood from his sword. "One of the oldest in the Villain's *Book of Dirty Tricks*. You all right, Katana?"

"I'm fine," Katana said, rubbing the grit out of his pale eyes. "Is my sister unharmed?"

"Mostly." Kris padded down from the hill, the last of the mercenaries dead or fleeing behind her. "A few nicks and scratches, but they're nothing compared to what it would have been without your spell."

"Good," Cyrus said. "I wasn't expecting them to come right out of the am*bushes* like that."

Katana groaned. "Can't you be serious for one moment? I want to ask you about the ley-lines."

"The what?" Cyrus said.

"Oh, *leaf* him alone," Kris said, grinning and giving her brother a playful cuff on the head.

Cyrus grinned. "*Wood* you, please? I'm tired of all your *vine*ing."

The cat-mage growled. "The ley-lines, Cyrus. I have to ask you about what happened back there. Where did that lightning come from? How did you do that?"

Cyrus shrugged. "I don't know. Glad it worked, though." He shook his head and put an arm around the Katheni girl. "Anyway, you were amazing, Kris. Especially for a weedy girl."

"Speak for yourself, twig," she retorted.

"No, I'm serious! For not being a Hero, that was pretty impressive stuff."

Kris looked at Cyrus and giggled. "For thinking your mentor's habits are annoying, you certainly sounded a lot like him."

"How do you mean?" Cyrus asked, wiping the blood from his blade.

"You were narrating, just like Reginald does."

Cyrus blinked. "What? No, no I wasn't. You must have been hearing things."

"I was hearing *you*, narrating," Kris insisted. "You even quoth something toward the end there."

Cyrus took off his hat and scratched his head. "Eh, I doubt it. There's a greater chance that I'd give up Heroics and become an investment banker than that I'd pick up *that* habit, of all the ones available. I spent years writing down Reg's narrations. That's more than enough for me."

Kris smiled, laughing again. "Either way, that was tiring. I can't remember when I've ever fought that hard for that long."

"I feel a bit drained myself," Cyrus said, then abruptly sat down. "Maybe we should go to the carnival."

"What?" Kris and Katana asked in unison.

Kris frowned at the strange expression resting on Cyrus's face.

"If we don't leave now," Cyrus said, "then it's like stars during the afternoon. They're there, but only a good scrubbing will get rid of them."

"Cyrus? What's the matter with you?" Kris said tensely, looking into Cyrus's eyes. His pupils were dilated, almost to the point where she could no longer see color in them.

"Kris?" Cyrus asked, putting a hand on Kris's furred cheek. "I don't feel so good. The music won't stop, and there's a monster making sandwiches of my brain. Can we see the puppy?"

Katana grasped Cyrus's hand, feeling his wrist. "His pulse is racing! This is bad, sister. I couldn't find *Spectrum Antivenin* in either of my books, and I don't know what kind of poison it is, so I can't treat it. All I can do is slow it down."

"You mean . . . " Tears began welling up in Kris's amber eyes.

Katana shook his head. "He's not dead yet, sister. Don't give up hope. Cyrus said we're only a little ways from Mir. I'm sure someone there can help him." The black Katheni looked into the desert. "If he lasts that long . . . "

Chapter 25

THE CIRCLE OF NO MAGIC

In which Reginald finally Sees the Keep of Five Flames,
Converses with an Exterior Decoration, Puzzles over Ancient
Curses, and Encounters a Dropped Maiden

THE MOUNTAINS OF the Morning comprised the majority of what were referred to as the "Barrier Mountains," a mountain range that described a nearly perfect circle around the Keep of Five Flames.

Two miles within the interior of the mountain chain lay a forest where magic did not function. All creatures with magic in their blood, such as Dragons and gryphons, nymphs and pixies, felt weakened and uncomfortable within this area. Once inside the walls of the Keep, magic resumed its functioning.

This de-sorcelled zone was referred to as the Circle of No Magic, named so by Lord Colmarian the Headstrong, a man responsible for other creative names such as the Sea of Water and the Tall Mountains. The Circle of No Magic was a thousand times stronger and more effective than even the most potent magic-suppressant spells in existence.

The effect seemed to be generated by the Keep itself.

From an aerial view, the Keep appeared to be a normal tower, made from granite and obsidian. It was far from normal, however. At its top, it split into five separate turrets. Each turret had, at its pinnacle, a pipe from which sprang a flame that never went out. Each flame burned a different color. One was brilliant red, another phosphorescent blue, the third a hot white, and the fourth an angry dark crimson.

Rising above these four was the fifth turret, from whence sprang a flame like no other. Those who had flown overhead claimed many things about the tower and the flame atop it, most of which conflicted with one another. Some said that the fifth flame was clear, possessing no color at all, merely flickering with light. Others said it was of all colors at once, never staying the same for more than a second.

No matter what the truth was, the Keep itself had fascinated Heroes and Villains alike since before the Twenty-Minute War. Legends said that the Keep had been built by the Creator Himself, and that at the top of this fortress He stored the Key to Ruling All Creatures. Thus, on several occasions, parties of either Heroes or Villains—and once, a party comprised of both—had assaulted the Keep, seeking this ultimate treasure.

Every attempt failed. Failed with lethal consequences.

The Guild of Heroes issued an edict that no Hero group may attempt the Keep in parties of fewer than seven. The Brotherhood of the Black Hand declared that any group of fewer than five Villains caught entering the vicinity of the Keep was to be ignored and left to its doom. Of course, these edicts were sometimes ignored, but most Heroes and Villains recognized the futility of such an assault on the Keep.

Reginald, however, was not one of them.

As soon as Reginald rode Wraith into a sufficiently large clearing in the woods, Keeth swooped down and landed next to him.

"Well, how have you been?" the Dragon asked.

"Exceptional, of course," Reginald replied. "How far is it to the Keep?"

"Only a few more hours, at the rate you're traveling," Keeth said. "I'm afraid I won't be around much longer, though. While I waited for you to come out of the woods, I happened to meet my cousin Skyvar. He told me that my uncle Nivonis is ill and near death."

"I'm sorry to hear that," Reginald said.

Keeth shifted his weight, staring up at the storm-darkening sky. "Don't be. It is his time. Nivonis has lived for nearly twenty-three centuries. He is one of the few left who lived before the Twenty-Minute War. The only reason this is important at the moment is that Nivonis has named me as a possible heir to his hoard."

"But you're a nephew, right?" Reginald asked. "Isn't your cousin the son? Shouldn't he be the one to inherit it?"

"Yes and no. In normal situations, yes. Skyvar, Nivonis's eldest would typically receive the hoard. It seems, however, that I am the only one of Nivonis's relatives who has not offended him in some way. Uncle Nivonis is rather a grouchy and spiteful old Dragon, you see. At any rate, he has named me as possible heir and now demands my presence before the week is out. I cannot fathom why, though," he said, rubbing his green-scaled head against a tree. "We've not spoken in nearly three decades."

Reginald backed Wraith up to avoid the shower of bark fragments dislodged by Keeth's hard scales. He removed his helmet and sat up straight in his saddle. "Well, Keeth, son of Barinol, whose sire was Kisanth the Great, wherever your path takes you, I shall wish you the best of luck. But I am still anxious to finally see the Keep of Five Flames. Shall we continue together for the time being?"

"For a while, yes. I'll meet you in the clearing northwest of here," Keeth said, and began flapping his great, leathery wings. He was soon out of Reginald's sight.

Midmorning, Reginald arrived in the large clearing where Keeth was sunning himself. All around the glade the woods had thickened to the point where the trees twisted around each other in sinister shapes, and the foliage blocked out almost all sunlight. The heavy, wet smell of decaying plants hung in the air like a pile of shed leaves in the fall. But here in the clearing, a few flowers sprouted from the turf near a half-buried log, a welcome burst of color in the monochrome dim green of the forest. Keeth's wings barely fit in the space, even partially folded.

Reginald dismounted and peered through the underbrush and fallen trees. "The Keep is right through here?"

Keeth nodded his large, scaled head. "It is, and I can go no further. Beyond that broken tree just there lies the Circle of No Magic. To even breathe in there would take supreme effort for me." He gave the Hero a curious glance. "What is so important that you must go into a place that has killed more Heroes than my immediate family has?"

"I have had a Divine Vision," Reginald replied. "A man made of light showed me the Keep and told me I must go there. One does not argue with the gods, son of Barinol."

Keeth shrugged his scaled shoulders. "Do what you must, Crimson Slash. I'm afraid I must leave you now, for my uncle is an impatient old creature and does not like to be kept waiting."

"I understand." Reginald began donning his greaves and crimson-barred breastplate. "Well, then, wish me luck, son of Barinol?"

"All the luck in the world won't save you if you do something stupid in there," Keeth said dubiously. "Just try to keep your head on your shoulders."

Reginald chuckled. He swung back up onto Wraith, drew his sword, and rode into the woods.

The forest air was cool and damp, almost chilly, despite the fact that it was midsummer. The patchy sunlight filtering through the dense tree canopy was just enough illumination for the overgrown path. The closer Reginald got to the Keep, the stranger and more twisted the shapes of the trees. Their ancient trunks pressed in upon him on all sides.

He guided Wraith along the shadowed path cautiously. Though he was a brave and courageous man, he was not an idiot. Many a Hero had been lost while attempting to get near the Keep, let alone enter it. *And that is half the challenge,* Reginald thought.

A subtle change overtook the air. Reginald felt it, a sensation he had never felt before. It was like having been covered by a warm and fuzzy blanket, then having it slowly pulled off. He shivered and regarded the pommel of his gigantic sword. The normally glowing shard of ruby embedded in the weapon was nothing but a dull gem. That meant the *Eversharp* magic that enchanted the blade was gone. Whether permanently or temporarily, Reginald could not tell.

A few feet farther, the trees gave way to a large grassy space dominated by an imposing grey-and-white stone edifice. Reginald dismounted Wraith and gave the black charger a pat on the flank. "Stay here a bit, Wraith. I shall return anon."

After tying Wraith to a conveniently twisted tree, Reginald stepped out from the forest to look up at the Keep.

The first obstacle was a sheer, smooth wall, well over seventy feet tall. Despite its great height, a trained Hero with a standard-issue ten-foot pole could vault over it with no trouble. Reginald, however, lacking even a non-standard *eleven*-foot pole, was not tempted to try.

Soaring above the top of the wall was the massive tower known as the Keep of Five Flames. It shone in the midmorning sunlight, as if built entirely of white marble. No windows or arrow-slits broke the smooth white surface of the tower. Reginald had never seen such an intimidating structure, nor one that had killed quite as many brave and strong men. Reginald stepped back to get a better view, but could see only occasional flickers from the flames that reputedly burned eternally from the top.

Reginald began to walk around the wall, looking for an entrance. The wall, he found, was perfectly round and smooth. At length he came upon a blackened mark on the wall. As he leaned to touch it, he found that the scorch mark completely surrounded a small gate in the wall. And in the center of the gate that was in the center of the scorch mark, he saw one tiny divot.

The divot was the only sign left by the Villainous Mortimer Stoneclaw and his notorious attempt to penetrate the wall using a device crafted by an alchemist.

The alchemist called the device a Kanon. It had been a long, metal tube, mounted on a small cart. It was designed to knock down walls with more power and accuracy than a catapult. Its fuel was a vile, sulfurous-smelling powder, and its ammunition a steel sphere packed with the same powder that Stoneclaw's alchemist fired at the wall.

The device had functioned perfectly, but with unanticipated effect. When fired, the Kanon rolled back rapidly on its cart, crushing the surprised alchemist. The projectile struck the wall and detonated as planned, but only barely scratched the smooth surface. While Stoneclaw stood pondering both the ineffectiveness of the Kanon and the death of his alchemist, a raging bolt of fire arced down from the top of the tower, incinerating him and melting the device into slag.

Reginald turned from the divot and examined the ground across from it. Scuffing up a tuft of moss he noted a rusted patch of melted metal beneath it. *Everyone who has tried to force their way into the Keep has been killed. If only there was someone to ask for permission to enter . . .*

A whirring of wings interrupted his thoughts. Looking up, Reginald saw two phoenixes cavorting about in the air.

The golden-red birds twirled about each other, chirruping happily. To untrained eyes, the birds would seem to be nothing more than strangely colored hawks or some other bird of prey, with their sharp beaks and hazardous talons. But Reginald noted the orange tufts of feathers atop their heads, a definitive marking of the species. The fact that they left streamers of magical fire in the air as they flew was another important pointer.

The phoenixes flashed across the clearing, trailing harmless fire, and landed atop the wall. Reginald, not wanting to be rude, waved at them, for phoenixes have long been suspected of having rather high intelligence for birds.

Reginald looked more closely at them. How were they still producing magic fire inside a supposedly magic-free zone?

The larger phoenix bobbed its head once in Reginald's direction. It turned to its companion and chirruped a few times. The smaller bird replied with a low whistle. The first phoenix, evidently having decided something, swooped down and landed on Reginald's shoulder. It was a lesser phoenix, and thus resembled a large bird of prey, only with a tuft of feathers atop its head. Its plumage colors ranged from bright yellow-orange on its legs to dusky red head-feathers. It chirruped, took a piece of Reginald's sleeve in its beak, and tugged gently.

Reginald blinked, then smiled. "Greetings, little phoenix. Are you here to show me what my Vision was about?"

To Reginald's surprise, the fire-hued bird bobbed its head and took off, flying to the small gate. Reginald followed, curious. He had once heard an Old Myth that phoenixes were special animal messengers of the Creator, but he hadn't been expecting such intelligence from a mere bird.

The phoenix landed on the head of an ugly, horned gargoyle adorning the wall beside the gate, and chirruped again.

Why hadn't he seen the gargoyle before? "Well, bird. What is this you've shown me?"

The fiery bird merely flapped its wings and squawked.

Reginald regarded the gargoyle. The squat statue had been carved from some dense stone centuries ago, and time had taken its toll. Stains from decades of harsh weather had stained its clawed feet and hands, and some creeping vines grew across its spread wings, like one would pinion a bird. One of the horns sprouting from its head was missing, broken off by some unknown force. Its pitted, impish face would have looked almost comical if not for the fangs jutting from its lower lip. And its eyes, carved of black gems, looked almost as if they were following Reginald's movements.

"Hmm," Reginald said. "I suppose this gargoyle holds the key to opening the gate, then?" he said rhetorically.

The phoenix nodded, emitted a lilting chirp, and took off without a backward glance, swooping up and over the wall.

Reginald stared at the gargoyle for a long moment before speaking. "Ho, Gargoyle!" he hailed, feeling slightly foolish.

The tiny white gems in the gargoyle's eyes began to glow faintly, just strong enough to be visible in the patchy daylight outside the Keep's wall. "Whoooo?" it grated, dislodging some small songbird's nest from its mouth.

Reginald started. First magic fire, and now a magic statue? There was too much magic in this place for his taste. And *far* too much for a place where there was supposed to be none at all. "Gargoyle, mine name is—"

"Oh, another Hero," the gargoyle said. "Just wonderful." It looked at him skeptically. "Why is there only one of you?"

"O Gargoyle of stone and . . . well, of stone, I had a Vision of a shining man who led me to this place and put fire at the top. Those same fires I see burning atop it now, I believe. I further believe I am intended to enter the Keep successfully without being hindered or attacked."

The gargoyle chuckled, a gravelly noise like someone shaking a box of rocks. "Heh, I doubt it. No one gets in here without a fight or my say-so. And I never let solitary Heroes in. They just die too quickly. At least with a whole party there's usually a good show."

"Well," Reginald said, "I didn't think to bring a party with me. Is that a problem?"

The gargoyle scowled. "Maybe for you it is. You want to get massacred, go right ahead. Me, I'm staying right here, attached to this wall."

"Wait, are you saying you would let me in if I asked?"

"Of course, you nincompoop." The gargoyle sneered, its pitted stone face a picture of malicious glee. "I'd have to play around with you a bit first, but what do you think my blinkin' job is?"

"See here," Reginald said, becoming displeased with the insulting waterspout, "if your job is to let people in, why must you hassle them about it?"

"It's a perk," the gargoyle said with a grin, and spat a torrential cascade of frigid water on the Hero.

It drenched Reginald immediately, all six feet four inches, not counting the boots of him. Unfortunately, the boots were drenched also, and therefore had to be counted. Reginald spat water out of his mouth, which had been open to deliver a retort when the gargoyle had delivered its payload. "All right, you imbecilic exterior decoration, that's enough of that. All I asked for was entrance. I didn't need a shower."

"Two problems with that statement," said the gargoyle, crossing its weatherworn arms. "First, you needed the shower. You smell like you slept among a pack of dogs. And two, you never asked me to let you in. You just *talked* about asking me to let you in."

Reginald shifted between one foot and the other, hearing water squelch in his boots. "Well, I would indeed like to be let in."

"That's nice to know. I'd like a funny hat with a siren to scare off birds."

"Look here, gargoyle, I'm on a Divinely Inspired Quest to get inside the Keep of Five Flames."

"Look here, Hero, I'm bolted to this wall. Don't we make an interesting pair? You not getting where you want to go, and me unable to go anywhere at all."

Reginald scowled. "That does it," he said, drawing his sword. "Prepare to suffer the Wrath of the Crimson Slash."

"Oh, that's going to be tremendously effective," the gargoyle said with a snort, blowing dust out its nostrils.

"Indeed," Reginald said, "but not as you suspect." He sunk his sword, point-first, into the grassy loam, and leaned his elbow on the hilt. And began to sing.

A lathe is a common tool, used by potters and carpenters alike. It involves a crank or foot-pedal to cause rotation around a central axis.

This axis can be vertical or horizontal, depending on the purpose. For example, a vertical axis with a plate attached atop it is excellent for rotating a lump of clay that a potter may shape into a jar. A horizontal axis with clamps on either end serves admirably to help a carpenter who is carving table legs. Finer and richer craftsmen have magical lathes that can rotate by themselves.

No matter how fine the lathe is, it invariably involves several wheels and belts, which, if not properly oiled, begin to squeak. Now imagine a lathe that has not been oiled for two years and was never put together properly in the first place, and grinds terribly. Imagine that it is a potter's lathe, on a vertical axis, and atop it is a large jar, full of irritable housecats. As a final stretch of your now sadly abused imagination, picture that this lathe is operating at full speed, with a madman attempting to use it as an instrument to play actual notes.

Drop this sound by about four octaves, and you have arrived at an accurate approximation of what Reginald's singing voice sounded like.

"There was an old lady, who chased her old dog
She chased her old dog 'round the room

And while she was chasing her old dog around,
She chased her old dog 'round the room!"

Reginald knew that both his singing and the song were truly atrocious, but he felt it was the only weapon he had that could reach the gargoyle. Toward the end of his seventh verse Reginald began to fear that his song was falling upon stone ears.

Unfortunately for the gargoyle, these particular stone ears were, in fact, not deaf. "Gaaahh!" it screeched, clapping stone hands over stone ears. "What is this, a pain concert? You should stop that before you kill someone!"

"You're right, I probably should," Reginald said. *"And while she was chasing her old dog around . . . "*

The gargoyle grimaced as Reginald continued singing. "No, I really mean it. You're going to break something if you keep making that racket!"

"That's entirely possible. *She chased her old dog 'round the room!"*

"Hero, you're beginning to annoy me!"

"Am I? What a shame. You annoy me by not letting me in. *There was an old lady . . . "*

The gargoyle began to sag from the wall, having given up his futile attempt to block out the sound. "Good gods . . . Why couldn't my creator have fashioned me without a sense of hearing?"

"Because you're supposed to hear people and let them in. Can't be helped if you ignore them and make sarcastic remarks instead. *"Who chased her old dog . . . "*

The gargoyle heaved an enormous sigh, and his white gemstone eyes glowed brighter. With the high-pitched shriek of long-unused gears, the gate swung wide, and an ancient portcullis slid open. "There," the gargoyle said resignedly. "Now will you cease that infernal racket?"

"Of course," Reginald replied. He half-bowed to the irritable waterspout, retrieved his sword, and made for the entrance. "My gratitude, O Gargoyle."

The gargoyle growled, sounding like someone shaking a box of gravel. "Just get in there so I don't have to listen to you anymore," it said. "I wish you'd just asked nicely to be let in. Then neither of us would have had to endure that torment!"

Reginald chuckled. "But I was just warming up! I have another song about a boy and his fishing cat—"

"*No!*" the gargoyle shouted, screwing up its face into a comical mix of sheer terror and profound irritation. "Just get your discordant posterior in there and get out of my sight. And pray that the guardians enjoy your atrocious singing more than I do."

Reginald stepped into the courtyard of the Keep of Five Flames and stared about him in awe.

Vines and creepers climbed the insides of the white marble walls, and unkept grass grew up through cracks in the stone walkway that led from the gate to the Keep. A dried-up fountain sat forlornly in the center of the broad courtyard, overgrown with vines. Above it all soared the massive five-pronged tower of the Keep itself. It looked just like a picture of an abandoned castle from the Book of Many Old Legends that was so popular among the day's youth.

Reginald let out a low whistle as he slowly walked into the long-forgotten courtyard, turning in a circle to admire the ancient edifice. "My . . . what a place."

A bird's chirrup brought him from his reverie. One of the phoenixes he had seen earlier sat perched, seemingly on nothing, bobbing through the air as it approached him.

Reginald started, seeing something physically impossible. Now, physical impossibilities were nothing new to Reginald, but this particular impossibility took place inside a zone where magic could not override the laws of physics. He scrutinized the phoenix's motions as it drew near. The fiery bird was riding on something. Something that made the sounds of horses' hooves on the broken stone walkway.

"You there," Reginald said in his Commanding Voice. "Whatever you be, I mean you no harm, nor do I mean to intrude on this ancient place."

"Of course thou dost not," a voice boomed from the empty air beneath the phoenix. "All who mean harm have hitherto got themselves in through unorthodox means."

Reginald glanced about, as the clip-clop of more hooves sounded all around him. Whatever his unseen unknowns were, they had him completely surrounded. Reginald triggered the release for the clasps which held his titanic sword to his armor, allowing the weapon to fall to the ground. He stepped back, careful not to make any threatening gestures.

"Mine name is Sir Reginald Ogleby," he said, looking about him for any signs of audience. "I have been guided here on a Quest, by a Shining Man. I am known as—"

"The Man of the Crimson Emblem," the voice interrupted. "We have known of thine coming for many years. Please, proceed to the fountain in the center of the courtyard." The voice was obviously masculine: a pleasant baritone with a good deal of power behind it.

The phoenix and its invisible mount moved to one side of the path, and Reginald proceeded down the ancient weatherworn stones toward the central fountain. He picked up his sword on the way, tucking it under his arm. As he walked, he noticed the ground churning in small patches, as if stirred by invisible horses' hooves. Reginald surmised that his unseen companions must be mounted on unseen steeds.

Upon his arrival at the fountain, a flare of trumpets shattered the silence. Where they were or who had sounded them, Reginald could not see.

"The Man of the Crimson Emblem hath arrived," boomed another voice. "Let today be marked as a celebration, for soon our captivity and curse shalt be at an end."

"Art thou certain then, that this be the man?" asked another voice from somewhere to Reginald's left. "Could not any number of Heroes or Villains bear an emblem of crimson?"

A third voice added to the discussion. "Nay, for hast not this one gained entrance by peaceful means? And dost not the Prophecy say—"

"Nikolai's prophecy?" asked a fourth. "Thou canst not take Nikolai's prophecy seriously. 'Tis not for naught he is called Nikolai the Vague."

"*Sometime in the future, some evil people shalt appear, and shall do many bad things. Then shalt some good people rise up, defeat them, and make everything better.*' Nikolai the Vague, Generic Prophecies, Volume the fourth," the third voice said smugly. "Naught can be said against the truth of this prophecy."

Another voice from the other side of the fountain piped up irritably. "Naught can be said in its favor, either. Nikolai would have made a better weather foreseer than a prophet. His mind was always partly cloudy with a chance of foolishness."

"I hate to interrupt you gentlemen," Reginald said, raising a hand, "but I came here on a Blessed Quest, and I still do not know how I shall gain entrance to the Keep, or even who you are."

The voices abruptly fell silent. The last of the hoof-falls ceased echoing across the courtyard, leaving an eerie silence in their wake. No insects disturbed the hush, no birds chirped. It was as if Reginald had stopped up his ears. Only the intermittent rustling of feathers disturbed the stillness as the phoenix alit on top of the fountain and began preening itself. Then Reginald's ears caught a few muttered and whispered words back and forth, and then the first voice spoke again.

"O Man of the Crimson Emblem, we are what remains of the great and noble Tenth Race, nearly destroyed by our tampering with Forbidden Magics, and cursed for the same," it said, echoing across the shade-dappled courtyard. "In accordance with the Prophecy—"

"The validity of which we yet dispute," added another disembodied voice.

"—we wait here, guarding the selfsame magic we once sought so that no man shall suffer our fate. We await the One who shall free us from our curse." The voice sighed heavily after it finished its sentence. "And it is our hope that thou, O Man of the Crimson Emblem, art the One in the Prophecy."

Reginald scratched the back of his neck, looking about him. "My apologies, but I cannot say for certain if I am 'the One' or not. But I believe I know who you are. You . . . you are all Centaurs, correct?"

There was no response.

"Demas," whispered one of the voices, "the Human cannot see thee nod sagely when thou art invisible."

"Ah, yes, indeed," said the first voice, a note of embarrassed irritation in its timbre. "How didst thou know I was nodding?"

"Never mind. Ask him how he knew we were Centaurs."

Reginald chuckled softly. "To start, all I heard of you were hooves. Seldom do horses, or even mounted knights, debate the validity of Ancient Prophecies. Second, in the Books of Old Legends that my mother read to me as a lad, I read that the Centaurs, when they still walked the land, were fearsome warriors. Who else better to stop attacking parties of Heroes or squads of Villains?"

"Other Heroes or Villains," grumbled another voice. "We have not the strength to stop full assaults. Otherwise that group would not have succeeded in entering the Keep."

Reginald started. "You mean the Third Assault? You were alive for that? I thought Centaurs only lived a few hundred years?"

"Under normal circumstances, yes," replied the first voice. "But when we misused the Forbidden Magics and destroyed our own people, the Creator didst frown on us and bestow a mixed blessing. First, He gave us freedom from the ravages of time. Not a surviving member of the Centaurs has aged another day from that point."

"In accordance with the Prophecy," said another voice.

"Shush. Thou'rt interrupting mine monologue," the first voice said irritably. "No weapons can harm us, save those with potent magics in them. But to leaven this gift, the Creator also cursed us with invisibility, and an instant revocation of the first blessing should we ever leave the Circle of No Magic. Now we may not depart from this forest, lest we age to death in an instant, nor can we see our own bodies or each other."

Reginald, silent until this moment, spoke up again. "So the Creator gave you a Mighty Magic Against Age, but also Inflicted Inconvenient Invisibility?"

There was silence among the assembled Centaurs. "Hero . . . " said the first voice.

"Demas, the Hero cannot see thee sadly shake thine head when thou art invisible," reminded another voice.

"So how canst thee?"

Reginald heard something very much like a whinny.

"Anyway," the first voice said, "thou hast it aright. Nor may we leave this Land without Weakening and being Overcome by Oldness. Sadly, speeches become silly when they are all alliteration, so cease and desist. As Predicted in Plethoric Perspicuous Prophecies, we— Aiiow!"

Reginald heard the sharp sound of someone striking a horse's rump. He chuckled. "Touché. So then, Demas and all noble Centaurs here gathered," he said. "I ask this of you: since you believe that I am the one to remove your curse, will you grant me entrance into the Keep?"

"Pray give us a few moments to consider, O Hero," Demas replied. "I shall consult mine brothers." The clip-clops of hooves sounded about the courtyard as the group moved away from Reginald and began conversing amongst themselves.

Reginald leaned back on the fountain and looked about the courtyard while he waited for the Centaurs' decision.

There were more creeping vines climbing the inside of the walls, but they seldom ventured below the reach of a mounted man. And when they did, they seemed to be torn off roughly. Apparently, though free from the ravages of age, the Centaurs still felt hunger. He looked up at the keep. Reginald felt Dwarfed by the soaring height of the tower and the impressive mysteries behind it. From where he stood, the tower seemed to have no top at all, as if merely disappearing into the sky at its peak.

Reginald's Reverie did not last long. Over the alliterative white walls swooped a distraught Dragon. Swatting aside a cloud of overused literary devices, Keeth landed in the court-yard, breathing heavily. His normally emerald-hued scales were fading into grey, and he seemed to be in extremely poor health.

"Reginald," Keeth said breathlessly, "you must come with me immediately."

Reginald hastily rose from his seat and strapped his titanic sword onto his back once more. "Keeth, I though you had other business to attend to?"

"I do, but there is a more dire a problem."

"What is it?"

"When I rose from the forest and flew toward the mountains, I saw a gryphon drop something large from quite a height. I flew over after the gryphon was gone and saw that it was a Human woman. She landed in a haystack, alive but hurt."

Reginald glanced in the general direction of where the Centaurs should be, then back to his draconic friend. "Son of Barinol, the Centaurs are deciding whether or not they shall let me enter the Keep. I cannot leave here until they do."

"Centaurs?" Keeth looked about the clearing with bleary eyes. "Perhaps it is because of the lack of magic, but I see nothing. Come, Reginald, this is a genuine Damsel in Distress," the Dragon pled. "If you don't come to her aid, my family will expect me to kidnap her, and I'd rather not deal with that kind of encumbrance at the moment."

Reginald groaned. "Ah, true enough. Very well, I shall aid this Damsel, but then return here. Go now, Keeth, lest this place overcome you."

Keeth nodded. "My thanks, Hero," he said, then struggled into the air and over the wall once more.

"Good Centaurs," Reginald hailed as he strode toward the gate by which he'd entered. "I fear I must depart for a time."

"What? And thou wouldst leave us here, without lifting the curse?" Demas asked in disbelief. "When we have awaited thee so long?"

"There is a Damsel, injured, just outside these woods," Reginald replied. "I must attend to her, and then I shall return, on my honor as a Knight of Bryath."

Though he could not see it, Reginald heard the rustling sound he had come to associate with Demas shaking his head. "No, Hero, we cannot let thee go," the Centaur said. "Release us from our curse, then thou mayst depart. This is a task to help others, rather than further thine own selfish glory."

"And you would have me abandon a helpless Damsel and take care of strong and healthy warriors like yourselves? Warriors who cannot die from heat or cold, nor sword or time?" said Reginald, frowning. "Who is it that is selfish, you say? I shall return. Farewell until then."

"Orilar! Drop thou the gate!" Demas bellowed. "Do not let the Hero escape!" The Centaur's invisible hands seized Reginald by his shoulders.

"My apologies!" Reginald shouted, leaning back and delivering a kick into the center of the Centaur's mass. The grip disappeared from Reginald's shoulders, and the fountain in the courtyard's center shattered under the impact of an unseen heavy object.

The Hero dashed for the gate. But the other Centaurs had heard Demas's call, and the ancient portcullis slowly creaked down, threatening to shut Reginald in.

But the Crimson Slash was not a Hero to be taken lightly. He reached the gate just before the iron points of the portcullis sank into the stone. Reginald took hold of the wrought-iron portcullis and heaved it upward.

With a shriek of stressed gears, the portcullis ceased its downward movement and crawled upward. The sound of galloping hooves sounded out behind Reginald. With a mighty heave, Reginald threw the portcullis high enough for him to duck under, laughing at the feeling of strain upon his Heroic muscles.

The portcullis slammed down behind him, and Reginald walked a few paces back. The sound of hooves diminished.

"Hero, wait . . . " said the voice of Demas, now full of sorrow. "Please, I beg of thee, turn not thine back on us. It hath been centuries since we had hope of the curse being lifted."

Reginald sighed. "Demas of the Centaurs, I said that I would return, and I shall. Bide your time until then. Surely after these many thousands of years you can wait another hour. After all, not every one of your prophecies can be wrong."

"Wouldst thou like to make a bet on that?" Demas said with a woeful chuckle. "Good luck then, Hero. We shall pray for thine swift return."

"Good-bye, Demas." Reginald turned and walked back toward where he had tied Wraith.

"Oi, Hero," said a gravelly voice.

Reginald glanced back up at the cranky gargoyle. "What now?"

"Didn't expect all your trouble to be in getting *out*, now, did you?" the gargoyle said with evil glee.

Reginald rolled his eyes and turned to leave once more.

"One last thing, Hero," the gargoyle said again.

Exasperated, Reginald turned around, only to receive fifty gallons of frigid water in the face.

The gargoyle chuckled. "Parting shot, Hero. Have a nice day."

• • •

An hour of navigating the overgrown forest later, Reginald passed from the cool shade of the forest into the heat of the afternoon sun on the grassy plain. It was a large hayfield that, due to an unusually dry and hot summer, had already been harvested into large stacks. One stack was smaller than the rest, or perhaps had once been the same size but was now somewhat scattered.

Keeth was there waiting for him. The Dragon looked much better now that he was no longer within the zone of no magic. Together, the two proceeded across the field. It was to the larger haystack that the Hero and Dragon made their way.

When they arrived, Keeth surged ahead of Reginald and bent his long neck over the haystack. "Excuse me, miss, but—aargh!" he bellowed, whipping his head back. Drips of deep crimson blood began trailing down the front of his head from a tiny puncture wound inside his right nostril.

Reginald eyed Keeth curiously. "I see the lady still has a weapon," he said, chuckling.

"If thad bas subbosed do be a jesd, I fail do see the hubor id id," Keeth snapped, snorting fire through his nostrils to cauterize the wound.

Reginald immediately adopted a more serious and Heroic facial expression. "Of course, son of Barinol. I see the problem. The Lady must be dealt with. Please allow me to handle this dangerous task."

"Is that sarcasm, perchance?" Keeth asked, twitching his snout.

"Of course not. Now, to the task at hand!" Reginald said. The Hero dismounted, donned a heavy gauntlet, and climbed the haystack.

• • •

Emily Cartwright couldn't move without pain shooting from her waist and down her legs. Apparently that gryphon had known what she was doing and dropped her in a haystack. But because of the height from which she'd fallen, she'd still been hurt, to the point that getting down was a near-impossibility.

To complicate matters, the Dragon that had flown over a few minutes ago was back and had just poked its scaled green head over the edge of the haystack. Being in no real position to fight off a Dragon, Emily had merely made a halfhearted thrust at it, landing a lucky blow inside its nostril.

Something disturbed the back of the haystack. Emily twisted to face the new threat and winced. She was in no condition to fight anything. How humiliating to escape the Villains and then die in a haystack.

But Emily was far from defenseless. At that moment, a man's head and upper torso emerged from the back of the haystack. "*Salamanders!*" the mercenary woman yelled, and swung her colichemarde with all her might.

The man was apparently expecting just such a welcome and blocked the blow with his gauntleted hand. Grabbing the thin blade, he yanked it from Emily's hand and tossed it to the ground. "Greetings, Miss," he said politely. "Mine name is Sir Reginald Ogleby, the Crimson Slash. The Dragon you so neatly punctured is Keeth, son of Barinol. Might we offer you assistance?"

Emily was taken aback. "What? You . . . Are you a Hero?"

"Of course, my lady. May I help you down from this haystack?"

"Well, I suppose so," Emily said cautiously.

The man named Reginald smiled. "Very well. Please take my arm, then."

Emily did so, trying and failing to suppress a wince as the Hero gently lifted her to her feet. She wobbled slightly as pain fogged and narrowed her vision. It was as if she was looking at this Hero through a tunnel.

Reginald gave the girl a concerned look. "Are you all right, miss?"

Emily groaned. She certainly didn't *feel* all right. It felt like she'd displaced some bone near her waist, and perhaps broken a leg. "No, actually, I don't feel so well," she said, giving the Hero a wry grin.

So, instead of helping Emily down, Reginald picked her up. "Keeth!" he said, before Emily could react. "Would you be so kind as to lower the lady and I down from here?"

The large green Dragon craned his neck over the pile again. "Only if you'll keep her away from the sword," he said, chuckling. The Dragon picked Reginald up by the back of his armor, as he had once before, and deposited both him and Emily on the ground next to the haystack.

"Here you go," Reginald said. He placed Emily gently on the ground and returned her sword, despite a dirty look from the Dragon. "Pray, tell me your name and what you were doing falling from the sky."

And so she explained. When Emily finished her tale about being summoned with all the other mercenary captains, of Voshtyr's plans to begin a war, and of being chased from Voshtyr's mountain keep, Sir Reginald walked a distance off and talked to the Dragon for a long moment. Finally, he returned to where Emily lay and sat down beside her.

"Keeth and I have decided," Reginald said, "to help you back to your mercenary outfit. You would not make it yourself in your state, so I offer you mine aid."

Emily smiled. "I appreciate it, Hero. But let me tell you something. You know why I survived that fall? It isn't because I'm a Hero myself, I'm not."

"You're simply lucky there was a haystack there," Reginald said.

"Not lucky," Emily said. "The gryphon dropped me here on purpose. Somehow she's tied in with my lost Uncle Gavin. She dropped me here so that, one, I wouldn't die, and two, Voshtyr would think I did die. You understand my position, right?"

Reginald scratched his head. "To protect you from what he would do if he thought you still lived and could bring word of his Diabolical Plot to the attention of a Hero."

"Right. The Salvinsel Salamanders don't side with Villains, ever. I don't know what the General was thinking, sending Captain Sakana and me there. Must have been the money. It was really, really good money."

Emily sighed and picked some hay out of her hair. "But after all this, I don't think she'll be getting involved in this one. Or if we do, it won't be on his side. General Allyn has this annoying Hero complex that dictates the Salamanders's involvement in Hero and Villain fights. Basically, she makes us right every wrong in the world. If this is one of those cases, and if we decide to do something about this Voshtyr fellow, we're going to need your help. And the Dragon's, if he doesn't mind. Our company gets along with Dragons pretty well, so having him around won't hurt anything."

"Anything I can do to help," Keeth said, bowing his neck.

Reginald glanced back to the spire of the Keep of Five flames as it rose above the tops of the trees. The very pinnacle of the tower was visible from here, its peak crowned with five dancing spots of light. "Well, perhaps. But I cannot stay long.

I have promised aid to another group and must return shortly. While my friend the Dragon and I both have some small quarrel with this Voshtyr and would love to be of assistance to anyone wishing to do him harm, I have prior commitments."

"We'll get you back in time for whatever it is," Emily replied, beaming. "The sooner we get there, the sooner we'll have that *orsobu pitchi* taken care of, and you can get back to your quest or whatever. Let's get moving."

And they did, west toward the camp of the Salvinsel Salamanders.

Chapter 26

HOME IS WHERE THE HEART IS

In which Cyrus is Well Taken Care Of, and Kris makes an Important Decision

THE THREE HORSES galloped across the increasingly sandy ground. Kris led the way, steering into the desert and praying silently to the Creator for a miracle. Katana followed, the reins of Cyrus's horse attached to his saddle. Cyrus was lashed down to his horse, murmuring random snippets of childhood memories, laughing, and dying.

After an hour of wandering the outskirts of the great Mir desert, Kris reined in her horse.

Katana pulled up beside her. "What's wrong, sister?"

A sob caught in Kris's throat as she attempted to answer her brother. "I . . . I'm lost. I don't know where to go, and Cyrus is . . . "

"Hey," Cyrus said weakly. "Who tied me to my horse?"

"Cyrus!" Kris leapt down from her mount and sprinted to Cyrus's side. "Are you all right?" she asked, untying Cyrus from his saddle.

Cyrus smiled weakly. "I'm fine, Katana. A little poison's not going to take a Hero down. I don't think . . . " His head lolled to the side, but he snapped straight back up, blinking.

"Don't die on us, Cyrus!" Katana said, gripping Cyrus's arm.

"Eh? Well, I wasn't planning on it, but Death comes whether you planned on him or not. Just remember," Cyrus said, stretching out his hand and stroking Kris's face, "this isn't your fault. I knew the risks when I took the Quest. Just, whatever you do, don't tell anyone you had to tie me to my horse. That would be *really* embarrassing . . . "

Tears flowed down Kris's face, darkening the fur below her eyes. "Cyrus, don't . . . "

Katana placed both paws on his sister's shoulders. "No time for grief yet, sister—look." He pointed west, where a sizeable cloud of dust had appeared on the horizon. "It isn't a sandstorm—it's people moving. With horses. We may have to fight for Cyrus one last time."

"Fight for me?" Cyrus said. "I can do my fighting by myself." He dismounted and drew his sword. "Just point me in . . . the right . . . direction . . . " He staggered for a moment, and regained his balance. "I said I'd get you . . . to Mir . . . and I will . . . poison . . . notwithstanding . . . " The young Hero squared his shoulders at the approaching riders, and abruptly fell to the ground.

Kris knelt next to Cyrus, shaking his shoulder. "Cyrus?" she cried. "*Cyrus?* No . . . not now, we were so close . . . *Cyruuuuuuus!*" Kris screamed into the sky, the sound absorbed by the wind and heat blowing from the desert. After a moment, Kris wiped her eyes, looked at the approaching dust cloud, and drew her short sword.

• • •

Sand and shimmering heat.

A cool cave full of crystals beneath the water . . . a moon-lit beach . . . a leopard Katheni girl . . . the splashes of skipped stones rippling across the river . . . the heavy, pleasant scent of a well-oiled leather combat harness . . . swimming in the rain . . . a friendly green Dragon . . . a spicy soup made from sea-turtle and amras seeds . . . the scratchiness of Father's beard . . . the silly clown at the festival . . . stars seen from a rooftop . . . a giant fish with blades for fins . . . crying after a spanking for tipping cows . . . nutty ale, cool to the throat and warm to the belly . . . sand and heat . . . the murmurings of a dozen snarling voices . . . lights . . . colors where they don't belong . . .

Blackness.

Too warm.

Cyrus gradually opened his eyes. He lay on a thin bedroll of some kind, inside a large, white tent. For some reason, his eyeballs felt dried out and the inside of his mouth tasted terrible. He glanced about for a waterskin. His eyes lit not upon the object he sought but a grey-furred Katheni with spectacles, sitting in a chair across from the bedroll and reading a book.

"Well, well. The Human has awakened," the Katheni said. He wrinkled his nose and picked up a walking-stick from its place beside the chair. "It appears Bar'at has saved the day again."

"Where am I, and how long have I been out?" Cyrus demanded. "Where's Kris? Where's Katana? Where are my *kahrestin* pants?"

The Katheni snorted. "Cease your questioning, Human. I had to physically pry Kris Baravaati off of you and make her brother cast *Heavy Eyelids* on her so she could get some sleep. She has bothered me nonstop for three days about you, so the sooner you are out of my tent, the better."

With titanic effort, Cyrus raised himself up on an elbow. "Three days? I've been out for . . . Where did you say my pants were?"

The Katheni's jaw hung slightly open as he stared at Cyrus. Then he shook his furred head. "You Heroes never cease to amaze me. You should not yet be able to move at all. So cease!" he ordered, tapping Cyrus lightly on the head with his walking-stick.

Cyrus, unexpectedly weak, fell back onto the bedroll. "Will you tell Kris . . . "

"No, I will not. No visitors until you are sufficiently recovered, nor until I am sure you have no contagious diseases. Now, stay there, and I will fetch you some water."

Cyrus spent the day in bed, still weak from the poison. The following morning he felt much better, and sat all the way up, much to the astonishment of the grey-furred Katheni healer.

"It isn't natural for Humans to heal so quickly," the healer muttered, "not from a poison that potent."

"You said it yourself: it's because I'm a Hero," Cyrus said. "You can see I'm all better already, so can I get up now?"

The healer glared at Cyrus. "No, you might suffer a relapse, and then I would be blamed," he said, and began mixing a flaky green powder into a small bowl of water.

"If I *don't* relapse, then it will be an amazing tribute to your healing abilities."

The healer harrumphed. "I have been the healer of this tribe for forty-seven years. I don't need a cub telling me how to do my business, much less a Human one. Now stay here. I must go and get another medicine for that poison." The healer stomped, as much as the Katheni with their padded feet could, out of the tent.

Cyrus lay still a few moments, then began removing the bandages on his shoulder. There was some blood on them, and the skin was slightly discolored around where the quarrels had struck, but the quarrel wounds themselves were healed.

"Psst!"

Cyrus craned his neck to see where the sound had come from.

"Behind you! Come on, get out of there!"

Cyrus rolled off the bedroll and got to his knees. Kris beckoned from beneath the back wall of the tent.

"Get out of there before Bar'at feeds you some of his nasty green slop!" Kris grabbed Cyrus's hand and helped him under the tent, then practically smothered him with an intense, full-contact hug. Katana and two younger Katheni also waited for him outside.

The desert sun beat down on an impressive sight. The Katheni village was comprised of over a hundred white tents and covered wagons. All of them clustered about a central oasis containing a small lake and multiple palm trees. The desert sparkled for miles around, nothing but sheer dunes as far as Cyrus could see. Inside the village, Katheni cubs sprinted about, playing and fighting with each other as their parents reclined in the shade of tent awnings, watching their progeny play.

"Well, Cyrus!" Katana said, clapping Cyrus on the shoulder. "Welcome back to the land of the living!"

Cyrus winced, but smiled. "Oh, come on, Katana. It wasn't that bad, was it?"

Katana nodded soberly. "It was touch and go there for a bit, but you seem fine now."

Kris rubbed her head under Cyrus's chin, purring softly. "It is good to see you well, Cyrus. We feared for your life."

Cyrus returned Kris's embrace. "Yeah, so did I. You managed to fight off those riders without my help, then?"

"Oh, no," Katana said, looking at his claws. "They were hardly foes. It was a scouting party of the tribe, sent out to see what that battle with Landrus was about. They brought you here as fast as they could, and the tribe healer got to work. He wasn't too optimistic, but he'd never seen a Hero's recovery abilities before."

Cyrus scratched his head. "I thought you were going to cast *Spectrum Antivenin* on me."

"I don't have it," the cat mage replied. "It's in one of the books I didn't bring with me. And once we got here, old Bar'at said that it was an especially rare kind of poison that he couldn't identify. Yet you survived. Well done, Cyrus. And now your Quest is over."

"What? You mean this is . . . ?"

Katana grinned. "Yes, it is, and you've delivered my sister and I safely here. Quest completed, Cyrus. Welcome to Mir."

Cyrus stood in the sand for a moment, his jaw hanging open slightly. Then he grinned broadly. "Well, what do you know about that? I guess that makes me a full Hero now, eh? Everything except the paperwork."

"And a Hero most brave and bold you are," Kris said, kissing him on the cheek. "Does the paperwork matter that much?"

Cyrus grimaced. "Oh, you have *no* idea . . . "

One of the young Katheni poked Cyrus in the thigh. "Is this a friendly Human?" she asked.

"Eh, I'm friendly enough, I suppose," Cyrus answered.

The Katheni child was no more than two feet tall, and had pointed ears with little tufts of light brown fur at their tips. Her cheeks were tufted as well, like those of a bobcat or lynx. Her thin ponytail of sand-blond head fur bore a dark pink bow to hold it in place.

"Why do you ask? Do you get a lot of unfriendly Humans around here?"

Kris grimaced. "Salvinsel isn't the only place where slave traders think of the Katheni as a commodity."

"I see. And I bet one like this," Cyrus said, hefting the other young Katheni into the air and catching him again, "is worth quite a bit."

"That's not funny, Cyrus," Katana interjected. "It's a serious business. So serious, in fact, that the council is trying to decide what to do with *you*."

Cyrus put the giggling Katheni boy down. "What? Me? Wait, I didn't do anything wrong, did I? All I did was deliver you and Kris here!"

Kris dusted sand out of the little girl's fur. "It's just because you are Human. The fact that you were helping brother and I is major testimony in your favor. But because of the slave traders . . . "

"The council is likely to be suspicious of all Humans," Cyrus said. "I understand. It doesn't really bother me, then. So, now that we're done ruining a nice sunny day, who are these two?" Cyrus asked, pointing at the young Katheni.

"Oh, of course, where are my manners? Children, introduce yourselves to Cyrus," Katana said.

"I'm Zamindar. Mommy named me after the King," said the tiger-striped Katheni boy whom Cyrus had thrown into the air. "You're really strong, mister."

"My name's Bella," said the girl, and made a short curtsey, her tufted ears bending slightly. "Krissy and Katana are our cousins."

Cyrus shook their paws. "Pleased to meet you both. You live here, right?" he asked. Both young Katheni nodded. "I guess that would make you Mir cats then, wouldn't it?"

Katana groaned and clapped a paw to his forehead.

Kris made a wry face and poked Cyrus in the side. "We're no mere cats, Cyrus. That was terrible. You should be ashamed of yourself."

The young Hero chuckled. "So, when do I get to meet your uncle, Kris?"

"He's coming from the capital to help the council decide what to do with you. Don't worry, though. I'm his favorite niece, and you've been such a great help to brother and I, that he couldn't possibly do anything mean to you."

Cyrus spent the remainder of the day with his Katheni friends and their cousins.

Kris and Katana showed Cyrus around the village, introducing Cyrus to her friends and relatives. At first, whenever a cub strayed too close to Cyrus, its parents would swoop it up and run away. But the farther through the village they got, the more the Katheni's fear lessened. A few even offered Cyrus some food and let their cubs climb up the obliging Hero. He winced at their sharp claws, but realized that he was breeding good will among Kris's family and tolerated it for her sake.

Besides, it wasn't him they were afraid of, he knew. It was the slavers. *I hope their chief understands that I'm not one of those miscreants . . .*

Kris grabbed the Cyrus's arm and shook him. "Pay attention, Cyrus."

"Eh? Sorry, what?"

Kris sighed and indicated a white Katheni with brown-tipped paws, tail, ears, and face. "I wanted you to meet Jaava. Jaava, meet Cyrus."

The white Katheni male bobbed his head. Cyrus seized his paw and shook it heartily. "Pleased to meet you, Jaava. Are you related to Kris and Katana also?" Cyrus asked.

"As much as any Katheni is related to one of another tribe," Jaava replied. "Her mother is my mother's cousin. Though I regret even the slightest relation, because she ignores me on account of it. If she paid more attention, we would make a beautiful couple," he said, rubbing Kris's ears.

Kris elbowed Jaava in the ribs. "You jerk! Being related to me is a high honor!" she said good-naturedly. "Anyway, I thought you were out with the Haj. What are you doing back?"

"The Haj returned about half an hour ago," Jaava answered. "I'm actually free this evening, if you want to—"

"Really? Uncle's back?" Kris pounced Jaava, knocking him into the sand, and sat on his chest. "Where is he?"

The white Katheni pushed Kris off and sat up, brushing sand from his fur. "He's in the elder's tent, probably talking with the council. I wouldn't . . . " he started, but was interrupted by a spray of sand as Kris abruptly ran toward the center of the village. "Wait, I . . . " He growled. "Grr, females. Katana! You need to teach your little sister some manners!"

The cat-mage turned his attention from a tigress about his age clad in a dress of several green hues and laughed at the heap of white fur. "Shunned again, eh? Not much has changed since the feast of the Great Eclipse, I see."

"Oh, come on, Katana, you know that my intentions are honorable!" Jaava protested, shaking his head to get some errant sand out of his ears. "She just refuses to pay any attention to me at all . . . "

"What's a Haj?" Cyrus asked.

"It's what we call our chieftain," Jaava explained. "His name's Wasara, but Haj is his official title." He glanced down the dunes where Kris had just run. "I swear, that girl will be the death of me . . . "

Cyrus chuckled. "All right, so what's the feast of the Great Eclipse, then?"

"A stupid get-together we had once," Jaava said sulkily.

"Oh, thanks, that was exceptionally helpful. Katana? What's the feast of the Great Eclipse?"

Katana whispered a few words in his female companion's pointed ear. She tilted her striped head coyly, standing on one footpaw and leaning herself against the black Katheni for a moment before nodding and disappearing into one of the myriad tents.

The cat-mage sighed and turned to Cyrus. "Do you remember that eclipse five or six years back that supposedly destroyed Bryath castle? Well, we had—"

"Oh, it did destroy the castle," Cyrus said. "Reg told me all about it. It was this Arch-Villain named Voshtyr. The eclipse didn't really do the destroying. That was more the work of this spell called . . . " He realized he was babbling. "Sorry, go on."

"Anyway," Katana said, "the feast of the Great Eclipse was a feast in celebration of the sun's return. I know this sounds a little superstitious, but we Katheni regard the sun as the Creator's face. Many thought that when He hid His face at an unscheduled time, it was a sign that the End of the World was at paw. Therefore, when the eclipse passed without the world ending, we were naturally very relieved. And we held a celebration."

Katana sat down on the sand and began idly tracing runes in it with a claw as he continued. "All the tribes came together to rejoice and thank the Creator. Father, Kris, and I came with a delegation from the Salvinsel tribe. While here, Kris became infatuated with a young lion and totally ignored Jaava. We're third cousins, so the relationship is sufficiently distant that the tribe would have allowed him to court her, but she simply ignored him in favor of the lion." The runes flashed and animated a patch of sand into a miniature sand golem that quickly dissipated, but not before clobbering one of Jaava's toes with its tiny fist.

"And she still hasn't seen the light," Jaava complained, rubbing his toe. "Now she's hanging on the neck of a hairless *Human*," he said, grinning at Cyrus. "I can't imagine what it is she sees in you."

Cyrus smiled. "I beg to differ on the 'hairless' score—"

"I don't want to hear about that," Katana protested, sticking his paws in his ears.

Cyrus chuckled. "Heh, don't worry, Jaava. I don't know what she sees in me, either."

Kris crawled up to the back of the large central tent, lifted up a corner, and snuck a peek inside. A dozen Katheni sat around a dimly smoldering fire inside, the smoke venting through a hole in the top of the conical tent. Most of them were old, venerable silver beginning to tinge the fur of their paws and faces. The council. At the head of the circle sat a large, golden lion, his mane a mass of shadows in the dim firelight. Kris suppressed a shriek of delight. Her uncle was here!

"That is a foolish plan," the lion said, glaring at a bobcat Katheni with tawny fur and tufted ears. "We are not going to kill him. First, it is against our laws, and second, it is impractical. The Human is a Hero: anyone foolish enough to try killing him would merely anger him. An angry Hero is not the best thing for the survival of our tribe, Talvan. Do you want your irrational hatred of Humans to endanger the tribe?"

The bobcat Katheni merely shrugged and picked up a clay cup from the serving board at their footpaws, draining it before replying. "And what if he is a pawn of the slavers? Will your unquestioning acceptance of other Races be any better for the tribe than a little caution?"

A leopard Katheni whose spots had faded nearly grey spoke up in a raspy voice. "A little caution is far different than outright murder, Talvan." He turned to the lion and half-bowed. "But neither can we trust him entirely, O Haj. He may be here to spy us out and report on our defenses."

"Oh, I doubt that," said a smaller Katheni with very tall ears. "He did deliver some of our supposedly dead kin back to us at risk of his own life, which I remind you he nearly lost despite what Bar'at could do for him."

"Not to mention how young Kris is treating him. She acts as if they are courting!" growled a tiger. "I doubt that the daughter of Marcellus the Wise would have such bad judgment, though her taste is strange."

Kris surreptitiously stuck her tongue out at the tiger.

A jaguar raised his spotted paw. "My suggestion is that for the time being, we trust the Human, but keep an eye on him. If he acts suspicious, we will reconsider," he said.

The lion nodded. "An admirable suggestion. We shall vote upon this matter."

The elders reached into small pouches hanging at their waists and removed small stones, placing them in a small pile near the Haj's footpaws. The Haj looked at the two small piles of polished stones in the sand. The piled white stones outnumbered the blacks ten-to-two. "It is decided," he said. "The Human may stay among us for a time. Rimar, I would ask that your youngest son take the task of watching the Human."

The jaguar nodded and placed a paw on his chest. "He will be honored to do so."

At that moment, a paw clamped down on Kris's tail and dragged her from her place at the edge of the tent. "And what are you doing?" Jaava asked. "I told you not to interrupt the council!"

"I didn't!" Kris spat, clutching her tail protectively. "I just wanted to see Uncle, that's all."

"Well, you can wait until they get out," Jaava said, peeved.

"We *are* out," boomed a voice from behind them.

Both Katheni jumped and spun to face the lion who had been inside the tent. "Uncle Wasara!" Kris cried as she pounced him.

Haj Wasara caught Kris in a muscular hug and swung her around in a circle, nuzzling her nose with his. "Kris, my kitten! It is good to see you well. We heard that slavers wiped out the Salvinsel tribe. It is good to find that not all rumors are true."

"Uncle, didn't any of the others make it here?" Kris asked. "There were seven other groups that left Salvinsel headed for Mir. They're not here?"

Wasara put Kris down and looked at her. "No, no others from Salvinsel are here yet, but take heart, some may yet arrive. But enough of that. Where are my nephew and the Human who delivered you to me?"

"His name is Cyrus, Uncle, and he's right over here. Come on!" Kris said, grabbing Wasara's large paw and pulling him to where Cyrus and Katana sat in the sand.

• • •

"Ah! Cyrus! Here comes the Haj," Katana said, pointing behind the young Hero.

Cyrus stood up to greet an enormous, maned Katheni. "You must be the Mir Haj," he said.

"No, I'm perfectly real, I can assure you," Wasara said, chuckling. "I am Wasara, Haj of Mir. You must be Cyrus. I have heard much about your exploits." He placed a massive paw on Cyrus's shoulder.

Cyrus was only a little intimidated by the Haj. He was by far the largest Katheni he had yet seen. Wasara stood well over six feet tall and seemed even taller thanks to his magnificent brown-gold mane. Considering that the average height of a mature Katheni is just over five feet, Wasara towered over his tribe. Not only was the Haj tall, he was well-muscled and comported himself as if he owned the entire desert, which, in fact, he did. Cyrus, however, was a Hero in all but formality, and Wasara was greeting him as a friend.

"I am Cyrus Solburg, Hero, Second Class, son of Jeremiah Solburg of Starspeak. I am honored to finally meet you, Haj Wasara. Your niece has told me much about you and your tribe." Cyrus bowed.

"No need to be so formal, Hero," Wasara said. "You have done my tribe and me a great service by returning our lost kin to us. We invite you to stay with us a while and enjoy yourself. You will stay, will you not?"

"Of course he will," Kris said. "He's not fully over his poisoning yet. Besides, you enjoy our company, don't you, Cyrus?"

"I enjoy your company very much. Er . . . I mean I enjoy all your company, in general. I'd be, uh, delighted to stay," Cyrus managed, flushing slightly.

"*He's* over the poison," Katana said, rolling his eyes. "It's Kris that isn't."

"Very well, it is settled," Wasara said. "I welcome you to Mir, Cyrus Solburg." He smiled and pointed all the fingers on his right paw at Cyrus.

Cyrus stared at the paw and wondered how to respond.

"Here," Wasara said, "place the tips of your fingers against mine. It is a Katheni sign of friendship, a sheathing of the claws. There, like that," he said as Cyrus did as instructed. In unison, Cyrus and Wasara drew back their hands, Wasara's formidable claws retracting as he did so. "Good. Now, I need to speak with my niece and nephew. I have assigned a cub the task of guiding you around and getting you anything you might need. I shall see you tonight, young Hero."

Kris, Katana, and their uncle sat in the shady oasis around which the tents of the village clustered. A hot wind blew sand across the dunes, occasionally sending a spray of it stinging against Kris's face. The sunlight slanted in from the west, throwing evening shadows from the trees and tents of the village. Shrubs hogged the space at the water's edge, and the green floating pads of the Brackren Oasis Lily dotted the surface.

The two told Wasara of all the things that had happened since their departure from their home, both good and bad.

"I am amazed that you two managed to survive all that," Wasara said.

"Well, we wouldn't have, save for Cyrus's help," said Kris.

Katana snorted. "Half of it was Cyrus's *fault*. Another quarter was Reginald's, and the last was Kris's for getting us tangled up with them in the first place. It amazes me what a tail lying across the road can get a person into."

"Shut up, Katana." Kris collected a double-pawful of slimy oasis mud and dumped it into her brother's lap.

"Kris! Blast, I just put this robe on too. I'll get you for this, sweet sister."

"I look forward to your attempt," Kris said, grinning maliciously. Katana left to remove the mud from his robe. Kris made to leave also, but Wasara motioned for her to remain.

"I must have a word with you about Cyrus, Kris," Wasara said.

Kris looked puzzled. "What do you mean?"

Wasara sighed. "I need to know exactly what your feelings for him are. It is obvious to anyone with a single eye in his head that you two have feelings for each other. For my sake and the sake of the tribe, I must know what is going on."

Kris leaned over the oasis and plucked a lily, tucking it behind her right ear. "I don't really see how that is the business of the tribe, or even your own, Uncle. However, I will tell you that I only wait for Cyrus to ask me, and—"

"And what?" Wasara interrupted. "Do you think a Human will take you as his mate? Don't be foolish, girl. You do not know this man."

Kris frowned. "I know him better than you do, Uncle. I have traveled with him this past month, and I know that he is a good man, full of kindness and courage. I know that he lives for justice and would die to protect me. What more could I ask for?"

"That he be of your own race," Wasara replied. "It would make far more sense for you to mate another Katheni. If you go with this Human, you will never know the joys of raising your own cubs. You will be pointed at and stared at wherever you go. People will whisper about the Katheni who mated a hairless Human." He placed an enormous but gentle paw on his niece's shoulder. "Neither would you fit into Human society, kitten. It is for the best that Cyrus delivered you here. Now you can live life as you were meant to—here with us."

Kris turned away, tears welling up in her eyes. "But . . . I love him . . . more than I ever loved anyone before . . . " She swallowed, took a deep breath, and turned back to her uncle, fierce determination filling her. "And I intend to go with him when he leaves Mir."

Wasara was silent for a long moment. A pair of Dragonflies flitted across the oasis's surface, chasing each other in happy loop-the-loops before flying back off. The sun sank behind the western dunes, dropping the village into dusk.

Then he laughed softly. "Ah, kitten, you are so like your mother. She would not listen to our father when he told her not to mate Marcellus, either. I suppose it runs in the family. But look," he said, ruffling Kris's head-fur, "good resulted from her disobedience. I am not your father and have no authority to tell you what to do. Do as you like. Mate this Human if you must. And I wish you two the best of happiness."

"Thank you, Uncle. I'm sorry to disappoint you," Kris said, hugging him. "Since my father is . . . since he isn't here, I guess I needed *someone* to defy."

"Anytime, niece. Anytime."

Chapter 27

WARS AND RUMORS OF WARS

In which the Five Continents are Embroiled in War,
and Reginald Encounters an Old Friend

GENERAL LEVILARAS STEPHENS of
the Basilisk Brigade, a famous company of
elite Elven mercenaries, landed his ships on
the shining, shell-strewn sands of Lorimar's
Glass Coast.

It did not take long for the High Elves of Lorimar to dis-
cover his arrival, nor for the Elven House of Lords to cor-
dially invite such a famous personage to the coastal fortress in
which they held their Summer Parliament. The Elven Prime
Minister was there personally, and took Stephens's hand to
officially welcome him to Lorimar.

Not since King Randall Bryath the Third had heeded his
advisors and instituted the income tax had trust been so sadly
misplaced. Shouting "Death to the High Elves!" Stephens
plunged a wave-bladed dagger into the frail Elven leader's
chest. The Elven Prime Minister was immediately avenged.
Neither Stephens nor his contingent of men left the fortress
alive, for Elves are deadly archers even when taken unawares.

But Stephens had accomplished his fell purpose. The High
Elves immediately blamed the Low Elves for hiring Stephens

to carry out the slaying and declared war. So began the first Elven civil war in over thirteen centuries.

The Median Elves sided with the Low Elves, as they do about 50 percent of the time. Joining them were the Dark and Twilight Elves. But this alliance was more than matched when the High Elves were joined by the Mean Elves, the Mode Elves, and the little known Average Elves. To their banner came also the Light Elves, the Morning Elves, and the Late Afternoon Elves, who would only fight after lunch but before dinner. Soon, the entire Elven race fought itself.

The actions of General Stephens were repeated across the known world. Disguised in the uniforms of the enemies of each country they attacked, mercenary groups in Voshtyr's employ committed atrocities and acts of war. Soon the entire world was turned upside down.

On Salvinsel, the Demon Division laid siege to Kamish Castle, pinning Baron von Kamish and his son, Turner von Kamish the Solid Wall inside the castle's impenetrable defenses. On the frozen Northern continent of Novania, assassins from the Chaos Company slew the Frost King and two of his sons in their sleep, throwing the slow-moving, neutral government into disarray. The Orcish mercenaries, the Horendis Horde, ravaged the countryside of Landeralt. They were finally stopped at the Black Ford by Emperor Vladimir Xanathosson and his Army of Darkness™.

Finally, on Centra Mundi, Voshtyr personally attacked and decimated the castle of Shallot-by-the-Lake.

It was not a pretty battle. After Voshtyr's magical assault, the few remaining defenders huddled behind the battlements, fearing the next flight of wyverns. Plus there was an especially vicious female gryphon fighting for Voshtyr, who repeatedly picked off the best defenders from the wall and dropped them from lethal heights. The wyverns and the gryphon had killed more of the Shallot soldiers than Voshtyr's archers and magic artillery combined. Every five minutes or so, a flight of the scaled beasts shrieked by, dropping glass spheres filled with explosive fire magic. They killed the Captain of the Shallot Guard in the third pass.

However, the defenders began to turn the battle to their favor. Lieutenant Willis took over for the slain Captain, shooting down five wyverns with the castle's siege ballistae. His men rallied, courage flared, and the tide of the battle almost turned.

Then Voshtyr himself led a charge. Using the potent magic of a stolen, crystallized soul, he fired a Siege-Grade *Impact Beam*, knocking down not only the castle gate but also leveling a long piece of the wall.

Though disheartened, Willis's defenders rallied and pressed forward to close the gap. Voshtyr's forces charged the weary defenders. The soldiers of Shallot lasted nearly fifteen minutes, despite the horror an Arch-Villain can bring to a battlefield.

Voshtyr strode into the midst of the melee, wielding a new-forged black falchion: *Antagonist*. The blade was a ray of darkness on the sunny day, hewing its way across the battlefield, reaping souls and leaving death in its wake. Voshtyr had forged his new blade, like its precursor, from Darkmatter.

The reader must understand a bit about Darkmatter.

At the climax of the Twenty-Minute War, at the nineteenth minute and thirty-seventh second mark to be specific, three giant meteors bore down on the world. The saints Michael, Helm, and Greaves immolated the falling stars with holy magic, diverting the Star of Power from its target and shattering the stars of Death and Anger.

When they shattered, their momentum was not lost. Their pieces scattered across the surface of the world. Wary of these fragments, Saint Helm ordered that they be found and destroyed. Many were. However, some pieces buried themselves deep into the soil and rock.

Over the centuries the fragments that were never found gradually corrupted the minerals around them. The vile crust of deadly black material that resulted was darker than the thoughts of a poet in a graveyard. Dwarves soon discovered it, naming it *borok gat mors*, the stone that kills. The Elves named it *shalucomalus,* the eater of light. To Humans, it was Darkmatter, and it was deadlier than any poison.

Mining Darkmatter is a hazardous task. To start with, raw Darkmatter produces horrible burns on contact with skin. Second, breathing in even ten grains of the stuff causes massive bleeding of the lungs and brain. Smelting and forging it is complicated, as they must be done in total absence of sunlight, or the raw Darkmatter will evaporate. Any anvil or hammer used in the forging process gradually becomes tainted by the Darkmatter, ultimately turning unstable and brittle.

But if Darkmatter smithing is successful, the end result is fearsome. The smith produces a blade carved of darkness, a black weapon that eats light and excretes death. A cut inflicted by a Darkmatter weapon is almost invariably fatal, for it causes Human flesh to explode like alchemist's flash powder. If the wound itself is not fatal, the resulting infection inevitably is. Any armor or metal repeatedly struck with a Darkmatter blade becomes tainted and brittle, much as the tools of the cursed blade's forging do.

There are drawbacks to Darkmatter weapons, however. First, they are banned by all upstanding governments. Even the Hereditary Evil Empire prohibits them, though this is more because of concerns regarding patent infringement than safety concerns. Second, many of those known to wield Darkmatter weapons have developed tumors, experienced breathing problems, gone blind, and finally died prematurely. It is a risky material, used only by the most foolhardy, the most brave, or suicidal Villains.

Voshtyr was none of those. The blood of Demons flowed in his veins, and this gave him ample protection against the ill effects of Darkmatter. He wielded *Antagonist* with supreme confidence, slashing his way through the ranks of the Shallot defenders.

At the height of the battle, Lieutenant Willis himself sprang through the rank of soldiers in front of Voshtyr and aimed a precise cut at the Arch-Villain's neck.

Voshtyr caught the sword in his bare left hand, blade ringing against his metallic palm. "Almost good enough, Human. I am impressed."

The Arch-Villain chuckled and yanked Willis's sword from his hand. Swift as a diving hawk, Voshtyr sheathed his falchion and plunged his metal hand directly into Willis's chest. He withdrew his fist clutching a crystalline image of the unfortunate soldier. A brief flash, and Lieutenant Willis's body slumped to the ground, a surprised expression on its face. Voshtyr pocketed a small opal and turned to his next opponent.

After that, the massacre ended in minutes. Not a single man, woman, or child had escaped. Voshtyr smiled, the blood of the young dripping from his pointed nose.

• • •

Slashback shook her wings and folded them to her furred back. It had been another easy victory under Voshtyr's banner. The only flaw was that she'd had to fight alongside those smelly wyverns. The gryphon disliked wyverns, for they had all the unpleasant qualities of Dragons, with none of their intelligence. They were large beasts, resembling small Dragons with no forelegs, and owning more teeth than any creature had a right to.

At any rate, the battle was over. Slashback began walking to Voshtyr's tent to discuss their next move. She felt a soft touch on her left wing and stopped. Cocking her head, Slashback saw a man in a dark cloak beckon to her and step behind an enormous pile of rubble. Curious, she followed warily. When she stepped behind the pile, the man removed his hood, revealing raven-black hair and distinctive facial scars.

"Good to see you, Slashback Ricor."

"Serimal?" Slashback gaped. "You are still alife? How iss that possible?"

Serimal smiled his friendly half-smile. "Oh, I am injured, to be certain. Spending any amount of time in an Iron Maiden is detrimental to one's health. But Voshtyr is a poor swordsman, and my fiancée is an Elven princess. How could I *not* survive?"

"You must not stay here," Slashback warned. She looked around at the camp.

Goblins were everywhere, as well as Minions and Henchmen in abundance, stacking and setting fire to the corpses of the defeated defenders. The black tents of Voshtyr's army covered cages containing other, less reasonable, Mythological beasts. Were *any* of these creatures to find Serimal, the game would be up.

Slashback pushed Serimal father behind the rubble with her beak. "Stay down. If Koshtyr sees you, he will kill you."

"Actually, I'm here to kill him," Serimal said. "Not just yet, perhaps, but soon. Normally the von Steinadlers do not kill family. But Voshtyr is family no longer. Aside from trying to kill me, my half-brother has started several needless wars, all to power his pet project."

"How—"

"How do I know about his plan? Please, Slashback. I'm not as dense as a Hero. He set the accursed thing up in *my* castle basement, after all. I also know he's been planning this for a long time. You think that was his own spy network he was using to keep track of young Solburg? Hardly. Voshtyr's been at this insane venture for years. It's the reason he tried to kill King Bryath six years ago.

"See, Bryath has a ring that allows the wearer to use magic within The Circle of No Magic surrounding the Keep of Five Flames. Voshtyr wants the treasure at the top of the Keep—whatever it is. Unless I miss my guess, Voshtyr needs that treasure to power his dreadful Device. And in order to get into the Keep with his powers intact, he'll need that ring. If he assembles his device, Slashback, it will be the end of us all. I *will* stop him, but I need your help to do it. "

"And you are needing my help for what?" the gryphon asked.

Serimal placed a finger on Slashback's beak. "Silence, gryphon. If Voshtyr finds me before I am fully recovered, I will most certainly be killed. All I need from you is that you keep that beautiful blue eye of yours on my half-brother at all times. Tell me where he goes and who he collects to commit his petty atrocities for him. If he wants to start a worldwide war, by the gods, I will make sure the other side is ready for him. And here," Serimal removed a locket with a very long chain from his black cloak and handed it to the gryphon. "This is for you."

Slashback eyed the locket curiously. Extending a cautious talon, she opened it. Inside were two miniature paintings, one of a handsome young man, the other of the same man as a boy, cradling a gryfflet in his arms. Alkaline tears welled up in Slashback's eyes. *Gavin.*

Serimal smiled. "I recently received that from a Miss Emily Cartwright, who I believe is related to an old friend of yours. Farewell, Slashback Ricor." Serimal stepped back and vanished as quickly as he had appeared.

Slashback placed the long chain about her neck and slipped the locket between some feathers. Mixed emotions swirled in her eagle-like head. But no—time enough for confusion later. Now it was time to do what Gavin would have done. Slashback turned and headed for Voshtyr's tent.

"No survivors, then?" Voshtyr asked.

Slashback shook her head. "I make two aerial passes hoffer the castle ruins. No people haff surfieft."

Voshtyr allowed himself a cold smile. Things were working out exactly on schedule, with no mishaps so far. "Excellent. We cannot afford the Guild of Heroes learning of our deeds just yet. My thanks for your report, Slashback," Voshtyr said.

The Arch-Villain sat down in one of the padded collapsible chairs in his large, black meeting tent. A central table held a war map of Centra Mundi, pinned to the surface with four daggers with skulls for pommels, each securing a corner of the map. A fire burned in a brazier behind him, generating more shadows than it did light. Which was just the ambience he intended.

"Soon," Voshtyr continued, "we will control enough of Centra Mundi to find that irritating Crimson Slash. When we do, gryphon, he is all yours. Now, go and find me Duke Tremel. I wish to speak with him."

Slashback dipped her beak in a gryphonic salute and left the tent.

Within minutes, Duke Tremel, a muscular man with streaks of white in his otherwise black hair, pushed the tent flap aside and entered. "You wanted to see me, sir?"

"Yes, I did." Voshtyr drew another red circle on the map on the table. "Roger has informed me that he did not hire one of the mercenary groups for which we had scheduled interviews."

"Yes, sir, that would be the Salamanders, sir," Tremel answered. "Their emissary left the assembly, but I believe the griff picked her off so word couldn't get back to them."

Voshtyr sighed. "Yes, Slashback took care of their envoy, but that isn't sufficient. I don't want some unclaimed group of mercenaries becoming a loose ballista. That has been a problem for armies such as mine, historically. They could very well be planning to attack me when I least expect it, perhaps as revenge for killing their girl, and I wish to keep that sort of nuisance to a minimum. Tremel, I need you to take an infantry division and some hand-picked men and remove this possible threat. Here is what you must do . . . "

"Emily! You are safe, thank the gods!"

A woman in black-enameled armor pulled Emily Cartwright into a strong embrace. "Koshiro told me that a gryphon had snatched you," she said, "and when you failed to return, I thought you had perished. What happened to you that you took so long to get back?"

The two women stood just outside a large camp. The white tents bore the banner of a flaming lizard rampant, the emblem of the Salvinsel Salamanders. Several men milled about the field outside the camp, sparring with wooden swords, while others cooked a pair of deer over some of the multiple fires that already burnt to light up the dusk of evening.

"It's complicated, General Allyn," Emily said, wincing. "It starts with a rude Arquellus and ends with a gryphon, a Dragon, and a Hero."

Allyn looked puzzled. "You want to take those one by one?"

Emily smiled wearily. "I would love to explain it to you, General, but at the moment my legs and back feel like I've been stomped by a golem, and I may pass out before I finish telling you. Suffice it to say that you need to be prepared for an attack by our prospective employer. Voshtyr didn't take very kindly to impatience." Seeing the puzzled expression on the General's face, she grinned apologetically. "If you like, ma'am, I can give you the brief version before I see the medic . . . "

"That isn't necessary, Captain. Go see the medic, immediately." General Jael Allyn gently herded Emily in the direction of the medical tent. "Did you happen to bring the Hero you mentioned with you? We can always use another strong man on our side."

"Yes, ma'am. That's him, standing next to the Dragon I mentioned."

Allyn looked where Emily was pointing. The crimson bar on the Hero's shield gleamed in the setting sun. "Did he say who he was?"

"He's the Crimson Slash, ma'am."

A smile tugged at the corners of Allyn's mouth, but she quickly hid it. "The Crimson Slash, you say . . . "

"Yes, ma'am. Why, is there something wrong?"

Allyn shook her head, black tresses blowing across the snake etched on her breastplate. "No, nothing at all. Now, get to the medic, double-time. Raul!"

An exotic-looking man with glossy black hair and deeply tanned skin approached and saluted.

"Help Captain Cartwright to the medic's tent, and tell Captains Sakana and Karvash to start organizing our defenses against a possible surprise attack. If we *are* attacked, I want it to be as little a surprise as possible."

Reginald put the pack down. "It's too late to return to the Keep of Five Flames today. I suppose we'll have to ask this General Allen if we might spend the night here. I don't relish the prospect of sleeping in those woods."

The two stood on a low hill just outside the large mercenary camp where they'd deposited Emily. Aside from the bustle that accompanied the setting of the sun in any military setting, the outskirts were quite deserted.

Keeth shrugged, as much as Dragons can. "It is probable that they will not mind us spending the night here," Keeth said. "You did return a missing soldier for them, after all."

"Still, it is better to ask permission," Reginald said, scanning the rows of tents spread out across the field. "I've had my share of unfriendly encounters with mercenaries."

"I appreciate the courtesy," said a woman from behind Reginald. "But I can confidently offer you a tent for the night, Crimson Slash."

Reginald turned and was confronted by a woman nearly as tall as he was, wearing white tights and shirt, a metal-plated skirt, and a breastplate with an ebon snake etched in the front. "Black Viper?" Reginald said, trying to mask his surprise.

"Four years, and that's all you can come up with, Reginald?" the woman asked. "You haven't changed one bit, I see."

"Well, I suppose I haven't, Miss Allyn. But I wasn't expecting you. My, you look the same as when . . . Well, as when you went by another name and . . . fought beside me. What are you doing with these mercenaries?"

The woman glanced back at the tents. "Oh, the Salamanders? I command them. I suppose you could call me General Allyn now, if you wanted to. But please, Reginald, 'Jael' will do fine."

Reginald nudged Keeth in the ribs. "You hear vowels—why didn't you tell me that Emily Cartwright had pronounced Allyn with a *y*?"

Keeth made a hurt expression. "You didn't ask. I thought you were being witty when you said 'Allen.'"

Reginald ignored the Dragon. "Very well, Blac— Jael. But I forget myself. I wanted to thank you for your hospitality."

General Jael Allyn smiled. "You can thank me by joining me for supper. We have much to catch up on. Meet me at my tent in three hours."

"Of course," Reginald said.

"And I wouldn't dream of intruding," Keeth said. "I can delay my visit to Uncle Nivonis no longer. Farewell, Crimson Slash. May we meet again."

Reginald pounded Keeth's neck with manly affection. "Safe travels, son of Barinol."

Keeth dipped his head and took to the air. He soared above the mercenary camp, the tents a flock of sheep on a grassy hill. The Dragon banked north and headed for the Mountains of the Morning.

That evening, the Crimson Slash and Jael Allyn met over supper in the tent reserved for the Salamanders' commanding officer.

It was obviously a military tent, judging from its sparse décor and lack of trappings. But the few pieces of furniture there were surprisingly comfortable. The white walls reflected the light from a glowing white orb, a magical lantern of some sort, resting atop a pedestal. Another orb to one side of the room radiated coldness into the tent's interior. Apparently Jael allowed herself the luxury of magical climate control, if nothing else.

Over roasted venison and potatoes Reginald told Jael of their encounter with Lydia the White Tiger, who used to be Jael's apprentice. Jael was most upset about Lydia's turn to Villainy. They spoke of Cyrus and how he had become a Hero, Second Class after assisting in Reginald's escape from the Swamp Keep. Finally, their discussion turned to the Salvinsel Salamanders and the job Voshtyr had recently offered them.

"I never officially severed ties with the Guild. They let me keep my Heroic Name, and still ask me to do things for them from time to time," Jael explained. "They contacted me a few days ago and asked that I investigate this Voshtyr fellow." She took a bite of potato and chewed for a moment before continuing. "They were particularly concerned that he might have been the one who recently stole the Three Terrible Turbines from the Sharkwater Channel Museum of Magic. Apparently these turbines can be combined into a larger device, one that—"

"Would threaten all Heroes, and possibly Destroy the World, if assembled," Reginald said, nodding. "The Guild told me much the same thing before I went to Demonkin's keep in the swamp. So, what was it you did?"

"Well, I decided it was worth the risk. The Guild was sending me there anyway, and like any good mercenary commander, I was interested in a job that paid so high. I had no idea it was this dangerous or that Emily wouldn't return." Jael sighed and slumped in her chair. "I should have gone myself instead of sending proxies. Sometimes I think I'm getting too old for the Hero business, Reginald."

"Nonsense," Reginald said. "You're only forty-two. You've a goodly number of fighting years in you yet. Myself, now, I may be retiring soon. Cyrus was my fourth squire, and he's turned out better that any of the others. I've done my part for Good and raised my share of the next generation of Heroes." He put his wineglass down and took Jael's hand in his. "But you, Jael, you're the commander of a successful mercenary band. Don't give up yet."

Jael smiled. "Reginald, stop that. You're still acting like you did when we were squires during the Landeralt campaign."

"Those were good times," Reginald said, returning the smile. "Fighting against Xanathos Klominarson and his Empire, making fun of our masters . . . "

"Eating unidentified foods."

Reginald grimaced. "Ugh, pray, don't remind me of that. I had to drink an entire bottle of brandy to get the taste out of my mouth."

"You always were one for a drink, Reginald." Jael smiled wickedly. "But you never could stand up to me in a drinking contest."

"Now just one moment," Reginald protested. "I recall winning well over half of those!"

Jael took the wineskin off the table and placed a heavy glass decanter on it instead. Glorious amber liquid swirled and sparkled inside the flask. "Oh, of *course* you did. But today," she said, "you will lose once more."

"I accept your challenge. Do your worst, woman!" Reginald said, and filled two tumblers to their brims.

Chapter 28

CEREMONIAL

In which a Happy Event Occurs,
and the Chapter has an Irritating Ending

CYRUS WAS BEGINNING to feel out of place with the Katheni of Mir.

It was the second day after returning to consciousness, and with his returning wits came a growing sense of unease. It was certainly a nice place, and the Katheni had warmed up to him immensely. Few if any still acted hostile toward him, and most even seemed to approve of Kris's attitude toward him. But still he felt oppressed by all the strangers and the complete lack of Human faces. Thoughts of what would happen when he left the village plagued him.

"I don't know if you like cheese, Mister Solburg," the young jaguar boy said, "but we do make some very fine goat cheese here in Mir."

Wasara had assigned the boy to guide Cyrus around the village. He was young, not more than thirteen years or so, but he carried himself with the air of a professional tour guide that knew their location inside and out. His name was Benjara, he'd said, and he was handy with a needle and thread. He wore a tan vest and white trousers, and his left ear bore a single brass loop.

"Cheese is good," Cyrus replied absently. "You know what, why don't you get me a piece?"

Benjara perked up. "Oh, I would love to! Stay right here, I will return immediately!" He sprinted off toward wherever it was the cheese was located.

Cyrus did not stay right there. What he needed right now was some solitude. And that was what he found beneath the shade of a wide-branched desert palm tree in the oasis.

What's my problem? Cyrus asked himself as he sat down and leaned against the tree. I've completed my Quest and can become an official Hero. I want to stay with Kris, but this is her home, not mine. I'll have to go, and soon. But can I just leave her here? I wish I could ask her what she wants without being all awkward about it. If she wants to come with me, I can't ask her to stay here. But I can't take her with me, either. A Hero's life is dangerous. She would be in danger if she stuck with me. Plus, it seems absurd to bring her all the way out here only to make her leave again. If I could only ask her . . .

"Cyrus?"

"Hello, Kris," Cyrus said, pleased by Kris's serendipitous appearance. "Have a seat."

Kris did so. "I must speak with you, Cyrus," she said. "First, I want to thank you for all you have done for brother and I."

"Don't bother, Kris," Cyrus said, "it was nothing. It was my Quest, after all."

Kris winced. "Be that as it may, I also have one question to ask. It's . . . it's a bit more personal, though."

Something began to jump around in the back of Cyrus's mind, squealing wildly with glee. It was promptly told to button its lips by the cynical part of his mind. The rational part of Cyrus's mind interjected that since the noisy, gleeful bit was part of a brain, it technically had no lips. Cyrus's temper got angry and threw a metaphysical punch at the metaphysical head of the rational part. Cyrus collected his thoughts, put them back in order, and began to worry about having a multiple-personality disorder.

"Cyrus?" Kris was looking at him rather strangely. "Are you all right?"

"Err, no. If I was all right, something would be wrong with me," Cyrus said. "What were you saying?"

"You do realize what my situation is, don't you?" Kris asked, looking down and tracing pointless patterns in the soft sand with a furred finger. "I . . . you're very important to me, Cyrus, and I don't want to be separated from you. Even though you brought me home, if you're leaving . . . I don't want to stay."

Cyrus sat still for a moment. "Kris," he said slowly, "I have fought Orcs, bandits, Villains, Vampires, Ogres, and tax collectors. I've raided the underwater lair of a Hydra. I've dived off cliffs, scaled mountains, drunk the flaming essence of a Starfire plant, and thrown a powerful Wizard from the top of his own tower. None of these things seems difficult compared to what I am about to attempt. I'm so used to making light of everything that when it comes to being serious or speaking for a purpose, I fail.

"I've never told a woman what I really think of her, not once that I can remember, probably because it would usually get me slapped. So forgive me if this doesn't come out exactly right."

Cyrus took the Katheni girl's hand and stared into her eyes. "Kris, we've known each other for barely a month. In that time, I've seen many qualities in you that I like. I can't imagine anything I would like better than to have more time to get to know you better. But I am, after all, a Hero. I go into dangerous places on purpose. *And I don't want you hurt.* I care more about you than any thirty-seven other people put together. If you were to come with me, you might get injured or killed, and I don't know if I could stand that.

"So I leave it up to you. I recommend that you stay here. Your kin will take care of you and you'll be safe. I could even come back to visit once in a while between Quests. But what I want . . . " He swallowed. "Kris, if you want to come with me, I would ask that you marry me." Cyrus took a deep breath and tried not to hold it.

Kris was remarkably silent, her shoulders shaking a little. When she looked up, tears streamed down her face, darkening the fur beneath her eyes. "Of course, Cyrus. I love you more than any life I could possibly have without you." She threw her arms around Cyrus.

Cyrus held Kris tight. *Thank the gods I didn't botch that up.*

"Hero Cyrus!" shouted Benjara. The jaguar boy seemed to suddenly notice that Cyrus was in a full embrace with the niece of the tribe's leader. He didn't seem to know exactly what to do with himself. He coughed gently into a closed paw. "Erm, the Haj requests your presence . . . "

Cyrus released Kris, stood up, and brushed the sand from his trousers. "Why, what happened?"

"We've captured another Human, and he wants to know if it was with you," the Katheni said. "Now, come along."

Kris and Cyrus followed the page to Haj Wasara's tent. Inside stood the Haj and two jaguar warriors. The warriors held tightly to the arms of a Human man. To Cyrus's amazement, he recognized the man: it was the priest whose burnt church had mysteriously disappeared.

"Master Solburg," Wasara asked Cyrus, "do you know this man?"

"Hello, Cyrus," the priest said sheepishly. "Looks like I wandered into the wrong desert."

"Yes, I recognize him," Cyrus said. "He's a priest. Kind and harmless, I'd say. He's got some odd magic, though, so keep an eye on him."

The Haj nodded to the warriors, who released the priest. "Very well. As you are a friend of Cyrus, I shall let you go, for now. But know that we mistrust Humans here, as a matter of principle."

"I understand," the priest replied. "Complete, unthinking trust, in a world containing evil and evil people is not the most intelligent thing. I shall offer no complaints."

"You need not worry yourself, Haj," Cyrus said. "I'll vouch for him. In fact, I'll keep an eye on him for you."

"Very well," Wasara replied. "Go, then."

Outside the tent, Cyrus seized the priest's arm. "What are you doing here, priest? What happened to your church? How did you—" He stopped as the priest raised a hand.

"I am more than I seem, Cyrus Solburg," the man said. "You may ask me three questions, and no more, for my old body is tired after traveling this far."

Cyrus scratched his head and ran his fingers through his hair. The priest still wore the same gold-trimmed black robe, and his dark hair was just as unkempt as before. "All right, then," Cyrus said. "First, who are you, really?"

The priest chuckled. "I am a servant to all, and King over them. I am the opening paragraph of the world's first book, and the period at the end of the last written line. I sit here, flesh and blood, yet people deny my very existence."

"That doesn't answer my question," Cyrus said, furrowing his brow.

"It does, indirectly," the priest said, grinning. "I didn't say that I would give you straight answers to your questions, only that you could ask them."

"Fine. In that case, I'll be more specific with my next question. How did you make that church disappear?"

"Magic," said the priest, wiggling his fingers at Cyrus. "You could call it magic of a higher order than that which the Elementalists and Highseekers use. It is a gift from the Creator. Now, before you ask your third question, think it over carefully."

Cyrus thought a moment, cleared his throat, and spoke. "All right, priest, my third question is this: will you perform a marriage ceremony for Kris and I?"

The priest smiled. "Good lad! I knew you'd get around to the important question eventually. Of course I will, but hadn't you better inform her relatives of this? They might want to hold some sort of celebration."

"Well, I'm not sure. Some of them are still a little iffy on the whole idea of my being here, let alone marrying one of them. Tell you what, I'll ask the Haj. Don't go anywhere, priest," Cyrus said, pointing warily at the priest.

"I wouldn't dream of it."

• • •

"You *what?*" Haj Wasara said.

"I came to ask your permission to marry, or take as mate, or whatever the Katheni call it, your niece, Kris."

Cyrus and Wasari stood in the Haj's tent. Some odd Katheni furniture decorated the tent—chairs designed to accommodate tails and such. A tapestry of the rising sun hung from one wall, and the same emblem decorated the thin blanket atop a futon on the floor. Both the back and front flaps of the tent were open to let the gentle breeze through, keeping the tent a decent temperature.

"I spoke with Kris moments ago," Cyrus said, "and she shares my feelings. I ask this of you because I'm not sure how your tribe would take it, what with the slaver problem and all."

Wasara smiled. "I know of this already, Cyrus Solburg. My niece spoke to me yesterday. She was simply waiting for you to ask. And now let me tell you something," he said, putting a heavy paw on Cyrus's shoulder. "Three years ago, one of our bravest and most well-liked males fell tail over ears in love with an Istaka girl from a wandering tribe which passed through our lands.

"As you probably know, the Katheni are on worse terms with the Istaka than we are with Humans. After suffering the initial storm of criticism and harsh feelings, the two were mated right here, in this very village. They even lived here for a year or two before a wounded mage passed through and gave the girl a spellbook. They are still together, founding a kingdom or something. You know: typical mismatched-couple activities. But that's a different story."

Cyrus blinked, wondering if this story was good news or not.

Wasari chuckled. "In short, my boy, you have my blessing, and the tribe won't blink an eye if you want to have the ceremony right here—this very evening, in fact."

"This evening?" Cyrus started. "Isn't that a little—"

"And now to plan the ceremony feast!" Wasara clapped Cyrus heartily on the shoulder. "For my favorite niece's ceremony, nothing must be missing. There must be food and music and decorations . . . Benjara! Stop lurking out there and come in!" he shouted.

A young jaguar Katheni poked his head into the Haj's tent. "Yes, sir?"

"Go and tell your father and Lorrian that Kris is to take a mate this night. I need everything prepared for a grand festival. Now, get gone! There is little time to waste!"

The jaguar bobbed his head and disappeared from the entrance. Wasara turned back to Cyrus. "All will soon be prepared. For now, find somewhere to be that isn't in the way and isn't near my niece. It is, after all, ill luck to see your mate before the ceremony."

"You're rushing me, Haj," Cyrus protested.

"You're not anxious to mate my niece?" Wasara said, quirking a tawny eyebrow at him.

"No, it's not that," Cyrus answered. "I just had this great idea for a wedding gift, and I need you to help me get it before this evening."

It was late evening by the time the preparations were complete. There was much cooking of foods and moving of the tents to clear a space for the ceremony. There was a briefing for Cyrus on what the ceremony contained and what he must do. Finally, there was the matter of the procurement of proper clothing.

His regular garb was mostly dirty or damaged from the fight with Landrus and his men, and the ceremony required fresh attire. Someone spirited away Cyrus's regular clothing, along with his sword, chainmail, and floppy blue hat.

The leopard boy Benjara, having some skill as a tailor, helped Cyrus dress in appropriate finery for the ceremony. "If you would stop moving, the pins would not poke you! Now hold still," Benjara insisted.

Cyrus grimaced. He'd combed his mess of flame-red hair for the first time in several months and received a trim, so he was presentable. However, the only garments that were of a size to fit him were some of Haj Wasara's, and they needed some adjusting. Benjara was in the process of taking in the shoulders of a fine white shirt with gold embroidery, which for some reason involved an uncomfortable number of pins. The most irritating thing was that young Benjara did not cease talking the entire time. The leopard, having a captive audience, was practicing his Central.

Central is the speech used by all Races when they wish to communicate with one another. It is easy to learn, and none of the races have much difficulty speaking it.

The language supposedly originated among Humans, who found the Elven language far too difficult for everyday use. Elves and Dwarves, finding each other's tongues too complicated, learned the easy speech of the Humans instead. Orcs followed suit after noticing how many violent words were included in its vocabulary and how many sentiments could be expressed in monosyllables. Even the reclusive Avierie, the birdfolk of the northern mountains learned a little for trade purposes.

• • •

And so Benjara inflicted his proper Central on Cyrus. "I do envy you, mister Solburg," he said. "Kris is one of the prettiest girls I have ever laid eyes on. Not only that, but she can hunt, and from what I have seen, she is very good with cubs. Of course, you are Human, so she will not be having *yours*, but that is beside the point. She is the very model of a Katheni woman. I do question her taste, though. Of course it is not my business, but why would someone prefer bare skin rather than soft fur? It seems strange to me, and—"

"I recommend that you stop talking before you say something derogatory about Kris," Cyrus warned, wincing as a pin poked him in the shoulder. "Are you done yet?"

Benjara backed away, admiring his handiwork. "Well, yes, I suppose. If you must leave now, the clothing will not fall apart, but I still need to—"

"It's fine, thanks. Good job, Benjara. If you keep this up, you'll make a fine tailor someday. Hey, wait a minute," Cyrus said, feeling his pants. "Are these pants supposed to be drafty?"

"Oh, my, I forgot that you have no tail," Benjara said, chuckling. "Here, hand me the breeches, and I will sew the tail-hole shut." In no time at all, Benjara's deft paws stitched the hole closed. "Now, I think everything else is ready. You had best get out there."

"Thanks, Benjara." Cyrus grinned and shook the young leopard's paw. "Perhaps someday I'll have you custom-make me some garments."

"I would be honored, mister Solburg. Now get out there. You don't want to keep everyone waiting."

• • •

The sun trailed shimmering waves of golden heat as it began disappearing below the sand dunes. The white hide tents of the Katheni village dotted the outsides of the oasis like sand-grazing sheep. Katheni bustled about, clearing a semicircle in their midst to make room for the celebration that was to take place there shortly.

Dozens of Katheni of all fur patterns and colors helped set up long benches and tables in the sand. At the front of the empty semicircle was a raised dais hung with green cloth and golden sun-disks. In the center of the dais was a trestle-table with a pair of high-backed chairs, reserved for the bride and groom. Off to the side, Katheni cubs under the careful supervision of a pair of adults built a bonfire pile. It was to be lit after the celebration started.

From the back of the semicircle the smells of roasting goat and other herdbeasts drifted out over the clearing and the workers. More guests began filtering into the clearing, bedecked in finery far different from what Cyrus had ever seen before. As Kris had told him before, Katheni clothing seemed to be designed for the sake of beauty rather than function or even modesty.

One of the most popular female garments appeared to be made of nothing but seven sashes. These were worn wrapped around the body to show the most fur possible, while still retaining token modesty. Jewelry was quite common, with ear-loops being the most popular, followed by ornamental armbands, brooches, and things that looked like jeweled collars.

Katheni, Cyrus learned, loved celebrations, and this one was no exception. Guests now streamed in from all corners of the camp, cramming the clearing to watch the unusual mating ceremony. And then the priest and Wasara took their places at the front of the dais. Katana gestured at the pair, then out at the crowd, his paws glowing slightly.

A buzz of conversation erupted as Benjara and another young Katheni male escorted Cyrus to the pavilion. It was the first time some of the assembled had seen the injured Hero, and comments flew about concerning everything from why Cyrus wore the Haj's garments to speculation as to why so many Katheni chose strange mates in this day and age.

"And here he is," Wasara proclaimed. "Now we may begin."

Several Katheni seated on a low bench near the pavilion began to play an uplifting tune, using a flute carved from bone, a forked flute made of some kind of greenish wood, a set of reed pipes, and a tall skin drum. On some cue, the villagers' chatter faded to an expectant hush and they turned as one. Cyrus followed their gaze and was stunned.

There was Kris, flanked by four bridesmaids, advancing slowly through the center of the clearing. She wore a flowing green dress, bedecked with scales that glittered like a thousand emeralds. From her pointed ears hung thin gold hoops with pieces of jade dangling from them. Her speckled fur gleamed like radiant gold, but her smile outshone her fur. When Kris arrived at the pavilion, she took Cyrus's hand in her paw. Cyrus shook himself from his reverie and smiled. The bridesmaids took their places at either side of the couple, and the ceremony began.

"Children of Mir," the priest said, his voice carrying quite well over the crowd thanks to a voice-amplification spell cast by Katana. The priest still wore his black robe, but wore another vestment atop it: a white apron with shoulder pads, decked with five gemstones in a plate on the apron's front. His hair, for once, was combed, making him look much older and more austere. "We are here today in the sight of the Creator to witness the union of Cyrus son of Jeremiah Solburg, and Kris, daughter of Marcellus Baravaati. We are here to share their joy and to celebrate their love.

"Marriage is a gift from the Creator, through which husband and wife grow together in love and trust. It is life made holy by the Creator, a sign of unity and loyalty that all should uphold and honor. It should not be entered into lightly, but reverently and responsibly in His sight. Cyrus and Kris are here this day to enter this life, together.

"Katheni mate for life, a trait uncommon in the society of today. Society will look down on these two for being uncommon—not only in appearance but in commitment and steadfast love. But these two will triumph, for love conquers that which the sword cannot. Now, who gives this woman to mate?"

Haj Wasara stepped forward. "In the place of her father, I so give." Then he bent down to whisper to Cyrus. "And if you mistreat her, I will snap your neck."

The priest stifled a chuckle and continued. "Cyrus Solburg, do you take this woman to be your wife, to forever love and cherish her in sight of the Creator who sees all things visible and invisible, plain and hidden?"

Cyrus's heart raced as it did before a major battle. "I do."

"And Kris Baravaati, do you take this man as your mate, to love and to honor always, before the Creator who gives all life and takes away?"

Kris's smile became, if possible, even more radiant. "I do."

"Then as tokens of this union, each will present the other with a gift. Cyrus?" the priest looked at him.

Cyrus turned and took a burnished copper-colored buckler from Benjara. The shield bore the coat of arms of the

International Guild of Heroes blended with the rising sun of the Mir Katheni tribe. At Cyrus's request, Wasara had talked the tribe's maker of weapons into creating it in time for the ceremony.

Cyrus placed the shield in Kris's gentle paws. "I've always thought of a ring as a foolish thing to give as a marriage symbol. It's a circle, ending at the same place it starts. With a symbol such as that, the marriage is probably doomed," he said with a self-conscious chuckle. "Instead, I give to you this shield. It is my pledge that I shall always love and protect you, so long as breath remains in my body."

The assembled Katheni murmured approvingly, and a few of them clapped their padded paws.

Kris took the shield and handed it to a bridesmaid. Then she turned to another bridesmaid and took from her an ornate silvered scabbard containing Cyrus's sword. "My gift to you is this scabbard," she said, handing the sheath to Cyrus. "As a sword needs a scabbard, so a Hero needs a home to return to. It is a pledge that there shall be no fighting or discord between us, only love and harmony."

A gentle sigh rose from the crowd. Someone in the crowd gave a two-toned, slightly rude whistle. Jaava, Cyrus assumed. The sun had finished setting, and several of the workers who had been setting up tables now lit torches and the bonfire to provide light. The roasting meat smelled so good it was hard to keep his stomach from rumbling.

When the exchange had concluded, the priest spoke once again. "By these tokens, the pact is sealed. If any of you knows a reason that these two may not wed, say it now." No one spoke, and the crowd waited silently. "Very well. In the sight of the Creator, with the blessing of the Haj, and in the presence of you all, I declare Cyrus and Kris Man and Mate. Cyrus, you may kiss your bride."

Needing no further invitation, Cyrus did so, sweeping Kris off her feet. An enormous cheer erupted from the crowd.

The priest smiled beatifically. "I now have the distinct honor of being the first to introduce you to Mr. and Mrs. Cyrus Solburg!"

The musicians broke into a lively piece, and spontaneous dancing broke out amidst the crowd. Several roast herdbeasts were brought in, and Cyrus led Kris down to the center of the trestle-table reserved for them so that the feasting could begin.

The celebration lasted until the sky was black and strewn with stars. The dancing of the Katheni was mesmerizing, as they leapt and twirled in agile fashion by the flickering light of a bonfire. Kris and Cyrus sat at the table at the head of the circle and watched the celebrants enjoy themselves—whenever they could tear their eyes from one another, that is. The fire flared in the desert night, the Katheni danced, and the evening seemed as if it might last forever.

Then the slavers attacked.

Chapter 29

CONFLICT AND CONFLAGRATION

In which a Battle is Fought, and a Greater battle Foreseen

REGINALD AND JAEL Allyn stopped after five entire flasks of brandy and called the match a draw. When Jael passed out, Reginald excused himself and staggered off to his tent, realizing that he was getting too old for this sort of foolish behavior.

The next day dawned clear and cold, the first day of Summerwane. Reginald crawled from his tent and put on his night-chilled armor. The mercenaries' camp had already begun to stir. Men set about collecting their weapons, packing up tents, and taking care of animals. Catching the scent of frying bacon, Reginald followed his nose toward the mess tent.

A young messenger stopped him on his way there. "Good morning, Crimson Slash," the boy said. "I have here a message from General Allyn. She requests that you join her in the battle pavilion in one hour."

Reginald nodded. "Tell her that I shall be there as soon as I break my fast." The messenger saluted and departed. Reginald found the mess tent and went inside.

After ingesting eight fried eggs, a rasher of bacon, and half a loaf of toasted bread, Reginald finally left the tent and headed toward the battle pavilion, a dark red, circular tent ringed with armed guards.

Inside, around a large collapsible table, sat Jael Allyn, Emily Cartwright, and an Orc in black-lacquered armor with what looked like a spoon emblazoned on it. A map of Centra Mundi dominated the table, with red and black pins stuck in it. Another glowing orb hovered near the pinnacle of the tent, at full brightness so that the interior was well lit. In fact, to Reginald, the room felt more like one of those clean white rooms you wait in for the doctor to call for you rather than a tent, only with less chance of being stuck with needles afterward.

"Ah, Reginald, there you are," Jael said with one eyebrow raised. "Now we may begin. You know Emily, of course."

"Good morning, Crimson Slash," Emily said, rising slowly from the table and offering Reginald her hand. Her blond hair was pulled back and put up in a military bun, held in place by what appeared to be a pair of very short daggers. Instead of the chainmail she'd worn the previous day, the young woman wore a suit of partial plate-armor, with leather straps keeping it together. The chestpiece bore the flaming lizard rampant of the Salamanders. The armor seemed somewhat loose, probably because of the bandages around her lower torso and the brace on her hip. "Finding the Salamanders to your liking?"

Reginald took Emily's hand and kissed it. "I've had many dealings with mercenaries in my time. This experience is by far the most pleasant."

Allyn cleared her throat. "Glad you like us, Crimson. Anyway, this is—"

"The Blak Spoon," Reginald finished. "It is good to see you again, Gorbar Karvash."

• • •

Orcs are the third-most plentiful race in the world. An Orc of average height stands six and a half feet tall and has skin of either a melon-green or pallid grey hue. Two extra-long teeth protrude from the jaw, sticking up an inch above the lower lip. All Orcs have yellow eyes. However, if you see an Orc with red eyes, stand back. His or her eyes are bloodshot from alcohol, blood-lust, or a rather deadly combination of the two.

Orcs have incredible strength and stamina. There are no better long-distance runners, swimmers, or overall athletes among the non-Heroes of other Races. Given their penchant for violence, both necessary and unnecessary, this strength is almost invariably abused in one way or another. Hence the antipathy toward Orcs. All Races either mislike or mistrust them, whether because of said random acts of violence or just because a seven-foot, green-skinned thug who cannot spell will make anyone nervous.

This violent behavior is the same in both male and female Orcs. In fact, the only time a female Orc is relatively mellow is during the first month after giving birth. This is foresight on the part of the Creator: the skull of an infant Orc takes about four weeks to fully harden. After that, the mother goes back to her violent self, and the infant is protected by its well-hardened head.

The Orcs' racial bent toward violence is mediated somewhat by their government, which can only be termed a "Thugocracy." Simply put, the unofficial king of the Orcs is whichever Orc can bash the previous leader's skull in. Considering the thickness of an average Orc skull, this is often quite a feat, but tends to lead to very messy "elections."

Not all Orcs indulge in violence just for the fun of it, however. Some channel their destructive energies into the positive career of a professional Hero. Gorbar Karvash, a Hero in Good Standing, had been smashing things in the name of Justice for well over ten years.

Karvash smiled, his fangs a dull yellow. "Et's good ta see you 's well, Crimson Slash. How did trainin' that whelp go for ya?"

"Cyrus is fine. He just finished his training and is now a Hero, Second Class," Reginald replied. "How did that alchemy training work out?"

The Blak Spoon scratched his ugly green head. "Nah, it di'nint go through. Too confusin'. I gave up an' smashed it."

"How do you smash alchemy?" Reginald asked in disbelief.

"With yer fist! 'Cuz all them little glass bottles breaks easy. Jes gimme a noice sharp axe any day. All that picking of flowers and roots and *bok* is for wimps," the Orc said, laughing.

"What, you already know all my troops?" Jael Allyn said with a chuckle. "At any rate, Gorbar is my second-in-command now. He manages the heavy combat divisions—"

"'Cuz I gets to do the smashing, see?" Blak interrupted.

"And Emily commands our archery and Magic Artillery divisions," Jael said. "As for you, Reginald, I hear that you have had some personal experience with this Voshtyr fellow."

"That I do," Reginald said, scowling. "He's a black-hearted, conniving scoundrel with no sense of morality or fair play. His villainy knows no bounds, and his megalomania is threatening the entire world."

"So, typical Villain, then?" Jael said.

"That's about right. The only difference is that he has, I believe, some Demon blood in him. That, and I chopped off his left arm, but he's got a new, mechanical one now."

Reginald sat down at the table spread with a terrain map. "His combat abilities are uncanny, and he can somehow steal people's souls, slaying them instantly. If I were you, I would think of some way to kill him from a distance. That would be the safest way."

"Well, we do have two artillery-class magi and a wizard who is a siege specialist, but I doubt that they would be sufficient," Jael said. "Besides, Voshtyr is well-protected. Thanks to Emily, I have a contact who knows much about how Voshtyr operates. Emily?"

Taking her cue, Emily Cartwright rose from her padded seat, moving stiffly due to the brace on her hip. "As grateful as I am for your rescue, Crimson Slash, you weren't the first to find me. A mysterious man in a black cloak showed up first. He never gave me his name, but he was a very handsome fellow with raven hair and stormy eyes. He claimed to have information about Voshtyr's army and to be friends with the gryphon that spared my life."

Reginald rested his head on a fist. "If the man you speak of is the same one I know, his name is Serimal. He's Voshtyr's brother."

"I see," Emily said, glancing at Jael before continuing. "He offered that information in exchange for my uncle Gavin's locket. When I gave it to him, he promised to deliver it to the gryphon, and left before you arrived. But the point is, he gave us some pretty juicy information."

"It's reliable and accurate, at that," Jael said, indicating the swarm of pins stuck in the table map before them. "From Emily's source, as well as our own spies, I have found out that Voshtyr seems to be attracting all manner of dark creatures to him, not to mention mercenary companies and an entire legion of the Synod's Dark Templar troops."

"Regrettably, I cannot help you," Reginald said. "I am on a Quest to free an Ancient People from a Terrible Curse, and by the Order of Importance in the Codex Heroic, my Quest clearly trumps your Battle. Have you contacted the Guild? They can definitely help you. I have no doubt that this scenario would be of interest to them."

Jael sighed. "I did. They put me on hold for nearly twenty minutes. Then this annoyingly chipper girl came on and told me that they already knew of Demonkin, and ordered us to be on standby should they decide to attack him. This despite all the information I sent them. So at the moment we only have five Heroes in my entire force: myself, Gorbar, the Silver Fish, the Red Death, and you."

"The Red Death?" Reginald said incredulously. "Was he not ejected from the Guild of Heroes for joining that 'Scythe of the Reaper' group?"

"Technically, yes, and got jailed to boot. We've got him on loan from Bal-Grimor prison, supposedly for 'community service.' But he retains all of his abilities—and his disposition."

Reginald grimaced. "I would rather he lost the disposition."

"Now, you're just saying that because he defeated you in that tourney," Jael said, smiling.

"He did not defeat me. He merely gained more points!" Reginald protested. "The two times I managed to hit him, I sent him sprawling. All he had were more total hits, none of them in vital areas. A victory is measured in life and death, not points."

Jael laughed. "One cannot say that he is the strongest Hero, though he may be the quickest."

"That's not roight neither," Gorbar interrupted. "Tha Green Falcon's quicker than tha Red Death. Tha Green Falcon could pick tha Red Death's pockits while 'e was fighting, and 'e'd never notice."

"At any rate," Reginald continued, "you cannot count me, for I depart within the hour. But you still have your other four: one delinquent supersonic assassin, a walking green battering ram, a long-winded master swordsman, and a female mercenary General. Few armies have counted so many Heroes in their number. What could possibly go wrong?"

Jael looked shocked. "Don't say—"

At that moment, a messenger burst into the tent. "General! Captain Daniels and his scout unit have engaged Enemy troops outside the west camp! He requests reinforcements!"

Jael dropped the chart she was holding and snatched up her flail case, glaring at Reginald. "You just *had* to go and say that, didn't you. 'What could possibly go wrong?' Have you completely forgotten your *'Do's and Don'ts of Precombat Banter'*?" She turned to the messenger. "Whose troops?"

"Their flag bears a severed demon's hand clutching a crystal," the messenger replied. "It's not a device we've seen before."

"Voshtyr," Reginald said darkly.

" . . . and Slashback, you must lead the wyvern division," Voshtyr said.

Slashback sputtered. "What? Me, lead tose scaly, smelly creatures?"

Voshtyr nodded, dipping a quill pen in an inkwell on his desk.

The tower in which they sat soared above all but one spire of his mountain keep and provided an excellent southern view of the forest countryside. The round room was probably the best-lit in the entire fortress, as daylight streamed in through multiple open windows.

Along one wall was an eight-foot-tall terrain map of the entire world, with the current boundaries of countries clearly printed on it. On the opposite wall was a similar map, except with different boundaries, and none of the same names. Voshtyr had explained it earlier as the present and future maps of the world, the latter bearing his radical changes to the geopolitical landscape. Magical lights denoted the current positions of the armies in Voshtyr's employ. It was his private war room.

Two chairs and a low couch were the only furniture in the room besides the desk. Voshtyr sat on one of the chairs, scribbling away at the parchment, while Slashback occupied the couch.

"The wyverns are a potent fighting force," Voshtyr said, "and our enemies—these pathetic Salvinsel Salamanders— have nothing to match them. The wyverns are, however, stupid enough to think of their own tails as food sources, so I need someone with a brain in her head to lead them to their target. We don't want a repeat of what happened during the Shallot campaign, do we?"

Slashback didn't object. The wyverns *were* stupid. During the initial wave of the Shallot bombardment, three of the wyverns had not dropped their payloads on the enemy. They waited until returning to the camp, where they nearly caught the ammunition dump on fire. "Fery well, I go. But what is it that we attack?"

"Their supplies, the barracks tents, the medical tent, what-ever burns," Voshtyr said, his eyes glowing as he began writ-ing runes on the paper. "Now go. We don't have all week."

• • •

Following a thousand of Tremel's foot-soldiers, Slashback soon arrived at the plain where Voshtyr had ordered them to attack the Salamanders. It was hardly more than a hilly field. A terrible choice for the mercenaries to camp. There was no cover at all, save tall grass, and grass was flammable. But it was a perfect attack location for her and the wyverns.

On a signal from Duke Tremel, the gryphon took to the air, followed by a flight of seven wyverns carrying explosive treasures. Slashback herself carried a tube of some sort with a conical nose. It was something Voshtyr and his Toadies had come up with, some sort of anti-personnel weapon. And, of course, she would have to drop it first before the wyverns would do anything. The witless beasts wouldn't drop their payloads without some kind of a signal. But if the wyvern in front dropped his, the entire group did. So it was up to Slashback to release her payload first.

The gryphon led the scaled, draconic beasts over the Salamanders' tents. One bore the logo of the Royal Apothecary service. The medical tent. Well, that would have to go first then. With a sharp cry, she dropped the tube and banked west. Seeing that as a signal, the wyverns did the same, their spheres sparkling with inner flame as they fell.

Slashback wheeled and flew back toward the supply depot for the next round of bombs, wyverns following like a V of atrocious, scaled geese. It was time for the Salamanders to burn.

• • •

"General Allyn, they've got *wyverns!*" yelled a camp cook while trying to douse an ignited mess tent.

Nearly a quarter of the mercenaries' tents were afire already, and the fires were spreading. The firebombs had caught the hilly grasslands on fire. Flames jumped from tent to tent.

To complicate matters, some kind of shell had slammed down in the midst of the maelstrom and sprouted a gatling crossbow. The weapon magically tracked movement and spat quarrels at anyone who got near enough to douse the spreading fire. The medical tent was already destroyed, and the mess tent would be next unless they dealt with it soon.

Jael Allyn directed a large group of men to start dousing fires and threw together a mixed unit of the few troops that had not been caught totally off guard.

Over the din of the burning camp rang the sounds of fierce combat. Swords sang through the air, some of them off-key, and rang against shields and armor. Shouts of victory mingled with screams of pain, and the pounding of men's feet and horses' hooves rumbled beneath it all.

When Reginald crested the hill, he found a battle already in progress. Two platoons of Jael's Salamanders were desperately trying to fight off nearly five hundred assorted foemen.

The Crimson Slash wasted no time. Drawing his five-foot sword, he dashed down the hillside. "Viper!" he called to Jael as he bounded down the incline. "We need archers and one of those artillery mages!"

"The fearless Hero barreled into the left flank of the enemy soldiers, his tremendous blade wreaking havoc!" Reginald narrated.

From the hill, he had seen that the opposing side was mostly composed of Human infantry, with a handful of Elven archers and a few heavily armored Orcs. In the center of the Villanic host stood two swordsmen and a mage, the swordsmen giving orders and the mage casting spells to bolster his men.

"The Crimson Slash carved his way through a dozen foot-soldiers before he was stopped by a particularly courageous halberdier," Reginald said. "The Hero's opponent wore little armor, and a dozen angry red scars marked his bare arms. The Hero hefted his sword and struck at the man, but the soldier dodged to the side and brought his halberd down on the inside of the Hero's elbow! Blood gushed from the wound as the Hero dropped his sword, swearing in pain."

The halberdier, though confused by the running commentary, knew an opening when he saw one and leapt at Reginald, swinging his pole-ax sideways, aiming it at Reginald's neck.

"The Hero successfully blocked the blow with the shield, which he still grasped in his left hand. Shoving the shield forward on impact of the halberd, the Hero threw the halberdier off balance and brought the rim of his shield down on the man's head. Blood burst from the man's nose and mouth as he slumped to the ground. Another victory for the Crimson Slash!"

Reginald winced at the pain in his arm as he picked up his sword again. *But the battle isn't over yet, Hero,* he thought. *No time for trivial things like blood loss.*

Jael crushed a foeman's helmet with her flail and barked orders to her own soldiers.

Her reinforcements had arrived not a moment too soon. The corpses of her men dotted the battlefield, alongside slain

Minions and Villains. The roar of combat, the shrieks of dying men, and the ring of steel on steel filled the air with horrendous din. The hilly plain was the site of a vicious melee. Into this, she and her reinforcements charged.

"Sam," Jael shouted, "take twenty men and get behind them. Raul, take those archers and get to higher ground. I don't want you hitting any of our men, we've got few enough as it is. Where in the Black Plains is Koshiro?"

"I am here, O fearsome Lady of the Salamanders," Koshiro Sakana—also known as the Silver Fish—replied, appearing as if out of thin air.

The Silver Fish was barely five and a half feet tall, with tanned skin and almond-shaped eyes, all signatures of his origin in the Eastern Islands near Landeralt. The Hero wore no visible armor, though his grey silk kimono had strands of lightweight silversteel woven through it. His single-edged blade was nearly eighteen inches longer than a standard katana, but he carried it with stately grace. His spiky black hair seemed out of place, considering the general neatness of his appearance, but he had assured many that it was a necessary feature for one of his rank.

"I shall unleash the unstoppable might of the *Jikan ga kakaru* style upon these fools if you only ask," he said, unsheathing the first inch of his blade.

"Just get out there and kill something," Jael snapped. "And try to remember that it's your sword arm that needs the exercise, not your mouth."

"As the General-sama commands," the Silver Fish replied, bowing, and was gone as quickly as he appeared.

• • •

Reginald had cut his way through the army until he was nearly within range of their commanding officers, but he found himself penned in by enemy troops. He parried almost everything they threw at him, but every now and then a blow got past his guard. His narration began to lack luster, and the Hero was losing both ground and blood.

Reginald stood a moment, considering dropping his guard and going on the attack again despite the constant blows raining on him, when a red blur and a rush of wind blasted past him, leaving corpses in its wake.

"Well, if it isn't the Crimson Slash," shouted the man in the red cloak as soon as he stopped.

"Greetings, Red Death," Reginald replied over the din, frowning. "I wasn't expecting you to help me, not after last time."

The Red Death looked as hurt as the three additional men he had just cut open. "Now, what do you mean by that? I meant to come back, I really did, but there were unavoidable complications!"

Reginald picked up a soldier and threw him at four of his comrades, knocking them all to the ground with a tremendous rattling *clang*. "Well, you didn't, and I had to face that platoon alone. Well, not entirely alone. Your friend the Yellow Sun stayed to help, but he is a priest and did very little actual fighting."

"Oh, you would be surprised how much fighting Yellow can do, despite his name," Red chuckled, slaughtering five pikemen and removing another's right leg with his curved grey blade. "Besides, I was trying to rescue your squire, remember?"

"Bartholomew needed no rescuing," Reginald said, leaping over a heavily armored Orc and crushing the soldier's armor with a swift blow from his gigantic sword. Blood still flowed from the cut at his elbow joint. "He had almost finished with his training at that point, and all he was doing was escorting the princess down the stairs. What could he possibly have needed help with?"

The Red Death's blade, *Zandira,* flashed less than a foot from Reginald's face, swatting a crossbow quarrel aside. "Well, she was quite the buxom wench, despite being a princess. Poor delicate thing—she'd never seen men die before. She may have needed some . . . comfort. I knew young Bart wouldn't be able to, being trained by you and all."

"Bartholomew wouldn't because he's a proper Hero. And you shouldn't talk: we both know you *couldn't* comfort her, even given the chance," Reginald said, grinning. "Now, who shot that bolt at me?"

"That would be me, Hero," spoke a man in a black cloak and platemail, one of the three leaders of the Villanic army. Reginald and Red had finally made their way to their destination. "I am Duke Tremel of Landeralt, called Tremel Ironhide."

"Honored to meet you," Reginald replied.

The Red Death finished massacring two ranks of swordsmen, then turned to face the Duke. "Hmm . . . I haven't killed a Duke recently . . . . Two Viscounts and an Earl, but not a Duke. Can I kill this one, Crimson?"

"No, this one belongs to Koshiro Sakana," said the Silver Fish, appearing behind the two Heroes. With that, he leapt into the air, the blade of his Daito glowing. *"Sakana muda yogen rashii jikan ga kakaru kudaranai tonde kógeki!"*

Koshiro's black spiky hair blew about, despite the total lack of wind. "The ultimate attack of the *Jikan ga kakaru* style! The shining force of a thousand souls, a blade which divides the shadow from the light and causes the mountains to tremble beneath its fury! A flame that consumes the darkness as the breath of Dragons consumes the dry grasses of summer, leaving divine smoke behind in a cloud of holy vapor! The bane of monsters, hope of orphans, thrill of women, and strength of men, bound together by the courage of a master swordsman, wielded against the corruption of the land!"

The Crimson Slash, the Red Death, Duke Tremel, and dozens of soldiers watched the Silver Fish hang in the air, uttering irritating descriptions.

Tremel turned to Reginald. "How long does that usually take?"

"Usually two paragraphs."

"Oh," said the Duke. "In that case . . . " He began winding his crossbow.

" . . . as the oceans overwhelm the land . . . !" Koshiro continued.

Duke Tremel placed a quarrel in his crossbow.

" . . . from the east to the west in a cataclysmic fury . . . !"

Duke Tremel aimed his crossbow.

" . . . in a conflagration seen from the heavens . . . !"

Duke Tremel fired his crossbow.

" . . . blasted from the—*ghurk!*" Koshiro took the crossbow quarrel in the chest and fell to the ground with a heavy thud.

With that, the armies, Heroes, and Villains resumed fighting each other. Reginald attacked the Duke, while Red leapt over them to attack the mage at the center.

A wall of steel met Reginald, and a wall of black fire met Red.

• • •

Jael lifted her horn to her lips and blew the retreat. Her scouts had just reported a massive army approaching from the south, and her small mercenary band was no match for it. "Let the tents burn!" she shouted. "Save all you can carry, and get going! Rendezvous at Shai'il Knoll!" she shouted. "Raul, where are Crimson, Red, and Silver?"

Raul shook his head. "They're still in the melee, General. Blak went down to get them, and he isn't back yet either."

"*Incoming!*" yelled a lookout, just before glass orbs burst all round them and an inferno sprang into being.

Jael fell to the ground and rolled, putting out her flaming clothes and hair. The blast killed the lookout immediately and set another half-dozen tents afire.

Jael scrambled to her feet and sounded the retreat once more. Then she mounted her horse and rode for the south end of the camp, where the medical tents had been evacuated, to prepare the wounded for transit.

Hurry up, Crimson, she thought. *And come back in one piece.*

"*Expuuuuuunge!*" yelled the Blak Spoon as he crushed two ranks of infantry with a blow from his titanic club.

The club was itself a marvel. Called simply *Bonk*, it was a bar of silvered steel nearly six feet long, an armspan thick, and had handgrips embedded in the sides. *Bonk* also had the unusual property of having no discernable weight to the wielder. The recipients of a blow from the club, however, felt the full weight, and very few things survived one.

Blak prided himself on three things: his enormous club (he always said that with a bawdy laugh), his ability to spell a few things correctly, and his collection of tiny silver spoons, each with the name and picture of a place on a piece of ceramic embedded in the handle. No one teased the Blak Spoon about his hobby of collecting such an absurd thing. Indeed, no one in his right mind teases an eight-foot tall Orc, especially not one with Heroic strength.

Voshtyr's soldiers broke and scattered beneath the Orc's onslaught. He attacked the rear of Voshtyr's army, which by this point had almost surrounded the beleaguered Salamanders. Blak's heavy iron boots squished through the bloody field as he clobbered man and beast alike.

Blak laughed and looked about for the other Heroes. The Silver Fish was easy to spot, sitting in a heap on the ground, nursing a crossbow-wound. The Crimson Slash and the Red Death were busy fighting a mage and a sword-wielding noble. As Blak watched, the Red Death blurred to nothing and then came into focus again behind the mage, who slumped to the ground in a spray of blood. Reginald was being driven back by the noble, whose body glowed a pale red as he hacked at the Hero.

Red materialized at Blak's green elbow. "It looks like our friend is having himself a bit of difficulty. What say you help him out a bit?"

"Wot? Why can't you do it?" Blak asked.

"Because I think Crimson is about to lose and is going to need to be carried, that's why. I can't exactly lift the lummox."

"Wotsa lumix?"

"You are, and so is Crimson. Oh, don't look at me like that," Red said, cringing at Blak's glare. "It's a compliment. It means 'a person with so many muscles that they're very heavy.'"

Blak grinned, his yellowed fangs protruding from his lower lip. "Roight then. I'll go and pick me up a lumix."

"There's a good Orc," Red said as Blak lumbered off in Reginald's general direction.

Red watched the Orc stride away. *Just wait until he comes back,* he thought. *I've got some more choice "compliments" for him.*

Red looked down at what he carried in his hands. It was the slain mage's tome of magic. It was a weighty, black thing, bound in something that felt disturbingly like Human skin. Smiling, the Red Death tucked it beneath his cloak and headed for the camp.

The three-note retreat call sounded across the blood-soaked plain. The Salamanders had not been routed, but they were in bad shape. The enemy had closed on them in a pincer formation and hammered at their flanks.

Reginald was too occupied to do anything about it, as he was engaged with a Villain and fighting with all his strength. Reginald broke his sword-lock with Duke Tremel and stepped back a pace.

"Going somewhere?" Tremel asked.

"Not until I finish this fight," Reginald answered.

He readied his blade to spring back into fighting, but at that moment the Blak Spoon grabbed him around the waist with a brawny, hairy green arm, and dragged him out of sword range.

"It's toim ta go, Crimson. No lollygagging about foitin' this chap." He turned to Tremel and swung *Bonk* at him. "Off with ya!"

The tip of *Bonk* barely caught Tremel in the breastplate, but it was enough to send him flying across the field. As the Duke flew, he managed to yell back to Crimson. "I'll get you next time, Crimson! Neeeext tiiiiiiimmmme!"

Reginald chuckled. "Classic Villain. Can't even be removed from a battle without some kind of parting remark, and an unoriginal one at that. Now, put me down, you lummox. I can walk on my own."

The remaining Salamanders had begun moving southwest, away from the attacking army. Thankfully the wyverns seemed to have disappeared for the moment, so their escape vector was clear. And thanks to the Heroes, Voshtyr's force was not in any shape to pursue them. Koshiro had gotten up and limped back to the group, though, leaving Reginald and the Blak Spoon as the only Heroes on the field.

"We need to rejoin Jael," Reginald said to Blak. "Where's Red?"

"Red sent me after you. We've got ta catch up wi' our army, they packed up in an 'orful rush. Come on, then, can't be 'avin some common soldier shoot ya while yer standin' still."

"Right. Let's get moving."

"They're currently out of range of anything but the wyverns, but we managed to inflict heavy casualties on their main encampment."

Duke Tremel, still decked in black armor, stood before Voshtyr in his watchtower delivering his report.

The private war room was just small enough to feel uncomfortably close with so many people in it. Voshtyr stood in front of his velvet desk chair, while Lord Roger Farella occupied the wicker chair near the window and Slashback dozed on the couch, snoring softly with a wing over her head. Her breathing blew her wingtips in and out gently as she slept. Roger toyed with a dagger, cutting nicks in its blade with the organic one protruding from his right arm.

"We believe that the Salvinsel Salamanders are now crippled," Tremel said, "if not put out of action entirely."

"Very good," Voshtyr said. "Get your dead to the Necromancer immediately while they are still fresh. When you return, speak to Roger about payment."

Tremel Ironhide saluted and strode from the room.

"Now that the Salamanders are out of commission, I control all independent armies south of Mir. Roger, have we received a report from Captain Landrus and his Mandrakes yet?"

Roger Farella shook his head, sitting up in his wicker chair near the window. "We couldn't reasonably expect a messenger back yet, and they took neither a mage nor trained birds with them." He dropped the damaged blade in his lap and folded his blue-scaled arms. "Besides, if our past dealings with this Cyrus fellow are any indication, you may have to go and get Cyrus yourself. Sending mercenaries after a man that unpredictable was not your brightest idea, Voshtyr."

"I asked for facts, Roger, not opinions. And I only sent mercenaries because my list of loyal followers *not* purchased with coin is a short one, and I couldn't be there myself. Has there been any word from my mercenaries in the other kingdoms?"

Roger pulled out a parchment scroll and referred to it as he spoke. "Rincar of the 'Horendis' Horde was defeated by Emperor Vladimir Xanathosson at the Black Ford. His Orcs scattered, but one of our agents managed to locate the

Landeralt tower during the confusion. It's under tight guard, and we believe it contains the Heart of Flames."

Roger rose and began pacing the tower floor. "General Glenmark commands the Basilisk Brigade now. Apparently his predecessor, the fool General Stephens, thought he could escape Elven archers. But he fulfilled his part: the Prime Minister is dead. Without his strong leadership, the Elven factions have turned on each other, and their allegiances change daily. The Sky Elves are fighting the Mountain Elves, the Jungle Elves are fighting the Forest Elves, the High Elves are in a territory dispute with the Middle and Low Elves, and—strangely enough—the Dark and Light Elves have joined forces against the Twilight Elves."

Voshtyr laughed. "With that many factions around, I'm surprised the Elven Parliament lasted so many thousand years."

"And that's not even half of them," Roger continued. "You can't forget the Sea Elves, River Elves, Swamp Elves, Desert Elves, Plains Elves, Volcano Elves, Brightstar Elves, Shadowfolk Elves—"

"Cease and desist, Roger!" Voshtyr shouted. "I've no wish to learn all the Elven factions, just the ones not under our control yet. In fact, I don't care about that either. Just tell this Glenmark to get as many of them under control as he can. How many of the world governments do we have in our grasp?"

Roger consulted the parchment. "Let's see . . . Well, as I said, the Elves are disorganized, and we can easily influence individual factions. We'll have the Elven Parliament under control by next month. Humans are more of a problem. Their Confederation is not one to fall apart easily. The most we can do is drive them apart with mercantile interests and hope that some of our candidates are elected in individual territories."

"Getting these stones is far too much trouble," Voshtyr grumbled. "And I thought starting wars to distract the governments would make my plans easier."

"It has," Roger said, running a scaled hand down Slashback's back between her wings. The gryphon made a rumbling purring noise, but remained asleep. "They're quite distracted, enough so to leave the Stones mostly unguarded. And as a bonus, they will be much easier to conquer once your P.L.O.T. Device is fully assembled and you are ready to attack individual countries."

"At least the Araquellae have already promised their loyalty, correct?" Voshtyr asked.

"Hrm, well, not exactly. My people are disinclined to intervene in these affairs. The current Neptarch is not in favor of our proposed coalition, and neither are twenty of the Salt Council."

"Then we kill them," Voshtyr said, waving his metal hand in dismissal. "Anyone foolish enough to disagree with us deserves what they get." He looked at Roger. "Oh, don't give me that ghastly 'pickled fish' look, Roger. I know you're related to the royal family. But when making bread, one must grind some grain."

Roger flared his nose-slits in anger. "The Araquellan Royal Family is well loved and hardly 'grain,' Voshtyr. If you kill them, you will lose all the support I've managed to scrape up amongst the Sea Peoples. Besides, I said only twenty of the Council fail to support me. If one or two of *them* were to suffer some sort of accident, then the majority needed to overrule the Neptarch would be mine."

Voshtyr smiled his most unpleasant smile. "One or two need to disappear, eh? I know just the fisherman."

Roger looked at him, aghast. "You wouldn't."

"Oh, it isn't like Araquellus blades sell for much on the black market," Voshtyr said, toying with a dagger and tracing the length of Roger's scaly arm with it. "And I am of course not familiar with people who would do illegal, murderous deeds for profit. Don't worry, Roger, your friends on the Council are *perfectly* safe."

Roger shifted uncomfortably and went back to the scroll. "As you well know, the Katheni, Istaka, and Avierie have no centralized governments. They can provide no resistance to any coherent force. On second thought, it might be better not to bother attacking them at all. The Ransha can be left well enough alone. So long as we stay out of their swamps and don't fish near their coastal nests, they will ignore us. The Dwarves, on the other hand, may pose a problem."

"Pose a problem?" Voshtyr repeated. "How so?"

"They weren't such a problem for us Villains before the Twenty-Minute War, when they were still ruled by the Underking, but now that they have become socialized . . . "

Voshtyr sank into the heavy, black-velvet desk chair with a sigh. "Right, I had forgotten. The 'People's Republic of the Underground.' Things were so much simpler back when most Dwarves were peasant miners and you only had to deal with their corrupt aristocracy. A few well-placed bribes and you could get whatever you wanted. Now you have to go through that ridiculous mockery of a council and president that they have."

Roger sniffed and brushed his yellow-gold cloak as if trying to remove some invisible dirt conjured up by speaking of the Dwarves. "As I said, they pose a problem because bribes don't work. I tried to bribe their president, but he had the nerve to turn me down. 'If you want to bribe a Dwarf,' he said, 'you must bribe all Dwarves. Everything below the ground belongs to all Dwarves, even foreign gold.'"

"And I suppose bribing the entire Dwarven race simply isn't economically feasible?" Voshtyr said, smiling innocently.

Roger scowled. "Honestly, Voshtyr, I try to keep your accounts in order, handle bribes, pay off your mercenaries—who are very expensive, I'll have you know—and what do you do? You make sardonic, sarcastic, uncaring, laconic, driveling remarks! How are you going to get anything accomplished when you can't even manage your own accounts?" The little blue man began hovering a foot off the ground as he spat his ferocious syllables.

"Calm down, my temperamental scaled friend," said Voshtyr, placing a hand on Roger's shoulder and gently directing his feet back to the stone floor. "I know that my treasury is limited, and I do appreciate your keeping track of it for me. But you must understand that some things are worth more than money. Conquering the entire world, for example. When the world is under my thumb, money will no longer be an issue. Now, stop fretting about the accounts and give me the briefest version you can of our status report."

Roger caught his breath, composed himself, and unrolled a sheet of vellum. "Governments conquered: Orcs and Elves. Allies to our cause: Synod, Orcs, Black Hand, Scythe, assorted mercenaries. Non-threat entities: the True Church, Merchant's Guild, and Seafarer's Union. Obstacles: the Dwarven People's Republic of the Underground, Hereditary Evil Empire, Guild of Heroes. And as for the Dragons . . . "

"Leave them out of my plans, Roger. They tend to stay out of Human affairs. If we don't provoke them, they won't get involved. Dragons are the main reason that fool Morival was defeated. No wonder he couldn't assemble the Device last time. I don't plan on making the same mistake." Voshtyr rose and stared out the tower window. "And if I am opposed by mere mortal races, anything less than Dragons, I can defeat them—with this." He gestured out of the window.

Roger couldn't see out the window from where he stood. He walked that direction, objecting as he came. "But, Voshtyr, Vladimir's Army of Darkness™ can cut any force to shreds! Even your expensive mercenaries—" Roger's voice faded away as he looked out the window.

Below and across the plain stretched an enormous army, black-clad and terrifying. Men, Orcs, and smatterings of other races camped upon the faded grass, spears and blades glinting in the dying light. Voshtyr knew that most terrifying of all to Roger would be the beasts, the dark and twisted beasts that strode about in the massive camp.

Wyverns shrieked and flapped overhead, man-faced Manticores stalked about the tents, smiling their alarming sharp-toothed smiles, and a Greater Hooded Basilisk sat atop an outcropping of rock, ignoring the squalor and noise below it. A few squadrons of Goblins camped outside the main group, as even Orcs found them too stupid and mean-spirited for rational conversation. A few ogres, two trolls, a conjured Fire Elemental, and a titanic Earth Giant rounded out the number.

Finally, to the west, since the wind was from the east, was a putrid force of zombified soldiers. Voshtyr had found a Master Necromancer about to be burned at the stake and interrupted the process. In return for his freedom, the Necromancer joined Voshtyr and created undead soldiers from their own and their enemies' dead, starting with the entire population of the offending village.

Voshtyr chuckled at Roger's dumb amazement. This force had simply not been there two days ago. To Roger it will have appeared to have materialized practically overnight. And indeed it had.

The fading light was blotted out entirely for a moment. Voshtyr smiled and pointed into the sky. "And there, my dear Araquellus, is one of my secret weapons. The floating Citadel of the Kinetics."

The Citadel of the Kinetics. No one knows exactly where the mysterious flying city has hidden over the years, nor when it will appear and strike next.

The Citadel was a fortress city that floated in the sky. Its grey, oppressive walls were scarred by the scorches and pits of years of warfare with the Nine Races. It had a cylindrical tower that rose above the rest of the city. Its pinnacle stared down on everything around it with the feeling of a malevolent glare. Over the centuries, some have jokingly suggested that the Kinetics just build castles in the sky and that they have their heads in the clouds. Over the centuries, those jokesters have quickly died.

And all around the central tower was a grey city, a city full of mysterious and powerful albino Elves. Legend has it that they can control the minds of others. All that is known for certain is that the city floats in the air without the aid of magic and that the few Kinetics seen have had power beyond that of any mage.

Their power is not magic. Rather, it is the manipulation of some invisible force. The Kinetics use this force to push, pull, move, or destroy whatever they need to.

And now, this unknown and unpredictable force had allied itself with Voshtyr. Woe to the Heroes, for this new threat was not one to be taken lightly.

Chapter 30

UNINVITED GUESTS

*In which some Stupid People interrupt the wrong
Wedding Celebration, and Cyrus is Captured*

INTO CYRUS AND Kris's nuptials came the sound
of battle.

Fire arrows thudded into the Katheni's outer tents,
causing the dried hides to burst into flame. From the
cover of darkness sprang thirty men armed with cudgels and shortswords, who began laying about them with their
weapons. The Katheni, who had been in a celebratory state,
were caught totally off guard and unarmed.

But not all the celebrants would be easy prey.

The semicircle of sand had emptied somewhat as the celebrants wandered off, having eaten and drunk their fill, wishing Kris and Cyrus the best of luck on their future. Some of
the workers had even removed more of the tables to make
more room for dancing by the bonfire.

At the first faint sounds of commotion, Kris sat straight
up in her chair, ears swiveling toward the noise.

Cyrus put his cup down and looked at her. "What's
wrong?"

"I just heard a scream," Kris replied. "Would someone go
see what happened?"

"I'll go!" Benjara volunteered.

Cyrus smiled at the jaguar boy. "Okay, Ben. Go for it. I doubt it's anything major, but if it is, don't do anything your father would think is stupid."

"Well, that takes all the fun out of it," Benjara complained, glancing at his father, who was dancing to spite the other members of the council, who merely sat at one of the benches, looking as if they were deliberately trying not to enjoy themselves and failing at it. "That includes practically everything."

"Just get going and find out what it was." Cyrus took a playful swing at his spotted shadow.

Benjara dashed off and left the newlyweds in peace.

Or it would've been in peace had it not been for Kris's relatives, who kept coming by the table in varying states of sobriety to wish them a happy life together.

"Here, try this," Kris said, holding up a small, baked, purple plant filled with chopped meat and breading.

Cyrus opened his mouth and Kris fed the comestible to him. Both smiled at each other, then Cyrus's expression turned to pain and Kris's turned to evil glee. Cyrus's eyes watered as he frantically searched the table, finally locating a tankard of desert ale. After gulping down three-quarters of it, he put it down, coughing.

"Whuh . . ." *cough* . . . "What was that? That was the . . . " *keff* . . . "Spiciest . . . " He had to stop and finish the ale. "What was that?" he finally asked.

Kris giggled at Cyrus's distress. "Alaks Cactus, with desert tapir, cornmeal, and firebelly peppers. I *told* you that my uncle's food could burn your mouth!"

"And here I didn't believe you. I take it back: there *are* some foods that I still find spicy. Can you get me that recipe?"

Kris smiled. "Sorry, Cyrus, it's a family secret."

"Then you can tell me! I'm part of your family now, or did you forget?"

Kris leaned over and kissed her new mate. "No, I didn't. Not for a moment."

At that moment, Benjara sped back into the clearing, eyes wide in fear. "Haj Wasara! Cyrus! Slavers are attacking the eastern tents!" He then fell down, clutching at an arrow protruding from his shoulder.

Panic, as it often does, ensued. Evil may lurk and Doom may impend, Night may fall and Day may break, but only Chaos and Panic ensue.

Cyrus leapt to his feet just as a rank of slaver archers appeared through the tents and fired a volley of flaming arrows at the platform. He heaved the table onto its side, spilling wines and roasts, and dragged Kris down behind it with him. The arrows thudded into the solid oak, followed by a second volley.

"What in the Hall of Shouted Obscenities is going on?" Cyrus yelled.

Haj Wasara overturned his table as well, then made a flying leap from behind his to the one Cyrus crouched behind. "Slavers," Wasara spat. "If you have betrayed my trust and this is your doing, Human, I will . . . Uh, what are you doing with that soup pot?"

Cyrus picked up the spilled tureen and emptied the remainder on the ground. Placing it on his head, he carefully peered over the top of the overturned table.

There were a lot of slavers out there. And what was that priest doing? He had abandoned his ceremonial vestments and was back to his plain black robe. Cyrus made to shout at him to stay out of the combat, but the priest took twelve steps and disappeared into thin air.

Cyrus blinked. Did the priest just—

An arrow rang off the pot, and he ducked back down. "There are probably forty or fifty of them," he said, removing the dinted pot, savory-smelling leek-and-potato soup trickling down his face. "No, I didn't do this, and I'm actually just a *little* upset with these *salaki* for interrupting my wedding celebration."

"See," Kris scolded, "this is why weddings should happen at the end of the book, rather than the middle."

"Shush, Kris. This is easily four-fifths through anyway," Cyrus replied before turning back to Wasara. "Haj, helping your people is my first priority. But I can't do that while I'm pinned down by those archers. As soon as I get them occupied, you two get out of here. Find Katana and get as many Katheni out of harm's way as you can. Haj, how high can you throw one of these wedding benches?"

Wasara looked puzzled. "What?"

"The wedding benches. I need you to heft one of them up and over this table, in the general direction of the archers. They're over there," Cyrus pointed to their right.

Wasara shook his maned head. "I couldn't possibly throw it far enough to hit them."

"You don't need to. Just throw it. Trust me." Cyrus reached over and dragged an end of a bench to within Wasara's grasp. "Throw it on three, ready? One, Two, *three!*"

Wasara spun, threw the bench, and ducked back down before the archers could target him.

Cyrus leapt over the table and into the air, catching the bench midflight and keeping it between himself and incoming arrows. He landed just in front of the archers, and with a sweep of the hardwood bench, toppled a half-dozen of them.

A commander yelled at the archers to "Fire at the fool!" They launched a volley at Cyrus, who interposed the bench between himself and barbed death. After catching nearly the entire volley on his makeshift tower shield, he picked it up and brought it down heavily on an archer. Bones snapped with a wet, crunching noise, and Cyrus dropped the bench between himself and the archers once more.

They fired again, with much the same result. Cyrus repeated his previous action, but by that time, some assorted thugs with swords and clubs had arrived. One took a swipe at Cyrus's exposed back, slicing through the Haj's fine shirt and scoring the flesh beneath.

Cyrus winced and swung the bench in a wide arc, crushing the slaver's rib cage and knocking two others back. But more slavers poured into the clearing, and Cyrus spun his impromptu weapon, dropping it between himself and a club-wielding maniac.

Then an Orc with a two-handed axe swung at Cyrus, shattering the bench into two pieces. Cyrus hesitated for a moment, then snatched up the two pieces and held them by the legs, the middle sections covering his forearms.

Catching a sword-blow on his left arm, he pivoted and smacked the Orc in the side with his other half-bench. He smiled as the slaver boss pointed at him, directing the entire mob in his direction. *Now this is one heck of a way to celebrate your own wedding,*

As soon as the archers stopped firing, Haj Wasara stood and directed his people toward the northwest corner of the camp, a pair of sword-length katars in his brawny paws.

"Take only what you can carry," he shouted. "The rest can be remade. Any able-bodied male that has a weapon, go get it and stay with your families. Those males without families, you will form the rearguard."

The Katheni scurried into their tents and came back out with only the most essential of their possessions. Neither the slavers nor the fire had yet reached these tents, so it was dark but at least safer than out in the clearing. The sand beneath their paws shifted slightly as they ran, and they could probably be easily tracked.

The moon looked yellow through the smoke of the burning tents, like a wheel of cheese. Only it was more like a Cheese Wheel of Doom, for nothing good was happening beneath its yellow light.

"Kris, go find your brother," Wasara ordered. "We need his magic."

"But Cyrus needs my help!" Kris protested.

"Your mate is a Hero, Kris. He can take care of himself. If you get involved, he'll be trying to protect you as well as himself, and he'll be injured. To help him best, stay out of his fight. But before you go, he may need your wedding gift." He pointed one of his blades at Cyrus's sword, still in its silvered sheath, lying behind the toppled table.

Kris picked up the sword and sped off.

Wasara turned to his people. "All right. The rest of us will guard the rear while our new brother slows the slavers down. Those of you who wish to fight, follow me!"

Cyrus beat the slaver's head in with a vicious blow, blocked two arrows with his improvised weapon, and bludgeoned a bald man wielding a net and club.

"*Cyrus, catch!*" Kris yelled, lobbing the sheathed sword over the advancing ranks of slavers.

In one continuous move Cyrus threw the bench pieces away, caught the sheathed sword, drew it from its scabbard, and lopped an incoming club into two harmless pieces.

Spinning, he knocked a slaver over with the scabbard and cleft a second's head from crown to jaw with the sword. Before Cyrus could yank the sword free, two burly men threw a net over him, tangling his sword-arm and his feet.

He struggled to get free but could not. The slavers closed in, laughing. The flames engulfed the wedding pavilion. Slavers swarmed into the clearing. One of them mounted the dais and grabbed Kris's wrist. She turned and struck at him, but he caught her other paw as well.

The world slowed down.

Cyrus felt energy in the air around him.

Somehow he sensed that it was particularly strong just to his left and below the ground.

Not understanding his own actions, he dropped the scabbard, shrugged at the net over his body, and lunged for the energy source.

In some fashion he understood that he had grasped it. He tried to lift it, but it felt so heavy it dragged his hand back to the ground along with it. He yanked at the energy and then let it snap back to the desert floor.

Dirt and sand exploded around him. A circular wave of earth raced outward from his position. The wave upended his foes, throwing the slavers from their feet. It knocked Kris free of the slaver's grasp as well, and she ran off to catch up with her uncle.

Cyrus found himself laughing. He realized he had once again used magic unintentionally. Cackling like a jackal, he removed the net while the slavers struggled to regain their feet.

They were dazed but quickly recovered. The slavers picked up their weapons and advanced on Cyrus.

Cyrus began to reach for the energy again, but before he could grasp it, two dozen bolts of electricity spattered the sand and the slavers. Cyrus saw Katana advancing across the dune, throwing more handfuls of shocking darts.

"Cyrus!" the black Katheni yelled. "Are you all right?"

"I'm fine, Katana. Thanks for asking." Cyrus picked up his scabbard and used it to beat down a slaver who had just managed to get to his feet again. "How many more of these goons are left?"

"Not more than ten or fifteen. You've already dealt with most of them," Katana replied, tracing a multi-sided shape in the air and setting a pile of men on fire.

"Who are they?"

"Just another group of Human slavers, Cyrus. They attack us all the time. Just like back on Salvinsel."

Cyrus watched Katana efficiently dispose of three more of their attackers, then turned back to his own fight. After another thirty seconds, the slavers started to lose heart, and some broke and fled.

He mentally felt about for more ley-lines. The power he'd just used was rapidly dissipating and was probably no longer usable. From a distance, he felt heat. And right above him, a fantastic tingling that just cried out to be snagged and turned to his purposes.

"Hey, Katana," Cyrus asked, tossing aside an unconscious slaver, "how much power can you handle in one spell?"

"You mean how much can I send out or how much can I be hit with and not die?"

"When you're casting. How much can you summon to put into the spell?"

"As much as I can. I try not to take any of it back on me. I just channel it at my foes mostly. I hardly absorb any. Why do you ask?"

"Then power up whatever Air spell you have ready," Cyrus said. "I'm going to give you more power than you know what to do with."

Katana nodded and began gesturing in the air toward the fleeing slavers.

Cyrus reached out again. Mentally he seized hold of the power in the air. He tugged against it, gauging its resistance. Finally he directed it at Katana.

Katana's fur stood on end as the electrical Air energy flooded into him. All at once the power overflowed through his fingers, spewing forth in dense clouds of short bolts similar to the ones he had fired earlier. But now they were five times bigger and numbered in the hundreds. They lit the desert oasis like a strobe light, brighter than a high-energy thunderstorm, and chased the slavers across the dunes.

Katana laughed out loud. He shouted to the sky at the incredibly fury Cyrus had channeled into his spell. He laughed so hard that tears flowed down his furred face, and he could barely keep his paws straight.

When Cyrus finally stopped channeling the energy, Katana dropped to his knees, staring at what he had just done.

Cyrus stared as well. Not a single slaver had survived the holocaust. They lay smoldering in heaps, the sand beneath them slagged to glass.

"Well, that was impressive," Cyrus managed. "Are you all right, Katana?"

Katana lifted his black-furred head, his voice raw from laughter. "I've never felt that much power at one time before.

Cyrus, do you realize what you did? You *broke* the ley-line and handed it to me like you would a hunk of rope."

Cyrus blinked at him. "Hmm."

"I've no idea how you did it," Katana said, "nor am I sure I *want* to know. That's the second time I have seen you tamper with raw elements. Cyrus, what you are dealing with is hazardous, unpredictable, and obeys no rules. It's something completely new. No, old. Essential. From the beginning. And it makes the magic I use look like parlor tricks in comparison."

"I think I'm figuring it out, Katana," Cyrus said. "Sometimes I can feel the power in the air. If it happens when I'm in a fight, I just grab whatever is handy and throw it at my foe. I don't think it's divine intervention, or even a cheap plot device. There's certainly no skill or style involved." He reached up for his floppy hat, but he'd left it in the tent to dress for the wedding. He chuckled. "It looks like I'm a magic-user after all. What will Reg think?"

"He'll think you're something special," Katana said.

Cyrus smiled. "What do you mean, 'I broke the ley-line'? Is that reparable?"

"Not that I know of," Katana replied. "And I wish you'd stop it. If you keep doing that, it will make it difficult if not impossible for me to use *my* magic. But don't worry about that right now. Where is everyone else?"

Cyrus glanced about. The Katheni had all run to the northwest, and the camp was deserted, save for himself, Katana, and the dead and dying slavers. Their clothes still smoldered, and not one moved. The tents beyond still burned, though the fire seemed to be dying as it ran out of fuel. And there didn't seem to be any more slavers on the way. "Well, everyone must have escaped. Looks like we took care of the threat."

"I'm not so sure," Katana said. "They should have brought more men to attack a camp this size. They should have had at least a hundred, and I didn't see their leader anywhere."

"How do you know who their leader is?"

"Wasara told me when Kris found me and brought me to you. He said that their leader is a man in a purple cloak, wearing a magnificent hat. Here, give me a moment, I'll try to *Farsight* Kris and see if they're all right." Katana walked back over to the scattered tables and retrieved a jug of water and a clay bowl. He poured some water into the bowl then gestured across it. He dipped one finger in, then watched the ripples. Within seconds, he stared up in shock.

"No," he said, breathlessly, "they aren't all right."

Theodore Ralkin looked over the field of battle. His men had the cat scum hemmed in against a desert cliff, almost completely surrounded. And where would the cats run to if they managed to slip out? It was desert for several leagues around in any direction, and there were no horses for them to escape on. In fact, it was just Ralkin, his men, and the handful of cats up against the cliff. And *his* men were the ones with spears, swords, and cudgels. The cats had almost nothing.

The large lion Katheni was obviously the tribe's chieftain. He stood at the head of the defenders, holding off his men. The lion swatted away two spears with his katars, but roared as a third punctured his left leg. The leopard-spotted female beside him slashed at one of the net-and-trident men, her shortword laying his face open.

The trap had worked perfectly, Ralkin thought as he surveyed the fighting. His forces outnumbered the Katheni at least five to one. And soon his diversionary group would finish their work at the wedding site and close on the cats' flank. Ralkin, commander of the slavers, chuckled softly to himself as he donned his purple cape and silver skull mask. It was time to make his theatrical entrance. As a finishing touch, Ralkin donned his magnificent feathered hat and pushed aside his bodyguards to stand atop a sand dune not far from the battle.

Ralkin was pleased. At this rate they'd have the cats subdued within five minutes. Even if only half of the cats survived to be sold as slaves, he would turn an enormous profit on this venture.

Suddenly, panic began to spread at the back of the slaver ranks. His men began to turn and flee. Ralkin turned to see what disconcerted his men.

A manlike shape shuffled slowly through the ranks, swinging a Lucerne Hammer and slaying anyone in its path. The figure bristled with arrows and javelins, and even had an axe embedded in its head, but still it shuffled on, killing at every stroke.

The hammer in its hands was a four-pronged metal head atop a seven-foot-long pole. On the backside of the hammer head protruded a single long spike. And the weapon had a spearlike point on its top. The weapon had been designed to destroy thick plate-armor, so the thin chainmail and leather armors of the slavers were no match for it. Every stroke decimated its target.

Ralkin paled beneath his silver mask. But then he steeled himself. No shuffling pincushion with a hammer was going to deprive him of his prize. Confidence returned as he unslung his greatbow from his shoulder and notched an arrow to the string. He had slain over fifty men with this bow.

Its name was *Pyre's Call*, a fearsome weapon constructed from a Darkmatter-Dragonsbone alloy, Dragonsbone being the only flexible substance dense enough to withstand the tainting influence of the otherwise unstable Darkmatter. Any archer wielding *Pyre's Call* required special gauntlets merely to hold the thing without being poisoned by it. The bow itself imbued any arrow fired from it with the terrible corruptive power of Darkmatter.

Ralkin drew back the string and fired.

The arrow struck the shuffling figure in the center of its mass, throwing it to the ground. The back-blast of the magicked arrow instantly killed three slavers who had been fighting the creature.

Acceptable losses, Ralkin thought. Smiling, he turned back to his soon-to-be-lucrative business. But his pleasure turned to dread as he heard screams erupt from behind him once more.

As Ralkin watched in horror, the shuffling creature picked itself up. The black arrow was still stuck amidst the rest of the arrows—and no more effective. In fact, rather than killing the creature the arrow seemed to be having the opposite effect. Now the shambling figure moved quicker, swung his hammer faster, and actually began to dodge some of the attacks thrown at it.

Shuddering, Ralkin notched *Pyre's Call* and fired again. His aim was off, and the arrow slew another of his own men. The creature did get caught in the dark energy backwash and began moving faster once more. It moved like a cross between a crack swordsman and a slobbering drunk, but was decidedly Human. Or was it? Ralkin couldn't see that it had any eyes. Its skin was grey, but it was too slim to be an Orc. And even an Orc couldn't take that many arrows and javelins without going down.

So he decided to add one more arrow. Ralkin's third arrow struck the creature through the skull.

Instantly a wave of black energy rippled out from the ground where the creature stood, and a high-pitched keening pierced the air.

When the black energy dissipated, Ralkin peered at the site. All the men who had been grouped around the creature lay prone, dead on the ground.

Only one figure remained upright. The man stood, befeathered by arrow fletchings and clutching a rusted warhammer, and slowly removed a blackened arrow from his left eye socket.

It was not Human, though it might once have been. With decayed lips, the zombie grinned maliciously and advanced upon Ralkin and his remaining slavers.

Cyrus and Katana dashed through the deserted camp. Most of the tents had burned to ash, and the scattered remnants of the feast and decorations were nothing but garbage on the ground. The air was thick with smoke, and it wasn't pleasant smoke either. It burned in Cyrus's lungs as he ran. It was like trying to breathe aerosol acid.

"What did you see with the spell?" Cyrus asked as they dashed past a blazing tent.

"Kris and our uncle are being attacked by more slavers," Katana said, leaping over a shattered bench. "Some kind of evil energy was distorting my spell. Whatever it was, we need to get there quickly!"

And they did. Within the minute, they encountered the group of Katheni.

But they did not seem to be in distress. They weren't fighting or running away. The Katheni watched wordlessly as a lone figure battled the slavers. Cyrus followed their gaze.

Few of the Human slavers stood and fought. One man stood against them, seemingly covered by arrows into his body. No matter what the Humans threw at him, the man they battled remained unharmed. As Cyrus watched, a swordsman separated the man's arm from his shoulder. That should've ended the battle, but the man merely picked the arm up, hammer still tightly gripped in its hand, and slew the slaver with it.

"It's Zaccheus," Cyrus whispered, not quite believing what he was seeing.

He gave the situation two seconds' thought. On one hand, their decomposing friend seemed to be doing fine. On the other, he was surrounded and likely to be dismembered by repeated attacks. Not that the dismembering would be fatal, but it would be incapacitating.

At the end of the two seconds, he sprang into action. He drew his sword and leapt into the melee.

As he ran, Cyrus realized he could sense the power around him. The ley-lines, Katana called them. Could he use it now in a smaller way than before? By sending a thought at the air energy nearby, he was able to sheath his blade in frost. Excellent.

He struck the nearest slaver, freezing and shattering his armor. The next fell in the same manner. Cyrus waded through the slavers, fighting his way toward the archer in the center with the purple robe, silver mask, and magnificent hat. Upon reaching him, Cyrus swept his frozen blade and struck at the bow in the man's hands.

Two things happened. First, the bow flew from the slaver's hands and skidded across the battlefield to Zaccheus's feet. Second, Cyrus's blade, upon impact with the Darkmatter alloy and weakened by fire and frost, snapped in two.

The archer's mask tracked the bow skidding across the bloody sand. His posture said this was not something he'd been expecting. But he quickly regained his composure and drew a blade, ready to face the now-unarmed man in front of him.

Cyrus adopted a defensive posture and dodged the sword, but the masked man was too fast. He lashed out, scoring him across the cheek. The blade bit through flesh and skipped across his teeth.

The masked man raised his sword for a killing blow—but an arrow stuck him in the side, and he was instantly enveloped in black flames.

With a shriek, the slaver dropped his blade and sank to his knees, flesh crisping and bubbling from the fell magic. The flesh burnt from his bones in mere moments, leaving a fragile and blackened skeleton in a badly oxidized silver skull mask. Cyrus looked away from the gruesome sight and turned to Zaccheus.

The zombie stood holding the mysterious black bow. As Cyrus watched, Zaccheus pulled a second arrow from his chest, notched it to the bow, and fired at an Orc who was bending down to tie up two unconscious Katheni. The second arrow had much the same effect on the Orc as the first had on the Human.

A backwash of dark energy flowed over Zaccheus's body. As it spread, patches of skin, muscle mass, and three more fingers began to regenerate. He raised his magically growing arms at the Humans and lurched toward them.

The slavers fled into the desert.

● ● ●

Kris and Cyrus sat near the remains of some of the tents near the rest of the wounded. And wounded there were.

Since the slavers had been trying to capture, not kill, the Katheni, there were many nonlethal injuries. Wounded Katheni lay about on the sand getting bandaged by those with slighter injuries, while the unharmed put out the fires on what remained of the tents. Benjara and Wasara moved about carrying those who couldn't walk over to the makeshift infirmary. Wasara heaved a huge sigh and sat down next to Cyrus, shaking his maned head.

Kris dabbed gently at Cyrus's slashed face. She used the end of a hot, damp cloth to wash away the blood. Cyrus winced, but sat still with his back against a rolled purple and yellow carpet outside a storage tent. It was midnight, or thereabouts, as far as Cyrus could tell. And to him it seemed that the whole "celebrating a wedding via violence" idea had been highly overrated.

"Well," Cyrus said, "this sure has been an unusual way to celebrate a wedding, eh, Kris?"

"I did not envision that my mating would turn out with half of my guests cut or clubbed," Kris said with a sad smile. "But at least no one was seriously injured."

"Hey, now! I count doubling the size of my mouth as a serious injury!" Cyrus protested.

"Only to those of us who have to listen to you," Wasara said, leaning his katars against the rolled carpet. "Benjara, as soon as you've finished helping Ravi, come and sew Cyrus's extra-large mouth shut. Kris, where is your brother?"

Kris looked about. "I haven't seen him since the fighting stopped. I believe he's tending to the wounded. No, wait," she said, pointing at one of the western tents. "There he is."

Beside the tent sat Katana, cradling the head of a young tigress in his lap. Kris walked over to where he sat. The girl was dead, and Katana sat oblivious to anything else, gently stroking her striped paw.

"Katana . . . ?" Kris said tentatively.

Katana looked up, eyes vacant. "Hello, Kris. How is everyone doing?"

"Who was this?" Kris asked.

"Her name was Marie," Katana answered, looking back down. "We loved each other once."

Kris started in surprise. "What? You never . . . you never told me you had someone . . . "

Katana smiled wryly. "We never told anyone. Father would not have approved, nor would Wasara. I promised her that day after the eclipse that I would return someday and take her far away, some place she'd never been before. Now she's gone somewhere far away without me, and I can't follow . . . "

Kris placed her paw on her brother's shoulder. "I'm so sorry, Katana."

Katana said nothing and returned to stroking the tigress's paw.

While waiting for Benjara to arrive and sew up his injuries, Cyrus walked over to where Zaccheus stood.

The zombie looked much better than he had the last time Cyrus had seen him. He now had a full compliment of fingers, almost a full head of hair, and decent muscle mass. His skin was no longer present only in patches, and no bones showed through the flesh. He had even regenerated his eye-balls, though they seemed to remain sightless. A few arrows still protruded from his back, but Zaccheus didn't seem to notice. He merely stood over Cyrus like a decomposing guardian angel.

Cyrus propped himself up against the rolled rug and looked up at him. "Zaccheus, I can't remember the last time it was actually good to see a zombie. How did you happen to be here just when we needed you?"

The zombie shrugged. "Ah followed you." His voice still had the quality Cyrus remembered, an airy moaning that one would expect to hear emanating from a tomb. Only with better diction than before.

"You've been following us the whole time? It must've taken you over a week to catch up with us."

"Yesh," the zombie answered. "Ohn foot, ah ahm shlower ghan you ahhr on horshesh."

"So what will you do now that you're here?"

"Leaf. You helft be, Ah helft you. Be aghr eben. Ah bill tacche shish bow," the zombie said, hefting his tainted prize, "ahnd gho. Perhash ah bill shee you aghaid shobday."

Cyrus took Zaccheus's cold hand, then shuddered and put it back on the end of the zombie's arm. "Farewell, then. I'll see you around. We'll probably meet again, since I'm a Hero and a good-guy zombie isn't something you see every day. Maybe if you regenerate some more teeth, I'll buy you lunch sometime, eh?"

The zombie nodded. With that, he plodded off, barely even limping now, far faster than his earlier shuffling gait. Cyrus watched him go, then went back to his spot, laid his head against the rolled rug, and drifted off to sleep.

A flash of light interrupted Cyrus's brief rest. Two men appeared on the desert sand, an old one dressed in a grey robe and a younger one clad in a deep green. Upon their arrival, they began to look around, and the green one produced a small wand, flicking it back and forth. Within moments, he turned, the wand pointing directly at Cyrus.

"You there!" the green-clad man shouted. "Stay where you are for a moment, if you please."

Cyrus blinked sleepily. It was still night, which meant he hadn't had enough time to heal yet. So stay put he did. He was wounded in enough places that rising might have proven difficult. "Who are you two?"

"I am Kemal Forsythe," said the man in green. "Associate of the Council of Highseekers. You have been causing much trouble, young man, and I intend to arrest you for it."

"Peace, Forsythe," said the old man in grey, his voice full of kindly wisdom. "You are rash, accusing this man when there are so many others present. Before arresting anyone, you must prove their guilt, or they must prove their innocence. My apologies, young man," he said to Cyrus. "My associate is hasty, and knows little of the legal ramifications of our situation. Might I have the pleasure of knowing your name?"

"Cyrus Solburg, Hero, Second Class," Cyrus answered, wincing at the pain in the side of his face. "And you two are?"

The grey man bowed, as did his associate. "I am Rastarian Riverstride. My young companion is my apprentice, Kemal Forsythe. We represent the Council of Highseekers, and is that a piece of potato in your hair?"

Cyrus put his hand to his head and pulled a small white chunk from his red hair. "Oh, that. Yes, I suppose it is. That's what comes of putting a soup pot on your head, I guess."

"At any rate," the older Highseeker continued, "the Council sent us to find out who or what has been causing such a disturbance in the ley-lines of late. After noticing first an unknown tension in a Water line, then an unusually heavy drain on a Fire line, we began to trace these occurrences. The next time it was again a Fire line, but this time it was broken, severed entirely. Do you mind if I sit down?"

"Not at all," Cyrus said, motioning for Rastarian to sit beside him in the makeshift infirmary.

Some of the other wounded looked over at the newcomers, but soon lost interest and returned to tending their own injuries. Benjara arrived with clean needle and thin thread, and began working on Cyrus. "So long as you don't mind if I get my face stitched up while you talk."

"That's perfectly all right, master Solburg. Now, as I was saying, this destruction of a Fire-line was grievous news to the Council. There are only four hundred or so Fire-lines in the entire world. With it destroyed, there is now a thirty or forty-square-league patch of land in eastern Centra Mundi where Fire magic is nigh unusable. You see our problem, master Solburg?"

Cyrus nodded gently, trying to move as little as possible while Benjara stitched his wound closed.

"So we strove to track whatever was destroying ley-lines," Rastarian said. His voice was wonderful, like the voice of everyone's favorite grandfather. "The next day, we discovered a damaged Air line, and it wasn't too long until our quarry broke one of those too. The Council uses Air lines to communicate with our satellite guilds and the League of Elementalists, not to mention the Guild of Heroes. We were nearby enough to appear within the day, and found dozens of slaughtered men and one destroyed ley-line."

Rastarian rubbed his grizzled chin. "Today, one after another, whoever this mad ley-line destroyer is damaged an Earth-line, broke another Air-line, and tied a Water-line in a knot. You can can see why this is an emergency, I hope. So here we are, looking for our culprit." He looked at Cyrus without expression "Are there any rampant, destructive Elementalists about?"

"I hate to tell you this," Cyrus said, "but I think your apprentice was right. I'm not too skilled at magic and haven't got control of it. I think your 'culprit' may," he swallowed, "be me. I'm afraid my ineptitude has been damaging your ley-lines, or so Katana tells me. Is there some way to repair them?"

The faces of both men hardened. "No, there isn't," Rastarian said, all the kindness gone from his voice. "And now you must come with us."

"What? Why?"

"Orders of the Council. We were to find the cause of damage to the ley-lines and either eliminate or capture it," Kemal said. "Lucky for you, we have decided on capture."

Cyrus leapt up, needle and thread hanging from his cheek, and reached for his sword. When he couldn't find it, he realized it was in two pieces, a hundred yards away.

Kemal pointed at Cyrus and mouthed strange words. Thin green strands like string shot from his fingertips, wrapping around Cyrus's arms and torso. Rastarian flung both hands out at Benjara, and an intense rush of wind flung the Katheni boy roughly away from Cyrus.

Cyrus flexed his arms and burst the strands. "Benjara, get Katana!" Cyrus yelled at the stunned leopard boy. Picking up one of Wasara's katars, he spun about, slashing at his opponent. Kemal interposed an invisible wall, turning aside the heavy punch-dagger. Cyrus struck twice more, once as a feint, the second laying open Kemal's left cheek and driving the apprentice Mage backward.

Benjara sprinted across the sand toward the rest of the Katheni. Cyrus hoped he would reach Wasara in time to send reinforcements.

But the fight did not last long enough. With two curt words, the elder Highseeker lifted Cyrus into the air and slammed him back down, knocking the air from his battered chest. With another command word, Cyrus's limbs went rigid, paralyzing him from the neck down. With a satisfied smile, Rastarian wove his hands in the net-like pattern of a multi-person *Teleport* spell.

"Kris! Katana!" Benjara shouted as he ran.

Kris and Katana stood up as the breathless leopard boy ran up to them. "Slow down, Benjara," Katana said. "You'll tear your wound open. What's wrong?"

"You've got to help Cyrus," Benjara gasped. "Two mages took him and vanished!"

Kris sighed. "This is tiresome. Having slavers interrupt your mating celebration is one thing. Having your mate stolen on your wedding night is quite another. I swear, it's like we're living in a bad adventure novel."

Katana growled softly. "My new brother-in-law seems to be nothing but trouble. I cannot trace a teleport spell, so all we can do is wait until he returns."

Chapter 31

RULES AND REGULATIONS

*In which the Rules of Magic are Outlined, Cyrus is Lectured,
and the Truth finally Dawns on the Forces of Light*

CYRUS WOKE TO the touch of a gentle night breeze on his brow. He sat up, expecting to feel pain as he moved, but felt none. He felt at his cheek and discovered that his wounds were all healed and the unfinished stitches in the corner of his mouth were gone. Nothing but a thin scar and scraped teeth remained as evidence of the cut. He saw that he now wore some kind of white acolyte's robe trimmed with light blue edging in place of Wasara's borrowed finery. Then he remembered what had happened to him.

He was outside, lying on an elevated stone pavement. The moon shone through heavy grey clouds, and Cyrus could see he was on the top of a dizzyingly high tower with four points shaped like the claw of a massive stone eagle. Around Cyrus was a ring of chairs, and in those chairs sat the widest variety of mages he had ever seen. They were of all Races and wore robes spanning the spectrum. Some were dressed in all black, some in all white, while others were totally inHuman and wore nothing. For example, a titanic Grand Basilisk dominated an entire section of the circle.

A young man in the largest chair at the head of the circle tapped his staff on the ground thrice. The buzz of muted conversation ceased as he rose and walked toward Cyrus. "He is awake," the young man said. "Greetings, Cyrus Solburg, and welcome to the audience chamber of the Council of Highseekers, though 'chamber' is a bit of a misnomer."

The man's age was hard to determine. He moved with youthful grace but carried himself with an air of ponderous wisdom and authority, and he had deep creases around his eyes. His hair was silver, whether from premature age or magic, Cyrus could not tell. He wore a robe of indefinite color. It seemed to shift from one hue to the next faster than Cyrus could think.

"It has been a long time since I saw you last, Cyrus. You were only a child of nine years when I left Starspeak. Do you remember me?"

Cyrus stared into the man's eyes. There was something there, but just barely. "I think so, but I couldn't tell you. That's almost half my life ago."

"Oh, I think you can, Cyrus. After all, you were sweethearts with my dear sister, who you encountered again only recently."

"William?" Cyrus said incredulously. "William Weatherblade?"

William smiled. "At your service, master Solburg. Welcome to my tower."

Cyrus looked about him. "Your tower? Wait, does that mean that you're the Grand Highseeker?"

"I'm afraid so," William answered. "I told them it was a terrible burden to lay on a man so young, but they refused to listen. Of course, when you wield as much elemental energy as any twelve of them put together, people do become intimidated and wish to saddle you with a title that keeps you from harming them. But enough about me. Today, we are here to talk about you." William offered a hand.

Cyrus accepted it and pulled himself up. "What about me?"

But William had already turned and walked back to his chair. "Today, we pass judgment on one Cyrus Solburg, accused of destroying ley-lines," he said in a stentorian voice. Several unruly members of the circle booed softly. "Witnesses against this man, step forward."

Two men stepped up, one from a chair and the other from behind it. Cyrus recognized them at once as Rastarian Riverstride and his apprentice Kemal Forsythe.

"What evidence have you?" William demanded.

"We have investigated the damage to the lines," Rastarian said, "and the locations of this damage follows the same path this man did. He has admitted that he tampers with magic while knowing nothing of its use."

Cyrus made to speak, but found that he could not utter a word.

"Circumstantial," William snapped. "Could he not have been followed by the true cause of the damage? And any peasant with a trace of magic in him tampers with magic while knowing none of its rules, yet that causes no damage."

There was a *Shut Up* spell on him, Cyrus realized. He began to *feel* the spell wrapped around his throat, preventing speech. Somehow he understood that the spell was tentatively connected to the Air line hovering over the tower. He raised a hand to his throat and began to feel along the edges of the impediment. A mage across the circle from Cyrus frowned and began weaving his hands. The spell tightened its grip. Cyrus gave up and listened.

"True, but he is different," Rastarian insisted. "His aura is not unlike yours, Grandmaster. Allow me to demonstrate."

Sprinkling a pinch of powder on the ground, Rastarian collected a small blob of greenish energy between his hands. Walking over to where Cyrus stood, he stretched the blob into a thin sheet of energy and tossed it onto Cyrus. A gasp rose from the assembled magicians as the air about Cyrus glowed a dusky gold for several seconds.

"Fascinating," William drawled, as though nothing in the world could have been more boring. "So he has a trace of power. This proves nothing."

Kemal Forsythe scowled. "Since you seem so bent on defending this boy, what *will* you accept as evidence?"

William Weatherblade, Grand Highseeker, fixed Kemal with an icy glare. Literally. Frost crept up Kemal's boots, freezing him to the floor. "I accept all evidence, Forsythe. Yours simply isn't solid enough to convict him. Reasonable doubt yet exists. Besides, he obviously knows nearly nothing about magic."

"Well, we must educate him, then," another Highseeker spoke up. He was a kindly looking old man with a bushy white beard.

"You would be the one to do it, Halmer Blackfence," William said. "You still teach *MAG 101* at Rubic's Academy, do you not?"

"I do." Halmer stood up and stroked his white beard as if lecturing a class. "Well, young man," he said to Cyrus, "what *do* you know about magic?"

Halmer gestured at Cyrus, and the Shut Up spell fell away.

Cyrus rubbed his throat. "Umm, it hurts to get hit with it. It's complicated to use. And . . . it comes in lines?"

The elderly wizard put a hand to his forehead in disgust. "This may take a while, Highseeker. The Council may wish to adjourn until I am able to get this boy straightened out."

"An excellent suggestion," William agreed. "The Council will now recess for a two-hour break. Halmer, take Cyrus to the Library and educate him there. I am in need of sustenance. Farewell."

With that, William disappeared into thick air. Then the thick air disappeared also, leaving only thin air.

Cyrus and Halmer Blackfence sat in the Highseekers' Library in enormous leather chairs. A table rested between them, with several books, an inkwell and pen, and a short stack of blank parchment on it.

The book-lined walls of the Library stretched back for several furlongs and disappeared into the darkness, taking up two entire floors of the enormous round tower. Rich tapestries adorned the few walls not covered in books, and exotic rugs lined the aisles between bookshelves. The dry air was filled with the musty smell of old books, mingled with the scents of new ink and leather bindings. Cyrus and Halmer sat before a cheery fire, which for some reason, exuded cold instead of heat.

"So how does magic work, exactly?" Cyrus asked.

Halmer chuckled. "That, my dear boy, is a more complicated question than you think. Let me start with the basics." He picked up one of the blank sheets of parchment, then snapped his fingers. A quill pen appeared in his hand, and he began drawing columns and diagrams to illustrate his points. "Magic is divided into three schools: Magery, Wizardry, and Sorcery.

"Magery deals with the use of magic as a weapon. The League of Elementalists, lowly college though they be, have advanced this school quite far. Wizardry uses magic to create magical objects and to enhance mundane ones. For example, a good friend of mine once made a magic crossbow that automatically reloaded itself after every shot, improving the original bow. That is the essence of Wizardry. Sorcery, however, is a terrible thing, as it deals with the summoning of Demons, stealing souls, and all manner of vile necromancy. Few, if any, of the men on the Council traffic in this dark art."

"What about Alchemy?"

Halmer snorted. "Alchemy. Bah! Alchemy isn't *real* magic," he said disdainfully. "All alchemists do is mix random smelly ingredients together in their search for their 'Philosopher's Stone.' They call their mystical garbage 'science.' Ha! Pure hogwash."

Cyrus shrugged. "Alright, then. I guess a better question is, what powers magic?"

Halmer's eyes gleamed. "This world is governed by three forces, dear boy: the Elements, the Capital Letters, and the Arbitrary Numbers."

"Did you just capitalize all of those?"

"Don't interrupt. It isn't polite. The Elements are four: Earth, Water, Fire, and Air. Everything that exists is made up of some mixture of these four. The oft-mentioned ley-lines carry pure, unadulterated forms of these elements. A spell takes some of that energy and transforms it into something useful, be it a bolt of fire, or energy to power a golem. Essentially, it changes the pure energy into the physical manifestation of what the spell is designed to produce."

"Wait, what?" Cyrus scratched his head.

Halmer sighed. "Making something appear where nothing was visible. Creating fire when you weren't holding anything flammable. For the sake of simplicity, call it crafting your own things from their essence. Spells, then, are like instruction books, recipes for making various types of things.

Like long-distance fireballs, instant ice-cubes, and paralyzing gases."

"I'll take your word for it," Cyrus said dubiously.

"When a mage takes hold of some power from a ley-line," Halmer continued, unruffled, "it generates a field of that energy around him. The more powerful the mage, the larger and more powerful the field he generates. However, if you try to affect a field of one type—Fire, for example—with another spell of the same type, both will be turned aside. Thus, two mages shooting fireballs at each other will not be harmed, though I will not vouch for their surroundings."

Cyrus picked up a pen and began to draw on a piece of parchment. "So what you're saying is, if one mage," he said, drawing a circle, "fights another," another circle, "with the same element, both spells are diverted." He drew lines coming from each circle and turning to the right and left once they neared each other. "But if they are using different elements," he drew lines connecting them, "then both take the hit?"

"Exactly!" Halmer said, beaming. "That is the essence of magery. You have it! Indeed, the precise definition of a counterspell is using the same element to totally deflect your opponent's spell."

"But what happens in here?" Cyrus asked, indicating the space between the lines, where they parted to the sides.

Halmer's smile disappeared. "That is a void. At all costs, avoid being caught between two mages using the same element. It will tear you apart."

Cyrus shuddered. "So what about these 'Capital Letters'?"

"Ah, the Capital Letters! You already know the principle behind them. You know what the difference between a sword and a Sword is, do you not?"

Cyrus arched an eyebrow. "Whichever one is capitalized is stronger, and has some magical property, usually. I've
seen the difference in price tags on regular iron swords and
Enchanted Swords many a time, but I just figured that it was
a marketing ploy."

"Far from it, my boy," Halmer corrected. "The Capital
Letters lend power to otherwise less significant objects, and
also have an important stabilizing influence on the other two
types of magic. For example, a pair of running shoes may be
good for taking a walk in or participating in a race. But if you
want to cover a thousand leagues in a day, then you will need
Shoes of Running."

Cyrus ran his fingers through his hair. "And it's only these
Capital Letters that give objects this power? It isn't based on
the Elements?"

"Exactly, and no. The Capital Letters lend power of a different type than that of the Elements."

Cyrus thought for a moment. "So if I have a clod of dirt,
it's nothing special, but if I have a Clod of Dirt, then it would
be?"

"Erm, some Dirt of Clodding? Hmm, I suppose so,"
Halmer said. "But it would have to sound more grandiose,
and have more Capital Letters in order to be effective. It would
need to be a Clod of Dirt of the Immortals or something like
that. And," he said, raising one finger, "it would need to be
part of a set of one of the Arbitrary Numbers, which brings
me to my next point."

Cyrus looked at his wrist and wished someone would
invent the wristwatch.

"The Arbitrary Numbers are a great source of power. Their
energy is unstable and unpredictable, but it surpasses that of
the Capital Letters. The Arbitrary Numbers are One, Three,
Five, Six, Seven, Nine, Ten, Twelve, and One Hundred."

"You just capitalized all of those too, didn't you?"

"Yes, as I should. When combined with the Capital Letters, the power of the Arbitrary Numbers becomes stable. And incredible. To bring back my sword analogy, let us say that a master smith forges some swords. If he forges four, there is nothing special. Four not being an Arbitrary Number, you see. But say he wished to create a set for the Seven Elven Lords. Then, when he forges the Seven Swords, they are magically of exquisite craftsmanship, far better than he thought he could make. These blades will have magical or magic-resistant properties. Do you follow?"

Cyrus nodded. "I think so. That's why there are Five Titans, Twelve Gods, Nine Races, and all that?" The library's cold fire popped, sending an ice cube into Cyrus's lap. He brushed it off and looked back at Halmer.

"Precisely," Halmer said. "But keep in mind that the higher the number, the lesser the effect. It becomes diluted, you might say, the higher you go. If you compare a set of Three Enchanted Swords to a set of Five Magic Blades, the Three will be noticeably better than the Five. So if you wished to create a very powerful weapon—"

"Then it would need to be one of the Three Silver Longswords of the Frost Giants or something like that. I get the impression that the more syllables something has attached to it, the stronger it is, too," Cyrus said, cynically.

"Yes, but only if the number of descriptive words adds up to one of the Arbitrary Numbers," Halmer corrected. "But in principle, you are right. And here's the real power, boy. When you add the Letters, Numbers, and Elements, you have the whole soul of magic. Add another layer of power by making your number of effects or descriptions into an Arbitrary Number.

"But be careful, you can overload yourself or the item you are trying to make. For example, a few centuries ago a half-crazed sorcerer styled himself a Dark Lord after creating the *One Indestructible Flaming Evil Magic Ring of Invisibility*. He thought he was quite the Ultimate Evil. But the ring itself was so powerful it caused all kinds of havoc among the people who got hold of it once he was slain. They finally had to destroy the thing by throwing it into the volcanic fires of its forging. So, to sum up, there are four Elements—"

"Wait," Cyrus said, "shouldn't there be Five Elements? To be an Arbitrary Number?"

Halmer shook his head. "Should, perhaps, but there are only four Elements. Alas. Four Elements are the source of power for spells. Capital Letters provide stability and are indicators of power. And Arbitrary Numbers, which can infuse almost any object with power, provided that the object in question comes in a set of one of the Numbers. Any questions?"

How many students per year in your class die of boredom? Cyrus thought, but said, "Nope. None at all."

"Then we must return to the Council. They will be waiting for us." Halmer rose and offered Cyrus his hand.

The young Hero took it, and in a flash, they were at the top of the tower once more.

The weather had worsened while they were inside, and rain now poured from the sky, turning the top of the tower into a windswept Pond of Slickness. The mages assembled within moments, and the Council resumed, now with glowing domes above their chairs to shed the rain. The sun had not yet come up over the eastern horizon, but the sky had begun lightening the dark grey of the rainy night. The Basilisk had spread its wings over its head to create a shelter, and it was underneath the wings that Cyrus and Halmer stood.

Rain, Cyrus thought, listening to the rain drumming on the Basilisk's membranous wings, sounding like rain on a cloth tarpaulin. Rain. He hoped that didn't mean that something *else* bad was going to happen. He'd had enough bad things happen already today.

"So, now that you know how the world of magic works, master Solburg," William said, "what have you to say about the charges leveled against you?"

"Not much," Cyrus answered. "I seem to be using elemental magic just the way everyone else does, only with no framework of spells."

"Lies!" yelled Kemal Forsythe, Rastarian's apprentice. "He was right there, practically standing on top of a broken Earth line!"

Cyrus rounded on the young mage. "You call me a liar in this august company?" he said, feeling for his missing sword. "I'll have you know I am a Hero, Second Class, in Good Standing with the Guild of Heroes!" He vaguely wondered if he'd be more persuasive to this audience if he spoke in sentences of three, five, or ten words.

"It is indeed a serious accusation, Forsythe, Riverstride," William said, looking first at the agitated apprentice, then his elderly master. "Would you care to back that statement up with some proof? Perhaps a trial by combat?"

"Yes, I do. Have at ye!" Kemal Forsythe shouted, quick-launching a mid-size fireball at Cyrus's head.

"You fool!" Rastarian Riverstride shouted at his apprentice. "Challenge him at your own peril!"

Cyrus had noted the weather conditions, however, and was prepared for another sudden attack. He leapt aside. The flaming projectile splashed harmlessly against magic walls that had instantly come up around the circle to protect the other mages from harm.

Since his sword was still in two pieces, and now a completely unknown distance away, Cyrus *reached* out for a line. He could almost see them this time, floating in the air, running through the earth, gliding along the stream at the base of the tower——all full of pure, beautiful energy. Cyrus grabbed the shimmering blue Water line and snapped it off. He didn't mean to—because that was how he'd gotten in trouble in the first place. On the plus side, it did come away much easier than the previous lines had. Perhaps he was getting better at this.

The assembled mages gasped as the line snapped. Their horror compounded as Cyrus guided the line along his arm and *threw* it at Forsythe. An enormous stream of crystalline water geysered forth from Cyrus's hand at high pressure and slammed the elderly mage against the invisible wall behind him, adding more water to the already slick surface of the tower. Cyrus dropped the line and let the drenched mage to his feet.

Electricity crackled as Forsythe began preparing a spell. Some insight came to Cyrus that the spell would be an Air spell: *Hellbolt,* to be precise. It made sense, thanks to Halmar's lecture. Any electrical attack would prove very effective against a foe using water attacks, especially in the rain.

So Cyrus knew what to do. He took hold of the Air line, snapped it off, and cast it away from Rastarian like a rotten branch. The power abruptly went out of Riverstride's spell. It fizzled in his hands, not even becoming a *Purgatorybolt.*

"Wait!" Forsythe said peevishly. "It was my turn! You performed your attack already. Now it is time for mine!"

"Turn?" Cyrus said quizzically. "What do you think this is, some kind of game?"

The young mage cursed and created a cloud of fiery darts, which he threw en masse at Cyrus.

Cyrus dashed forward and dropped under the flaming projectiles, sliding on the rain-slicked stone. Two darts caught his robe on fire, but the rain quickly quenched it. Then he found a Fire line and twisted it. It broke as well, and Cyrus reached for the Air and Water lines he had already used. Finding them, he braided the three lines into one coherent strand and pointed them at Forsythe.

The green-clad mage didn't even have time to scream before a brilliant beam of white energy poured from Cyrus's outstretched hands and vaporized him, robe and all.

When the light faded, Cyrus stood alone, staring at the flickering light of the failing magic walls. He blinked. Forsythe was gone. He hadn't meant to kill him—there had just been too much power there. Maybe Reginald was right about magic after all.

The Highseekers murmered angrily amongst themselves. Cyrus could pick up snippets of "He just broke the lines!" and "murdered a Highseeker" and "Weatherblade can't defend him now . . . " The Grand Basilisk even rumbled something about turning Cyrus to stone before he could do more damage.

William Weatherblade rose from his chair. "Well done. I would say that your victory proves your innocence." Then he grimaced. "However . . . "

"However what?" Cyrus said.

"However, you just broke three ley-lines, right in front of a jury of mages who were trying to convict you of breaking ley-lines." William grinned wryly. "I guess trial by combat isn't always accurate."

"Oh," Cyrus said, rubbing his head. "I guess I did. Well, that's enough evidence for me. I plead guilty."

At that moment, a trap door in the tower roof opened, and a liveried page scurried up from it. "Master Weatherblade!

Master Weatherblade!" the page said, all atwitter. "We are under attack!"

Cyrus glanced down from the incredible height of the tower platform. Rain dripped from his soaked hair, falling down the dizzying drop to the ground below.

Assembled at the base of the tower was an army, near invisible in their black armor thanks to the darkness and the clouds. As he watched, a patch of blacker blackness appeared in the midst of the dark army and hurled itself at the tower. The stone beneath their feet shook at the impact of the bolt.

"Why are the *Walls of Defense* down?" A mage in a topaz-colored robe screamed.

"Because our friend here," the Grand Basilisk growled, indicating Cyrus, "just broke the lines which kept them up."

Cyrus ducked his head. "Oops."

Another mage wove his hands in a magical pattern, then looked up in shock. "I can't cast anything! The lines are broken!"

"Not all the lines are destroyed," William said calmly. With a flick of his wrist, multiple enormous points of sharp rock burst from the ground far below them, impaling and scattering the dark host below. "Everyone evacuate the tower as quickly and efficiently as possible."

A distraught mage piped up. "How? The Air line is broken and we cannot teleport!"

Cyrus snorted. "Try taking the stairs. You do have stairs, don't you?"

Another wave of dark energy shook the tower.

"I mislike this situation," William said. "No one would be so foolish as to attack the Tower of the Highseekers. Unless . . . "

Cyrus stood at his shoulder, looking down. "Unless what?"

"Unless the reports we've been hearing of a dark army massing and being led by a demon spawn are true. I received a report a few days ago that a man by the name of Voshtyr had begun to—"

"Voshtyr?" Cyrus started. "The Crimson Slash was captured by Voshtyr Demonkin and held in the swamp keep. I recently had to fight to free him. The local authorities never did find Voshtyr after the fight. Even the Guild of Heroes turned up nothing. He is dangerous, William. If he's building an army . . . "

"Not building, built!" squawked a raven perched atop one of the four stone spires. It flew down to where Cyrus and William stood, blurring as it went. When it landed, it had become a tall, black-haired youth with murky purple eyes, clad in a black silk doublet and hose.

Cyrus reached for his sword, cursing himself for his short memory as he once again noticed the weapon's absence.

"I have come to deliver an ultimatum," the raven man said. "My master Voshtyr demands the immediate surrender of the Highseekers and their tower."

"Not likely, *orsobu pitchi*," William said pleasantly. "Fly back and tell your master that the Highseekers do not yield."

"Pity. And it was such a lovely tower. Very well, then, I shall leave you to your deaths. Honestly, we were expecting more resistance. What happened to all your vaunted wards? We got right up to your front door without you noticing!"

William smiled again. "Young man, you are making it very difficult for me to not kill the messenger. If you are leaving, leave."

Had the man had feathers at the moment, they would have been ruffled. "All right, all right, no need to be rude. I will leave at once. Good-bye, and enjoy your doom!" Shifting back into raven-form, the man flew into the black stormclouds.

As soon as the raven had flown, William clapped twice and summoned a black crow with silver-tipped feathers. "Crow, take this message to the Heroes' Guild." He pulled a small stick and a piece of parchment from his robe, scrawled a brief note, and attached it to the crow's foot.

"*Corn?*" quorked the crow.

"Not yet, crow. The men at the Guild of Heroes will have plenty. Go now." He tossed the bird into the air and watched it fly for a moment.

Cyrus tapped William on the shoulder. "What was that?"

"A Stormcrow," William replied. "The League of Elementalists breeds them for intelligence and Air affinity. They are the second-fastest species of bird in the world, out-matched only by the Sky Kite. Sky Kites are rare and difficult to train, though, so Stormcrows are a much better choice for message bearing."

"And is that what I think it is?" Cyrus said, pointing down to the base of the tower.

"Only if you think it's a battering ram."

Cyrus looked down. Black armorerd soldiers pushed a massive battering ram with a troll-headed steel cap. They rolled it right up to the main gate of the tower.

"We should probably be leaving," William said. "Though I don't know why they are bothering with that thing. Those doors are solid, certainly. But they're unlocked."

"Unlocked?" Cyrus said in disbelief.

"How many times have I told the Council that we rely too heavily on magic? But no, they said, no one could pos-sibly break the Ancient Wards we had in place." William shook his head. "I suppose they were right. The Wards are indeed intact, but you seem to have deprived them of their energy supply, master Solburg." William chuckled.

"Besides, we're Highseekers. Relying heavily on magic is what we do."

Cyrus and William rapidly descended the dimly lit, twisting stone staircase. The rest of the council had already fled. Reaching the Library, they dashed inside. William went straight to the M section. "Aha! Here it is," William exclaimed. "*In Case of Emergency*, by Eustace Beverly Morival."

"Morival? The same Morival who caused the Twenty-Minute War?" Cyrus asked.

"I'm afraid so. Beastly name: *Eustace Beverly Morival*. Don't you think?" William said, pulling on the small red book. "Living with a name like that would make me want to kill every living thing on the planet too."

Behind them, the cold fire went out and the fireplace swung aside, revealing a secret passageway.

"This passage was one of his many brilliant ideas," William said, stepping inside. "Fortunately, it wasn't one of his twisted, evil, sadistic ones as well. Follow me!"

Shouts and the tramping of heavy boots ascending stairs echoed up the stairwell leading to the Library. Cyrus hurriedly ducked inside the passage.

The escape tunnel was smooth and gently illuminated, though Cyrus could not see how. Probably magic. The floor, walls, and ceiling were all made of interlocking tiles, almost seamlessly put together and smooth to the touch. Their footfalls echoed inside it, as if they were running through a large empty building.

"I just remembered something," William said as they ran. "You know how I said that this passage was not one of Morival's sadistic ideas? I'm afraid I was not entirely honest.

There are two slightly sadistic things about it. First, there is DOS."

Cyrus looked at him in confusion. "All caps?"

William smiled, still running. "DOS!" he called. "Boot up!"

A sulky ruby glow began emanating from a large gem embedded in the wall ahead of them. With the sound of stone scraping on stone, a large portion of the back wall fell away onto the floor, carrying the gem along with it.

William stopped in front of the wall, Cyrus at his back. Before Cyrus's eyes, the chunks of stone rattled around and lifted themselves up, forming around the gem into the shape of a bulky Humanoid. Within moments, the golem fully assembled itself. The construct nearly filled the passage, its grey stone bulk pitted and scarred from many battles.

"ENTER NAME:>" it grated.

"Weatherblade, William A., Grand Highseeker. Code word: *Habrá Cadávera.*"

The golem's two beady red eyes, small gems also, dimmed briefly, then the golem spoke. "NAME AND CODE WORD ACCEPTED . . . INSTRUCTIONS:>"

William glanced at the open doorway behind them down the tunnel. "There are some distinctly unfriendly people following us. Remove them."

"ILLEGAL COMMAND: REMOVE."

William sighed. "Just kill them all."

"KILL COMMAND ACKNOWLEGED. FATALITIES REQUESTED = TOTAL." It paused. Then: "ERROR READING FROM MOTOR SECTOR, ABORT, RETRY, FAIL?"

"Motor sector?" William said. "One moment." Removing a small piece of rock from the golem's midsection, he adjusted the large red gem inside. "Retry," he said after a moment's work.

"LOADING MASSACRE.EXE. PLEASE STAND BACK."

"That," William said, "is our cue to leave."

He and Cyrus scampered further down the tunnel. The golem began plodding back the way Cyrus and William had come, a decidedly homicidal step in its lumbering gait.

"William," Cyrus said as the fugitive pair dashed down the tunnel.

"Yes?"

"You said there were two sadistic things about this escape passage. But a golem doesn't seem very sadistic."

"Oh, it's sadistic all right. Just not for the men I sent him to attack." William almost tripped on a bit of stone as they passed through a mysteriously rough section of the tunnel. "It's sadistic for the person trying to use the thing! It's that stupid 'operating system' personality that fool Morival designed for it. I'm almost certain he purposefully designed it to be that obtuse, giggling with evil glee at the prospect of what a nuisance it would be to future Grand Highseekers. No, the truly sadistic part is right here." They stopped at a small stone box protruding from the wall.

Cyrus peered at the box curiously. "What's that?"

"Traps." William opened the box and began flipping switches. "Castration trap, check. Spinning blade trap, activated. Boiling acid trap, *Spontaneous Human Combustion* trap, and monkey trap: check, check, check."

"Monkey trap?"

William stared at Cyrus, eyes full of muted horror. "You don't want to know."

• • •

The tunnel terminated in a small, round room. It looked like someone's stone guest room. It was sparsely furnished with a small wardrobe, a desk and chair, and a large wooden chest. William went straight to the desk and removed a small packet of powder from the drawer. "Here," he said, "sprinkle this in a circle around yourself."

Cyrus did so. Circle complete, he turned back to William. "What are you going to do?"

William smiled a tired smile. "If those Villains want this tower so badly, they can dig it up. I'm rather glad you didn't break the Earth line, Cyrus. Otherwise this would be much more difficult. Any place in particular you want teleported to?"

"Back to the village in Mir, where your minions scooped me up," Cyrus answered. "I sort of have a new bride there, probably wondering if I've changed my mind."

"Very well. However, the men who 'scooped you up' were most certainly not minions. They were real people, one of whom is no longer with us, thanks to you. By the way, I'd love to ask you how you *combined* three ley-lines, but now is not the time. Nor is it time to catch up about life in the Citrus Isles. I wish you'd shown up several days ago, in fact. But back to my point. Only Villains use minions. I may not be the nicest or most polite mage around, Cyrus, but I am certainly not a Villain."

He said a few words in the Elven tongue, then turned back to Cyrus. "Now, time for me to bury myself alive."

Cyrus cocked his head. "But . . . you're going to get out once you do, right?"

"Well, there was only enough Powder of Teleportation for one person, so no. I'll wait for a bit, just in case, but don't count on it. If you see my lovely sister again, slap her upside the head for me, will you?"

"Hold on just one s—"

"Good-bye, Cyrus." William snapped his fingers, and rings of light encircled Cyrus until he saw nothing but light.

The Stormcrow flew through the night, a swarm of unnatural buzzing creatures pursuing it across the darkling sky. He had to reach the place where the loud men were. The loud men would protect him, and they always had corn.

Releasing a burst of Air energy, he sped up and veered sharply to the left. The nasties followed, still slowly gaining. But there was the city, and only a few more wingbeats away lay the nest of the loud men.

The headmost nasty landed square between the Stormcrow's wings and bit hard. The crow squawked and dropped, shaking the nasty free as he fell. His wings grew heavy, as though he were becoming a bird of stone, not flesh. With his remaining strength, he dove through an open window, into the nest of the loud men.

"Here," said the Green Falcon, laying his cards on the small table. "Read 'em and cry for shame."

Four men occupied the watchtower of the Heroes' Guild Headquarters. The Green Falcon sat playing a candlelit game of cards with a knight wearing a full suit of dark purple plate-mail. The Yellow Sun walked calmly back and forth reading a prayer book, while a tall, blue-haired warrior in azure breast plate and greaves sat in the corner, sharpening a particularly deadly looking axe.

"*Cahil kopek!*" swore the man in violet armor. "You have the luck of a demon!"

"Or his own trick deck of cards," Yellow suggested. He walked across to the window and stared out at the pouring rain. "I hope one of you is paying attention to the weather. Something bad is bound to happen . . . " The air inside the stone watchtower was stifling, smelling of ale and sweaty armor, and he needed fresh air.

The man in purple grabbed the deck of cards from Green and began sorting through them.

"*Kahrestin,* Purple!" The Green Falcon cried, trying to pull his deck out of the knight's lobstered gauntlet. "Give me those back, you poor sport!" The two struggled back and forth.

Yellow was about to break up the fight when a crow shot through the window, skipped off his shoulder, and slammed into the table, scattering cards everywhere. Before the four men could react, seven horrible insects, each nearly the size of a man's head, followed the crow in and set upon the poor bird.

"Yellow!" shouted the man in blue as he leapt from his chair in the corner. "Fire these things!"

Green became an emerald blur, snatching the belea-guered crow from the table and slashing at the insects with the curved knife in his free hand, slaying one. The Purple Paladin grabbed a second insect in his gauntlet and crushed it, puce ichor oozing from between his fingers. The third insect met its fate at the hands of the man in blue, who swatted it aside with the flat of his axe, then stomped the stunned creature.

The remaining four creatures shrieked and sizzled as they burst into spheres of pure, white flame. When the ash settled, the Yellow Sun lowered his hands. "Those were creatures twisted by magic and spawned by darkness. May they be banished back to whatever dark place gave them birth."

The man in blue took the the injured bird from the Green Falcon and examined its leg. "The crow has a message." He worked to get the strip of parchment off. The crow flapped weakly and squawked in protest.

Green stood on a chair and peered at the message over the warrior's shoulder. "'Highseekers attacked and defeated,'" he read, and looked incredulously at the others. "'Rumors true, Voshtyr credible threat. Rally forces at once, else darkness falls. Signed William A. Weatherblade, Grand Highseeker.' Holy smokes, Blue, we have to tell Guardian about this at once!"

"*Corn?*" the crow croaked softly.

"Here, little one," Green said, removing some corn from a jar by the window and placing a kernel in the bird's beak. He stroked the dying bird's feathers. "You did your job well."

The crow emitted a soft, happy *quork* and died, the sweet taste of corn on its tongue.

Chapter 32

LOOSE ENDS

In which there is Much Buildup,
and the Armies prepare to Battle

THE POWDER OF Teleportation was several years past its expiration date, so Cyrus materialized ten feet above the sand.

He hit the dune hard and rolled, coming up with his hand on where his sword hilt should have been. Seeing no immediate threat, he straightened up and surveyed the area. He was back at the Katheni encampment in the desert of Mir. Not much had changed in the time he had been gone. The tents still smoldered merrily, and the Katheni tended their wounded with consummate skill. The rain apparently hadn't reached the desert yet, but clouds still hid the sunrise.

"Cyrus!"

Cyrus didn't even bother to brace himself against the inevitable. Kris tackled him and knocked him flat into the desert sand. Inevitable also, but more enjoyable, were the kisses that came next.

"What happened to you?" Kris said between quick kisses. "I was so worried. Don't leave me like that. You missed our wedding night."

"Missed? It's still kinda dark," Cyrus said, kissing her back. "If you haven't been to sleep yet, it's still night."

When the pair finally sat up, Cyrus spoke first. "We need to leave at once. Voshtyr has formed an army. He just took over the Tower of Highseekers with it. That's where they took me. Where's your brother?"

Kris scowled, but got up. "He's with Wasara, getting the wounded ready to move. Where is Voshtyr and his army now?"

"I have no idea," Cyrus admitted, rising also. "But we need to get away from here. If you recall, he still holds a bit of a grudge against me."

Benjara approached the newlyweds. "Cyrus! Cyrus is back, everyone!" The young leopard ran to him in concern. "Are you all right, Cyrus? Let me see your—your wound is . . . it's completely healed."

"I'm fine, but we're about to be in danger," Cyrus said. "Where is Wasara?"

"Right here," Wasara said, stepping through a gathering mass of curious Katheni. "Where did you disappear to, and what's wrong?"

"Long story," Cyrus said. "The important part is that Voshtyr, the Villain I spoke of earlier, is back, and he's raised himself a dark host of some sort. They just took out the Highseekers."

"They killed a Highseeker?" Wasara said. "That's not—"

"No, not *a* Highseeker, Wasara. I mean *all* of them."

Wasara balked. "But the Highseekers have protected our northwest border for a thousand years!"

"Not anymore." Cyrus brushed sand off his unfamiliar robe and looked at the Katheni cleaning up their destroyed village. "My advice is that you take your tribe southeast, as far as you can get from the tower of Highseekers. I'm going back that way to see if I can find out what he's up to, and tell Reginald and the Guild about it."

Wasara nodded his maned head. "Sound advice. I shall inform the Council immediately. Anything we can do to help you? Perhaps Katana can—"

"You'd best keep brother with you," Kris said, standing up and moving very close to Cyrus. "He's the only one around who is competent with magic."

"Hey, now," Cyrus protested. "I'm competent, just unorthodox. Wasara, thank you for your offer. But I think the only thing you could help me with is new clothes. I'm tired of wearing this funky dress." He pulled at the white robe the Highseekers had burdened him with.

"I will keep Katana here," Wasara said. "After all, Kris now has you to protect her." He looked Cyrus's clothing up and down. "What happened to my finery, dare I ask?"

Cyrus rubbed the back of his neck. "I'm afraid they took your clothes, Haj, but I kind of need mine back."

Wasara chuckled grimly. "Very well. I'll have Benjara to fetch them. Benjara!"

The jaguar boy stepped away from tending the wounded. "Haj?"

"Go and get Cyrus his clothing and armor."

Benjara dipped his head, then sped off to get the requested items.

"Well," Wasara said, "we have precious little time to waste. If that army is as close as you say, then we must leave right away." He unslung one of his katars from his brawny back and handed it to Cyrus. "Fare thee well, Cyrus Solburg. May this keep you and my niece from harm."

"My thanks, Haj Wasara," Cyrus said, accepting the katar and bowing.

"And now we must go." Wasara turned back to his tribe. "Benjara! Oh, blast, I sent him off already. I suppose I must do my own paw-work for once. I shall inform the Council of this immediately . . . " The Haj walked off toward the remains of the tents.

Benjara returned momentarily and handed Cyrus his blue shirt and chainmail, which had both been cleaned and repaired. The shirt looked much better and less torn, and the chainmail had been burnished brightly by diligent paws. "Anything else you need, Mr. Solburg?" the jaguar boy asked.

"No," Cyrus replied, shaking Benjara's paw. "You've done more for me in the last two days than I could possibly express my gratitude for. I'll see you around, eh, Ben?"

"Upon that you may make a wager on the value of your footwear!" Benjara said, looking pleased with himself.

"I can what?"

Kris giggled. "I think he means 'bet your boots.' You still need work on your Central, Benjara."

Benjara shrugged. "Come around again, Mr. Solburg, and I'll have someone to practice on more frequently. Farewell." He smiled at the pair, then went off to find Wasara, who most likely had another errand for him to run.

Cyrus turned to Kris. "We'll need to leave right away too."

"Are you certain," Kris said, pressing herself against Cyrus and looking up into his eyes, "that we need to leave *right* now? It is still our wedding night, after all."

Cyrus's face flushed, but he put his arms around Kris's shoulders. "No, now that you mention it, I'm pretty sure that we have a few hours . . . "

"And my uncle and brother can take care of what needs done in the meantime," Kris said with a raised eyebrow. She pulled aside the flap of an undamaged and serendipitously unoccupied tent. "Here, this will do nicely." They entered together, and the author promptly pulled his nose out of their business.

The brigadier paced back and forth in the predawn grey, stomping across the churned earth at the foot of the Tower of Highseekers and slapping a rider's crop into his left hand. Large spikes of stone still protruded above the ground from the Grand Highseeker's elemental attack. One still had an unfortunate soldier impaled on it.

Two Minions repeatedly shooed a dark-haired youth dressed in black silk away from the impaled corpse, despite his protests of hunger and insistence that the soldier was already dead and it didn't matter. An orderly stood on some shattered stone, amusedly watching the Minions contest the hungry raven-man. Other Minions and Henchmen, as well as some Lesser Villains, milled around the base of the tower, patrolling for escaping Highseekers.

"Where are those fools?" the brigadier asked the orderly.

"I s'pose that depends on which fools you mean, sir," the orderly replied.

The brigadier scowled. "The fools I sent into that tower to get the Grand Highseeker! They should have been back an hour ago!"

"Well, sir, they came out with all them mages they captured, then went back in to get their leader. We ain't seen 'em since."

Just then, a lone figure limped out of the Tower doors.

"Bring that man to me," the brigadier ordered. Two soldiers brought the gibbering man before their commanding officer. "Report, soldier. Where's the rest of your platoon?"

The man laughed maniacally. He had multiple cuts on his face and hands and what looked like an acid burn on the side of his neck. "Dead! All dead and knocking on the door! Knocking on Death's door from the inside, trying to get out!" He cracked up in insane laughter.

The brigadier dropped his riding crop. "Dead? How?"

"The golem, the acid, the monkeys—oh gods, the monkeys! Get them away from me!" he screamed, and began clawing at the soldiers holding him.

The soldiers struggled to hold him, and one looked at the brigadier.

He sighed and drew a hand across his neck. The soldier nodded, turned, and put the raving man out of his misery.

"That could have gone better," said the brigadier, turning away. "Take the corpse away, and get me more volunteers."

"Sir!" shouted a sentry. "The Tower!"

The brigadier spun to look at the tower, and nearly lost his feet as the ground beneath them began to rumble and shake violently. "Retreat!" he yelled, already running away. "All men fall back!"

It took the Tower of the Highseekers almost an entire minute to slide underground. Once the entire height of the tower was below ground level, massive slabs of rock exploded from the rim of the hole and fell atop the tower, sealing it beneath the surface.

The brigadier swore a blue streak all the way back to the fortress. They had defeated the Highseekers with minimal casualties and captured many of them, but Lord Voshtyr would not be pleased with the loss of their magnificent tower.

• • •

Cyrus woke gently. His skin stung from a dozen or so shallow scratches. They weren't major, and they'd heal by mid-morning at latest.

Beside him lay his bride, purring softly. Her head rested on his chest, and he stroked it. Then he ran his hand down the beautiful, soft length of hair that Kris called her "head fur." The tawny deep yellow complemented her fur perfectly. It fell down across her shoulders, and a lock hung in front of her face, as it always did. Her gentle breathing slowly blew the lock back and forth, like a light breeze.

Cyrus smiled. He knew he'd made the right choice. She was beautiful, strong, kind, intelligent, and no slouch at pun wars, either. He kissed Kris's head.

She stirred, emitting a puzzled "Mrr?"

"Shh. Back to sleep, my love. Time enough to face the day later," he said, stroking her hair. She sighed contentedly, nuzzling her head into his shoulder. Cyrus smiled again and drifted back to sleep.

"So it has come to this, then," Richard Guardian mused.

The Guildmaster of the Guild of Heroes sat at his ironwood desk, staring at the image of the Green Falcon. Green's Token lay on the desk surface, atop four inches of paperwork regarding war reports and rumors of a dark army massing in the northwestern quarter of Centra Mundi. The grey morning light streamed though the window behind him, casting the normally dim office into a slightly less dim gloom.

"We have no choice, Green," Guardian said finally. "Muster all the Heroes you can find. Pull them from current

Quests if you have to. I will call up the civilian reserves and call on the heads of all countries to support us."

He leaned back in his chair and looked at the map of Centra Mundi on his wall. "But it sounds as if we have precious little time. The Highseekers were less than a hundred leagues from us. Voshtyr's entire army could be here in a matter of days." He looked back at Green. "Once you get hold of enough men, head north for the Tower of Highseekers. Try to secure the southern end of the Vale of Dreams."

"We'll get started on that right away, sir. How many do you think we'll need?" Green asked.

"Get a few dozen and some common soldiers. And keep in touch. After I sort all these briefs out, I may have further instructions for you."

"You've been sorting undergarments?"

"Good-bye, Green."

Green grinned, then saluted. His image disappeared.

Richard Guardian sighed. He was Guildmaster over the Guild of Heroes, the most powerful force for Good in the world. But if the report the Green Falcon and the others had delivered was true, an Arch-Villain was on the loose, rampaging about the countryside with a dark army. With war suddenly on every front and in every kingdom, the Heroes were spread thin. He shook his head. The Highseekers gone? He still couldn't believe it. And what of the Device this Voshtyr was reportedly assembling? The afternoon scouts had brought reports that the Citadel of the Kinetics had been sighted! Was this it? The end of all things? All at once Richard Guardian felt two hundred years old.

"Guardian?" said a soft voice. The wraithlike Elf named Destiny entered the room and placed a weightless hand on Guardian's shoulder. "You called for me, Richard?"

"Yes, Destiny, I did." Guardian opened a drawer and removed some boxes from it. "The Green Falcon is about to activate Clarion for the first time in two centuries."

"Clarion? Then you have chosen to fight Demonkin in the seat of his power?"

Guardian looked Destiny in her pure-white eyes. "We have no choice now. We must destroy his army. We must eliminate his supporters. We must recover the pieces of the P.L.O.T. Device. We must destroy Voshtyr Demonkin, and we must do it *now*, lest he destroy the Guild and what you saw in your vision come true."

"I can no longer see Voshtyr Demonkin," Destiny replied, closing her eyes. "His power has grown too great. I can only pray that Clarion has clearer sight than I."

The speaking horn on Guardian's desk chimed. Guardian almost smashed it in irritation, but picked it up roughly instead. "What, Saliriana? This had better be important."

"The Crimson Slash is here to see you," the Elven secretary said, "with the remnants of the Salvinsel Salamanders, as well as the Silver Fish, the Blak Spoon, the Black Viper, and the Red Death. He says they were almost wiped out by Voshtyr Demonkin," she said cheerfully. "Shall I schedule them for this afternoon after the boat christening?"

"No, I'll see them right now," Guardian said, scowling. "And cancel all my appointments for the rest of the month. Something diabolical is afoot, and I am going to stop it if it takes me 'til the End of All Things."

He hung the horn back up and turned to Destiny. "How will this end, Destiny?"

"In a very, very long final chapter," she replied. "And I fear it will not be happily ever after."

• • •

Reginald pushed open the large double-doors leading into the Guildmaster's office. He'd been there many times before, but the spaciousness of the interior still amazed him.

"Come in, Crimson," Guardian said from across the room, wheeling himself out from behind the desk. "Saliriana tells me you're with the Salamanders. How is the Black Viper doing?"

"She is well," Reginald replied, "as are the Blak Spoon and the Red Death. The Silver Fish suffered a quarrel wound, but is recovering. The health of my compatriots aside, I have dire news for you, Guildmaster."

"Have a seat, Crimson," Guardian said, indicating one of the chairs in front of his desk.

Reginald did, and proceeded to tell Guardian of the events surrounding first his own capture and fight against Voshtyr, and then the attack of the Salamanders by Voshtyr's forces.

Guardian was quiet for a few moments and drummed his fingers on his desk, obviously thinking the news over. The drumming echoed dimly in the spacious room, muffled by the carpeting and the wall hangings.

"Crimson," he said finally, "I have multiple confirmations that this Arch-Villain is at least an Epsilon-class threat. And you have had dealings with him before."

"If you count him handing me my head, then yes, I have," Reginald replied, grimacing.

"But you know his methods and his failings better than any Hero. Therefore I task you to lead the assault I am organizing against his forces."

Reginald balked. "Me, sir? Lead an army?"

"Not just any army, Crimson." Guardian turned his chair to face Reginald. "The largest army of Heroes since the Twenty-Minute War. It will take more than a handful of Heroes to defeat this Arch-Villain, and since we've not seen a Hero of Legend for over a century now, you are our best hope for catching this Voshtyr Demonkin off guard."

Reginald took a deep breath. The stunning amount of honor and responsibility Guardian had just laid on his shoulders was, well, stunning. But someone had to defeat Demonkin. And if no one else would, why, the Crimson Slash was more than equal to the task.

Reginald stood. "Very well, Guildmaster, I accept." He bowed deeply. "But if I am to gather such an army on short notice, I ask your permission to use Clarion."

Guardian nodded curtly and wheeled himself back behind his desk. "I have already sent several of the Spectrum Heroes ahead of you to scout the battlefield. I believe the Vale of Dreams would be a good place to make your stand."

"Indeed." Reginald saluted Guardian and turned to leave.

"Crimson."

"Sir?" Reginald turned back around.

"Destiny tells me that the Fate of the World may Hang in the Balance of this encounter. Should you fail, the world may fall into Darkness." Guardian looked out the window into the grey sky. "However, if you should succeed, this old man will step down as Guildmaster and let you take his place."

Reginald nodded, his chest filled with pride. "Then I shall not fail you. Farewell, Guardian."

"Farewell, Crimson Slash."

● ● ●

Reginald stood in a large dome-roofed building. The cavern-ous room was dominated by an object resembling a titanic trumpet. It was over twelve cubits high, made of solid brass, had a chair connected to it, and a specialized helmet to put on once you sat down.

Needless to say, no one took Clarion lightly.

Reginald sat down in the chair and took the helmet in his hands. He'd heard that Clarion would instantly cripple the minds of anyone who called upon her without good reason.

More magic. He shuddered, but quelched his fear. This was for the Greater Good.

He donned the helmet.

Suddenly Reginald found himself standing alone in a vast space of whiteness. No variation marked the endless plain of pure, flat, white, nothing. White flat earth, white flat sky.

"Greetings, warrior," a soft female voice said.

Reginald turned slowly, expecting to see someone behind him. There was no one.

"I am *CLARION*. Who are you?" the voice asked in a conversational tone.

"Mine name is Sir Reginald Ogleby, the Crimson Slash," Reginald answered. "There is an emergency, and—"

"And you wish to summon all Heroes to your aid," the voice of Clarion sighed. "Very well. This is my purpose, and I will fulfill it. It just . . . "

Reginald quirked an eyebrow. "Just what?"

Clarion's voice sounded disappointed and wistful. "It seems such a short time since the last Hero called upon me to summon his brothers to fight. But I suppose that it has been a long time for you. Have you learned nothing in the intervening period?"

Reginald thought a moment. "All we have learned is how to kill each other more effectively," he answered bitterly. "Swords are stronger, magic more potent and far too commonplace, and every day holds a new innovation. And here we stand, on the brink of another Twenty-Minute War."

"No," Clarion said sadly, "you will not get off so easily this time. Farewell, Crimson Slash. Your friends will hear my call. Go now."

The white light in the white world became more and more intense, and a clear and brilliant trumpet note rent the air. Clarion had sounded.

Reginald gasped and sat up.

He was back in the Clarion chamber, unharmed and still sane. Feeling an odd buzzing sensation, he reached inside his Token pouch and withdrew his personal Token, a thin silver disk with a single red bar across it. He pressed it in the center to receive the message, and Clarion's voice rang out.

"To all Heroes of all Races, who are scattered about the world, greetings. This is the Clarion call of the Guild of Heroes. Dire trouble has arisen. Voshtyr von Steinadler, also called Voshtyr Demonkin, has amassed a dark host greater than has been seen in two thousand years. This day, he has attacked and defeated the entire Council of Highseekers.

"This call goes out as a summons. Assemble south of the Vale of Dreams on Centra Mundi within the next three days, or all will be lost. To repeat, assemble south of the Vale of Dreams on Centra Mundi in three days, or all will be lost."

• • •

"So we goes in and we smashes his army," Blak said. "Wot's wrong with that plan?"

Gorbar Karvash the Blak Spoon, Jael Allyn the Black Viper, and Dante Vertigo the Red Death sat at a table in the main hall of the Guild Headquarters building.

Groups of Heroes stood about the atrium speaking with one another about the bulletin from Clarion. The hushed buzz of concerned conversation reverberated off the marble columns and domed ceiling of the Guild's interior. Even the Cheerful Elf receptionist at the front desk looked less chipper. The news they had all heard via their personal Tokens had been sobering.

"First off, Blak," Red said with a condescending tone, "we have to find said army before we can smash it. Second, this is an *Arch*-Villain we're talking about. I'd imagine he's quite smash-resistant. And if he isn't, he's liable to turn that chunk of scrap metal of yours into a bouquet of flowers. I hear he's quite the puissant magic user."

"'E's a piss-ant?" Blak scratched his head. "'Ow's that dangerous? More's the reason to smash him!"

Jael elbowed Red sharply in the ribs. "Blak, he means he's a very powerful sorcerer. And sadly, he is not likely to fear *Bonk*, mighty weapon that it is."

"But he may fear the combined might of the entire Guild of Heroes," Reginald said, pulling out a chair and sitting down with the group.

"Reginald," Jael said, "do you think we can defeat this man?"

"I have reservations," Reginald replied, "but if we can muster even half of the Guild's strength, we may have a chance. Guardian has tasked me to lead the assault. Which means that my Quest—and those long-suffering Centaurs—will have to wait until this is all over. I just hope my Vision wasn't anything urgent . . . "

"Well, I can't say I'm sorry for you, Reginald," Jael said, flashing her friend a disarming smile. "Another strong sword-arm and courageous leadership are exactly what we need right now."

Blak rose from the table and clapped Reginald on the back. Reginald looked as if he'd had all the wind knocked out of him. "Well, I's behind you, Crimson. My arm's yours, as long as ya's need it."

Jael suppressed a snicker. She'd told Blak more than once that his friendly gestures were not always received as well as he'd intended them.

"It's only a short distance to the Vale from here," Reginald said, "and the supply train would take care of any needs I would have, so I suppose I can leave Toboggan here at the Guild." He sighed deeply. "I must alert Cyrus to this. I pray he calls me soon. He hasn't his own Token yet."

"Where is he?" Jael asked.

"The Desert of Mir, probably. Unless he's finished his Quest already and is returning, in which case . . . " Reginald trailed off. "Oh, no."

Jael looked at him in alarm. "What?"

"If Cyrus is in Mir and turns southwest, he'll run right into the middle of Voshtyr's dark army!"

Cyrus ran right into the middle of Voshtyr's dark army.

As he and Kris crested the grassy hill two days' journey southwest of Mir, they were stunned by what they saw. Less than a league away, spread out across the flat plain, was a host of soldiers and beasts like nothing he or Kris had ever seen before.

Cyrus dismounted, the gentle breeze tugging at his usual blue shirt and floppy hat. He dropped to the ground and signaled Kris to do the same. Cyrus quickly led the horses to a shaded spot, then returned to Kris. They crawled into some bushes and crouched, observing the dark host.

They numbered in the tens of thousands, armored in black and bearing all manner of strange weapons. Even from that distance, Cyrus could read their standards, and this told him that almost a third of the assembled were Villains, some of them infamous. Rolf Cutthroat and his private force were there, as well as Tara Lastbreath and a large number of the Scythe of the Reaper. The banner of the Synod of Outer Darkness flapped black, crimson, and malevolent over a unit of men at least two thousand strong, a legion of the Dark Templars.

Nor were Humans the only race present. Orcs were represented by the "Horendis," "Hurendos," "Herrendous," and "Horrendous" Hordes. Each group's name was pronounced the same, but as Orcs have a penchant for misspelling things—and almost no creativity—there were at least six companies with virtually the same name.

There were a few Istaka present: the Scavengers, an elite mercenary group rumored to eat the corpses of their enemies. Some Fallen and Stumbled Elves formed archery and spellcasting divisions, backed up by a corps of Swamp Ransha, probably vengeful leftovers from the defeat at the Keep of Falling Stars.

Conspicuous in their absence were the Katheni, Avierie, and Dwarven races.

But their numbers were countered by other species. Goblins skittered and Giants lumbered about along the edges of the army. A few Greater and Lesser Basilisks slunk through the ranks. And a few Mythologicals—such as Manticores and Chimerae—stalked along in stately, hideous magnificence. Overhead flew several flights of wyverns, dense clouds of hideous gigantic insects, and a lone gryphon. In the far back, zombies limped and lurched their way along with the army's baggage train.

And off in the distance, hovering above a mountain range to the north, was what appeared to be a flying castle. Whatever magic kept that in the sky, Cyrus did not want to tangle with.

As Cyrus watched, the army began filing into and around a narrow mountain pass called the Vale of Dreams. Large though it was, and narrow as the pass was, the army moved far more rapidly than he would have believed possible.

"This can't be good," Cyrus observed. "Who are these people? What in the Terminal Twilight is going on?"

"An army this large," Kris said, "composed of such creatures . . . "

Cyrus pulled a *Token of Summoning* from his pouch, one bearing a bar of crimson across its plain silver surface. Cyrus pressed the token firmly, praying that Reg was awake.

A tiny projection of Reginald appeared, standing atop the token. "Lad, you're safe!"

"Yeah, I am. Reg, what's going on? And whose dark army is this?"

Reginald started. "You can see the army? Where are you?"

Cyrus looked about. "I'm about a league from the Vale of Dreams, north side. Reg, this army is huge! Tell me what's going on!"

"The news isn't good, lad," Reginald said. "That army belongs to Voshtyr Demonkin, the man who captured me almost a month ago. Cyrus, we activated Clarion, and Heroes have already begun to assemble here on the south side of the Vale. But we are few in number, and we were unable to come up with very many reinforcements. Guardian estimates that only half of known Heroes are available to fight. Many are either missing or fighting for their native countries in the wars Voshtyr started."

Cyrus looked back out over the mass of evil men and creatures. They were quite stately in their evil. He almost admired the uniform darkness they bore. Until he caught a whiff of long-dead flesh. Cyrus wrinkled his nose. He had less respect for armies that used zombies.

"Reg, there's some kind of flying castle to the northwest, and I think it'd take some serious magic to burn it down. But the Highseekers are gone. Demonkin took them out last night."

"I know, lad. The Highseekers succumbed before we even knew that there was an army building," Reginald said. "The Elven nations are in a state of civil war and could spare no soldiers. The Araquellae have declared neutrality, which is no surprise. And the Human Confederation only managed to come up with two thousand soldiers.

"The Solid Wall sends his regards, but cannot help us now, as he and his father are occupied fighting a siege force and protecting their peasantry. When we asked the government of Landeralt for support, they merely laughed at us for thinking they would help Heroes. Besides, they've troubles of their own. Someone broke into the Tower of the Inferno and stole the Heart of Flames, so the entire Army of Darkness™ is out trying to find it.

"The good news is we've been reinforced by two units of Dwarven infantry," Reginald said. "A squad of engineers, and one of their Thunder Runners. The League of Elementalists, after gloating over the defeat of the Highseekers for a bit, realized that they too are in danger and have sent us a unit of artillery mages. Even Old Rubic from Rubic's Academy is here, setting up magical barriers and such. Perhaps he can do something about that flying city. But that's all we have, lad. Can you spy on them for a bit, then get to the south end of the Vale of Dreams from where you are?" Reginald finished.

"I think so," Cyrus said warily. "There's an awful lot of them, but they're all focused on securing the north end of the Vale. They're moving fast, too fast for a force that size, so you be really careful, okay, Reg? They could be on top of you before you know it."

Reginald nodded. "Of course, Cyrus. Being careful is the first thing about being a Hero. My thanks for the warning, lad. I will make certain we're prepared. But whatever you do, lad, do not get yourself killed trying to help us. Don't play the hero."

Cyrus smiled. "You forget something, Reg—I *am* a Hero."

Chapter 33

DECEPTION

In which there is Betrayal and Blackmail and Voshtyr is Decidedly Evil

NIGHT FELL WITH a rapidity unusual for summerwane, as if the sun itself sensed the growing forces of Evil and wished to hurry itself away. A thousand fires burned amongst the encamped soldiers of Voshtyr's army, both in and around the Vale, throwing grotesque shadows from the beasts and lighting the darkness from within.

Just outside of this light, Cyrus and his bride crept.

They crawled as quietly as they could through the low brush growing along the mountain trail beside the Vale. It was precarious footing, and the right side dropped off three hundred feet to the valley floor below. Their goal was to make it past the enemy sentries and then on through to the southern end of the Vale of Dreams to join the Heroes who had assembled to combat Voshtyr.

They almost made it.

While crawling near the edge of the rocky Vale, Cyrus slipped. Muttering muffled curses, he grabbed onto a branch overhanging the three hundred-foot drop, and desperately scrabbled to get purchase on the rock with his boots.

He succeeded, but dislodged a chunk of rock from the cliff face in the process.

As Kris helped him up, Cyrus heard the rock smash on the valley floor. Shouts and curses rose from below. A brilliant beam of light shone up and outlined him against their cover-less surroundings. "Run!" he told Kris.

"No! Not unless you come too!"

"Kris, if you stay with me, you're going to be the cat-girl that gets killed defending the one she loves, and I can't have that!"

"But what if I'm the cat-girl who gets captured when she and her lover split up to avoid enemies?" Kris said. "Let me come with you, Cyrus!"

"We have no time for this." He pulled Kris along the rim with him, navigating by the light from below. An arrow pinged off the rock next to Cyrus's head, and he ducked. "Get to the southern end of the Vale as fast as you can. I'll be along quickly. If I don't make it, have Reg send someone after me, someone fast. The Green Falcon, if he's available. If I make it and you don't, I'll be right back to get you. Now go!"

Cyrus kissed Kris, and they broke apart, Cyrus heading south and west into the Vale, and Kris running dead south along the valley's edge.

Cyrus found a slope that would probably not be lethal to descend, and jumped. He landed on his feet and slid the rest of the way down to the grassy floor of the Vale of Dreams.

He ran as fast as he could toward the enemy army. And, considering the fact that he was a Hero, he ran fairly fast. As the walls of the valley melted into a blur, he suddenly remembered racing the Red Death on the Citrus Isles, all those many years ago. Only this time he was a Hero in his prime. And around him he sensed the presence of ley-lines.

His run terminated as he rounded a bend in the valley. There stood a squad of men in black armor. One bore a banner with a shattered hourglass on it, the banner of Malcolm Yesteryear.

Without pausing to think, Cyrus drew on the nearby Air line and spattered the men with a cascade of sheet-lightning. It lit the darkness with a brilliant flash, temporarily destroying his night vision. The stars and half-moon were not nearly enough to counter the burst of lightning.

Five of them went down immediately, their armor hardly making a clang as they hit the soft turf of the Vale's bottom. It was much greener in the valley than above it, for some reason, and had boulders and other excellent cover strewn about it, if Cyrus could but reach it.

But his bolt missed a dozen others, and three of them had magic armor, which dampened the effect. And they all had Knight Vision, so the brilliance of the flare had no more effect on them than would a dim candle. One of the three with the enchanted armor appeared to be a magic-user of some sort. He clasped his hands around the pendant hanging from his neck and began chanting. The other two rushed in between their mage and Cyrus.

Cyrus whipped a Fire line into his control and unleashed it on the three well-armored soldiers. The two in front raised their shields—both Not-A-Fake, League of Elementalists-Certified *Northern Lights* shields resistant to both Fire and Air magic—and deflected the fire. It splashed all around them, harming no one.

Then the air went cold and tingly to Cyrus's senses, as if all the energies in the air had just been stripped away from him. He reached for the Fire line again, but nothing met his grasp. The same was true for the Air line. Either all the ley-lines had disappeared, or that mage was interfering with his use of them.

Cyrus gritted his teeth, unslung Haj Wasara's katar from his back, and rushed at the center of the group.

A foolish mistake. Cyrus connected the dots a moment too late. These were the personal escort of the infamous Malcolm Yesteryear, a Villain of many years' experience. The Villain stepped from behind his troops and met Cyrus's rush with a sidestep and an outstretched foot.

Cyrus tumbled, katar spinning from his hand, and nearly struck his head on a seven-foot boulder. Leaping up, Cyrus grabbed the boulder and hurled it at the squad, crushing five of the remaining soldiers.

Then Yesteryear was on top of him. There was silver in the man's dark hair, a sign of his age, but also of his experience. No incompetent Villain lived long enough to get grey hair. The Villain threw a slash at Cyrus's chest with a wickedly glowing flamberge. Cyrus dodged backward, but the thin blade whipped faster than Cyrus could dodge. It cut through his blue shirt and chainmail, staining them with blood. Cyrus winced, but dove under Yesteryear's guard and tackled his legs.

Yesteryear went down, clubbing at Cyrus's head with the pommel of his flamberge and yelling at his soldiers.

The squad surrounded the struggling men. Two stepped forward and began kicking Cyrus in the ribs with their heavy metal boots. Cyrus grabbed a dropped sword from the ground, hamstringing one of the soldiers with it. Then the rest joined in and bludgeoned Cyrus into unconsciousness.

· · ·

"Lord Voshtyr!" A weasely looking soldier pushed aside the flap of the lavishly decorated black silk tent. "Captain Yesteryear has just captured a red-haired Hero and wants to know what to do with him."

Voshtyr, seated on a divan in the spacious black tent that served as his mobile headquarters, turned from his conversation with Roger Farella and stared at the nervous man. "The Hero in question wouldn't be about twenty years of age and have a female Katheni traveling with him, would he?"

The man nodded, stopped, then shook his head. "No, we didn't see a Katheni," he stuttered, "but he is about twenty. He was using unusually powerful magic, so we've got someone keeping a magic-suppressant spell on him."

Voshtyr sighed. "Hmm. It *might* be him. I was hoping Cyrus Solburg might pay us a visit. If a Katheni girl shows up in short order, I'll need to see the Hero. In the meantime, keep an eye on him. Heroes have a bad habit of escaping captivity. Keep him under a suppressant field at all times."

The weasely man saluted and closed the tent flap.

"Now, as I was saying," Roger continued, shuffling parchments with his blue scaled hands, "those areas are under our control, but they are unstable. We need to hold the reins very lightly there."

"Lightly? Don't you mean tightly?" Voshtyr asked, leaning back on the divan and taking a deep draft from his wine glass. "They're my territory now. I can do what I like with them."

Roger sighed. "I'm not trying to tell you otherwise, Voshtyr, but hear me out. You're not the first Villain to conquer large swaths of the countryside. The peasants are used to this sort of thing by now. What they expect is this: a Villain and his dark host sweep through their lands, burning, pillaging, and taxing whatever is left. Naturally, when a Hero shows up, they unite behind him and drive the Villain from their lands."

"They can't do that if I keep a tight hold on them," Voshtyr replied, irritated. "My father always said that peasants can be a nuisance unless you keep them on a short leash."

"And what exactly happened to your father?" Roger countered. "Murdered by . . . peasants, wasn't he? Dragged from his bed and stabbed to death by a mob weary of the heavy tax burden laid on them by his, er, unique management style. Besides, you would need to devote at least a portion of your army to suppression of revolts if you did it your way. And you can't afford to have your army off suppressing rebellion— you will need the entire force with you if you plan to defeat Emperor Vladimir Xanathosson."

Voshtyr scowled and set down his glass. "How do you expect me to manage my new peasants and still collect revenue at the same time, hmm? You just don't think these things through, do you?"

Roger stood from his soft, black-velvet chair and collected his pale yellow robe. "Voshtyr, what is the point of having an advisor if you refuse to listen to him?"

Voshtyr sighed. "Roger, my dear fish, Villains, as a rule, do not listen to advisors. My father certainly *never* listened to his advisors."

"Which is why very few Villains succeed at their diabolical plots," Roger said pointedly. "If you don't need my help, you may as well say so!" He began to float a few inches off the floor, and struggled to walk toward the door, an angry and determined expression on his face. Since his feet were not actually touching the stone, it was more difficult than it should have been.

"My apologies, Roger," Voshtyr said. "Please . . . sit down. Tell me your plan. Only then will I will judge its worth." As

Roger sat back down, Voshtyr continued. "I promise not to say anything until you finish."

A thin smile crossed Roger's scaled, blue face. "All right, then. If you wish to succeed where others have failed, here is what you do. Traditionally, once a Villain controls a region, he also takes control of its economy. *Do not do that.* No matter how much you study, and I know that you have precious little time for studying these days, you cannot possibly know what people will need or want at all times. It is better to leave the economy alone and let the market decide that."

Roger stroked an imaginary mustache. "Whatever people are willing to pay, they will pay, and merchants will only sell when they can gain from it. Prices and supply of wanted goods will adjust themselves, solving any supply line problems we might encounter. Even our disgusting friend Torval knows this principle."

"Speaking of our greedy friend, where is he?" Voshtyr asked, sitting up. "I haven't seen him for a few days."

Roger rolled his eyes. "He's off attending one of those conferences for Purveyors of Evil Products."

"Oh, a PEP talk," Voshtyr said with a chuckle, and slouched back onto his divan.

Roger scowled, but continued. "The next thing is taxes. If there is one thing that all peasants universally despise, it is the tax collector. Overburdening peasants with taxes takes away the little money that they could otherwise spend. If an area has no money to spend, few or no merchants will visit there, making the situation and poverty worse.

"The solution is this: do not tax individual peasants. Let them think they are keeping their money. Instead, impose a mandatory tax on merchants, say perhaps 10 or 15 percent of all sales. They will pay this by increasing the price of their goods by that same percentage. The peasants still pay their taxes, but unwittingly, when they buy things. This removes the visible agent of tax collecting, and if you do that . . . "

Voshtyr began clapping softly, an evil and amused expression on his face. "My, my, Roger. That is brilliant. Do you know, I believe you are more of a Villain than I am. If I do as you suggest, the people will see me as more of a hero than any real Hero ever was. I applaud."

"Thank you," Roger said, inclining his head. "I believe that—"

"Lord Voshtyr!" Another soldier, this one clad in chainmail, hauberk, and steel helm, poked his head in the tent-flap. "Captain Renaldo and his company have captured a female Katheni. What shall we do with her?"

Voshtyr leapt from his chair, a malicious grin splitting his visage. "Excellent, excellent. Bind her, while I pay a visit to our captured Hero. Whatever you do, make sure that *no one* touches the girl, understand?" He stared into the soldier's eyes, his own flaming red. "If someone does, it will be the last pleasure they ever experience. Now, go!"

The soldier backpedaled and ran for the far south side of the camp.

Voshtyr turned back to Roger. "I'm sorry, old friend, but your worthy idea must wait until I've had a little . . . chat with our young Hero."

Cyrus woke to the gentle tingle of healing magic. Opening his eyes, he saw that he was outside, and it was either twilight or sunrise. A balding priest in red and silver robes gently traced Cyrus's wounds with a thin reed wand.

"Oh, look," the priest said, "the Hero is awake. Ikarna, go get the General." A weasely looking soldier nodded and walked over to a large black silk tent.

Cyrus looked about more carefully. He sat in the dirt, a pair of manacles on his wrists, in the midst of the tents of the dark army. He was hemmed in on every side by the black tents of his enemies. The camp smelled of roast mutton, dung, body odor, and just a hint of putrefying flesh. Dawn's rosy fingers began to creep over the horizon, and Cyrus realized that he had been unconscious for almost the entire night. He sighed. He was well and truly captured.

Then he noticed the clawed helix-and-eye design on the sleeve of the man who had been healing him. This was no priest—he was a member of the Synod of Outer Darkness.

Cyrus gritted his teeth. "Who is this 'General'?" he forced himself to ask.

"Oh, I can't say," said the false priest, again leaning over Cyrus with his wand. "But I dare say you'll soon find out."

"Why are you healing me?"

"General's orders. I believe he has some plan for you which involves you *not* looking like you've just been kicked unconscious. Actually, you can ask him why. Here he is now."

Cyrus craned his neck toward the large black tent nearby. A man had stepped out and stood staring at Cyrus. He was a tall, handsome, and athletic man with raven hair, pointed ears, and softly glowing green eyes. Remembering the description Reginald had given him, Cyrus knew at once this must be Voshtyr.

"Ah, the notorious Cyrus Solburg, destroyer of ley-lines. The young man who has caused me so much trouble. You are very difficult to catch up with, you know," Voshtyr said pleasantly. "Greetings, and welcome to my humble camp." He gestured at the surrounding tents and men, then came around to stand in front of Cyrus. "I do hope my men have not put you through too much suffering?"

"Not unless you count a dozen boots to the head as too much," Cyrus muttered.

"Good, good," Voshtyr replied, smiling.

The false priest chuckled, then stowed his wand and pushed his way past a grizzled Istaka and a burly, grey-skinned Orc.

The Istaka, one of the wolf-people native to Centra Mundi, probably belonged to the Scavenvers, as he bore the distinctive scarring on his ears from their initiation ritual. The Orc had a shoulder tattoo of a serpent swallowing a sword and carried a leaf-bladed spear. He also bore a terrible grimace, one that looked like a mix between terminal irritation and constipation.

A Manticore shrieked behind them, quickly followed by the sounds of heavy blows against flesh. Apparently not all of the Mythologicals in Voshtyr's army were completely trained.

"Now that you are awake," Voshtyr said to Cyrus, "I have a small business proposal for you."

Cyrus spat on the ground. "Not bloody likely."

Voshtyr *tsked*. "Now, now, I was hoping you would at least listen to what I had to say. I suppose I overestimated your intelligence. Now, what I had in mind was this: I need you to send a message to your Hero friends over on the other side of this valley and tell them that we—and by 'we' I mean I and my army—have turned tail and run further north. In return, I shall forgive you for setting the Crimson Slash free and you can keep your life. You may even have a rank here in my army. There's even some special missions I would have you do, with great rewards. Do we have an accord?"

"*Siktir, pic.*"

Voshtyr frowned slightly. "Very well, I suppose you have every reason to be stubborn. After all, these are your friends we are talking about." The half-demon took the leaf-bladed spear from the grey-skinned Orc behind him and began paring his perfect fingernails with it. "I understand your reluctance. But there comes a time when a man must choose his loyalties carefully, and your time has just arrived. Who would you rather protect, Cyrus: your friends . . . or your wife? Galbrax, bring the girl here."

Cyrus tried to rise from the ground, but was shoved down by the Istaka, who growled menacingly in his ear.

Voshtyr chuckled softly. "My, my, Cyrus, you didn't really think you could defy me and suffer no consequences, did you?"

A second Orc approached, carrying a struggling Katheni prisoner with a burlap sack over her head. The Orc unceremoniously dumped the prisoner on the ground and ripped the sack away. Kris, gag in mouth, winced against the sunlight, tears matting the fur beneath her eyes.

"Kris!" Cyrus lurched forward in his bonds, but was pushed back by the point of Voshtyr's spear. "You monster! She has nothing to do with this!"

"Oh, yes, she does," Voshtyr said. "She has a very intimate connection to you and can be thus used as leverage quite easily."

"You don't know the meaning of the word mercy, do you?" Cyrus said, gritting his teeth.

"Mercy. Noun. Compassionate or kindly forbearance shown to an offender, enemy, or other person in one's power," Voshtyr said, smiling. "Synonyms: compassion, pity, and benevolence. I know the meaning, Solburg. I just choose not to show any."

The Villain's smile disappeared. "Now, let us revisit my proposal. You *will* contact your friends, you *will* tell them my army is gone, and you *will* be convincing, or I *will* turn this pretty girl over to my men to have a bit of fun with."

Kris sobbed and emitted a gagged scream as the Orc laughed and began fondling her.

"Stop it!" Cyrus yelled, cutting himself on Voshtyr's spear point as he half-lunged at the Orc and fell over onto his side. Apparently these manacles had been built specifically to restrain Heroes.

"Yes, Galbrax, stop that," Voshtyr said. He threw a bolt of pure darkness at the Orc's head, causing it to explode violently and spatter both prisoners with gore. The body collapsed at Kris's feet. Voshtyr kicked it. "I didn't give you permission to do anything. Yet." He pushed Cyrus upright with his soft, black boot. "Well, Solburg? The choice is yours. But I warn you, Galbrax was not—and even in his current condition is still not—the most unsavory creature in my army."

Kris and Cyrus looked at one another. Cyrus's resolve melted in the face of the pleading in Kris's eyes. "I . . . " His voice broke as he said the words, so low that he could barely be heard. "I'll do it."

Reginald reached into his pocket and removed his personal Token. When he activated the silvery disk, it stopped buzzing and Cyrus stood before him.

"Cyrus!" Reg exclaimed. "We were expecting you last night, but didn't dare mount a rescue without knowing where the enemy was. How are you, lad?"

"I'm fine, Reg," Cyrus replied. "Listen, I need you to tell this to whoever is in charge of your army. The big army I mentioned yesterday is gone. They packed back up and headed north."

Jael, watching over Reginald's shoulder, looked shocked. "What? How? Why?"

"The army. By walking, crawling, flying, and whatever the nasty things do. And I have no idea. Maybe they thought the north end of the Vale would be too difficult to hold."

Reginald rode at the head of an impressively large force of Heroes and common soldiers. Banners streamed in the morning breeze, pennants of Heroes from the Albino Albatross to the Zinc Zeromancer. The Heroes rode alongside their cohorts and apprentices, staring courageously ahead, as if determined to meet and defeat the threat head-on. The rolling grassy hills rang with the battle songs of several nations, all blending into a cacophonous but inspiring melody.

Rumbling along in the rear was a giant iron box atop rolling metal bands. The box was as wide as two freight wagons side by side, and almost twice as long. It was a Thunder Runner, one of the few mechanical innovations to come out of the People's Republic of the Underground since the Dwarves had abandoned monarchy in favor of socialism. It sported a gigantic ballista mounted on a rotating pedestal on its top, loaded and fired from the inside to protect the Dwarven team that operated it.

"Well, that would be me, lad. It seems I'm in charge of this force. If the enemy is gone, then we can take the Vale without a fight," Reginald concluded. "The nearest defensible place they could move a force that size to would be Seacoast Keep, and it would take them a year to breach the defenses there should they try to take it. We should be able to gather a sufficient force to defeat them in that length of time."

"No, Reg, I w—" Cyrus's image winced. "I would think, considering the political climate, that you might still have some

difficulty raising that many troops. But the valley—" again, a
wince, "is perfectly safe. I'll see you on the other side."

Reginald looked at Cyrus's flickering image. "Are you all
right, lad? You don't sound right."

Cyrus sighed. "I'm fine, Reg. Just tired. And sore from
sleeping on this rough ground."

Reginald cut the communication and slipped the token
back into his pocket. "Did he sound all right to you?"

"He seemed fine to me," Jael answered. "He said he was
tired. He probably didn't get any sleep last night, watching
the army move out. Why?"

"I just have a bad feeling about it, that's all," Reginald
said with a shrug. "If Cyrus was under duress, he would have
given me the MUD signal. It is probably nothing. Where is
General Guardian? Someone should probably tell him of the
change of plans."

MUD. Man Under Duress. This is the standard signal for
one Hero to give another when being forced to say something
against his will. The details on MUD procedure can be found
in Melvin Bryath's *Complete Guide to Heroics, Volume VIII*,
chapter 18, paragraphs i-xvi. But just in case the reader does
not have Bryath's exhaustive reference works available, the
author will provide a synopsis of this important procedure.

If a Hero is captured by his foes and forced to relay an
incorrect or outright false message to a fellow Hero, MUD
procedure is as follows. The phrase "or my name is mud" must
be convincingly worked into the message so as not to arouse
suspicion in the minds of his or her captors. The recipient of
a MUD message must not react abnormally during the communication, but upon termination of the message must cer-

tainly *not* do what he or she has just been told, and will instead mount a rescue operation, preferably with Guild assistance.

Reginald did not know it, but Cyrus had never read Volume VIII. His reading had ended at Volume VII, which contains interesting and helpful methods for conversing with Villains, but nothing on what to do if captured by one.

With that, the Heroes began marching directly into a trap.

Chapter 34

EPIC

*In which the forces of Light and Darkness Clash,
and One of them Loses*

CYRUS FELL, COVERING his head with his arms to ward off more kicks.

"That will suffice," Voshtyr said to the two guards who had been administering the beating. "That is all he deserved."

"Deserved?" croaked Cyrus.

"Yes, deserved," Voshtyr replied. "For freeing the Crimson Slash when I had him in my grasp."

Cyrus coughed, attempting to sit up. "But you said—"

"The agreement changed, remember? At first, I offered you forgiveness, freedom, and possible acceptance in my army," Voshtyr said, eyes glowing malevolently. "But no, my army was not good enough for you. You had to be Heroic and try to defend your friends. Unfortunately, that also meant defying me. And I am not one to be defied lightly, Solburg. Thus, the deal changed. Now all you get for the service of betraying your friends is the promise that my men will not harm your pretty kitty out there. No freedom, no rank, no forgiveness. And this . . . " Voshtyr said, kicking Cyrus in the stomach . . . "is for calling me a *pic.*"

With that, Voshtyr left Cyrus in the tender care of two surly guards: a one-eyed man and an Orc with a sword-swallowing serpent tattooed on his hairy green shoulder.

Kris fared better. She was thrown into a dim black tent and left entirely alone, save for an old woman who sat there watching the Katheni girl intently. Kris rose from rug the soldiers had thrown her on and explored the tent.

It was empty. Nothing hung from the black walls and there was no furniture, save for the low stool on which the old woman sat. The dirt floor bore no marks of having been dug in recently. She pushed open the front tent flap, only to have an Istaka snarl in her face, scaring her backward into the tent again.

So she sat, waiting for something else to happen. And still the old woman stared. Finally, Kris could not stand the stare any longer. "What do you want, crone?"

"To see," the woman said in an ancient, creaky voice. "To see your hand. Come here, child. I will not harm you."

Kris rose from the soiled rug on which she had been seated and walked to where the old woman sat. She extended her soft-furred arm, paw up, for the ancient woman's inspection.

After a moment's scrutiny, the woman gasped and sat straight up. "No, it cannot be! Master Voshtyr would not be such a fool. I must have read it wrong. Child, your hand again, please."

Kris obliged again, and this time the woman slumped on her stool. "It is. How wonderful and terrible. To think that I would meet the Huntress herself. My apologies to you on behalf of master Voshtyr, mistress. He could not have known."

"What?" Kris was severely confused. "Mistress? Huntress? Of what are you speaking?"

"You, mistress. You are the Huntress of the Prophecy, which means that poor fool Voshtyr will be the cause of the End." She cackled like a demented hen. "I apologize, mistress, but I must begone." The woman slipped from the tent.

Kris tried to follow, but was snarled at by the Istaka once more. This time she was not intimidated. "Who was that woman?"

The wolf shrugged. "Some harmless, demented woman. Lord Voshtyr found her about to be burned at the stake for witchcraft. Seriously, what is this world coming to when people execute you for a little curse that causes a breakout of Reaper's Plague?"

Kris frowned. "Harmless? Well, have a nice time preventing my escape. My mate will be along to slay you shortly."

"Shut your face and get back in the tent."

Kris stalked back into the tent and sat down on the abandoned stool. Outside, she could hear Voshtyr's army gearing up to move to war.

The army of Heroes marched down the narrow valley demarcated on one side by the Mountains of the Morning and on the other by the North Shore range. The Vale of Dreams was so named because tradition held that prophetic visions could be obtained by sleeping in it.

On this morning the valley was still and quiet. Not a breath of air stirred the foliage growing along its steep walls, not a bird disturbed the silence. Some of the soldiers began to grow uneasy at the silence, but they were reined in by the Heroes with them.

Jael placed a hand on Reginald's arm. "What is it, Reginald? Are you still worried about Cyrus? He said he's at the other end of the Vale. You'll see him soon."

"It isn't that, Jael. I just have this terrible sense of wrongness." Reginald looked about himself. "I am worried for the lad, yes, but more for the army we ride with."

"Is that a Sense of Wrongness, or just a sense of wrongness?" Jael asked.

Reginald scratched his helmet, then removed the helmet and scratched his head. "Without the capitals, I think. I'm no magic-user and have no skill with such things. But if something bad does happen, then it must have been the former. The whole setup of this battle gives me chills."

Cyrus knelt in a black tent, manacles around his wrists and ankles, bleeding from cuts on his head, arms, and chest. Voshtyr and his two Henchmen had beaten him until they tired, then had chained him to an iron stake.

If it had been a regular dirt floor, it would have been easy to pull the stake out and escape. But this was some kind of liquefied stone, which had then been hardened around the stake. Two guards waited outside. He could see them through the partially open tent flaps. One was the same burly Orc with the tattoo. The other was a one-eyed Human.

Cyrus's thoughts ran wild with fear for Kris. Had Voshtyr changed the agreement again? Had Cyrus betrayed the Heroes *and* lost Kris? Someone pushed aside the tent flap, and Cyrus nearly jumped out of his lacerated skin.

He blinked against the flood of sunlight, but then he saw who it was. Disgusted, he turned his head away. He almost hadn't recognized her.

Clad in full Villain gear, including black shirt and rose-red cape, stood Lydia Weatherblade—formerly the White Tiger. She stepped inside the tent. Her armor was an oddity. Though she wore normal greaves, no metal protected her torso, save for a shaped piece of metal across her bosom.

Originating in the Eastern Islands, the Breastsplate is a singularly useless piece of armor. Indeed, it is good for nothing more than putting a female warrior's décolletage on display. Despite its impracticality, it remains popular among Villains for its fashionable appearance and usefulness in distracting male Heroes.

"Cyrus? Oh, Demons and Demigods, they really hurt you, didn't they?" Lydia knelt next to her childhood friend.

"Not as much as you have," Cyrus said, looking at the ground. "Reg told me what you did, Miss Weatherblade."

Lydia winced. "It was . . . complicated, Cy. I couldn't have helped Crimson if I'd stayed. But now I can help you! I have the key to your manacles here. I can let you go if you promise to stay here and not join the Heroes."

"Free to stay put? Excellent," Cyrus said in a monotone, still not looking at the turncoat girl. "No. Get away from me, Miss Weatherblade. I want nothing to do with you."

"What?" Lydia balked. "You can't mean that, Cy. You can trust me!" Cyrus hadn't made eye contact even once. "Look at my face when I'm talking to you!"

"Which one?" Cyrus spat, meeting her eyes with an ice-cold glare. "I told you, Miss Weatherblade, I want nothing to do with you. I found someone who loves me and would never betray me no matter the circumstances. Now get away from me."

Lydia put a hand on Cyrus's cheek. "Cy . . . you're hurting me. Why won't you say my name?"

"Because Beelzebub is already taken," Cyrus said, turning his back to the girl.

Lydia stood, tears in her eyes, and yelled at Cyrus. "Fine! Die here, see what I care! You idiot Heroes and your honor, your morals, you make me sick! Seems to me you've just betrayed all the Heroes, you hypocrite. At least I hurt only one."

Cyrus winced. That was low. But he wasn't going to give Lydia the satisfaction of a response.

"When Voshtyr finally takes the world," Lydia shouted, "I hope he wipes you all out, you hear me? And then I can return and be a Hero, without your ridiculous names, your inane narrations, and your tired traditions. I'll be my own thing!"

"Nope," Cyrus said, "you're too far gone into Villainy. Listen to yourself. Only true Villains monologue."

Lydia slapped Cyrus. The sharp *crack* of palm across face filled the tent. Cyrus just went back to staring at the dirt. Lydia stood for a moment, then fled the tent.

Less than an hour later, Voshtyr's dark army had moved out, leaving behind only a few guards for their supplies and prisoners. Cyrus, still manacled to the stake inside the tent, knelt silently bleeding, his mind buried beneath a sea of worry and pain. He reached out with his mind, but still the ley-lines were gone. Perhaps he'd broken all of them in the area.

When did everything go so wrong? he wondered. *The Hero is supposed to complete his Quest, get the girl, and ride off to live happily ever after. And now all this has happened. I . . . I can't do this. I can't do anything at all.*

Cyrus came to the stark realization that he was completely powerless, powerless and alone, not knowing whether or not Kris was well or even still alive. Tears began flowing from Cyrus's eyes, dripping down onto the packed dirt of the tent floor. *When did it go wrong, and why? Why all this?*

When people are comfortable, they don't feel a need for a Creator. The priest's words rang out in Cyrus's mind once again. Suddenly he was back in the vanished cathedral, talking with the priest late at night. *It's only when things go wrong, or when they are suffering, that they cry out to Him.*

Cyrus sagged to the ground, neck bent and head bowed, tears flowing down his battered face. *Okay, okay. You got me, I surrender,* he prayed. *Whoever or whatever you are, I give in. I've fought you long enough. Maybe Mom was right, maybe you are there for me, I don't know. But I do know that I can't do this on my own. I can take a beating, I could even die, but I can't let anything happen to Kris. Please, I beg you: let me get her out of here.*

Cyrus's hand warmed slightly, as if sunlight had filtered through the tent walls. He looked down at his hand. A tendril of gentle fire worked its way down his right index finger and into the palm of his hand, where it flickered, then gained strength. Cyrus's eyes widened. It couldn't be . . . He smiled. The ley-lines were back. *All right, Creator. Let's do this.*

Of the two guards outside, Cyrus determined that the Orc was the greater threat, as the Human had addressed him as a Villain. To maximize the potential of the ley-lines in his grasp, Cyrus waited until the one-eyed guard had to go relieve himself. When the common soldier left to do his business,

Cyrus rose to his full height, broke a Fire line, and absorbed as much of it as he could.

For a second, his world was on fire. Then he released it, leveling and burning a hundred foot diameter circle around him.

The tent vanished in a whoosh. The chains around his legs and arms melted to slag. Unfortunately, his clothes vaporized as well. The magic-dampening wards that had supposedly been containing Cyrus's magic burned up in a flash. The Orc outside died immediately, weapon and armor consumed just as fast as flesh and bone. Cyrus had counted on that, which was why he had let the other guard live for a few moments more.

As the second guard came rushing back toward the conflagration, Cyrus scooped up a handful of blackened dirt. The guard, having not been anticipating an attack by a stark-naked Hero, swung his blade at Cyrus only halfheartedly.

Suddenly he had gritty blackness in his eye. He never got time to wipe it out.

Cyrus slammed his arm into the man's throat, flipped him off of his feet and onto his face, and slammed his foot into the center of the man's neck. The neck snapped. Cyrus picked up the man's curved sword and set off to find Kris.

And some clothes.

The first explosion went off with no warning whatsoever. Fire blossomed all around the Heroes and their men in the pass, killing several.

The next magical volley was more accurate and was accompanied by two flights of arrows. The Heroes could now see Villains all along the high edges of the narrow valley. They poured volleys of arrows and magic into the valley, raining destruction upon the unsuspecting Heroes.

A trap. A trap of such scope it was hardly believable.

Rallying, the Heroes and their remaining men returned fire, firing Fire, arrows, and fire arrows up at their attackers. But their short-lived retaliation came to an abrupt halt when the wyverns arrived.

With shrieks of animal glee, the scaled creatures dropped jars full of chemicals, acids, and assorted alchemic atrocities on the harried and hapless Heroes.

Nearly all the common soldiers died within the first few minutes. Any Hero attempting to leap out of the Vale, with or without aid of a standard-issue ten-foot-pole, soon became overwhelmed by the multitudinous Villains clustered around the valley's edge.

Worse still was the shadow cast over the Vale by a flying fortress, nay, an entire flying city, which floated in the air a mile distant from the battle as if watching the slaughter.

Roger Farella stood on a balcony of the floating city, leaning over the railing and watching the slaughter of the Heroes.

Beside him stood Voshtyr and Keltar, a Kinetic.

Keltar wore the same black robe he'd worn when visiting Voshtyr's fortress. The sunlight gleamed off his white hair and was probably burning his pale white skin. The albino Elf scanned the battle in the vale as if recording every detail, his hands gripping the railing with an excessively strong grasp.

The half-demon pointed out particularly impressive features of his well-planned ambush to the Kinetic. Keltar nodded slowly, his colorless eyes soaking up the carnage.

"And as you can see, the Heroes will soon be no more," Voshtyr said, running his flesh hand along the smooth white marble of the railing. "If this demonstration does not impress your Council, I doubt anything will."

The three stood on a projecting balcony of the great Citadel of the Kinetics, which floated menacingly in the sky less than a mile from the Vale of Dreams. The Citadel hovered above the ground, casting a shadow across the landscape far below. The spired towers and parapets of the flying city absorbed the morning sunlight, turning a dull and depressing grey. The tiles of the balcony were cracked and weatherworn, and a small statue of a seraph decorated one corner. The wind this high up was quite stiff. Voshtyr's cloak flapped wildly about him.

"You are indeed a man of cunning, Demonkin," Keltar replied softly, glancing at Voshtyr. "My trust in you seems well placed. But disturb me not with conversation. The entire Council watches this through my eyes." The pale Elf turned his gaze back to the massacre.

Voshtyr shrugged and turned to the Araquellus who was his accountant. "Well, Roger, it seems as if all our planning is finally paying off."

Roger covered his mouth with a light blue handkerchief. "Give me no credit for this, Voshtyr. I handle the accounts. Atrocities are your department."

At that moment, a massive fireball erupted a few miles away, away from the battle. Both half-demon and Araquellus stared at the column of smoke rising from the center of Voshtyr's near-deserted base camp. "What in the Nine Hells was that?" Roger said.

"Curse that Hero!" Voshtyr said, clenching his metal hand. "Causing trouble again, I see. You would think that putting guards on him and binding him with anti-magic wards and *HeroHolder* chains would suffice."

"You left Solburg at the camp?" Roger exclaimed, stunned. "That boy has all the earmarks of being a genuine Protagonist, Voshtyr—and you left him unattended?"

Voshtyr glanced at Keltar. Thankfully, the albino Elf remained absorbed in the happenings in the Vale. "He was done, Roger. I had him bound securely, with his wife as blackmail should he attempt escape. Nothing could have gone wrong."

"It just *did*," Roger spat, extending the blade ridges along his arms. "Now I have to clean up another of your messes. Stay here. Assure the Kinetics that everything is going according to plan. I will recapture our young Hero."

Voshtyr nodded. "Good luck, old friend."

"Save it. I have work to do," Roger said with a scowl, and leapt into the air. He twisted in the sky until he found an air current, and shot along it toward the smoldering camp.

Cyrus found clothes easily enough, and Kris was not far. Cutting down the guards without a second thought, he burst into the tent where they held her.

Kris jumped up immediately. "What took you so long?" she asked, kissing him. "Were you a little tied up?"

"Yeah, I could stake my life on it. Come on, no more bad puns. We need to get going."

"Very well, we'll consider it a tie."

Cyrus groaned from pain both physical and mental. "You're just bound to keep that up, aren't you?" He led the way out, slaughtering two more guards who had come to investigate the explosion. "Hey," he said to Kris, "you didn't happen to see where Voshtyr put my stuff, did you?"

"Third tent to the right," Kris answered, pointing at a fire-damaged tent. "I sure rope it's in there."

"Cord you *please* stop that?" Cyrus asked, digging through the remnants of tent. Finding his bag, he withdrew the Crimson Slash's token and pressed it repeatedly.

Nothing happened. Either Reginald was simply not answering or it was too late.

Cyrus threw the token back into the bag. "*Kahrestin*! He's not responding! Kris, we have to get to the Vale and help Reg!"

Kris nodded, picking up her shortsword and buckler from the pile of confiscated gear. She growled softly. "Let's go and show these Villains what a true Hero can do."

They exited the tent and sprinted down the road the way the army had gone.

With the crash of shattering stone and a rush of dust, something slammed into the ground between the pair and the Vale. When the dust settled, Cyrus saw that it was an Araquellus.

The blue-scaled man rose slowly from his landing on his feet and a hand, the organic blade ridges that marked his kind extending from the sides of his arms. "Solburg," he said.

Cyrus lifted the kora, the guard's curved blade. "Yeah, I'm Solburg. Get out of my way, Araquellus. I've got bigger fish to fry."

The Araquellus shook his head. "A racist pun, how witty. I dislike you already. But I can't let you into the Vale."

"Racist? Wait, that's not what I—"

The Araquellus sped toward Cyrus, fists flying and blades glistening.

• • •

The Yellow Sun raised his arms to the sky. A magical shield bubbled upward and began deflecting the rain of death falling from the Villains atop the cliffs. His shield stemmed the slaughter somewhat, and the bombardment slackened. The Heroes gained hope at the respite, but soon lost it again.

The reanimated dead of Voshtyr's army came pouring down the glade toward the Heroes, dropping chunks of flesh and tainting the air with their putrefied stench. The zombies attacked the men in the Vale with a fearlessness that only those already dead can muster.

The first Heroes they encountered were a purple-clad knight and a blue-haired giant. The Purple Paladin and the Blue Shock. They hacked at the reanimated corpses with a fury.

"Blue," the Purple Paladin shouted over the screams of his comrades and the incessant moaning of the zombies, "I think we're going to get buried in the undead!"

"I wouldn't worry," Blue replied, his fantastic double-bladed axe crackling with electricity. He swiped at a shambling corpse and cleft it in twain. On the backstroke, he released the stored energy and blasted a half-dozen of the zombies away. "We seem to be doing all right now that they've stopped shooting at us. That makes seventeen, Purple."

Purple swung his mighty blade in a horizontal arc, clearing a swath around the two. "You can't count zombies, Blue! They're already dead!"

The Blue Shock fricasseed another two corpses with a close-range spray of lightning, then decapitated a third. "Twenty. Yes, you can. If they move, and they're hostile, they count."

"Fine!" The Purple Paladin bellowed, slamming his blade down on the ground. A brilliant wave of violet violence slammed into the undead horde. It threw zombies in every direction, clearing a path down the center. "That makes twenty-eight!"

"You and your ranged attacks," Blue griped good-naturedly. "Shall we use that path you conveniently carved?"

"Of course," Purple replied, grinning fiercely.

The two dashed down the gap in the zombified first wave, toward the main force, sword and axe flashing in the morning sun.

Reginald vaulted up to the edge of the Vale, blade glowing red, and lashed out in all directions.

"The Hero struck at the cowardly Villains who had ambushed him and his brethren! He smote left and right with his mighty sword, slaying many. But his foes were too numerous and pushed the Hero back into the Vaaaaaaale!" he bellowed as he fell from the cliff's edge. He dropped back into the Vale of Dreams, crashing down the rocky slope and denting his breastplate yet again. He was going to have to stop fooling around and inform Guardian that this was indeed a trap.

"That was clever, Crimson," the Green Falcon said with a chuckle as he dashed by.

"I defy you to do better!"

Green shrugged, spinning his twin knives around in blurry circles. "Oh, I can. I just can't jump that high. If you'll pitch me up there, I'll do more damage than you could possibly imagine."

"Fie! I doubt it. Thou art a thief and a charlatan, not a warrior."

"I am not a charlatan! I know exactly what I'm doing!"

Reginald quirked an eyebrow. "But you are a thief . . . "

"Thieving is not my only trade, Crimson," Green said, pointing one of his knives at Reginald's face. "Now are you going to give me a boost or what?"

"Very well," Reginald said, grabbing Green by the back of his green doublet. "Cause some havoc for me, Green." With that, he threw the thief into the air.

"Green *Falcon!*" Green shouted, emerald energy bursting from the air around him as he shot upwards.

He landed with incredible grace right in the center of a large group of Villains. Without pausing, he began his attack, his two blades moving faster than even the Villains could follow.

The two knives in question were *Universality of Insanity* and *Irrelevance of Acquisition.* The blades were not terribly large. Indeed, their names were longer than the blades themselves. Nevertheless, the two knives were fearsome in the hands of a skilled Hero. Green severed bowstrings, hamstrung Villains, shredded spellbooks, and killed five men before the Villains had time to react.

But react they did, quickly penning him in with a wall of spears. The supersonic Hero backpedaled, ducking under multiple thrusts and spinning away from several more, but took one in the back and one in the shoulder.

One side of the pointy perimeter broke as blood spattered and Villains went down screaming. A red blur shot in and out of their ranks at a speed that nearly matched the Green Falcon's, leaving carnage in its wake.

"Red Death!" Green shouted to the blur. He whittled a foeman's spear down to nothing in less than a second and planted *Universality of Insanity* squarely into the soldier's eye socket. "Where in the Vaguely Defined Territories have you been? I almost finished this battle by myself!"

Dante Vertigo, the Red Death, stopped abruptly, the two men nearest him slumping with mortal wounds. "You? Don't make me laugh, Green. I'm glad you saved me some. What's your count?"

"Eh, I've been destroying equipment, mostly, so only forty-four."

Red shook his head, parried an attack from behind, and sliced his opponent into eight pieces with one liquid motion. "I think you're slipping, Green. Tell you what, if you break two hundred, I'll buy the ale tonight."

"Sure, and if you break *three* hundred," Green said, leaping backward, landing on and vaulting off a surprised Villain's shoulders, "I'll see what I can do about stealing you a crystallized Speed Demon for that sword of yours." With nine deft strokes, the thief cut all the straps holding the Villain's armor on, and it fell to the ground with a clang. "Deal?"

"Deal."

Forty-five seconds later, the two hasty Heroes leapt back into the Vale to meet up with their companions. The Villains still alive along that section of the cliffs stared about in sheer disbelief. The two Heroes had slain over twenty men and destroyed thousands of gold pieces worth of equipment in under a minute.

● ● ●

Cyrus parried the Araquellus's initial rush and ducked under two more vicious cuts. The air whistled over his blades as he struck repeatedly at Cyrus.

Several tents still smoldered from Cyrus's explosive escape. Thankfully all of Voshtyr's soldiers were otherwise occupied, and no one had come back to find out why the camp was on fire.

"*Kahrestin!*" Cyrus swore as a cut landed across the bridge of his nose. This Araquellus was faster and more skilled than any Villain he had ever encountered. Cyrus struck back with his kora, but the Araquellus crossed his blue arms, and the curved blade rebounded off the blade-ridges. "Who *are* you?" Cyrus demanded as his opponent leapt into the air.

The Araquellus shot past Cyrus, who barely managed to block the aerial cut, then landed atop the young Hero, his blades grinding against Cyrus's sword. "I am Roger Farella, Accountant to Villains!" He launched himself at Cyrus once more.

"Kris! Get out of here!" Cyrus yelled. "Get out of here and hide! You can't let the Villains recapture you!"

Kris nodded and sped away. Roger leapt into the air to follow her, but Cyrus grabbed his ankle and slammed the Araquellus into the ground.

"Oh, no, you don't 'That's *my* Katheni. Your fight is with me." Cyrus pointed the kora in Roger's face.

Roger lunged forward, bringing his organic blades together and snapping three inches of blade from the kora's tip.

Cyrus leapt backward, accidentally releasing Roger's ankle. The Araquellan accountant jumped up and pressed his assault, arm-blades ringing off the steel kora as Cyrus struggled to parry the rapid-fire blows.

Finally the blade, nicked and scratched from defending against the dense and sharp blade-ridges, snapped off at the hilt. Roger took advantage of the opening and launched an attack at Cyrus's face.

Cyrus's arms turned to stone, and he brought them up in front of him, deflecting the blow. "Hi there."

Roger stared at Cyrus's sudden transformation. "How . . . how did you . . . "

"Earth ley-lines, my friend," Cyrus said, wiggling his stone fingers. "Pity you can't access them. Now have at you!" The stone fell away, replaced with fistfuls of swirling fire. "Surprise. Time for a fish fry."

Raul Corazon, a lieutenant in the Salvinsel Salamanders mercenary army, took a crossbow bolt in the center of his chest and sagged to his knees.

"Raul!" Emily Cartright shrieked.

The Villains on the rim of the Vale were having a difficult time hitting any of the Heroes, thanks to the shield put up by that Yellow fellow, but some still got through, and one had found Raul.

Jael Allyn cast bolts of light from a black and silver gauntlet, picking crossbowmen off the rocky walls of the Vale, while two of the other Salamanders fired and reloaded a portable ballista at the larger Mythological beasts as they came into range.

Raul looked up at Emily with a glazed smile. "Take my unit . . . " he gurgled, and fell over.

Emily gritted her teeth. Her unit had been all but destroyed, and Corazon's had fared little better. Even between the two of them, there were hardly enough Salamanders left to form a defensive perimeter, much less win against the Villains.

Jael stepped up beside her, launching a bolt of light from her right gauntlet. The bolt spattered a crossbowman on the rim, and he fell into the Vale.

"That was my last charge," Jael said, looking at her smoking gauntlet. "We cannot take this. Emily, gather the Salamanders and fall back a hundred yards to protect the Yellow Sun. He's the only thing keeping most of those arrows and the magic off us. I'll join the rest of the Heroes to fight the beasts up front. Careful, though, the zombies have broken through the front line."

"Yes, ma'am," Emily said. "Have you seen Captain Karvash about?"

Jael closed her eyes. "The Blak Spoon took a ballista bolt to the bowels and we had to evacuate him. He's a hardy Orc, but even so . . . "

Emily nodded. "I understand, ma'am. Just—watch out!" Emily yanked her General down as a ballista bolt shot overhead and exploded, tearing chunks out of the rock walls.

From around a bend in the Vale stomped a nightmare. A tremendous Earth Giant—a one-hundred-foot tall behemoth with what looked like a siegeworks strapped to his back. Goblins swarmed over his body like fleas on a mangy dog, chittering in their barbaric tongue, climbing through the dirty, matted hair and operating the ballistae and catapults on the creature's back and shoulders.

Emily couldn't move. She stood frozen by awe.

"Cancel that order, Emily!" Jael shouted over the thundering of the Giant's footsteps. "Get away from that thing! The Salamanders can't handle something like that!"

Jael pulled Emily with her as they fled.

After a few stumbling steps, Emily saw a purple-armored Hero run up to them and halt. A small blue giant stopped beside him.

"Hold, Black Viper!" the Purple Paladin said to Jael. "Keep your men here. We need to hold that thing until our compatriots and Guardian arrive." Purple looked to the Blue Shock and ordered him down the valley and away from the Earth

Jael balked. "What? You can't expect common soldiers to stand against something like that!"

"They're all we have left!" Purple shouted. "We've less than fifty Heroes still alive in this godsforsaken valley. Blue is going for reinforcements, but the magic killed scores, the zombies took five, we lost almost a dozen to those poisonous giant bugs. Not to mention that this accursed Giant's killed almost a score in the last ten minutes alone."

"But—"

"*We hold here, Viper.* If that Giant gets through, say good-bye to the Yellow Sun and the *Protection from Projectiles* and *Spellstopper Shield* he has up. Without those, our wounded can't get out, the rest of our soldiers get bombarded, and all of us *die*. We can't afford to lose any more good men today. We hold here. Do you understand?"

Jael's face hardened. Emily thought she was going to defy him again, but even she, a non-hero, knew Purple was right. They had to hold the Giant until the Guildmaster arrived with reinforcements.

At that moment, Emily felt a bone-shaking rumble. It wasn't Guardian's chariot, nor was it the Giant's footsteps. Praise the Twelve, the Dwarven Thunder Runner had arrived.

• • •

The Thunder Runner. A red hammer emblazoned on the side showed that the valiant machine was property of the People's Republic of the Underground, and thus represented all Dwarves. It was the culmination of two lost technologies and Dwarven innovations in the fields of steam power and explosives.

The metal armor on the outside of the rolling box was nigh impenetrable. On top, the repeating ballista spat explosive bolts at the archers on the walls and the Giant in the center.

The Villains still on the Vale's edges recognized the threat immediately. They focused their fire on the armored vehicle, penetrating Yellow's wards by means of their concentrated fire.

But what did get through the shields was ineffective. The arrows glanced off the Thunder Runner's armor, and the magic merely turned the vehicle cherry-red for a few seconds. Even the jars of acid dropped by the wyverns failed to eat holes in the plating. The Thunder Runner rolled right overtop the straggling zombies, adding them to the bloody mess that already defiled the once-green Vale of Dreams.

The massive armored vehicle placed itself between the beleaguered Salamanders and the Earth Giant. Its top turret rotated upward, and it fired its repeating ballista at the wyverns, shooting down five and wounding two in the first volley.

Then the Dwarves inside switched munitions, loading the ballista with explosive arrows instead. The turret targeted the Earth Giant, and began bombarding it with the exploding rounds.

The Earth Giant roared and stumbled backward. Its Goblin crew returned fire with their siege engines. The disparity was immense. Neither bolt nor boulder dented the Thunder Runner's plating.

The machine's crew was a crack team of Dwarven engineers who knew the machine inside and out. One by one, the Thunder Runner picked off the Giant's siege engines, as well as bombarding the Giant directly whenever it regained its balance or got too close.

But the Villains could not tolerate being balked for long. Two Earth-affinity mages stepped to the rim of the Vale and each cast the same spell. The magical energy reflected back and forth between them, echoing and amplifying. When the final cry rang out, the section of canyon containing the courageous Thunder Runner closed in on itself with a resounding bang and the shriek of crushed metal.

With a roar of glee, the Earth Giant stepped over the smashed machine, and lumbered toward the Salamanders.

Blue, out of breath, ran up to Guardian's chariot. The Guildmaster scanned the Tokens on the central panel of his chariot. Almost all of them had gone dim. Nevertheless, he continued ordering and organizing the battle, keeping in direct communication with the Crimson Slash at all times. He ordered the survivors into various tactical formations, providing strategies and exit routes.

Guardian glanced up from the panel, shading his eyes against the midday sun. "Blue Shock. What's happened?"

"There's an Earth Giant in the Vale, tearing the troops up with siege equipment. We can handle that, but there's a fourth wave of Villains coming in right on its heels. And Guardian, they're all equipped with Darkmatter weapons. They even have a golem that appears to be made of the stuff. We can't manage it without onsite orders, sir."

Guardian nodded, pressing two more Tokens and barking orders to his escorts to follow him into the Vale. "Get in, Blue. You'll get there quicker if you ride along with me. Onward!" he said to the horses.

Blue jumped into the chariot, and the horses leapt forward into the Vale.

"There! Guardian is in!" Voshtyr said, putting down his spyglass and picking up a clay tube. With a snap of his metal fingers, he knocked the lid off the jar. A beam of fire and smoke burst forth, shining brightly even in the midday sun.

At the light-beam signal, a mage far below placed his hands on a crystal and spoke three command words. As soon as Guardian passed through the Vale entrance, a shimmering, bright green wall materialized behind him, sealing off the south exit of the valley.

Guardian did not notice, but his escorts certainly did. They died almost instantly as they tried to pass through the wall, their horses slain on contact and the flesh burned from their bones.

Voshtyr chuckled evilly and placed a hand on Keltar's shoulder. "And now, my friend, the real fun begins."

Keltar simply watched.

• • •

Cyrus bounced on the balls of his feet, wiping blood from his lip. Roger circled in front of him, breathing heavily.

In their battle they had cut up the turf, burned up more tents, dug holes, and exploded trees, and now the remnants of Voshtyr's camp were an absolute mess of garbage and debris.

Cyrus's arms turned to stone once more as he feinted right, ducked Roger's punch, and slammed his arm into the ground, pinning both of Roger's arm-blades beneath his own arm, and kicked the Araquellus in the face twice.

Roger shook his head from the blows, then performed a forward flip, with his hands and blades still on the ground. Turned upside down, he kicked Cyrus in return, knocking him flat, then locked his legs around Cyrus's neck and squeezed.

Cyrus clapped both hands onto Roger's shoulders and released an incredible burst of electricity into the Araquellus.

Roger shrieked, a strange noise that sounded like a cross between a Human scream and the cackling of a dolphin. But he was made of stern stuff, and grabbed Cyrus's wrists, pointing the young Hero's hands away from his torso.

Cyrus began blacking out from the pressure and lack of air. His vision blurred, and he blasted fire into the air at ineffective angles, trying to get the unreasonably strong accountant off him.

Roger rolled forward, using Cyrus's momentum to bring him to a sitting position atop the Hero's chest. "This is the end for you, Solburg. And make no mistake: I'm no fool like those traditional Villains. I'm not going to sit here and monologue, giving your reinforcements a chance to show up." Roger kept the pressure around Cyrus's neck. "It's really too bad. You would have made a fine servant for Voshtyr. With your abilities, you could easily have retrieved the power source for the P.L.O.T. Device, but you chose death instead."

Cyrus pried at Roger's legs. "What's . . . the power . . . source?"

"What do you take me for, a fool?" Roger placed the tip of his blade-ridge against Cyrus's face. "You think I'm going to sit here and tell you what he still needs so you can foil him if you manage to escape? No, my boy, you're doomed. I will reveal nothing. I don't monologue."

"You're . . . monologuing . . . about . . . not monologuing."

Roger blinked, then scowled. "No I'm— Bah, it matters not. You're alone here, Solburg. Your reinforcements aren't coming. They're dying like flies in the Vale. And I don't see your precious mate anywhere. She's deserted you as well."

"Wrong," Kris said, piercing the Araquellus in the back with her shortsword. "She never left!"

Roger shrieked in pain once more. He let go of Cyrus's wrists and twisted his blade-ridges backward to strike at his attacker.

Kris blocked the attack with her buckler and stabbed Roger again, right where a Human's right kidney would have been.

The Araquellus leapt into the air, writhing in agony as he gained altitude. Blood sprayed the scorched grass from his wound. "Curse you, Solburg! You will pay for this!" he screamed, shooting back toward the Citadel.

Cyrus looked up at Kris. "I thought I told you to go get help."

"I don't count as help?" Kris said with a grin.

"Hunh," he rubbed his neck. "Well, it worked out, I guess. But he was too strong even for me. Why did you—"

"I couldn't let him harm my mate," she replied, pulling Cyrus up. "Come on, we have to get to the Vale!"

Cyrus nodded. He looked around and spotted a horse pen a few dozen yards away. Good, they were going to need those. He pulled Kris into a tight embrace and began walking toward the pen. "Ol' fish gills needs to be more precise. He cursed 'Solburg,' but do you suppose he meant me or you?"

Emily nocked an arrow to her bowstring. Around her, the remnants of the Salvinsel Salamanders did the same with their own bows and the portable ballista. The Earth Giant was almost atop them. Why hadn't General Allyn given the command to fire yet? The Salamanders had all but lost, and the Purple Paladin lay back against a smashed ballista the Thunder Runner had knocked off the Giant's back, holding his side and favoring a leg.

"Hold your fire!" Jael held up a hand, ready to drop it as a signal. "Hold . . . "

Emily pulled back her arrow. Any time now, General.

Another rumble added itself to the thundering of the Giant's footsteps, reverberating in the stone walls of the Vale. More foes? Emily almost lost hope.

But actually it was the sound of hope on its way.

Guardian's chariot rumbled through the Vale, crushing stray zombies beneath its wheels and the horses' hooves. The gold scrollwork on the chariot glinted in the sun, and the wind flapped the banner of the Guild of Heroes that streamed from a spear in the chariot's weapon rack. A courageous pennant in the midst of slaughter. Emily took heart immediately, and looked back up to the Earth Giant.

"Fire!" Jael yelled. The archers loosed their arrows as the giant brought its foot up to stomp them. Instead, it got a sole full of arrows and javelins.

The Giant roared in pain and fury and ripped a chunk loose from the stone wall. The monster dropped it on the remaining Salamanders. Many, including Jael, had time to leap out of the way, but not so for Emily. She had time only to shove a wounded comrade out of harm's way before the rock was on top of her.

But she lived. Instead of crushing blackness, she felt the rush of wind. Strong talons carried her by the shoulders, and steady wingbeats carried her from the scene.

Slashback Ricor bent her feathered head down to look at her cargo. "Emli, I told you not to die," the gryphon scolded. "You are not fery gut at following instruction."

Emily breathed a massive sigh of relief. "You again. What's your name, griff?"

"I am Slashback Ricor. We hef much to speak of, Emli Catrite."

The two flew off to a safer location, Slashback's white wings reflecting the mid-afternoon sunlight.

The Blue Shock clapped Richard Guardian on the shoulder, then bailed out of the moving chariot. Guardian continued, thundering under the Giant and on toward the north end of the Vale.

Blue rolled to a stop and unleashed the last of his stored static on the Giant, singing hair and charring flesh.

The creature glanced down at Blue and roared its defiance. Blue realized that to this giant, he probably looked like a miniature version of one of the creature's ancestral foes, the Sky Giants.

The Earth Giant roared and swung at the Hero. Blue leapt back, the rush of air from the Giant's swing still bowling him over.

"Seeing his companion in trouble, the Crimson Slash leapt to his aid!" The Crimson Slash leapt down from the section of wall the Giant had torn away. "What say you, Blue? Can we take this fiend?"

Blue looked his friend up and down. Crimson was coated in sweat, blood, and grime. His silver armor was hacked to pieces, and what remained was so badly dinged that he wondered if it still afforded Crimson any protection at all. He actively bled from multiple wounds and had an arrow protruding from his left shoulder.

"If we do not, no one else will. Come, Sir Reginald," he said, clapping his hand on Crimson's shoulder, "let us make a stand!"

"If you provide a distraction, I shall assault the creature at the pinnacle of its height." Crimson hefted his large sword, which now had multiple nicks and dings in it that hadn't been there last time Blue had seen it.

"Then distract I shall. Fare thee well, Crimson Slash."

"And thou as well, Blue Shock."

With that, the two Heroes rushed the Earth Giant's ankles.

Reginald pounded across the short stretch between him and the Giant. As they arrived, Blue began hacking at the giant's tendons with his wicked axe. Reginald clipped his sword to his armor and leapt as high as he could, landing just above the giant's kneecap. He dug his fingers into the filthy, matted hair on the Giant's legs and began climbing up the beast.

The Giant bellowed in rage. It kicked at Blue, missing by a dozen yards as Blue dodged. Reginald smiled grimly. It appeared Blue could hold his own, so he could focus on the climb.

And climb he did. Reginald crawled up the Giant's side, grimacing at the horrendous smell of the beast. It was an unpleasant admixture of excruciatingly severe body odor and an improperly maintained compost pile.

As Reginald climbed above the Giant's waist, two Goblins manning one of the remaining siege engines on the Giant's shoulders looked down at Reginald and began chittering angrily. One shot an arrow past Reginald's head.

"Not to be deterred by something as miniscule as Goblins, the Crimson Slash drew his mighty blade and stabbed it into the Giant's side! Using the pommel as a springboard, the Hero launched himself upwards to the platform where the runty creatures stood, and knocked their fragile skulls together!"

The Giant roared as the blade penetrated his side. It lost all interest in the Blue Shock and reached across its chest to try and catch Reginald. In the process it accidentally dislodged the siege platform from its back.

Reginald fell with the platform, but pushed off it as he neared the Giant's waistline. "The Crimson Slash leapt from the falling siegeworks and caught hold of his mighty blade. Using the momentum of his fall, the Hero swung in a circle on his sword and catapulted upward, pulling his sword with him as he did so!" Reginald flew upward, landing handily atop the Giant's left shoulder. "Without further ado, the Crimson Slash began attacking the Giant's thick neck!"

The Blue Shock was no longer a concern. The Giant swung its open palm at Reginald to squash him as one might squash a mosquito.

The blow came so fast Reginald actually had no time to narrate. Instead, he braced his back against the Giant's bleeding neck and pointed his sword toward the oncoming hand.

The Giant smashed Reginald against its neck.

And roared in pain once more. It yanked its hand away, a dazed Hero clinging tenaciously to his sword. The sword had pierced the center of the Giant's palm, and now the sword and Reginald were stuck in it.

Reginald drew his sword out of the Giant's flesh and pointed it upward once more, shaking the dizziness from his head. *"Now, Blue!"*

From below, the Blue Shock shouted something that sounded like *"Gigabolt!"* A column of blue electrical energy arced up from the ground, charring a patch of skin on the Giant's temple.

The Giant smashed the side of his head to remove this new nuisance.

Unfortunately for the Giant, that was the same hand that contained a Hero and a very sharp sword.

Reginald's titanic sword drove into the side of the Giant's head. This time, there was no roar of pain, only a whimper. Dazed, Reginald plummeted from the Giant's height, barely having the presence of mind to yank his sword free.

As he fell, so did the Giant. It crashed into the Vale floor, collapsing more of the sidewalls as the impact shook the ground for miles.

Reginald landed not on hard stone, but in the brawny arms of the Blue Shock. Blue set Reginald down and gave him a quizzical look. "Art thou alright, Crimson?"

"There must be an easier way to slay a giant," Reginald complained, shrugging off the collapsed remnants of his battered armor. "Come, Blue. Guardian ordered me to help evacuate the Vale."

• • •

Other Heroes were not so lucky. After letting the zombies through for the common soldiers to deal with, a dozen Heroes had set up a defensive line near the north end of the Vale. The Heroes had taken a beating from the Mythological beasts as they passed by, and several had died attempting to slow or slay the Earth Giant. But now, they numbered only five, and two more died in a blast of dark energy from the approaching Darkmatter golem.

The construct was a fearsome thing indeed. Built on the same design as steel golems, it measured over seven feet tall and resembled a suit of armor. But its material was not steel. This one was made of Darkmatter.

The golem stomped forward, a light-eating shadow in the afternoon sun. Behind it came over a dozen Villains and sundry Minions and Henchmen—and even a few Toadies. The golem put the heels of its broad hands together, and another blast shot forth. That beam took one of the surviving Heroes in the chest, and the flesh burned from his bones in a horrid wreath of black flames.

The two remaining Heroes prepared to rush the golem in a Heroic Last Charge. But a rumbling from the rear halted them in their tracks. Guardian's chariot streaked past them, rushing to meet the golem and the advancing Villains head-on.

"Fall back!" Guardian yelled over his shoulder. "Retreat from the Vale! Get everyone out and to safety in Bryath or Voyage!"

The two Heroes nodded and retreated while their Guildmaster's chariot bore down on the Villains.

• • •

Richard Guardian pulled a silver-tipped javelin from the rack beside him and threw it at the Darkmatter golem.

The weapon crumpled and shattered on impact with the corruptive mineral, but not before it knocked open the visor of the golem's helmet-like head. The second javelin took the construct right in the helmet, shattering the gem affixed to the back of its head.

The golem exploded in a black cloud, sending chips and fragments of its substance in all directions. Some flew backward into the advancing Villains, killing many instantly, but others flew toward Guardian.

The horses took the brunt of it, whinnying in fear and pain as Darkmatter shards pieced their armor and burned their flesh away.

Guardian yanked a lever underneath the side-panel, releasing the horses as they bucked and reared. Within seconds, the chariot's wheels glowed golden, and the war wagon began moving under its own power.

Guardian took the flanged claymore from his sword-rack, pressed a specialized Token to sound the retreat, and guided the chariot toward the Villains.

"I am Richard Guardian the Swift Justice, Master of the Guild of Heroes! Prepare to Face Justice!"

Though the Heroes received the order and began evacuating toward the south end of the Vale, retreat was impossible. The green wall remained in place, killing any who tried to pass through it. To compound the problem, the Yellow Sun's wards began to fade, allowing magic and arrows to rain down on the few survivors.

Hope came in the form of a Dragon.

Shimmering green in the afternoon sun, it swooped down, breathing ignescent air upon the bow-wielding Villains. On its second pass, it swooped down low enough to see the surviving Heroes. Spying the Crimson Slash, it made a third pass, scooping the Hero up from behind the rock he was using as cover.

"Got yourself in a spot of trouble, Reginald?" the Dragon asked as they flew out of the scene of carnage.

"Keeth!" Reginald exclaimed. "I could not be gladder to see a creature! What are you doing back?"

"It turns out that Uncle Nivonis just had a chest cold," Keeth replied, banking left to dodge a hailstorm of arrows. "He was using his illness to see which of his relatives were loving family and which were vultures just waiting for him to die. He'll be fine in a week."

Reginald chuckled. "Well, I am glad that your relatives are all right. But quickly, you must put me down and get as many of the others to safety as possible!"

Keeth said nothing for a moment, then spoke. "I cannot, Reginald. Draconic tradition dictates noninvolvement in Human conflicts unless Dragons are threatened. I'm sorry, but . . . "

"To the Abyss with your tradition!" Reginald yelled. "At least rescue the Black Viper! She is important to me. If you won't do it, then let me down and I will!"

Keeth sighed, swooped low, and dropped Reginald. "Stay there!" the Dragon ordered. "I will be back momentarily."

He swooped back down into the valley and, true to his word, soon returned with Jael Allyn in his talons. Depositing her beside Reginald, he came to a graceless landing, hissing in pain; arrows protruded from his wings.

"Here, Keeth, let me remove those," Jael offered. "It's the least I can do for you."

"What about your troops?" Keeth asked.

Jael hung her head as she pulled the arrows from Keeth's membranous wings. "Dead. Most of them were killed in the initial magic bombardments, and the Giant killed most of the rest. Karvash is wounded, Corazon's dead, and Cartwright and Sakana are missing. I'm afraid I've failed as a commander."

"There's no shame in defeat, especially in such a dastardly ambush," Reginald said, taking Jael's hand in his. "Even Guardian didn't see this coming. Listen. I am going to bring down that magic wall so the survivors can escape. You must lead them to safety, do you understand?"

"Yes," Jael said, staring down into the valley. "But, Reginald, just you against all those Villains . . . ?"

Reginald turned away. "Do not worry about me, Jael. Lead the soldiers out of this hell, scatter them to the four winds, and go to Voyage Port. If I survive, we will sail together to Rondheim Port on Landeralt. Though it is a land of Villains, at least we will be safe from Voshtyr. He has crushed the only effective resistance we could have put up. Landeralt will be safer. He has not yet triumphed there. Now, go."

Jael's face set. "Very well. I will see you in Voyage Port in one week. Farewell, Crimson Slash. May the gods guide you."

"May the Creator smile on you, Black Viper," he replied, then turned to Keeth. "My friend, I know that there is a taboo against riding Dragons whilst in the sky, so could you fly over once and tell me which mage is keeping that green wall up?"

Keeth nodded and took to the sky. Within the minute, he was back. "It is a frail man, wearing robes the color of a vile storm. You cannot ride me, but I may drop you on him," the Dragon said, with a vicious, multi-pointed smile.

• • •

Hero and Dragon took to the sky, well out of range of arrows and all but the most accurate anti-air spells. As Keeth soared over the battle, he and Reginald could see the true extent of the devastation wrought by the Villains. Of the proud force of well over two hundred Heroes, scarcely fifty remained. The common infantry had fared as poorly, and the Dwarves and their Thunder Runner lay crushed in the center of the Vale.

"There he is!" Keeth bellowed down to the Hero.

Reginald, clutched in Keeth's hazardous talons, nodded. "Then drop me, son of Barinol! Any Hero worth his salt can survive a fall from this altitude."

The Dragon bugled a throaty draconic battle cry and complied, releasing the Crimson Slash.

"And so fell the Crimson Slash! From an incredible height, the Dragon dropped him to deliver death and doom to the treacherous Villains!" Reginald yelled as he plummeted. "Prepare to faaaaace Justiiiiiiiiiice . . . !"

Guardian hacked at a Villain in a round helm and red cloak, then yanked a lever on his chariot, spinning it around on its axis and crushing another Villain who had gotten too close.

Then a particularly swift Villainess wearing nothing but a breastsplate and disturbing black leather straps launched herself at Guardian, slashing her Darkmatter longsword across the Guildmaster's chest.

Guardian gritted his teeth. The black flames burned him but did not spread across his body. A side effect of the spell that had crippled him was that it bestowed on him a resistance to the deadly effects of Darkmatter. Before the Villain could recover from her surprise at his resilience, the Hero struck her down.

Seeing this, the whole cohort of Villains rushed Guardian at once, swarming his chariot.

The Guildmaster hacked and slashed at his foes, but there were simply too many. Before the minute was up, he had slain over twelve Villains, but they had taken their toll. Two spears with Darkmatter heads stuck in him, an axe was lodged in his shoulder, and a sword protruded from his belly, all burning away with black fire.

Guardian coughed as he slumped forward against the panel of Tokens. Feebly he pressed the one with his own insignia on it.

"Dad?" a boy's voice said from the Token.

"Trigger . . . " Guardian said, gasping, "take care . . . of your mother . . . for me . . . " He severed the connection, and turned a key in the front panel. A large red button labeled *Last Resort* popped up and lit with a fatal glow. More Villains rushed the dying Guildmaster as he slammed his hand down on the button.

Bright light and a deafening explosion filled the northern end of the Vale. Massive boulders, thrown free by the blast, rolled down and stopped up the valley's entrance. Every last Villain in the area was obliterated in the detonation.

Guardian, in a selfless act of Heroism, had saved what was left of his Guild.

"Do you hear something?" Tyler Nightraid asked, turning to a fellow Villain.

Both stood on the last line of defense for their Wall Mage. A few ranks of Minions and Henchmen, as well as a few Lesser

Villains, stood on the crumbling edges of the Vale to keep any Heroes from leaping out of the marvelous deathtrap Voshtyr had designed.

Though that seemed rather silly to Tyler. The Heroes kept doing things that eroded the Vale's rim—using everything from exploding ballistae bolts to knocking over Earth Giants. Why stand so close to such a precarious edge? It was merely common sense to stand back.

The Wall Mage stood behind them on a raised platform, his yellow-grey robes blowing in a nonexistent breeze. He waved his hands over a crystal ball of some sort.

As far as Tyler was concerned, the ambush had been boring so far. It was supposed to be this titanic struggle of Good versus Evil, and all. But not a single Hero had made it past the first two lines of Villains, even if they'd been stupid enough to try leaping out of the Vale to fight.

"Hear what?" the other Villain replied, removing his bat-faced helmet. "What be ye going on about now?"

Tyler glanced around, seeing multiple bored Villains and ugly creatures, but nothing making the sound he heard. "There's an odd noise around here somewhere. It sounds like . . . well it sounds faraway talking, growing louder by the second. And it's constant, like narration . . . "

" . . . the unstoppable might of the *Mors ab Alto* sword technique!"

A red flash fell from the sky, and suddenly the Villain Nightraid had been talking to fell apart in two pieces.

"Wh—"

Nightraid saw that a Hero had dropped from the clouds, but before he could react properly, the Hero ran him through, scattering Nightraid's demerit badges across the turf.

• • •

The Crimson Slash really couldn't blame the young Villain for not responding more appropriately. After all, what *is* the proper reaction to a Hero plummeting from the sky?

"The Crimson Slash turned and found his opponent on a small raised platform. The mage wore vile, yellow-grey robes, and quailed in fear as the Hero approached!"

Reginald's narration was correct. The mage fled, leaving behind the crystal sphere he had been using.

"But no mere mage could outrun the Crimson Slash! The Hero cut down the malicious magician, then whirled and smashed his diabolical device. The brilliant barrier crackled and faded as the Crimson Slash fought his way through the back lines of the Dark Host, carving a path to freedom for him and his brother Heroes!"

Cyrus and Kris galloped along the edge of the Vale on their stolen horses, nearing the south end just as the neon wall flickered and dissipated, freeing the few survivors to flee for their lives.

The two spurred their mounts to greater speeds. Cyrus had to find Reginald and save as many Heroes as he could. It was his fault they'd walked into the trap, and by the Seven Furies, he'd get them out of it.

Fortunately, the remaining Villains on the edges of the Vale were either concentrated on slaughtering the men in the valley or flummoxed at the loss of the wall that had been keeping the Heroes in the Vale. None paid any attention to the charging pair.

Kris lashed out from the back of her horse, knocking a Villain away from a tripod-mounted repeating crossbow. "Cyrus! The Heroes are almost out of the Vale, but look!" She pointed further down the Vale.

A fresh batch of Mythologicals—plus the bulk of actual Villains from Voshtyr's army—were bearing down on the fleeing Heroes. Cyrus judged the distances and came to a chilling conclusion: even if the Heroes made it out of the vale, they would be overrun within minutes.

He gritted his teeth and shouted over the pounding of the horses's hooves. "Kris, get on ahead, as far as you can from the mouth of the Vale. And I mean it this time. I'm going to cause some serious havoc here."

"All right, I'll meet you by that rock formation that looks like a Dragon over there," Kris shouted, and continued riding.

Cyrus slowed his horse to a stop a few dozen yards from the south entrance of the Vale. Wounded and retreating Heroes poured out of it. A multitude, but still far fewer than Cyrus would have liked. He dismounted and walked to the center of the Vale's mouth. The last of the Heroes ran past him, leaving him standing alone in the large gap between the forces.

Cyrus could see Voshtyr's army coming through the Vale. Manticores and Chimerae bounded forward, snarling in their bestial tongues. Villains in black and red shouted battle cries as they spurred their mounts onward or charged on foot. Arrows flew past Cyrus's head as a few frontrunning archers took hastily aimed shots at the last obstacle in the way of destroying the fleeing Heroes.

And an obstacle he was. Cyrus opened his mind to the entire area. There were six beautiful ley-lines nearby—floating in the sky, buried in the sides of the Vale, sunk in the river a league away.

Cyrus broke them all.

He bound all of them together in a massive energy braid. It was like being blasted with hot wind, immersed in freezing water, buried alive, and electrocuted all at the same time.

And then he let it go.

Pure white light blasted from his hands, immolating the sides of the Vale with catastrophic fury. Boulders shattered beneath the onslaught. Ionized air crackled in spontaneous lightning. The earth heaved and shook like a rug. And any Villain unfortunate enough to be caught in the light instantaneously ceased to exist.

More Villains streaked for the entrance to the desecrated Vale of Dreams to pursue the Heroes. But the earth and stone of the field beneath them slagged into molten death for any who touched it. Several ranks of Villains died as they fell into the quagmire, pushed on by the mass behind them.

Cyrus turned and mounted his horse again, his mind completely free of thoughts. He had created a molten, flaming barrier between the Light and Dark, allowing the fleeing Heroes to distance themselves from the dark host.

And flee they had to. For despite Cyrus's heroics—and because of his betrayal—the Heroes had lost.

Good had been defeated.

Evil had triumphed.

The Balance tipped to Darkness.

And the peasants never noticed.

EPILOGUE

Flight of a Hero

KRIS AND CYRUS entered the port town of Voyage. They were battered and weary, and to them the town smelled of defeat and fish. The grey sky reflected the bleak mood of the town's current inhabitants. Voyage was crowded with crestfallen Heroes, each seeking a boat to take him or her to a different and hopefully safe location.

The largest pier in town stuck out a hundred yards into the semicircular bay around which Voyage was built, and every boat moored there was crammed to capacity with fleeing Heroes. The destination didn't matter, so long as it was away. And the ship captains were perfectly happy to charge the Heroes to take them there. Bundles, crates, and barrels littered the pier, but no one seemed to care about their luggage, only their lives.

"Cyrus!" a voice called.

Cyrus turned to see the Crimson Slash and the Black Viper standing on the gangway of a large ship. "Reg!" Cyrus called. "Hang on one second!"

He and Kris dashed up the ramp to where Reginald stood. "Wow, Reg, am I glad to see you alive! I thought almost everyone was killed back there."

"Almost everyone was," Jael said sadly.

"Jael, I'd like to introduce you someone. Reg, you know her, but something important has changed. This is Kris. She's now my—"

"How can you show your face here?" Reginald demanded, his face a mask of disappointment and anger. "After what you just did!"

"What I did?" Cyrus blinked. "You mean what Voshtyr forced me to say? I tried to tell you—"

"You told me *nothing!*" Reginald pointed a finger in Cyrus's face. "You gave me no indication that *anything* was wrong! You are supposed to give me a MUD signal if you are under duress!"

"Hey, now! You never taught me anything about what to do under duress! I *tried* to tell you but you wouldn't get it. What, were you were looking for some obscure code word instead of being a normal Human and reading my body language?"

"This is not my fault, boy. *You* betrayed the Guild, and it's *your* responsibility to deal with the consequences!"

Jael put her hand on Reginald's arm, but he shrugged it off.

"You are a disgrace to the Guild, and you dishonor me." Reginald shook his head. "I am ashamed to have trained a traitor."

"Traitor? *Traitor?* Curse you, Reginald. I may not have been able to alert you to the danger, but don't you *dare* pin this on me!" Kris tried to say something, but Cyrus held up his hand. "After I escaped, I did everything I could to help the Heroes get away. You can't blame me for your failure to teach properly!"

"That does it, boy." Reginald turned around and stalked off toward the gangplank. "You're not deserving of a Heroic Name, and I'll have naught to do with you."

"Fine!" Tears of rage and pain sprang to Cyrus's eyes. "I won't take one then! I'll be a nameless Hero. Come on, Kris. I don't have time for this."

"*All aboard for Rondheim port!*" shouted a sailor.

Reginald looked back at Cyrus like he was about to say something else, then continued toward the boat without another word. Jael cast a backward glance at Kris and Cyrus, but followed Reginald down the pier and onto the boat.

Cyrus slumped onto a barrel, his head in his hands.

Kris put a soft paw on his shoulder. "Cyrus . . . "

"He's right," Cyrus said through clenched teeth. "It's my fault. I don't deserve to be a Hero. Maybe I can just go home. Do you think I could do that? Both of us? Hopefully Voshtyr doesn't know where I'm from, and nothing's gone wrong on Starspeak."

"I'll go wherever you do, Cyrus," Kris said, sitting down next to him and nuzzling his cheek. "Does this mean I get to meet your family?"

"My family," Cyrus repeated, his heart still racing. "I haven't been to Starspeak in almost six years. I don't even know what it looks like anymore, or if my relatives are still alive. But it is an isolated spot," he said, thinking. "We'd be safe there. Maybe. If there's no Heroes anymore, eventually *every* place will get overrun with Villains."

"But won't the Guild regroup?" Kris glanced hungrily at a man carrying a barrel of fish before looking back at Cyrus.

"Maybe. Not likely," Cyrus said, hanging his head. "If they do, it will have to be some kind of covert version. And who would lead it? Reg? As angry as he is, he'd go on the attack right away, and the movement would be doomed before it started." Cyrus laid his head on Kris' shoulder. "I think it would be better if we just laid low until we figure out what's going on. I'd especially like to know how Voshtyr was able to get so much power so quickly."

Kris nuzzled Cyrus's neck. "I hate how you and Reginald parted. You have to make that right. You two are too good of friends to stay mad at each other for long, right?"

Cyrus almost wept. But Heroes, even those without a name, don't weep. He hoped she was right.

Hey, Creator, he prayed, you think you could arrange some way for me and that big lout to reconcile? And while you're at it, maybe, you know, protect the world from being overrun by Villains.

It was strange, but Cyrus felt a little better. Like some of the load had been taken off his back. A quick image popped into his mind of the priest, laughing over his spiked tea back in the disappearing church. Maybe, just maybe, all wasn't lost.

He smiled at Kris. "I'll just have to try my hand at a normal life. And if my family's still on Starspeak, well, boy, will they be surprised that I got married."

"To a Katheni?"

"To anyone! They placed me as a terminal bachelor. And really, who else would I have married, eh? Heroes tend to marry either Elven princesses or some other kind of exotic bride. And you, my dear," Cyrus said, kissing Kris on the nose, "are as exotic as they come."

APPENDIX

Reference and Pronunciation Guide

Araquellus (Ah rah KELL us) *pl.* Araquellae—an
    Aquatic Race, skilled in mercantile interests
    and economics. Governed by a ruler called
    a Neptarch and his privy council.

Avierie (ah vee EH ree)—the reclusive Bird Folk of
    the mountains. This Race has a rigid and
    controlling tribal structure, characterized by
    shyness and hostility toward outsiders and
    non-Avierie.

Basilisk (BAA zill isk)—a large, draconic beast up
    to thirty feet long, possessing the power
    to temporarily turn an organic target
    to stone with a glare. Basilisks come in
    several varieties, including lesser, greater,
    Darkshroud, and Hooded.

Bryath (BRIE ath)—the ruling authority of Centra
    Mundi, a powerful kingdom in the southern
    half of the aforementioned continent. *Prop.*
    Dynasty of Kings who have ruled the
    kingdom of the same name for the last half-
    century.

Centra Mundi (CEN tra MOON dee)—equidistant
from all other continents, this landmass
could accurately be called the Center of
the World. Its primary features are its
racial diversity, varied terrain, and the
Keep of Five Flames. The seat of Human
government is based here, under King
Bryath III.

Filar (FY-lar)—a petty monarchy in the southwestern
area of Centra Mundi. Notorious for its
unscrupulous politicians.

Gauntlet (GONT-lett)—a heavy glove made of metal,
for protecting the hand. If you didn't already
know what a gauntlet was, you deserve to
be smacked with one.

Also: Lobstered Gauntlet—a gauntlet made of
overlapping plates. More flexible, but less
protective than a standard gauntlet.

Greaves (Greevz)—trousers composed of durable
cloth covered in overlapping armor-plates.
Myth. A Saint who participated in averting
the disaster of the Falling Stars during the
Twenty-Minute War.

Istaka (Is TAH kah)—a Race of sentient, bipedal
Canines, native to Centra Mundi and
Landeralt. They are swift hunters, and their
caste-based society is steeped in Creation
legends.

Katheni (Kah THENN ee)—this Race is comprised
of primarily desert-dwelling sentient
Felinoids. A non-interfering race, they move

about deserts such as Mir in regular routes
according to the season.

Kath Magi (Kahth MAH jee)—a Katheni trained in
learning magic by absorbing spells.

Landeralt (LAN der ahlt)—the eastmost of the Five
Continents, geographical location of the
Hereditary Evil Empire. Primary exports
are Villains and Mercenaries.

Ley-line (LAY line)—an invisible channel for
carrying Elemental energy, found in the air,
ground, or water. A tremendous source of
magical power.

Lorimar (LOW rim ahr)—the Western continent,
ancestral land of the Elves. "Discovered"
by Lord Colmarian the Headstrong during
an expedition to find the mythical paradise
island of the same name. *Myth.* the island
home to the gods and a race comprised
of only enlightened beings and true
philosophers. As yet undiscovered.

Manticore (MAN tih kor)—a monstrous quadruped
with a Human-like face. These are almost
invariably employed by the Forces of
Darkness, partly because of their fierce
combat abilities, but also because they just
plain look freaky.

Merope (Meh ROWpe)—a thriving mercantile
metropolis in the eastern fields of Centra
Mundi. This town is run by a council of
merchants, and each one's greed balances
out the others, making for a peaceful and

stable government with everyone's best
interests in mind.

Mir, Desert of (Meer)—located in northern Centra
Mundi, this desert is home to the world's
largest tribe of Katheni. It is characterized
by severe summer sandstorms, and
relatively mild winters. Home of the Alaks
Cactus and the notorious Firebelly pepper.

Morival (MOE rih val)—an evil sorcerer, cause of the
Twenty-Minute War.

Novania (No VAHN ee ah)—the Northern continent,
half of which is permanently covered in
snow. Ruled by the Frost King and his three
sons. The world's best brandy, as well as the
famous firewine and frostwine, are brewed
here.

Ogleby, Reginald (OH gell bee, REH jinn ahld)—
known as the Crimson Slash, this Hero has
participated in many battles and Quests
over his lifetime, such as the Battle of Three
Streams and the Nine-Day Siege.

Ransha (RAHN sha)—a fearsome Race of Humanoid
lizards. They primarily live in swamps,
though some varieties live on ocean coasts.
Hard scales protect them from harm, and
their tribal society reveres the elderly and
worships their ancestors.

Salvinsel (SAL vin sell)—the Southern continent,
famous for its mountains and deserts, both
renowned for richness in valuable minerals.
Also home to the People's Republic of

the Underground, and a good number of Katheni as well.

Von Steinadler, Serimal (Vohn STY nadd lur, SEH ri mahl)—trueborn son of Benjamin von Steinadler. Despite his true birth, this man was second-born and did not receive his rightful inheritance. Brother to Voshtyr von Steinadler.

Von Steinadler, Voshtyr (Vohn STY nadd lur, VOSH teer)—illegitimate son of Benjamin von Steinadler. Also called Voshtyr Demonkin due to uncanny magical talents, this Villain once attempted to assassinate King Bryath III and was sentenced to death. Brother to Serimal von Steinadler.

SPLEEN

Acknowledgements

This is the page where the author lists some of the people who helped him write his book. If you are uninterested in this, or do *not* wish to hear about my squeaky, psychotic, mass-murdering roommate, please skip on to the back tab of the dust jacket, if there is one, for it will undoubtedly be more interesting because it has a picture of me on it.

I could not have written this book without help from a whole bunch of wonderful, insane people. Well, I could have, but it would have been so bad that it would never have seen print.

First, I must thank my proofreader/editors, Dylan Thompson, Joseph Raborg, and George Allen, my college roommate. Not only did they endure the terribly rough first draft, but they also actually remained conscious enough to help me revise it. Kudos, guys, I owe you. Probably lunch or a free copy of the book, or both. Just watch and see, though; these men will undoubtedly become great. In order, they will probably become a world famous chemist, the Pope, and a lovable, psychotic, squeaky mass-murderer.

Thanks to my younger brother Alex (though I am loathe to say it), who has a much keener eye for detail than I do. Without his helpful and vicious editing, the first chapter of the book would have had no scenery whatsoever, and no one would *ever* have known what was going on in the first part of chapter 2.

Approximately two hundred gallons of thanks go to A. J. Cada, Avery Smith, Alex Paulus, Owen Gruner, Garrett Powell, Ian Rutledge, Anthony Maess, and the other guys from Trinity Baptist Church. These guys *are* most of the Heroes and Villains in the book.

To explain, and also to explain why some parts of the book seem like a video game, the material the book is based on is actually from a series of adventure games I created back when I was ten. The guys and I would go outside after church, or during the adult Bible studies, and play a wonderfully inane turn-based live adventure game called, simply, *Quest*. I played non-player characters and ALL of the bad guys, such as the smelly and carnivorous "Spoo," and my buddies played the Heroes. They saved the world at least once a year every year before I left for college.

From this gleeful monstrosity sprung many of the ideas used in creating Voshtyr, the Crimson Slash (who was actually one of our NPCs), and many others. Without the guys, the ideas would have withered and disappeared. Thanks, guys. Here's to many hours of our Backyard RPG.

Thanks to Dr. John Freeh, professor of English at Hillsdale College, for teaching me words like *Effulgent* and *Uxorious*.

Thanks to Ben Nygaard, for keeping me alive during my first week at college.

And thanks to you for buying this book and putting me through college. Unless you borrowed this book from your local library, which is okay, or stole it from somebody, in which case, the Silent Assassin will kill you in your sleep tonight.

—Mitchell Bonds

LaVergne, TN USA
08 February 2010
172364LV00002B/44/P